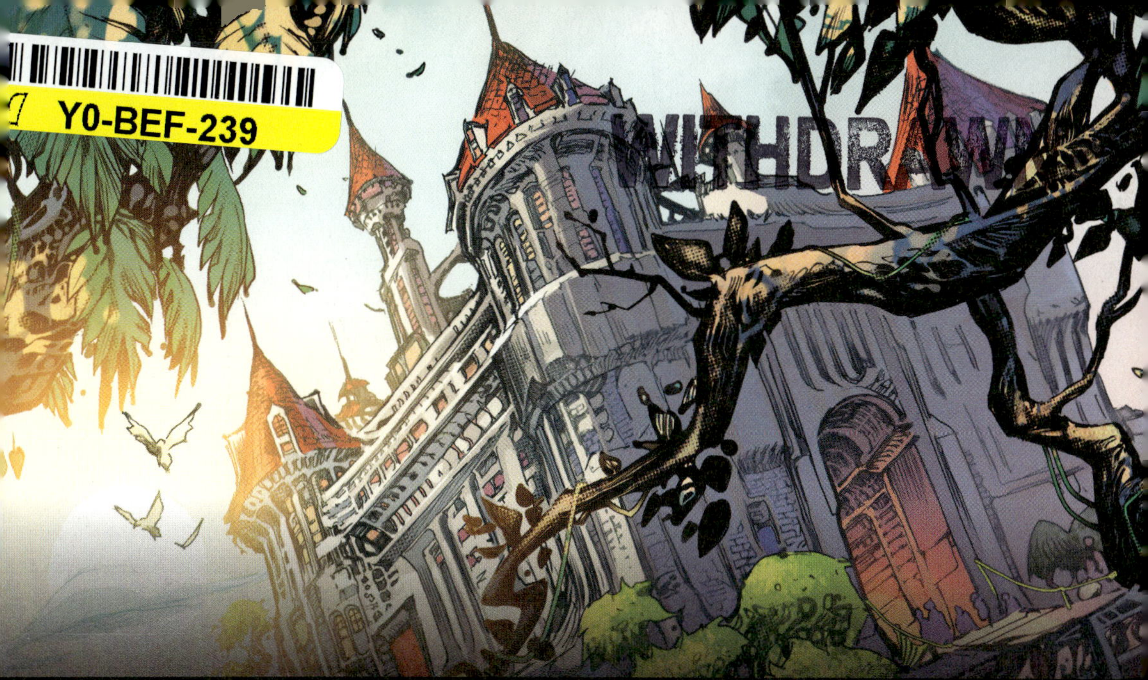
WITHDRAWN

DEATHSTROKE INC.

VOL. 1

KING OF THE SUPER-VILLAINS

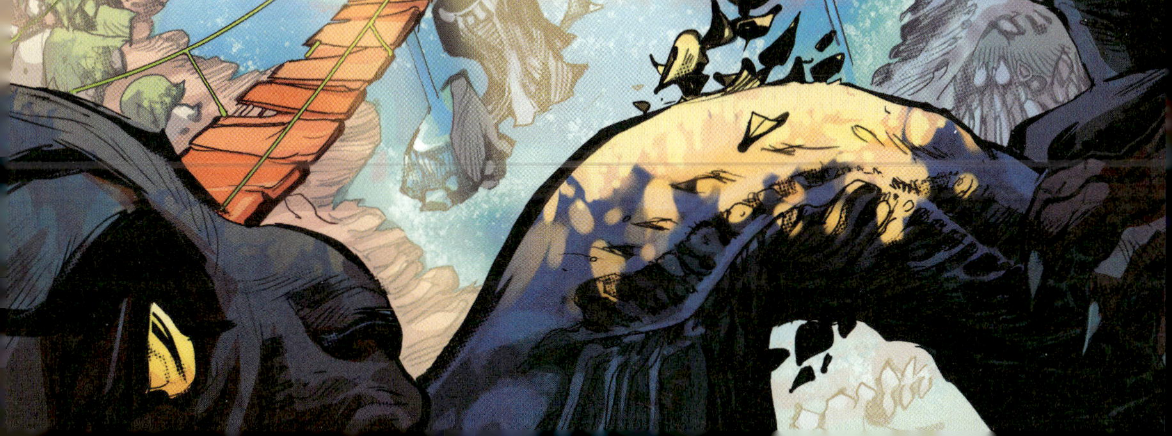

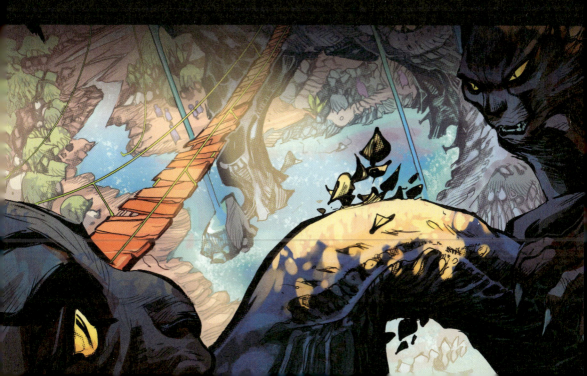

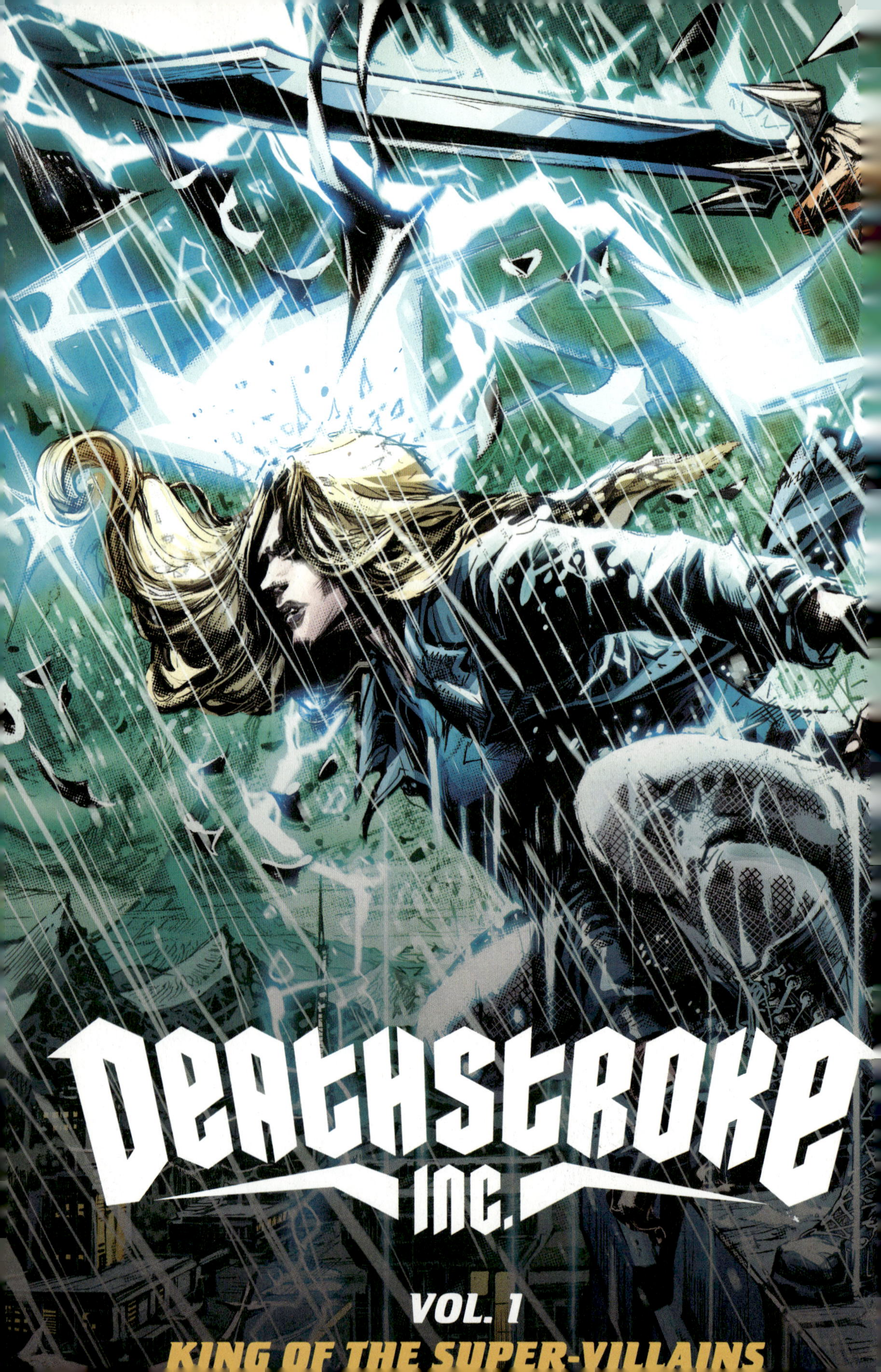
DEATHSTROKE
INC.
VOL. 1
KING OF THE SUPER-VILLAINS

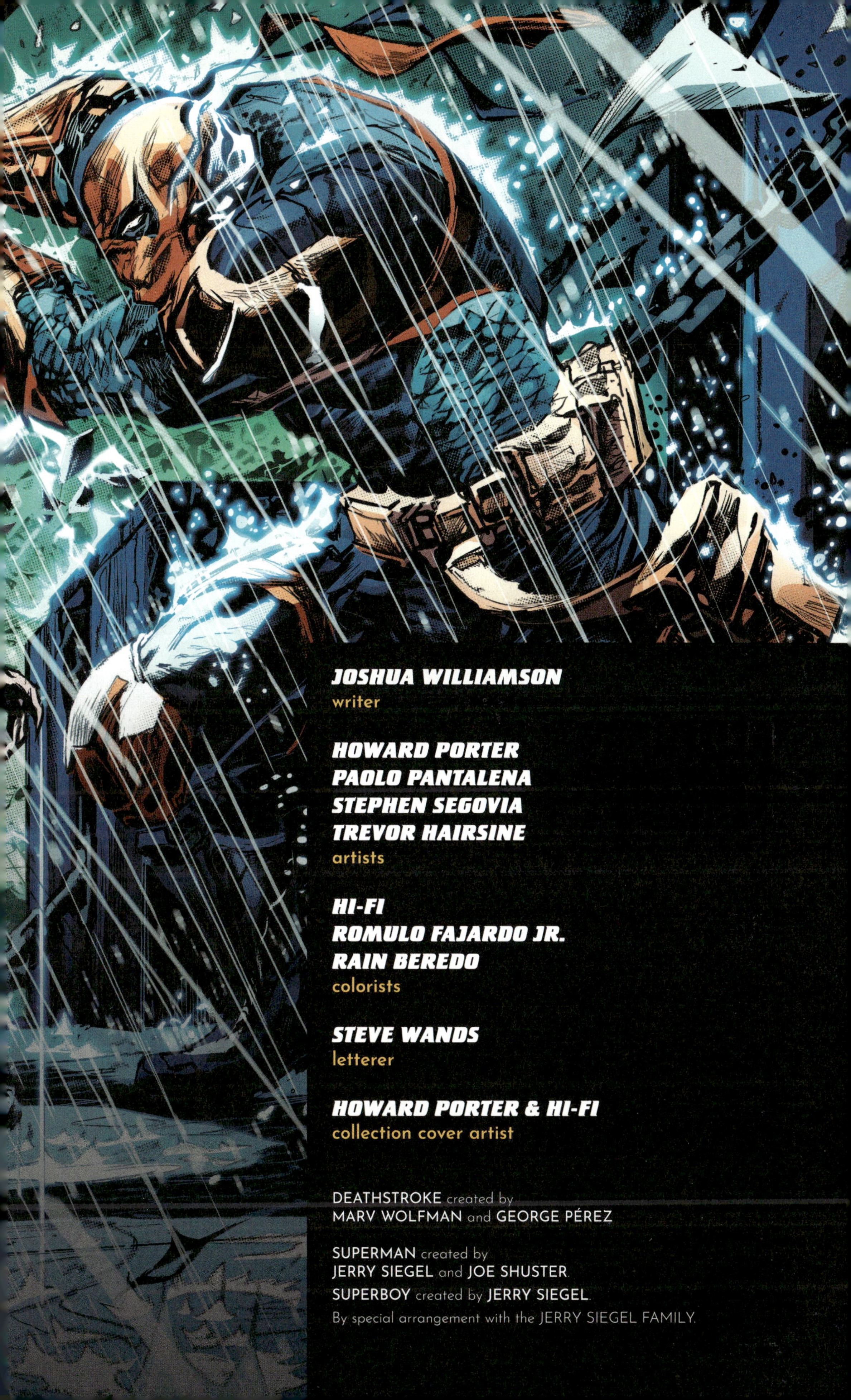

JOSHUA WILLIAMSON
writer

HOWARD PORTER
PAOLO PANTALENA
STEPHEN SEGOVIA
TREVOR HAIRSINE
artists

HI-FI
ROMULO FAJARDO JR.
RAIN BEREDO
colorists

STEVE WANDS
letterer

HOWARD PORTER & HI-FI
collection cover artist

ROB TOKAR & BEN ABERNATHY Editors - Collected Edition
BEN ABERNATHY Editor - Original Series
BEN MEARES Assistant Editor - Original Series
STEVE COOK Design Director - Books
MEGEN BELLERSEN Publication Design
CHRISTY SAWYER Publication Production

MARIE JAVINS Editor-in-Chief, DC Comics

ANNE DePIES Senior VP - General Manager
JIM LEE Publisher & Chief Creative Officer
DON FALLETTI VP - Manufacturing Operations & Workflow Management
LAWRENCE GANEM VP - Talent Services
ALISON GILL Senior VP - Manufacturing & Operations
JEFFREY KAUFMAN VP - Editorial Strategy & Programming
NICK J. NAPOLITANO VP - Manufacturing Administration & Design
NANCY SPEARS VP - Revenue

DEATHSTROKE INC. VOL. 1: KING OF THE SUPER-VILLAINS

DC Comics, 2900 West Alameda Ave., Burbank, CA 91505
Printed by Transcontinental Interglobe, Beauceville, QC, Canada.
6/13/22. First Printing.
ISBN: 978-1-77951-657-2

Library of Congress Cataloging-in-Publication Data is available.

PEFC Certified
This product is
from sustainably
managed forests and
controlled sources
PEFC™
PEFC/01-31-106   www.pefc.org

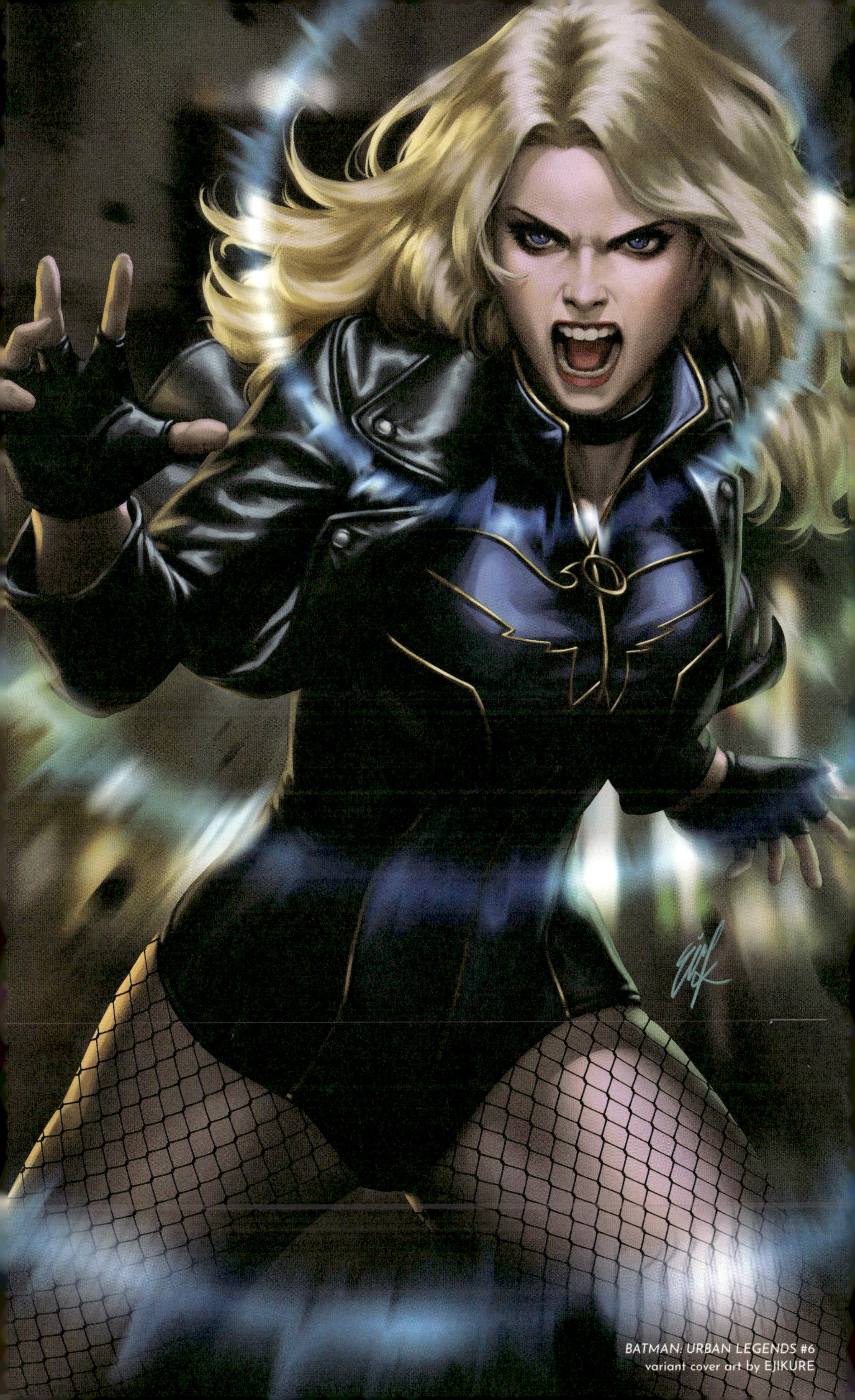

BATMAN: URBAN LEGENDS #6
variant cover art by EJIKURE

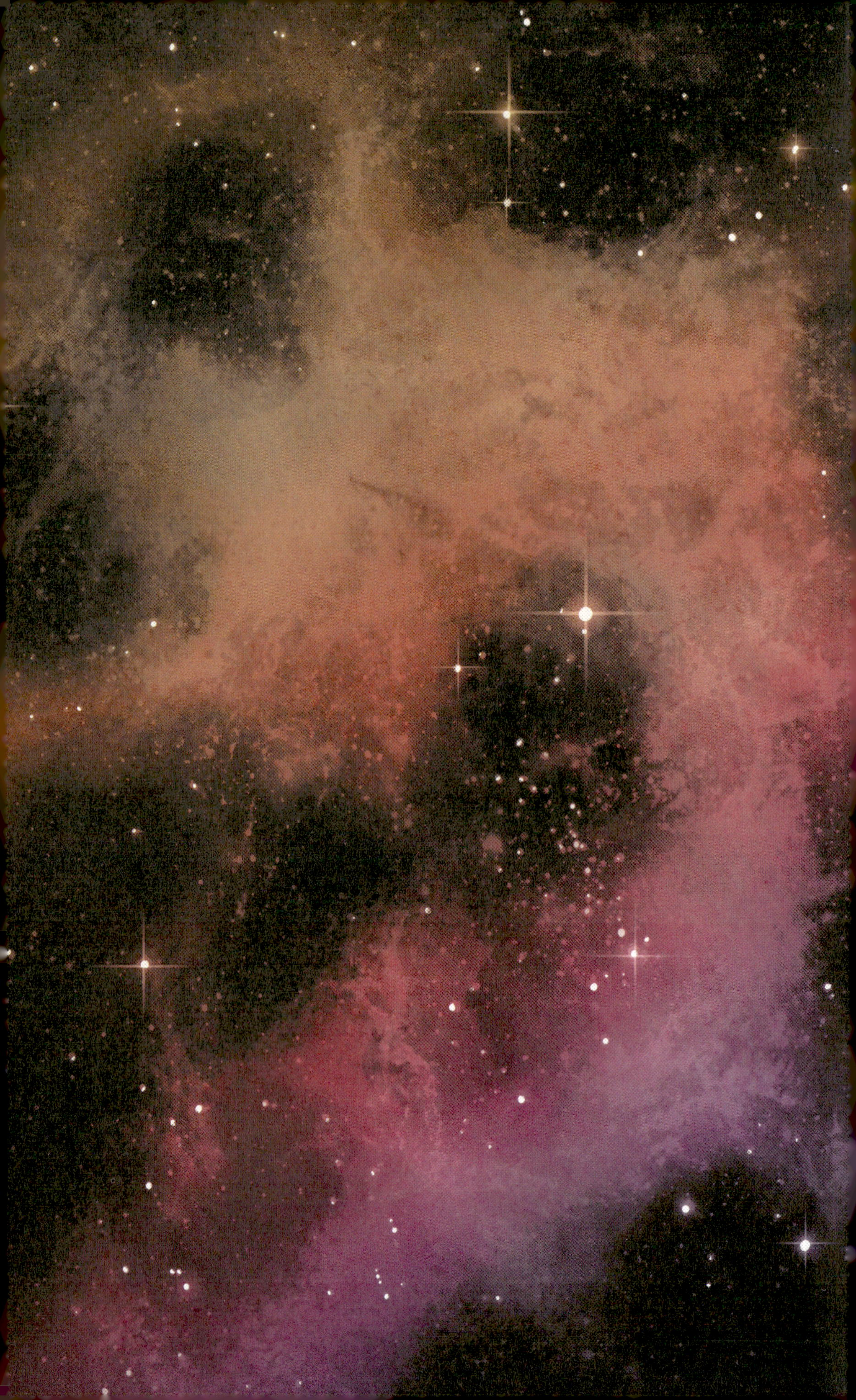

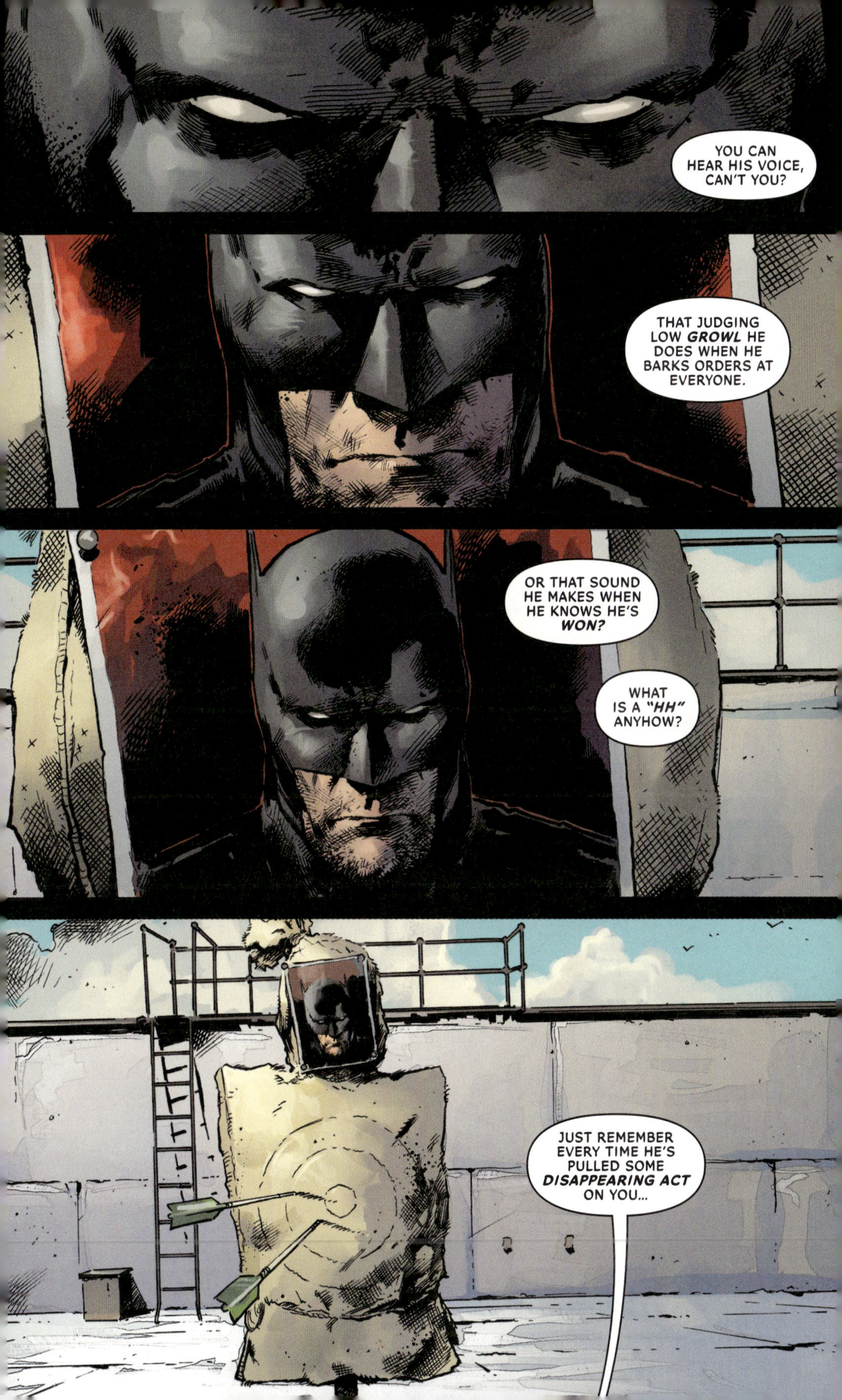
YOU CAN HEAR HIS VOICE, CAN'T YOU?
THAT JUDGING LOW **GROWL** HE DOES WHEN HE BARKS ORDERS AT EVERYONE.
OR THAT SOUND HE MAKES WHEN HE KNOWS HE'S ***WON?***
WHAT IS A ***"HH"*** ANYHOW?
JUST REMEMBER EVERY TIME HE'S PULLED SOME ***DISAPPEARING ACT*** ON YOU...

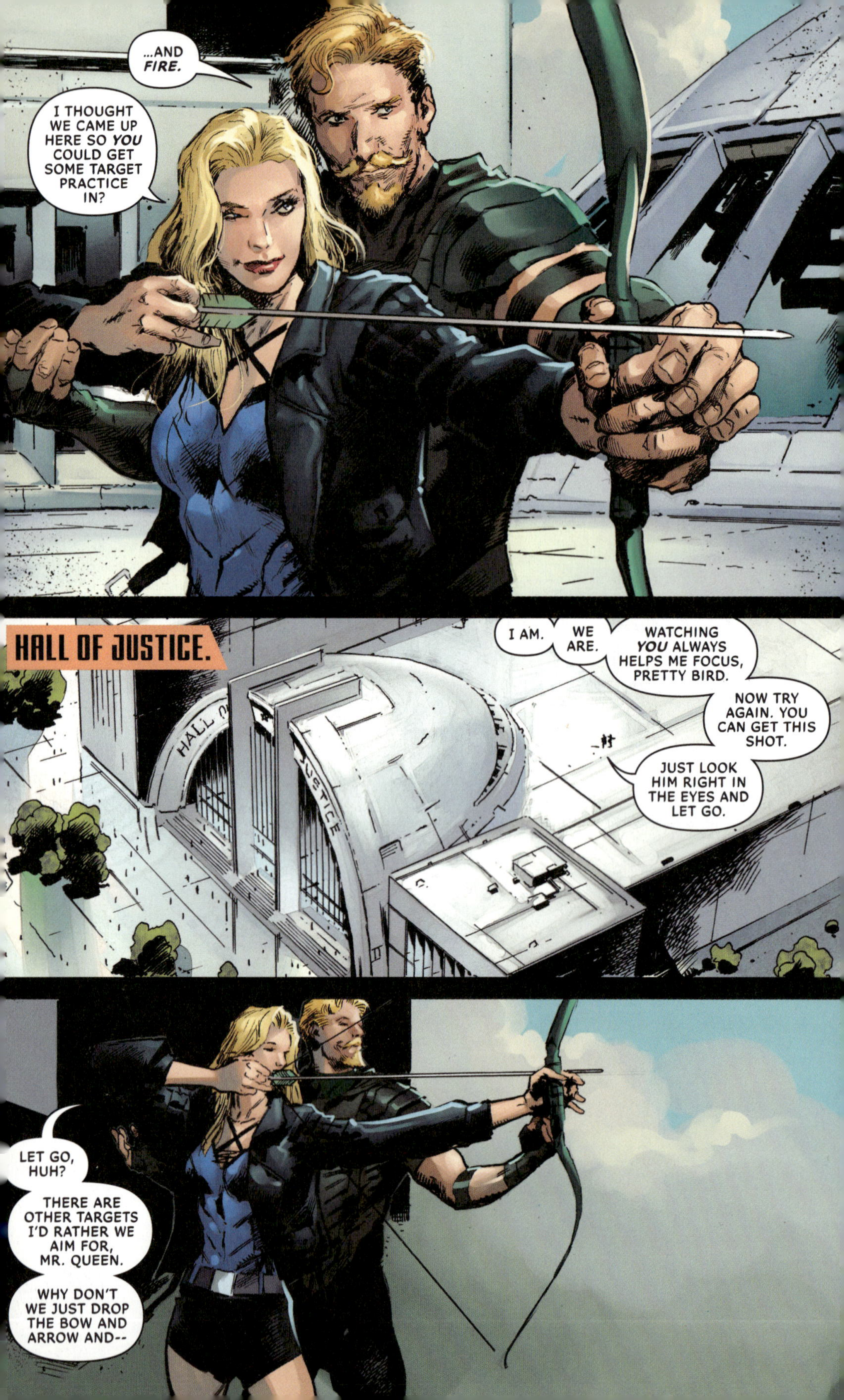
...AND *FIRE.*
I THOUGHT WE CAME UP HERE SO *YOU* COULD GET SOME TARGET PRACTICE IN?
HALL OF JUSTICE.
I AM.
WE ARE.
WATCHING *YOU* ALWAYS HELPS ME FOCUS, PRETTY BIRD.
NOW TRY AGAIN. YOU CAN GET THIS SHOT.
JUST LOOK HIM RIGHT IN THE EYES AND LET GO.
LET GO, HUH?
THERE ARE OTHER TARGETS I'D RATHER WE AIM FOR, MR. QUEEN.
WHY DON'T WE JUST DROP THE BOW AND ARROW AND--

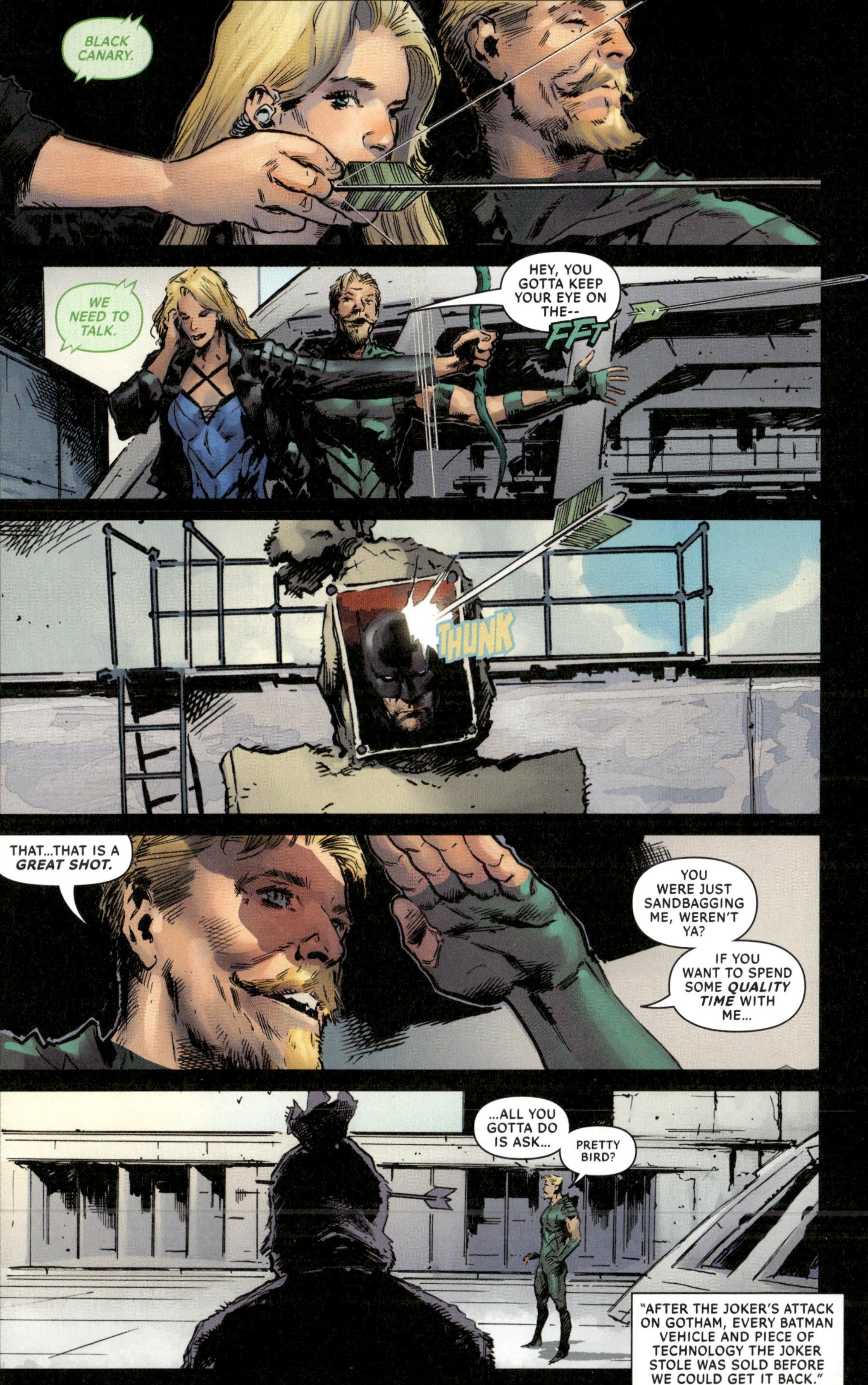
BLACK CANARY.
WE NEED TO TALK.
HEY, YOU GOTTA KEEP YOUR EYE ON THE--
FFT
THUNK
THAT...THAT IS A *GREAT SHOT.*
YOU WERE JUST SANDBAGGING ME, WEREN'T YA?
IF YOU WANT TO SPEND SOME *QUALITY TIME* WITH ME...
...ALL YOU GOTTA DO IS ASK...
PRETTY BIRD?
"AFTER THE JOKER'S ATTACK ON GOTHAM, EVERY BATMAN VEHICLE AND PIECE OF TECHNOLOGY THE JOKER STOLE WAS SOLD BEFORE WE COULD GET IT BACK."

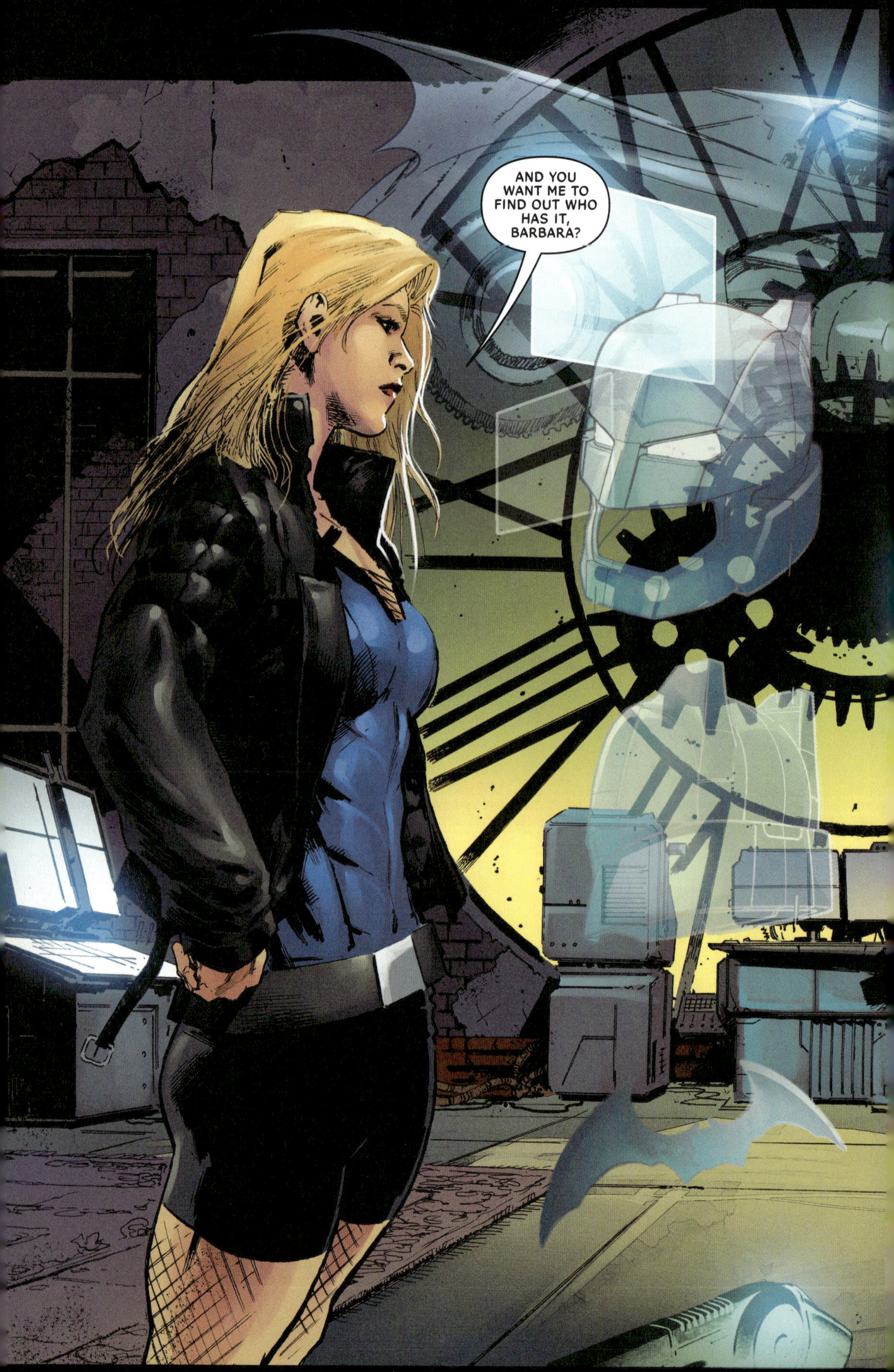
AND YOU WANT ME TO FIND OUT WHO HAS IT, BARBARA?

OH, I KNOW WHO.

THE BUYERS ARE A NEW BRITISH COMPANY CALLED T.R.U.S.T.

IT STANDS FOR "TRANSPARENT RESEARCHERS UNITED FOR STRATEGY AND TECHNOLOGY."

THEY LEFT A PAPER TRAIL. THEY MADE IT ALL LOOK VERY LEGAL.

TOO LEGAL, TO BE HONEST.

I KNOW SMOKE AND MIRRORS WHEN I SEE IT.

AND I DON'T LIKE THE IDEA OF BATMAN'S TECH IN *ANYONE'S* HANDS, LET ALONE A SECRET ORGANIZATION'S.

SOLO

WRITTEN BY JOSHUA WILLIAMSON
ART BY TREVOR HAIRSINE
COLOR BY RAIN BEREDO
LETTERS BY STEVE WANDS
EDITED BY BEN ABERNATHY

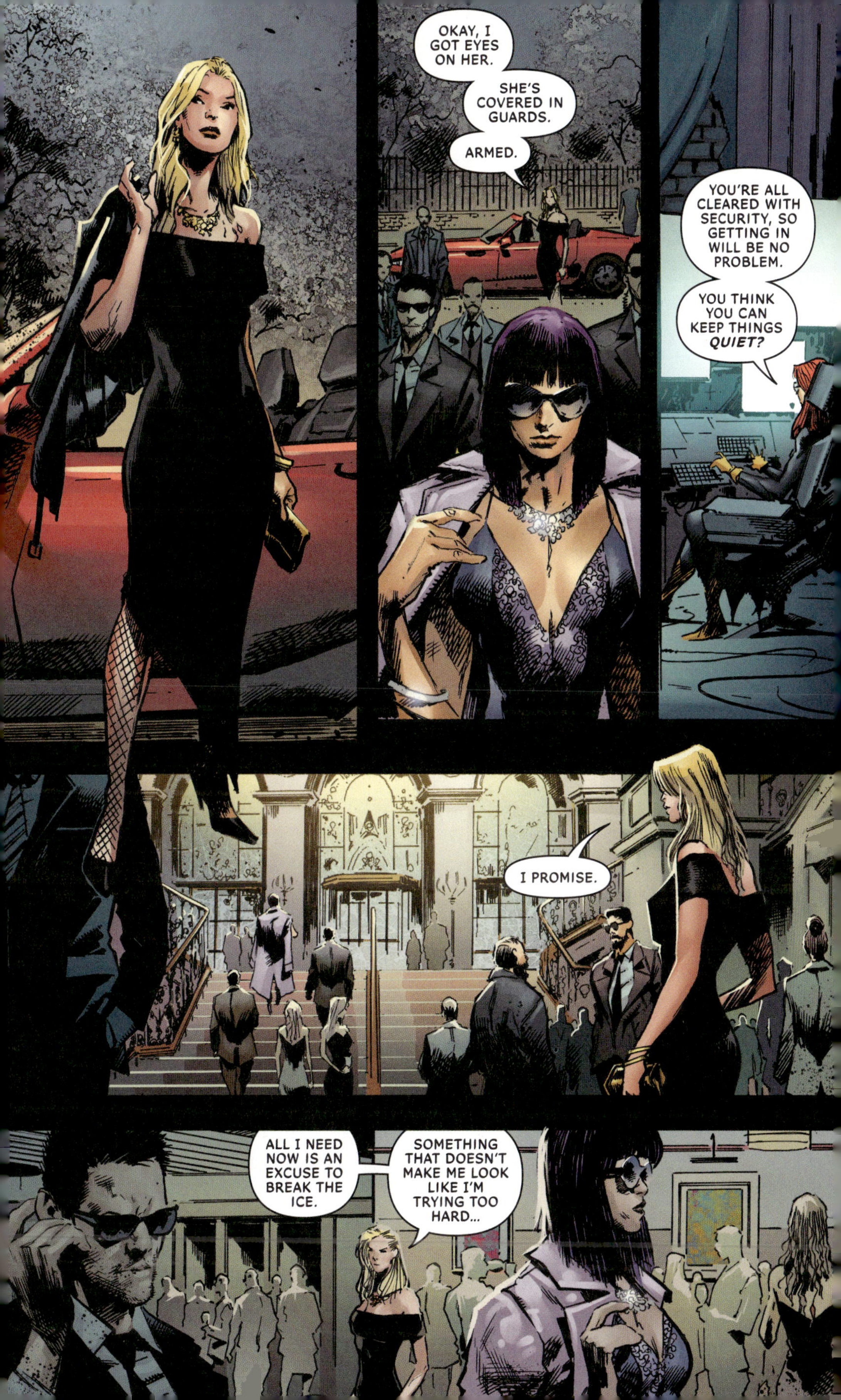
OKAY, I GOT EYES ON HER.
SHE'S COVERED IN GUARDS.
ARMED.
YOU'RE ALL CLEARED WITH SECURITY, SO GETTING IN WILL BE NO PROBLEM.
YOU THINK YOU CAN KEEP THINGS *QUIET?*
I PROMISE.
ALL I NEED NOW IS AN EXCUSE TO BREAK THE ICE.
SOMETHING THAT DOESN'T MAKE ME LOOK LIKE I'M TRYING TOO HARD...

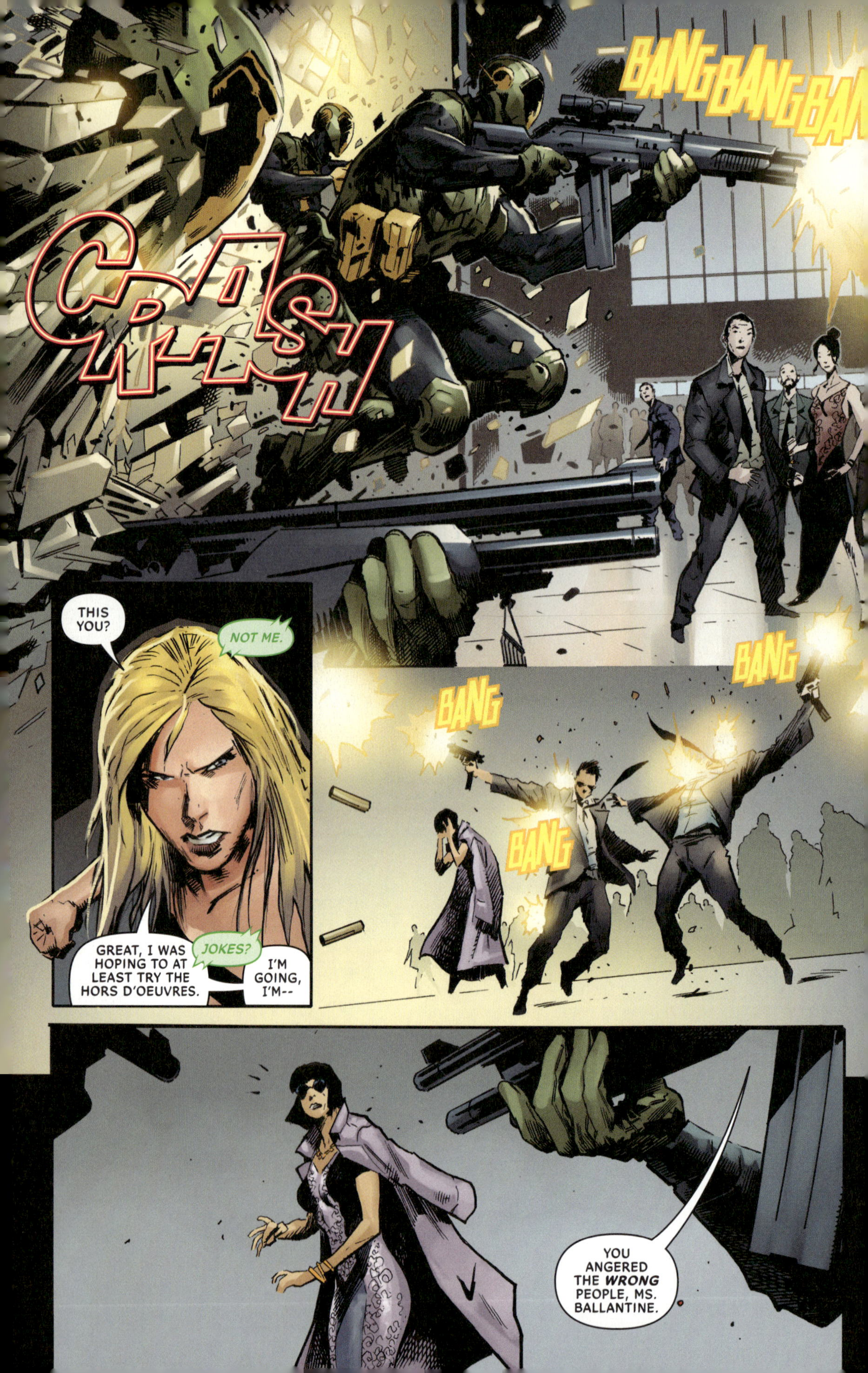

CRASH
BANG BANG BAN
THIS YOU?
NOT ME.
BANG
BANG
BANG
GREAT, I WAS HOPING TO AT LEAST TRY THE HORS D'OEUVRES.
JOKES?
I'M GOING, I'M--
YOU ANGERED THE *WRONG* PEOPLE, MS. BALLANTINE.

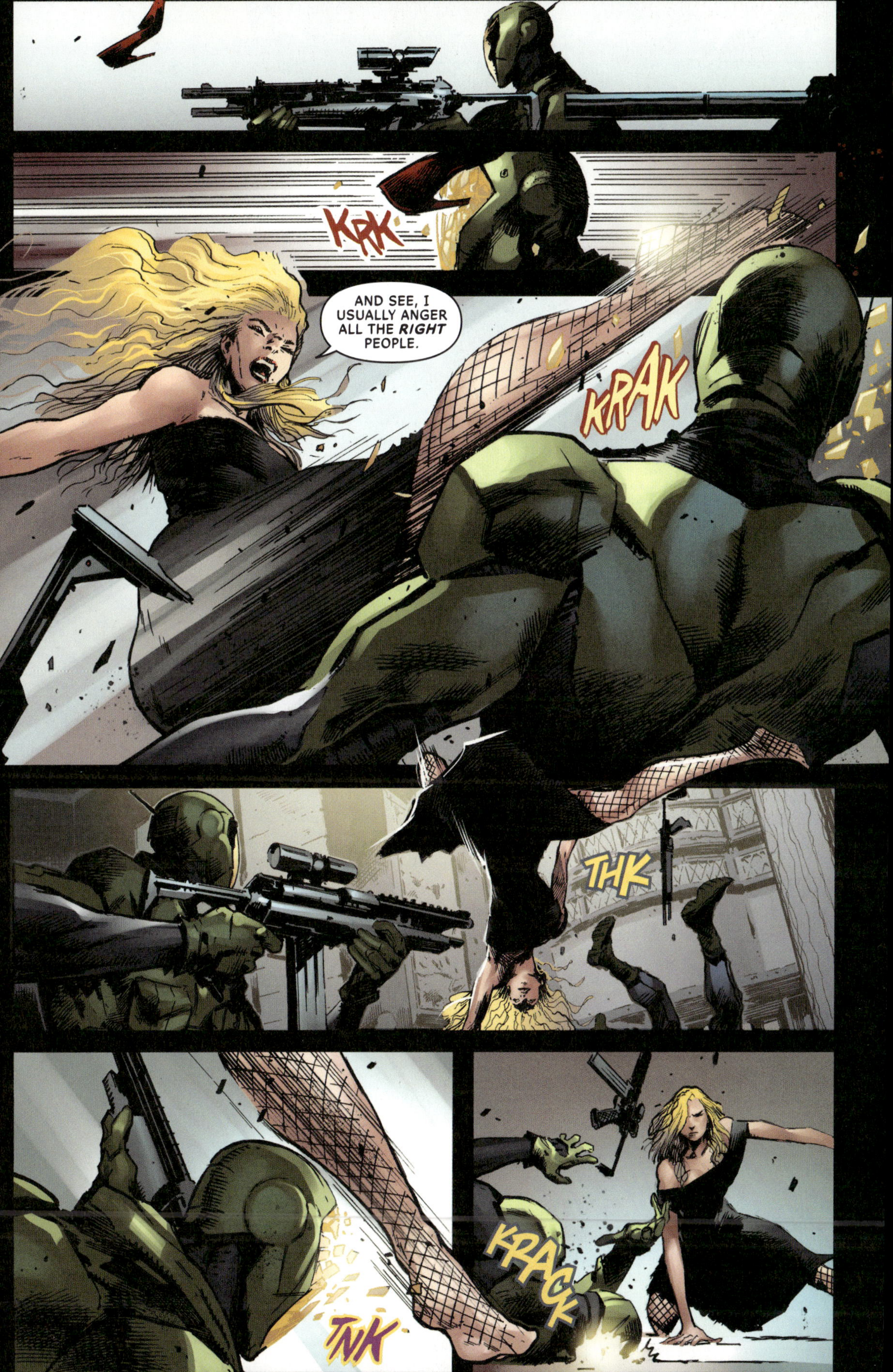
KRK
AND SEE, I USUALLY ANGER ALL THE *RIGHT* PEOPLE.
KRAK
THK
TNK
KRACK

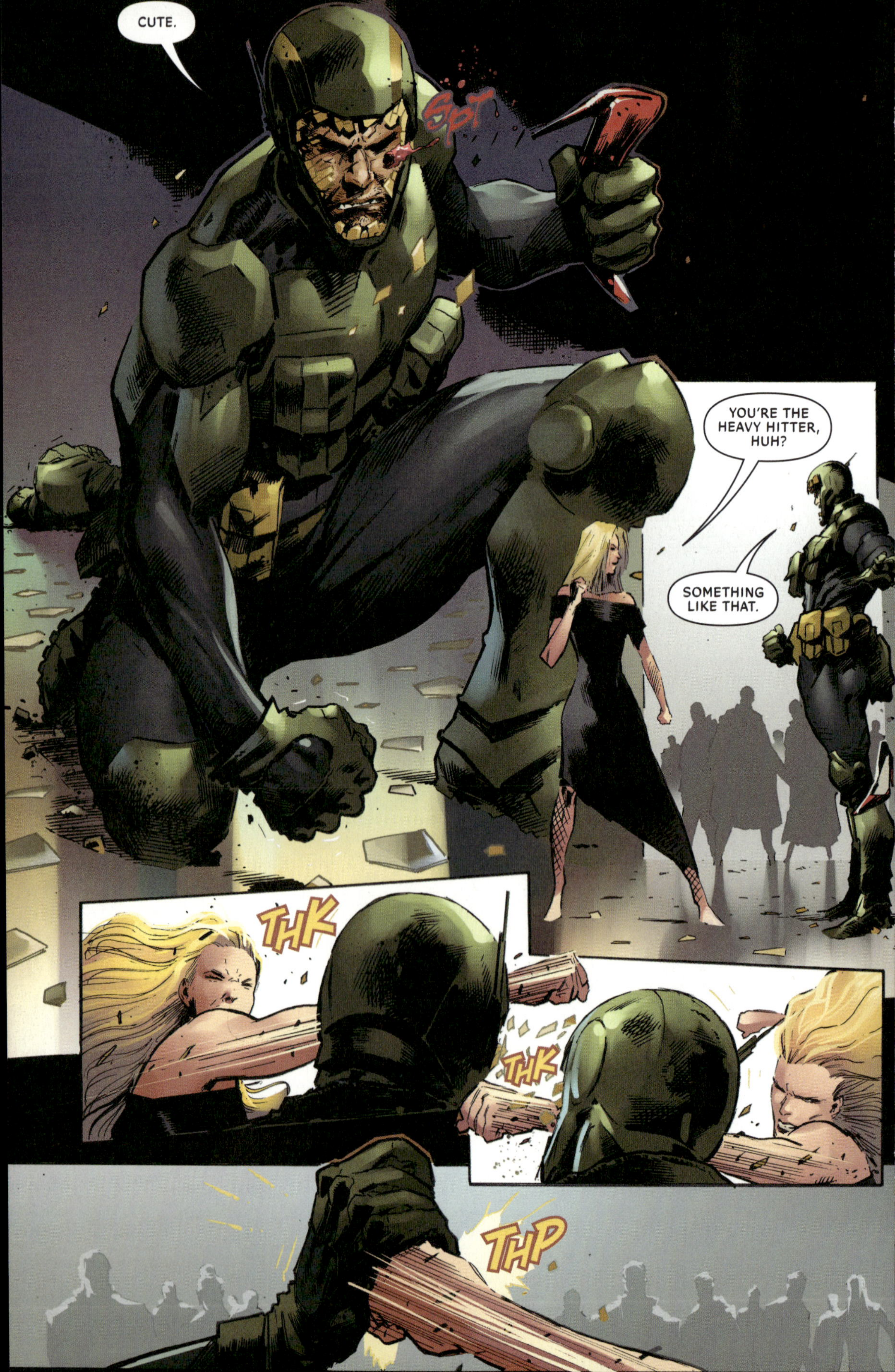
CUTE.
SPT
YOU'RE THE HEAVY HITTER, HUH?
SOMETHING LIKE THAT.
THK
THK
THP

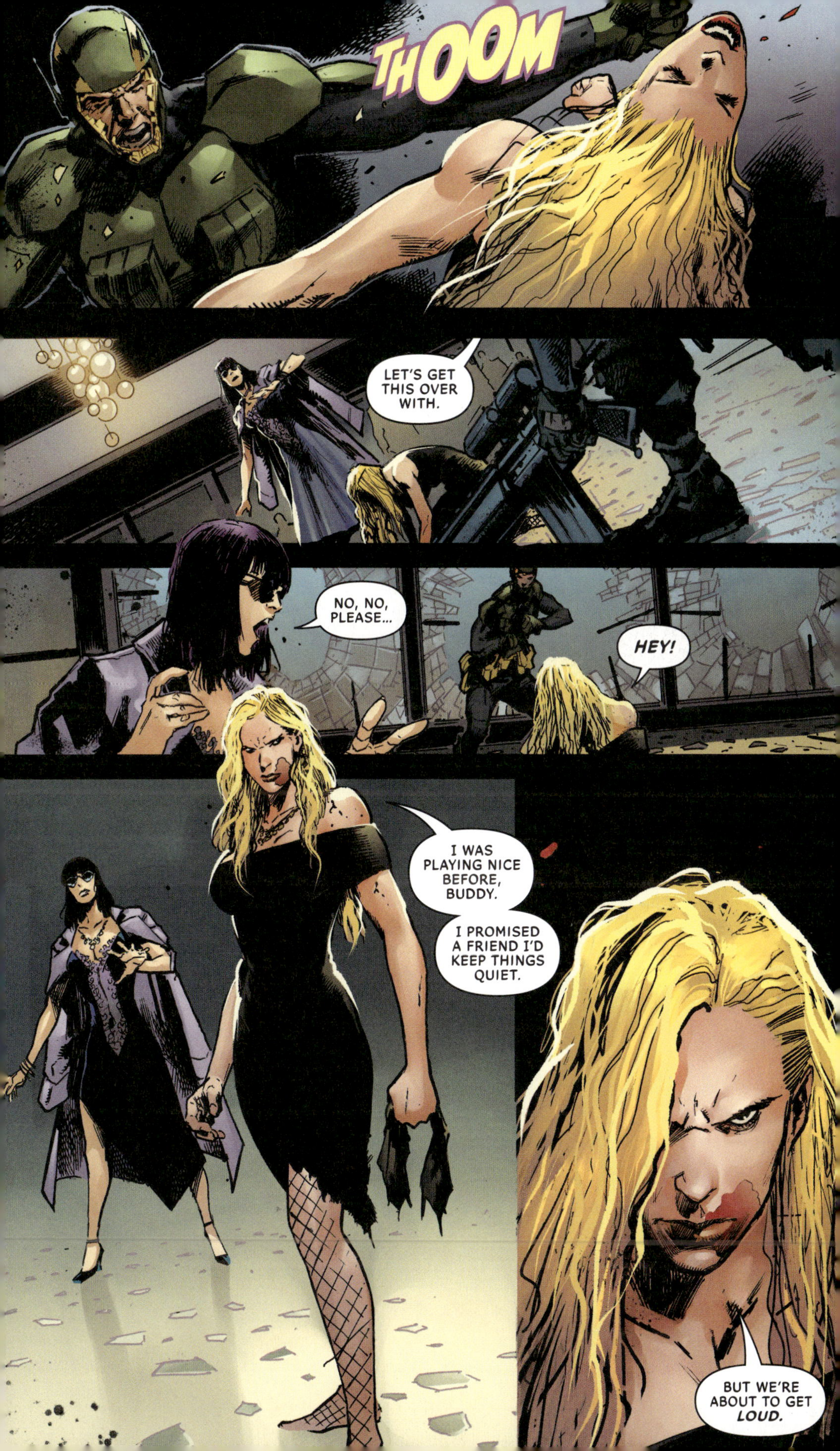
THOOM
LET'S GET THIS OVER WITH.
NO, NO, PLEASE...
HEY!
I WAS PLAYING NICE BEFORE, BUDDY.
I PROMISED A FRIEND I'D KEEP THINGS QUIET.
BUT WE'RE ABOUT TO GET *LOUD.*

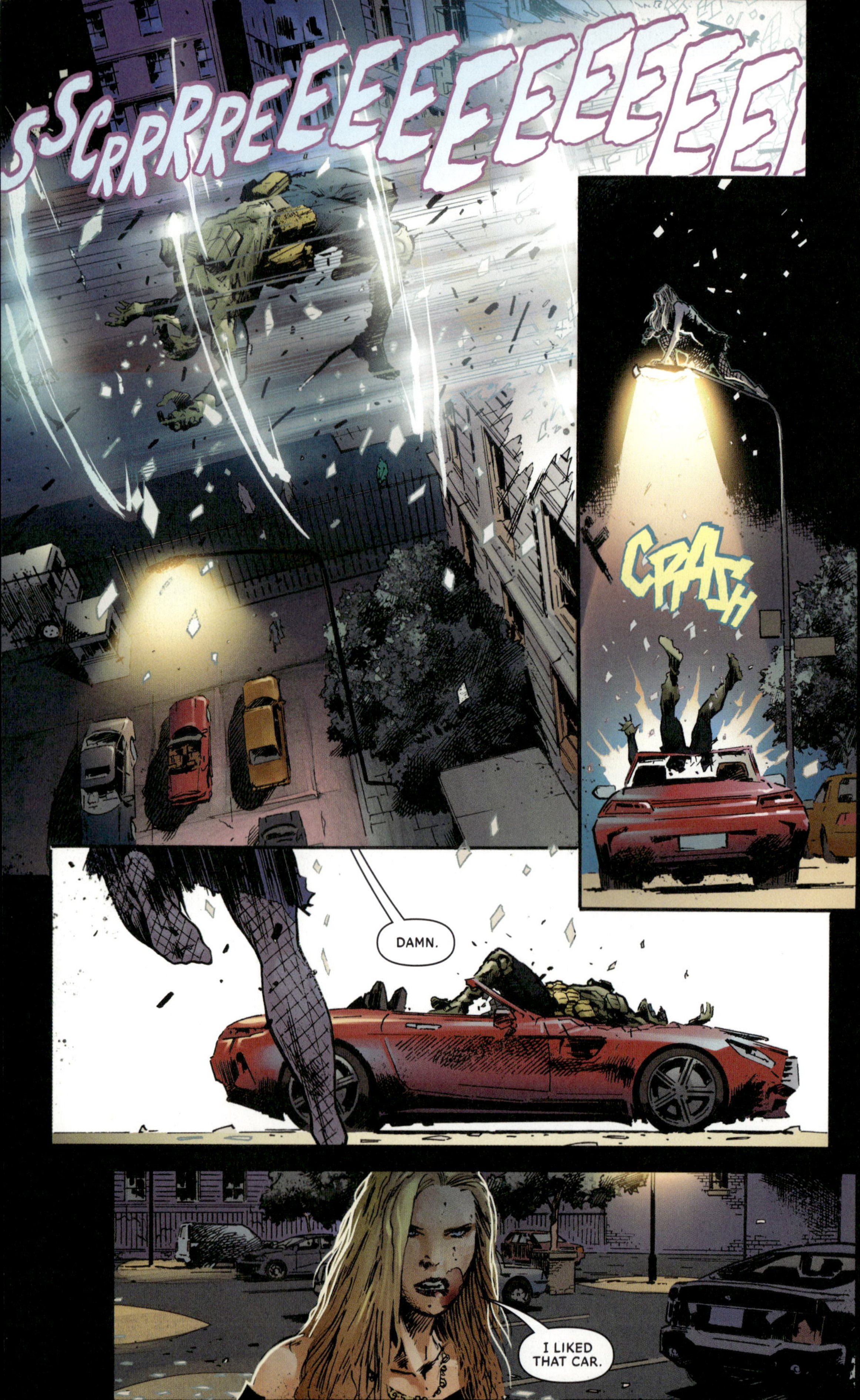
SSCRRRREEEEEEEEEEE
CRASH
DAMN.
I LIKED THAT CAR.

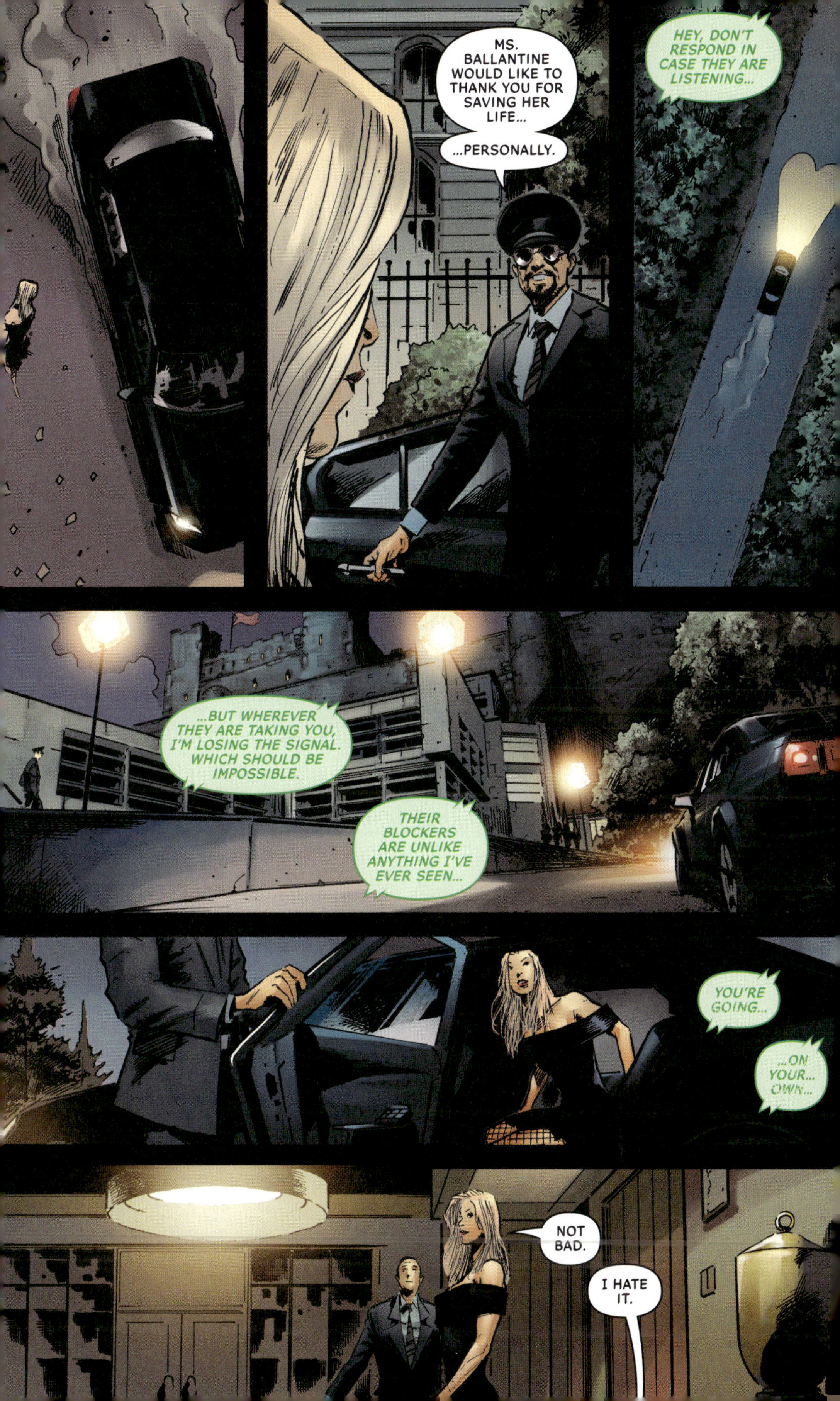
MS. BALLANTINE WOULD LIKE TO THANK YOU FOR SAVING HER LIFE...
...PERSONALLY.
HEY, DON'T RESPOND IN CASE THEY ARE LISTENING...
...BUT WHEREVER THEY ARE TAKING YOU, I'M LOSING THE SIGNAL. WHICH SHOULD BE IMPOSSIBLE.
THEIR BLOCKERS ARE UNLIKE ANYTHING I'VE EVER SEEN...
YOU'RE GOING...
...ON YOUR... OWN...
NOT BAD.
I HATE IT.

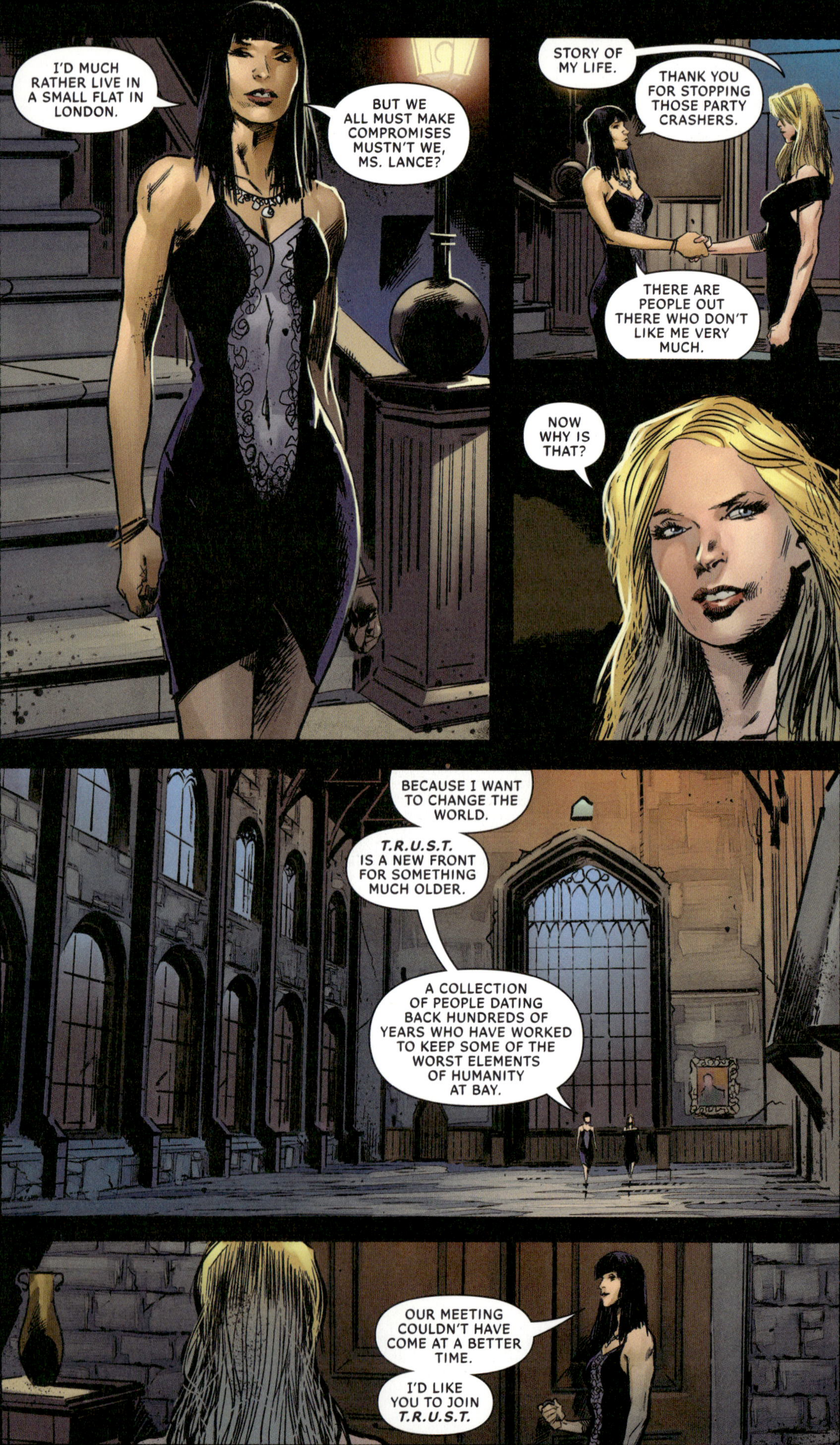
I'D MUCH RATHER LIVE IN A SMALL FLAT IN LONDON.
BUT WE ALL MUST MAKE COMPROMISES MUSTN'T WE, MS. LANCE?
STORY OF MY LIFE.
THANK YOU FOR STOPPING THOSE PARTY CRASHERS.
THERE ARE PEOPLE OUT THERE WHO DON'T LIKE ME VERY MUCH.
NOW WHY IS THAT?
BECAUSE I WANT TO CHANGE THE WORLD.
T.R.U.S.T. IS A NEW FRONT FOR SOMETHING MUCH OLDER.
A COLLECTION OF PEOPLE DATING BACK HUNDREDS OF YEARS WHO HAVE WORKED TO KEEP SOME OF THE WORST ELEMENTS OF HUMANITY AT BAY.
OUR MEETING COULDN'T HAVE COME AT A BETTER TIME.
I'D LIKE YOU TO JOIN *T.R.U.S.T.*

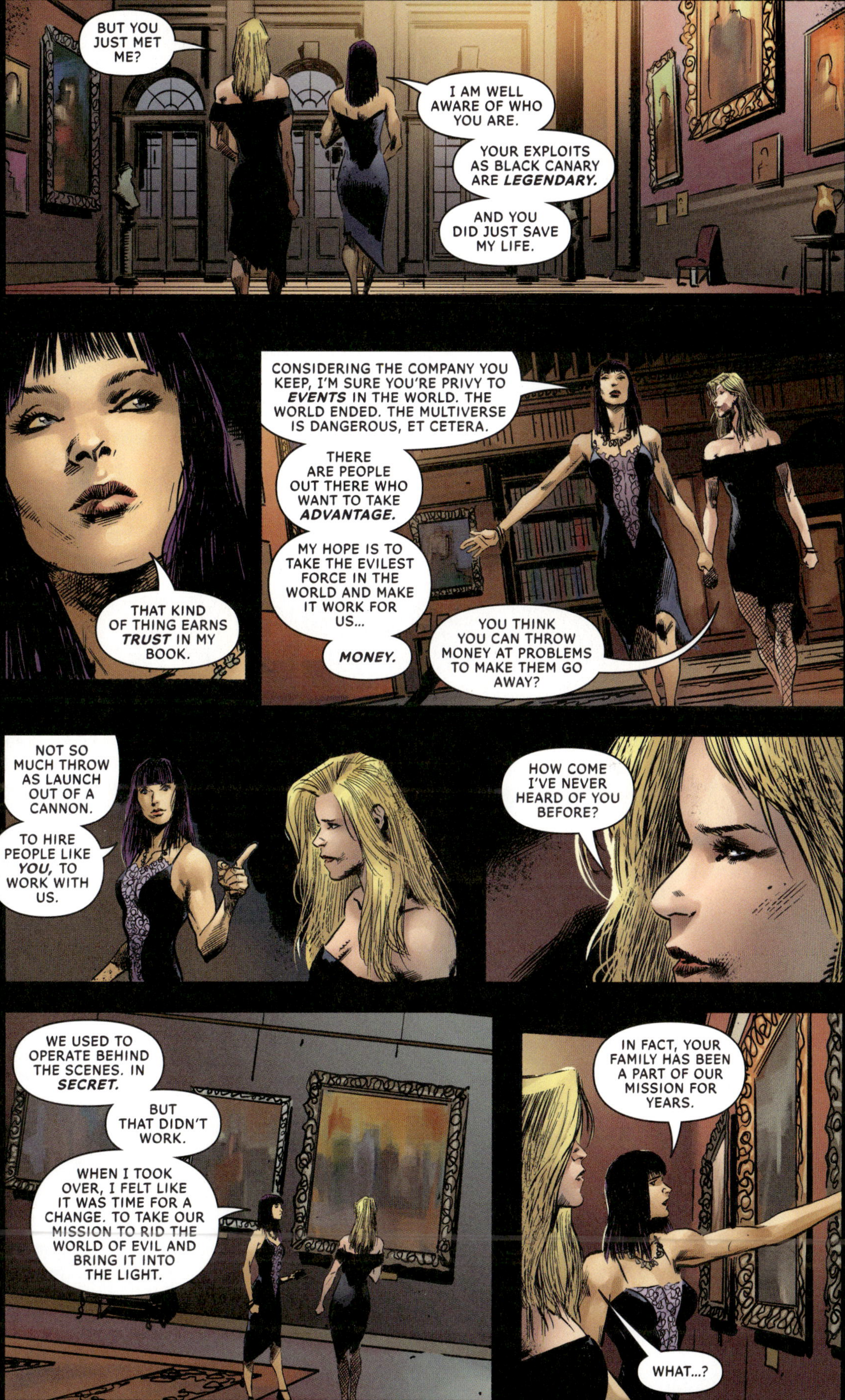
BUT YOU JUST MET ME?
I AM WELL AWARE OF WHO YOU ARE.
YOUR EXPLOITS AS BLACK CANARY ARE *LEGENDARY.*
AND YOU DID JUST SAVE MY LIFE.
THAT KIND OF THING EARNS *TRUST* IN MY BOOK.
CONSIDERING THE COMPANY YOU KEEP, I'M SURE YOU'RE PRIVY TO *EVENTS* IN THE WORLD. THE WORLD ENDED. THE MULTIVERSE IS DANGEROUS, ET CETERA.
THERE ARE PEOPLE OUT THERE WHO WANT TO TAKE *ADVANTAGE.*
MY HOPE IS TO TAKE THE EVILEST FORCE IN THE WORLD AND MAKE IT WORK FOR US...
MONEY.
YOU THINK YOU CAN THROW MONEY AT PROBLEMS TO MAKE THEM GO AWAY?
NOT SO MUCH THROW AS LAUNCH OUT OF A CANNON.
TO HIRE PEOPLE LIKE *YOU,* TO WORK WITH US.
HOW COME I'VE NEVER HEARD OF YOU BEFORE?
WE USED TO OPERATE BEHIND THE SCENES. IN *SECRET.*
BUT THAT DIDN'T WORK.
WHEN I TOOK OVER, I FELT LIKE IT WAS TIME FOR A CHANGE. TO TAKE OUR MISSION TO RID THE WORLD OF EVIL AND BRING IT INTO THE LIGHT.
IN FACT, YOUR FAMILY HAS BEEN A PART OF OUR MISSION FOR YEARS.
WHAT...?

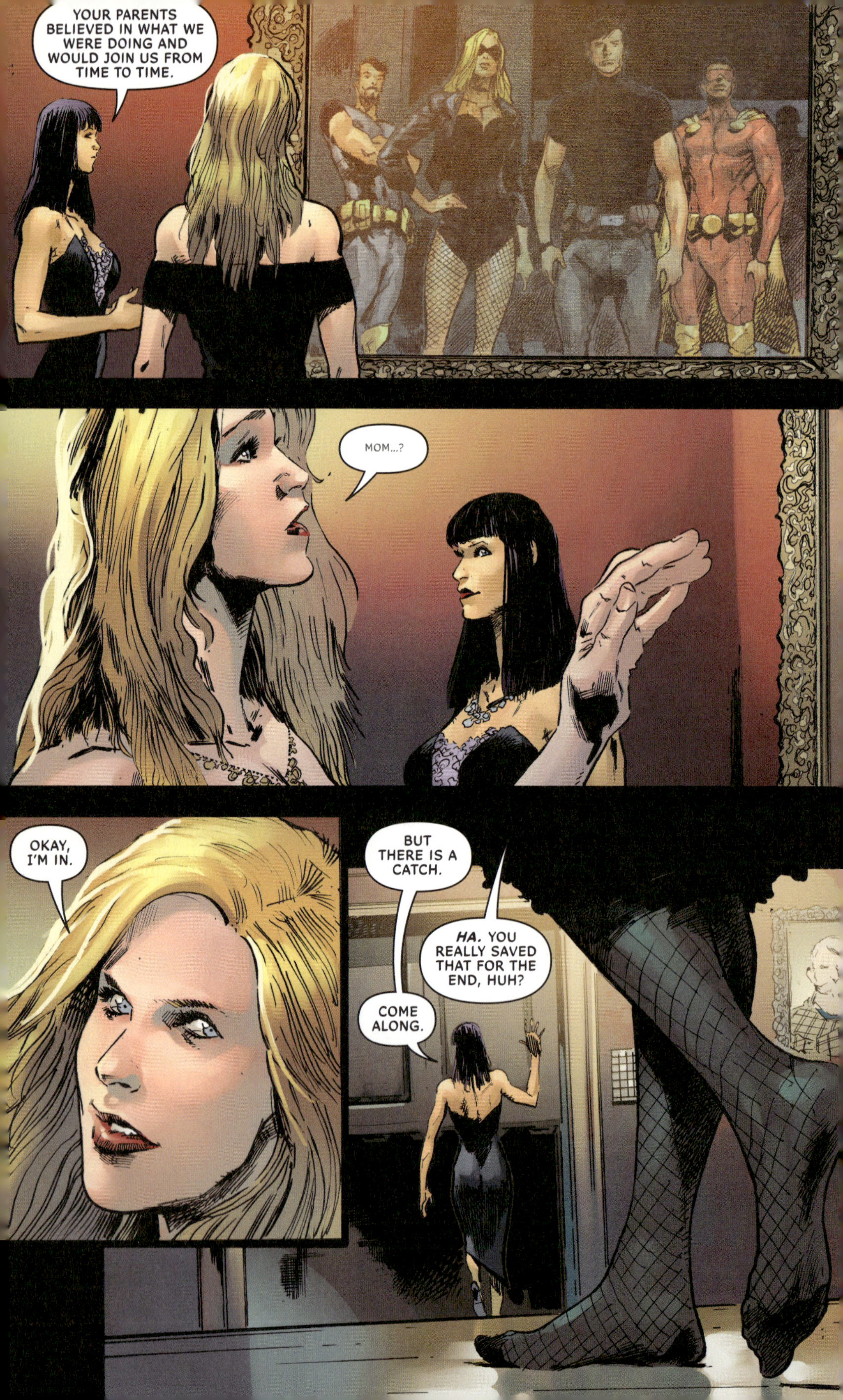
YOUR PARENTS BELIEVED IN WHAT WE WERE DOING AND WOULD JOIN US FROM TIME TO TIME.
MOM...?
OKAY, I'M IN.
BUT THERE IS A CATCH.
HA. YOU REALLY SAVED THAT FOR THE END, HUH?
COME ALONG.

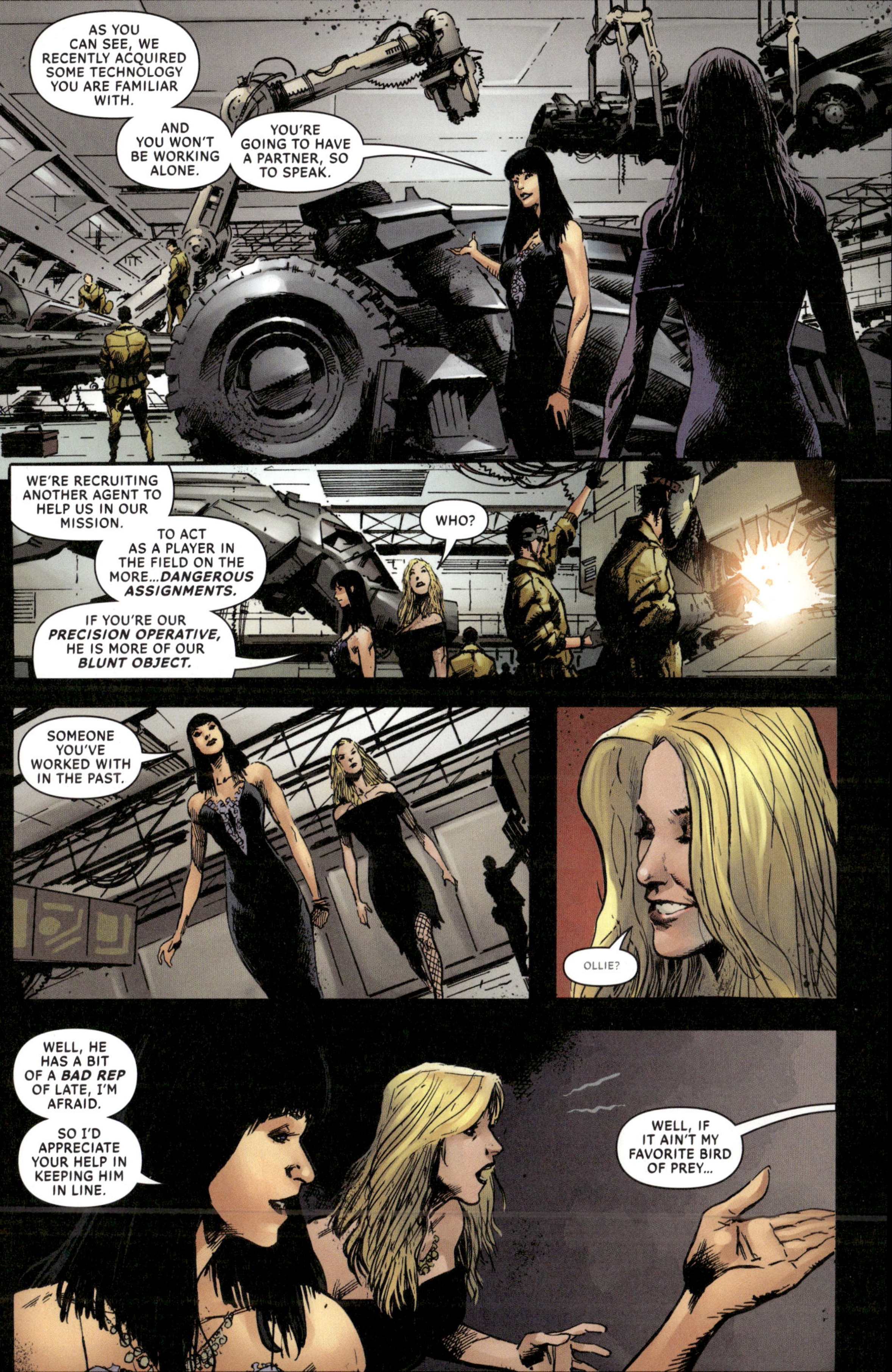
AS YOU CAN SEE, WE RECENTLY ACQUIRED SOME TECHNOLOGY YOU ARE FAMILIAR WITH.
AND YOU WON'T BE WORKING ALONE.
YOU'RE GOING TO HAVE A PARTNER, SO TO SPEAK.
WE'RE RECRUITING ANOTHER AGENT TO HELP US IN OUR MISSION.
TO ACT AS A PLAYER IN THE FIELD ON THE MORE...*DANGEROUS ASSIGNMENTS.*
IF YOU'RE OUR *PRECISION OPERATIVE,* HE IS MORE OF OUR *BLUNT OBJECT.*
WHO?
SOMEONE YOU'VE WORKED WITH IN THE PAST.
OLLIE?
WELL, HE HAS A BIT OF A *BAD REP* OF LATE, I'M AFRAID.
SO I'D APPRECIATE YOUR HELP IN KEEPING HIM IN LINE.
WELL, IF IT AIN'T MY FAVORITE BIRD OF PREY...

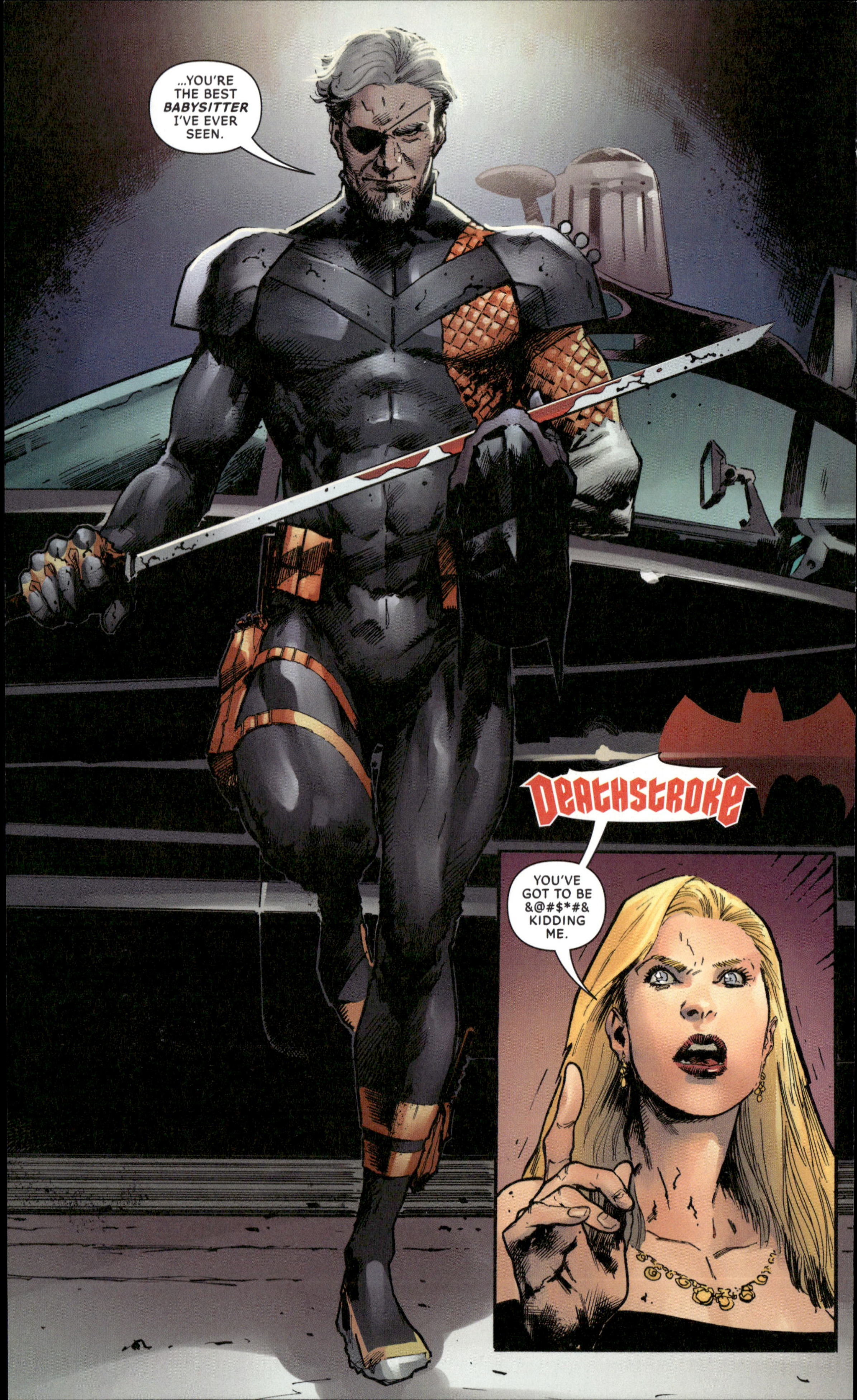
...YOU'RE THE BEST BABYSITTER I'VE EVER SEEN.
DEATHSTROKE
YOU'VE GOT TO BE &@#$*#& KIDDING ME.

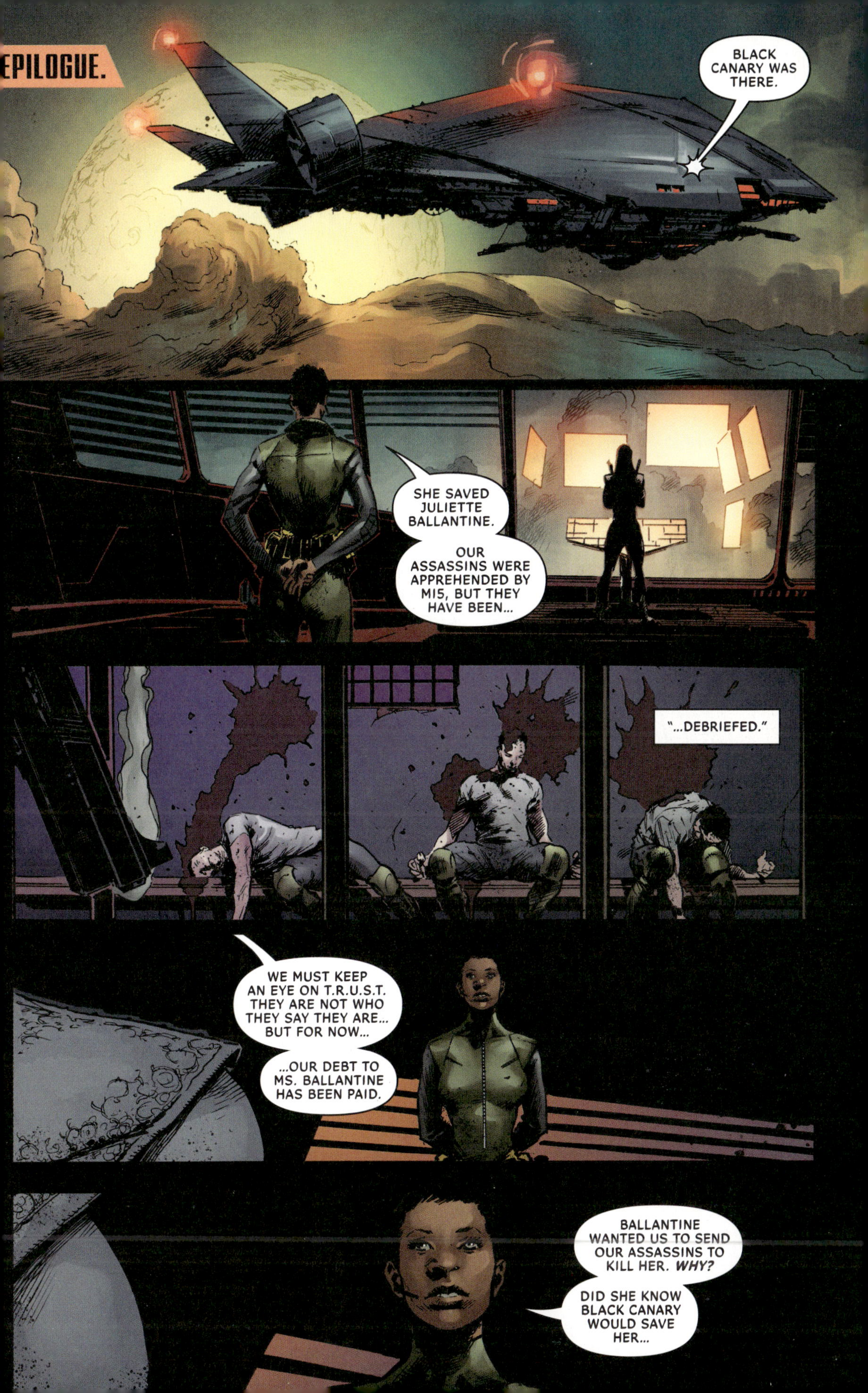

EPILOGUE.
BLACK CANARY WAS THERE.
SHE SAVED JULIETTE BALLANTINE.
OUR ASSASSINS WERE APPREHENDED BY MI5, BUT THEY HAVE BEEN...
"...DEBRIEFED."
WE MUST KEEP AN EYE ON T.R.U.S.T. THEY ARE NOT WHO THEY SAY THEY ARE... BUT FOR NOW...
...OUR DEBT TO MS. BALLANTINE HAS BEEN PAID.
BALLANTINE WANTED US TO SEND OUR ASSASSINS TO KILL HER. *WHY?*
DID SHE KNOW BLACK CANARY WOULD SAVE HER...

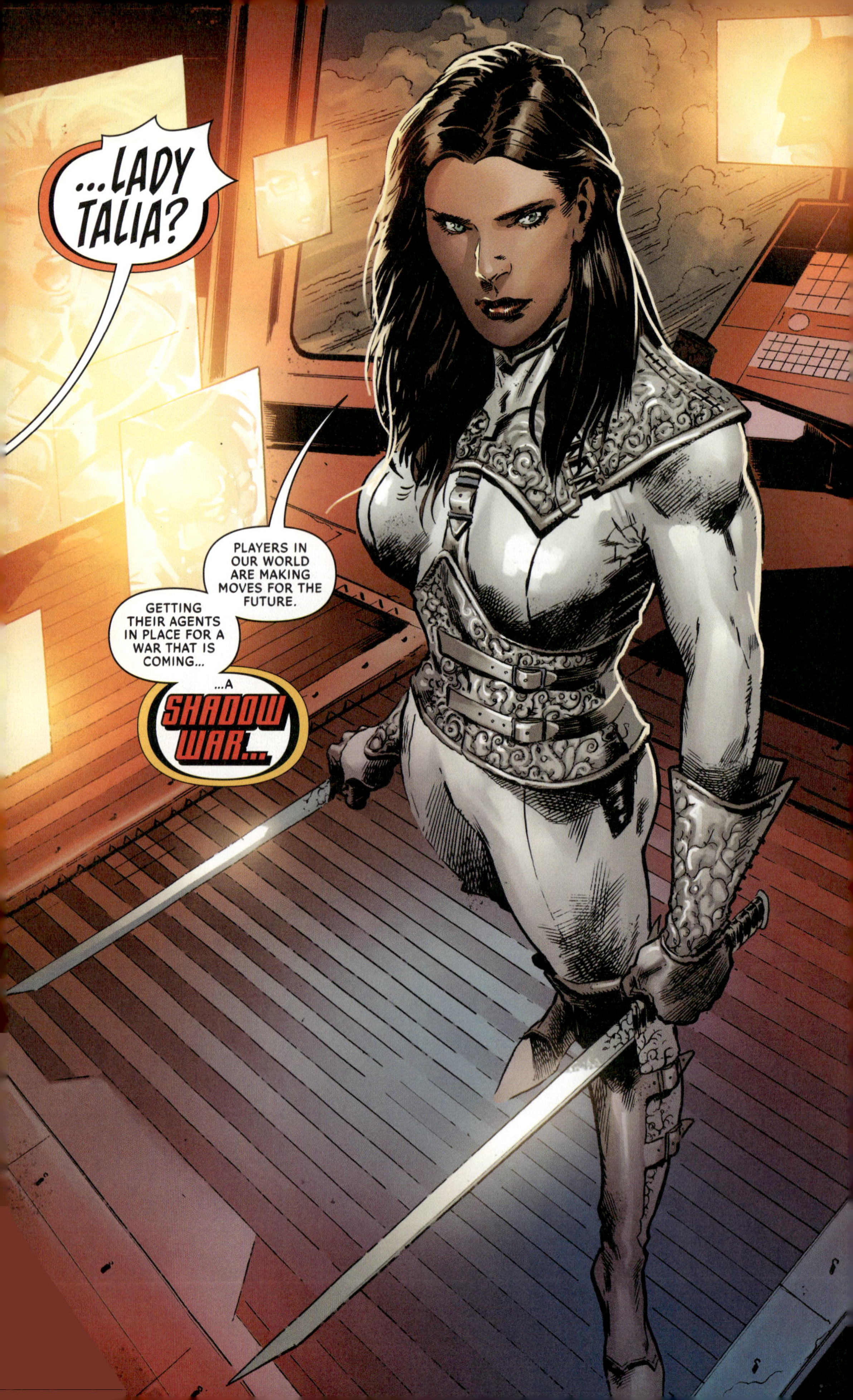
...LADY TALIA?
PLAYERS IN OUR WORLD ARE MAKING MOVES FOR THE FUTURE.
GETTING THEIR AGENTS IN PLACE FOR A WAR THAT IS COMING...
...A SHADOW WAR...

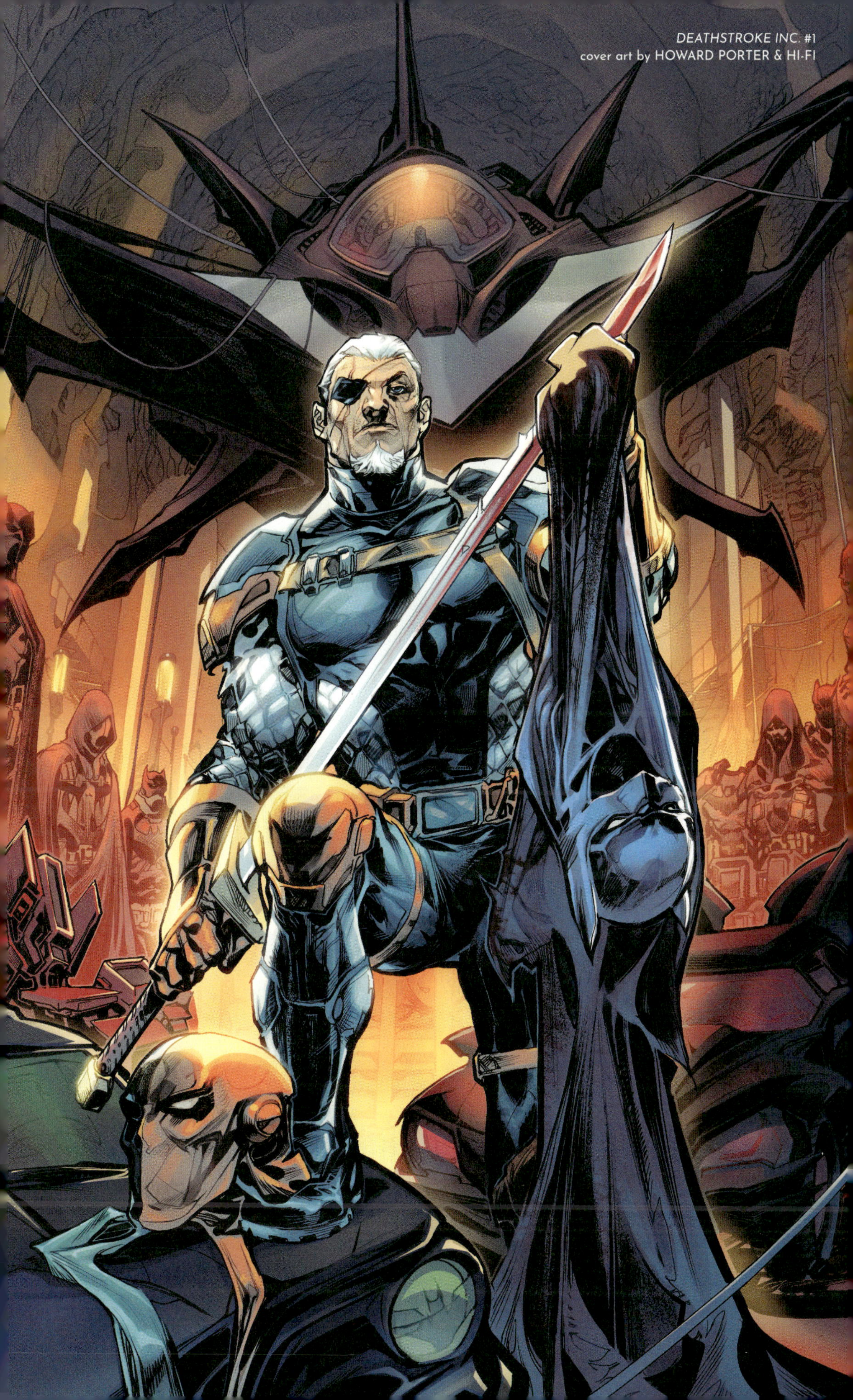

DEATHSTROKE INC. #1
cover art by HOWARD PORTER & HI-FI

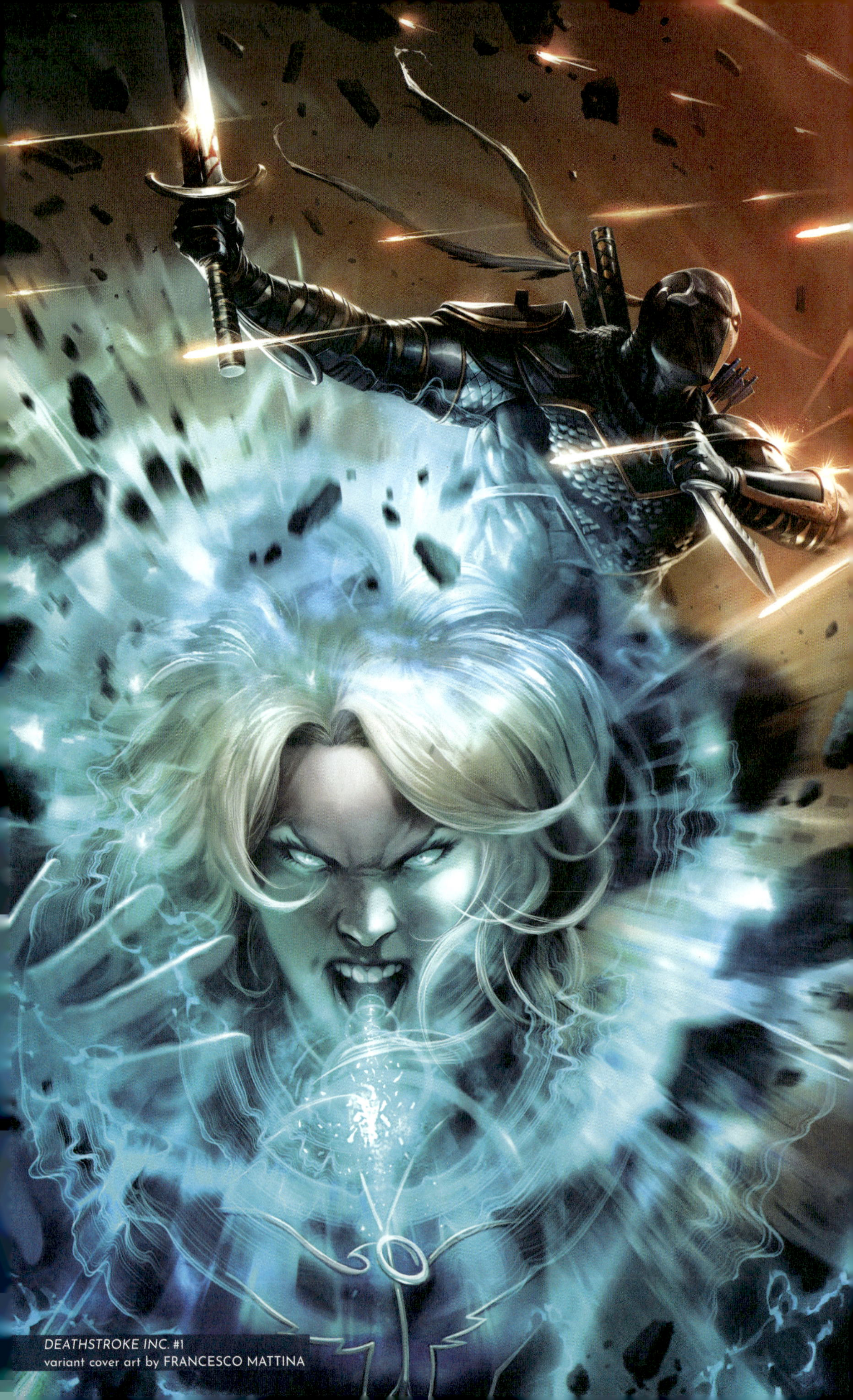

DEATHSTROKE INC. #1
variant cover art by FRANCESCO MATTINA

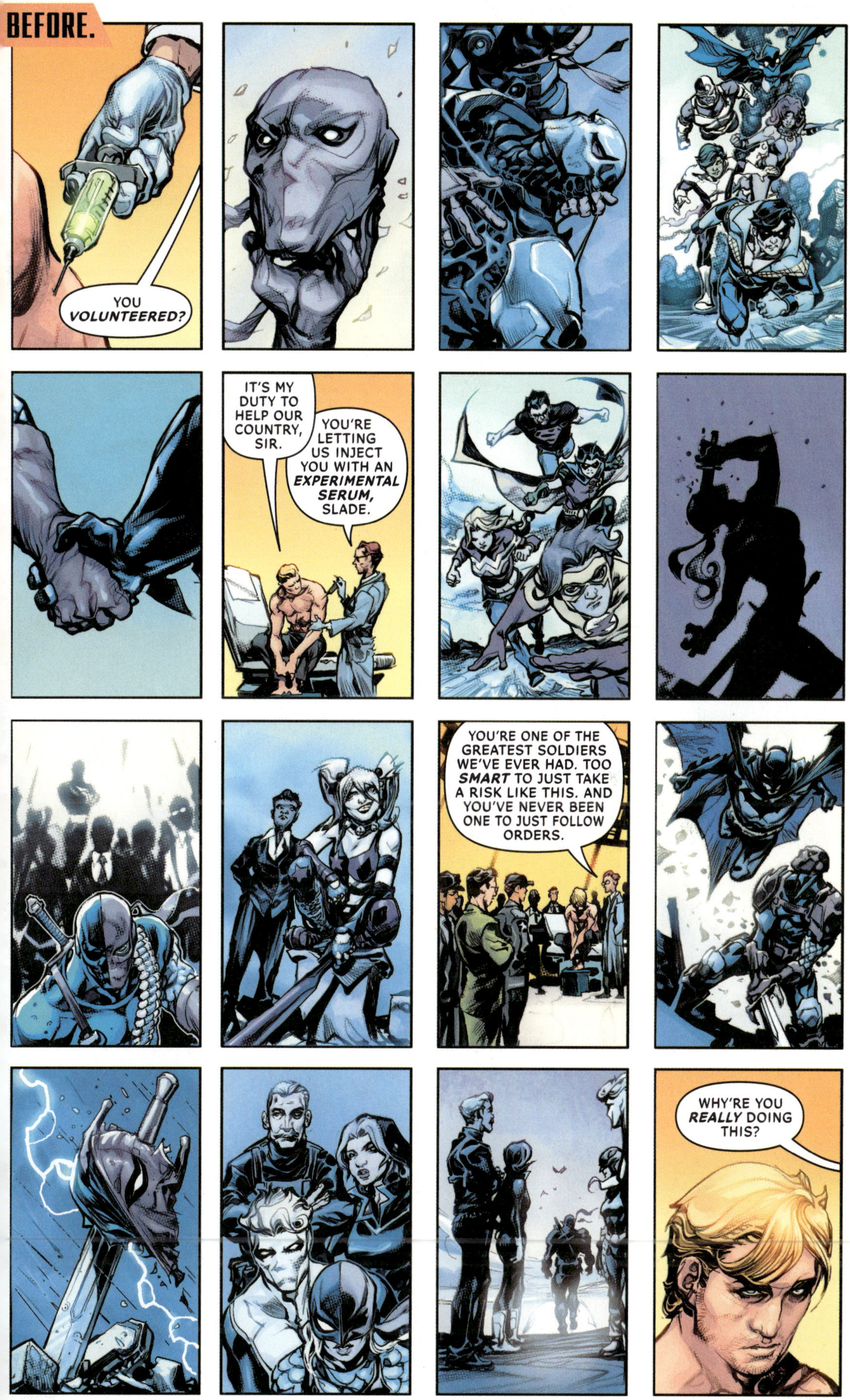
BEFORE.
YOU VOLUNTEERED?
IT'S MY DUTY TO HELP OUR COUNTRY, SIR.
YOU'RE LETTING US INJECT YOU WITH AN EXPERIMENTAL SERUM, SLADE.
YOU'RE ONE OF THE GREATEST SOLDIERS WE'VE EVER HAD. TOO SMART TO JUST TAKE A RISK LIKE THIS. AND YOU'VE NEVER BEEN ONE TO JUST FOLLOW ORDERS.
WHY'RE YOU REALLY DOING THIS?

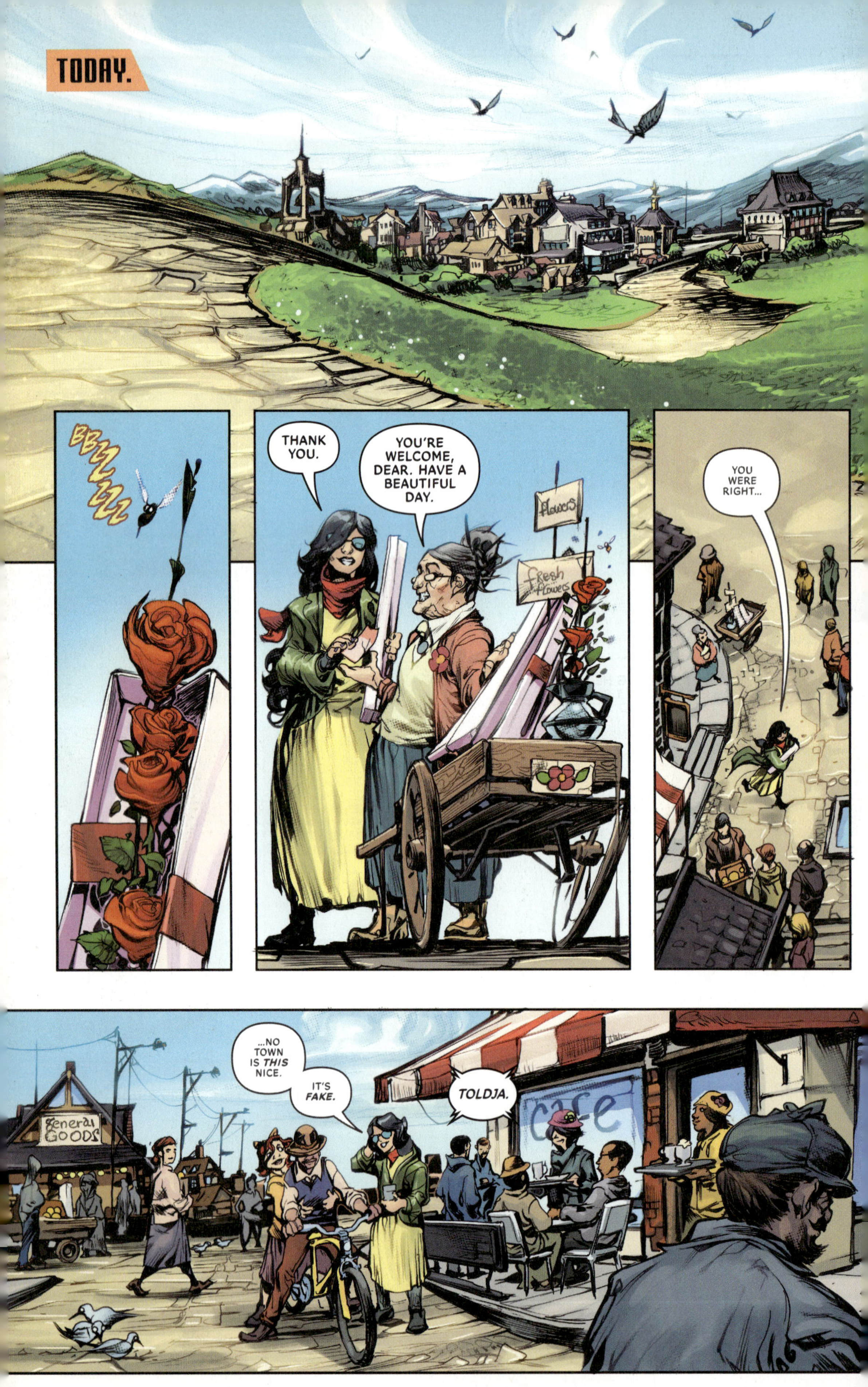
TODAY.
BZZZZZ
THANK YOU.
YOU'RE WELCOME, DEAR. HAVE A BEAUTIFUL DAY.
Flowers
Fresh Flowers
YOU WERE RIGHT...
...NO TOWN IS *THIS* NICE.
IT'S *FAKE.*
TOLDJA.
General GOODS
Cafe

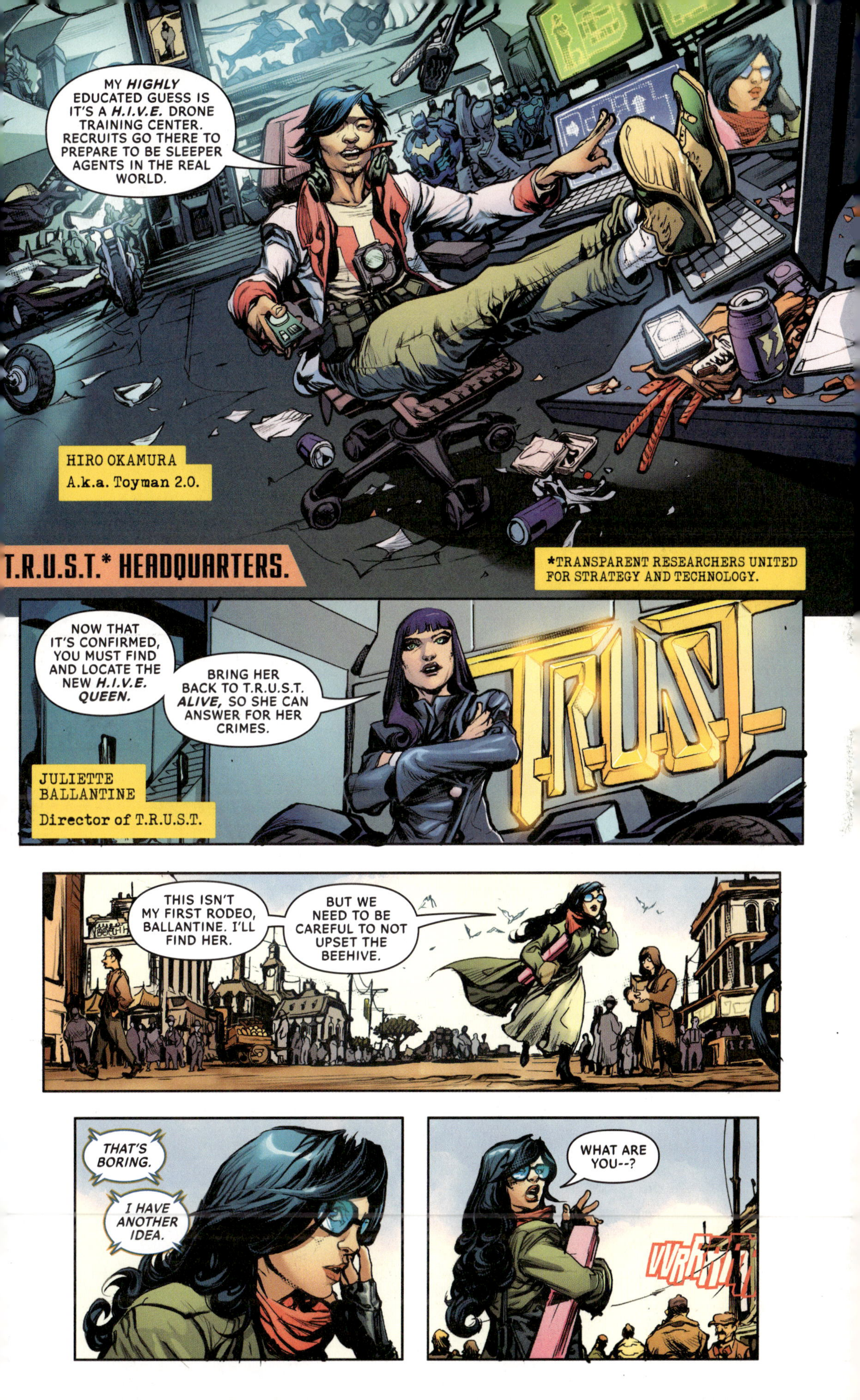
MY HIGHLY EDUCATED GUESS IS IT'S A H.I.V.E. DRONE TRAINING CENTER. RECRUITS GO THERE TO PREPARE TO BE SLEEPER AGENTS IN THE REAL WORLD.
HIRO OKAMURA
A.k.a. Toyman 2.0.
T.R.U.S.T.* HEADQUARTERS.
*TRANSPARENT RESEARCHERS UNITED FOR STRATEGY AND TECHNOLOGY.
NOW THAT IT'S CONFIRMED, YOU MUST FIND AND LOCATE THE NEW H.I.V.E. QUEEN.
BRING HER BACK TO T.R.U.S.T. ALIVE, SO SHE CAN ANSWER FOR HER CRIMES.
JULIETTE BALLANTINE
Director of T.R.U.S.T.
T.R.U.S.T.
THIS ISN'T MY FIRST RODEO, BALLANTINE. I'LL FIND HER.
BUT WE NEED TO BE CAREFUL TO NOT UPSET THE BEEHIVE.
THAT'S BORING.
I HAVE ANOTHER IDEA.
WHAT ARE YOU--?

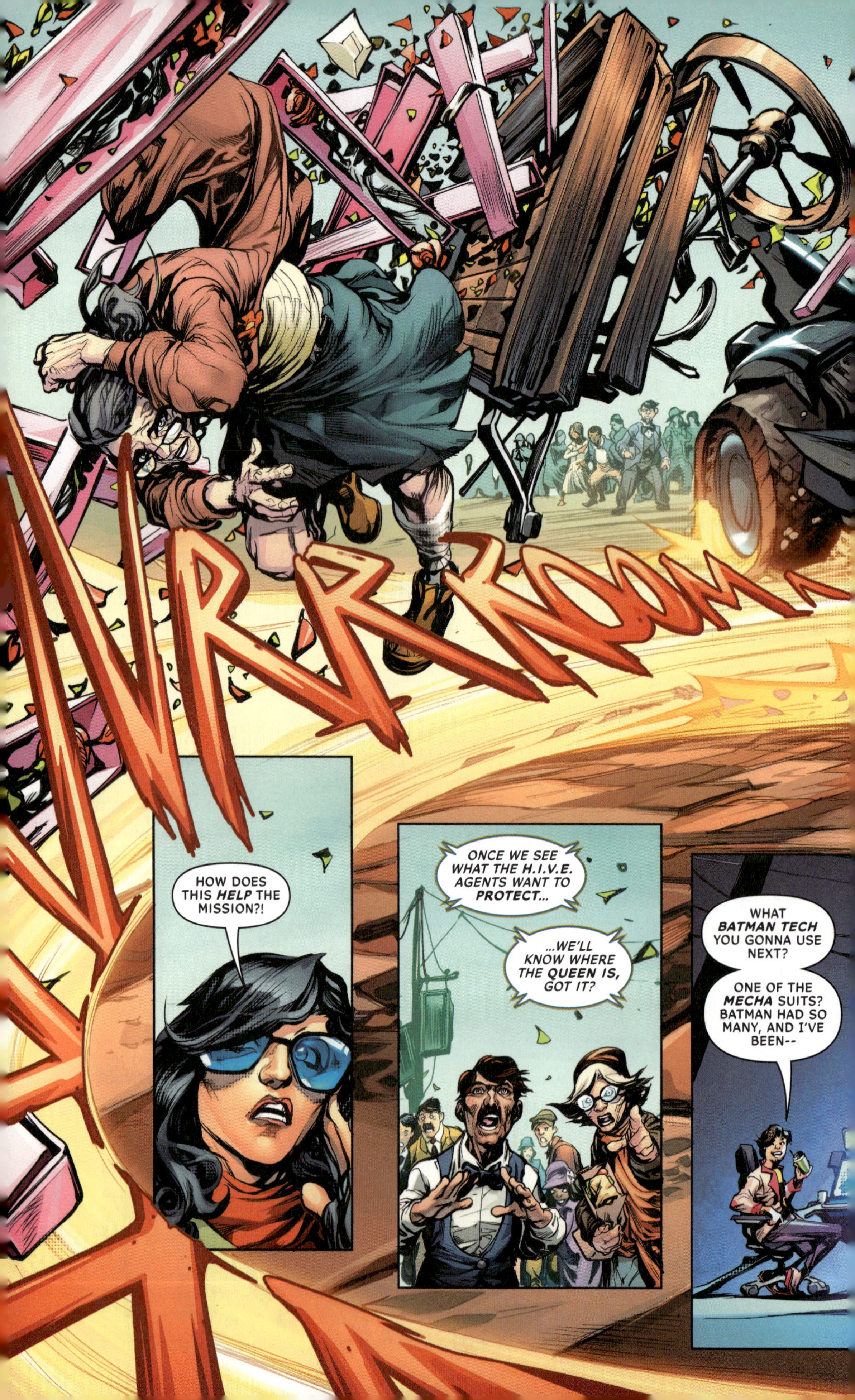
VRROOM
HOW DOES THIS HELP THE MISSION?!
ONCE WE SEE WHAT THE H.I.V.E. AGENTS WANT TO PROTECT...
...WE'LL KNOW WHERE THE QUEEN IS, GOT IT?
WHAT BATMAN TECH YOU GONNA USE NEXT?
ONE OF THE MECHA SUITS? BATMAN HAD SO MANY, AND I'VE BEEN--

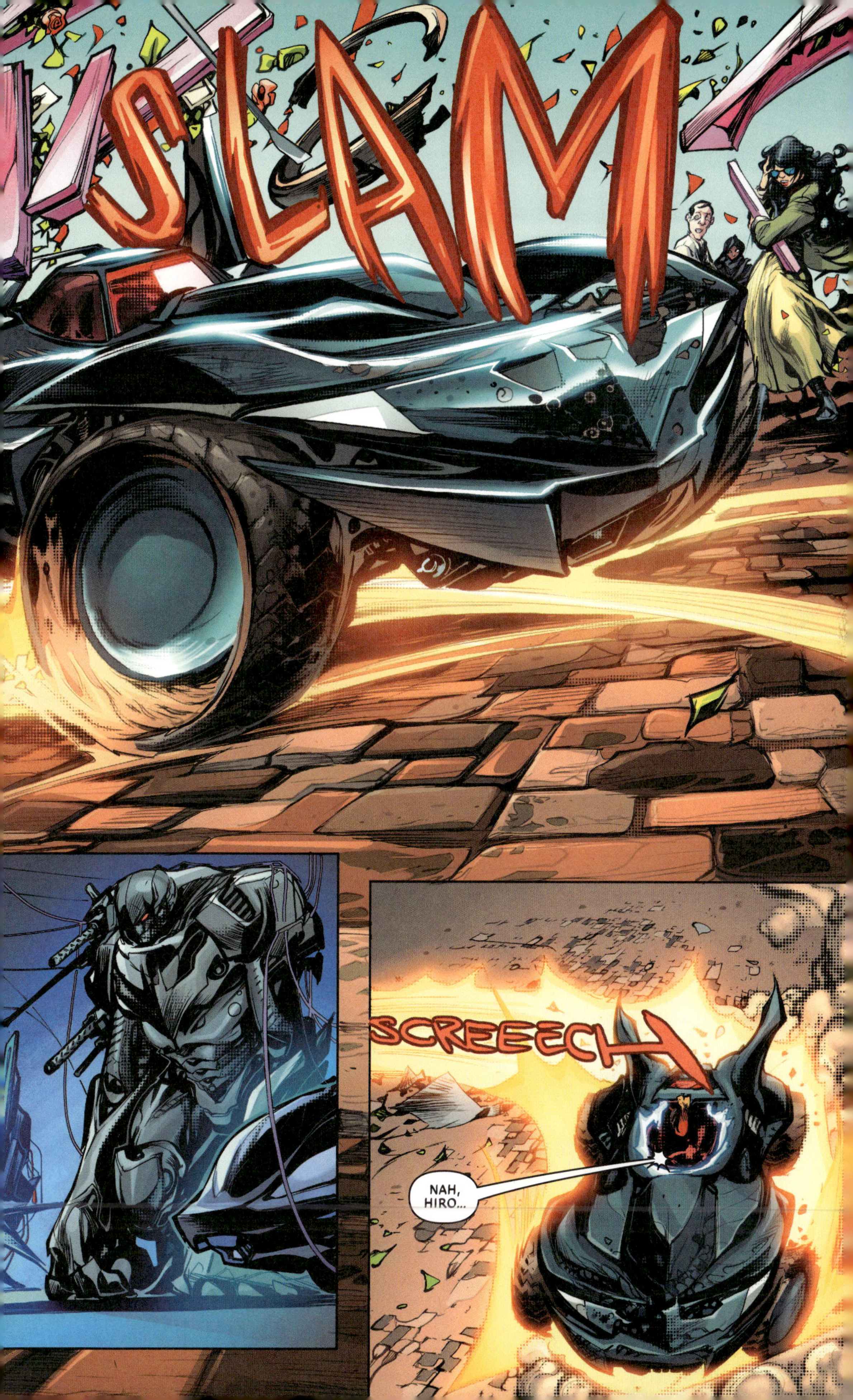
SLAM
SCREEECH
NAH, HIRO...

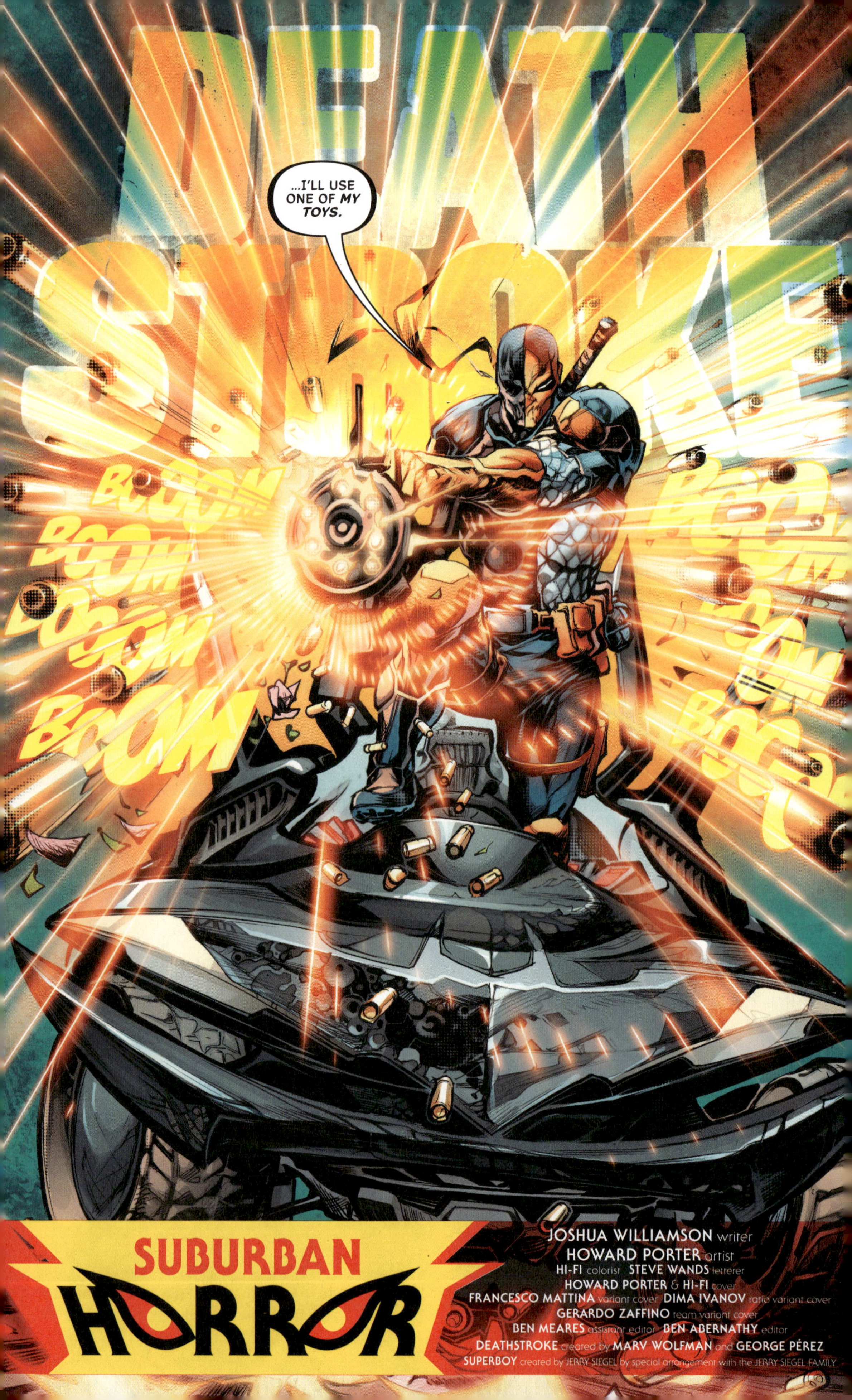
DEATHSTROKE
...I'LL USE ONE OF MY TOYS.
BOOM
BOOM
BOOM
BOOM
BOOM
BOOM
BOOM
BOOM
SUBURBAN HORROR
JOSHUA WILLIAMSON writer
HOWARD PORTER artist
HI-FI colorist STEVE WANDS letterer
HOWARD PORTER & HI-FI cover
FRANCESCO MATTINA variant cover DIMA IVANOV ratio variant cover
GERARDO ZAFFINO team variant cover
BEN MEARES assistant editor BEN ABERNATHY editor
DEATHSTROKE created by MARV WOLFMAN and GEORGE PÉREZ
SUPERBOY created by JERRY SIEGEL by special arrangement with the JERRY SIEGEL FAMILY

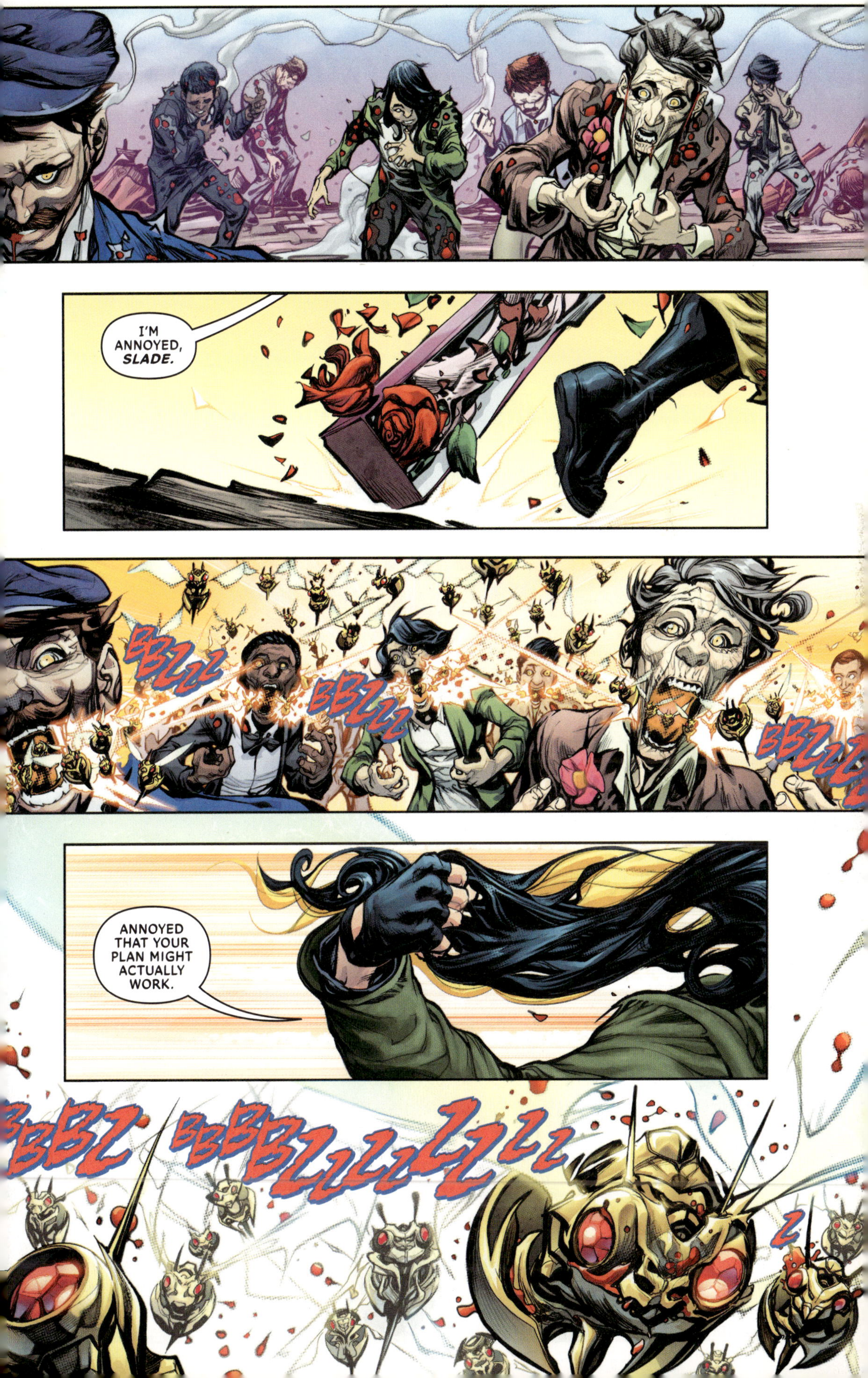
I'M ANNOYED, *SLADE.*
BBZZZ
BBZZZ
BBZZZ
ANNOYED THAT YOUR PLAN MIGHT ACTUALLY WORK.
BBBZ
BBBBZZZZZZZZZ
Z

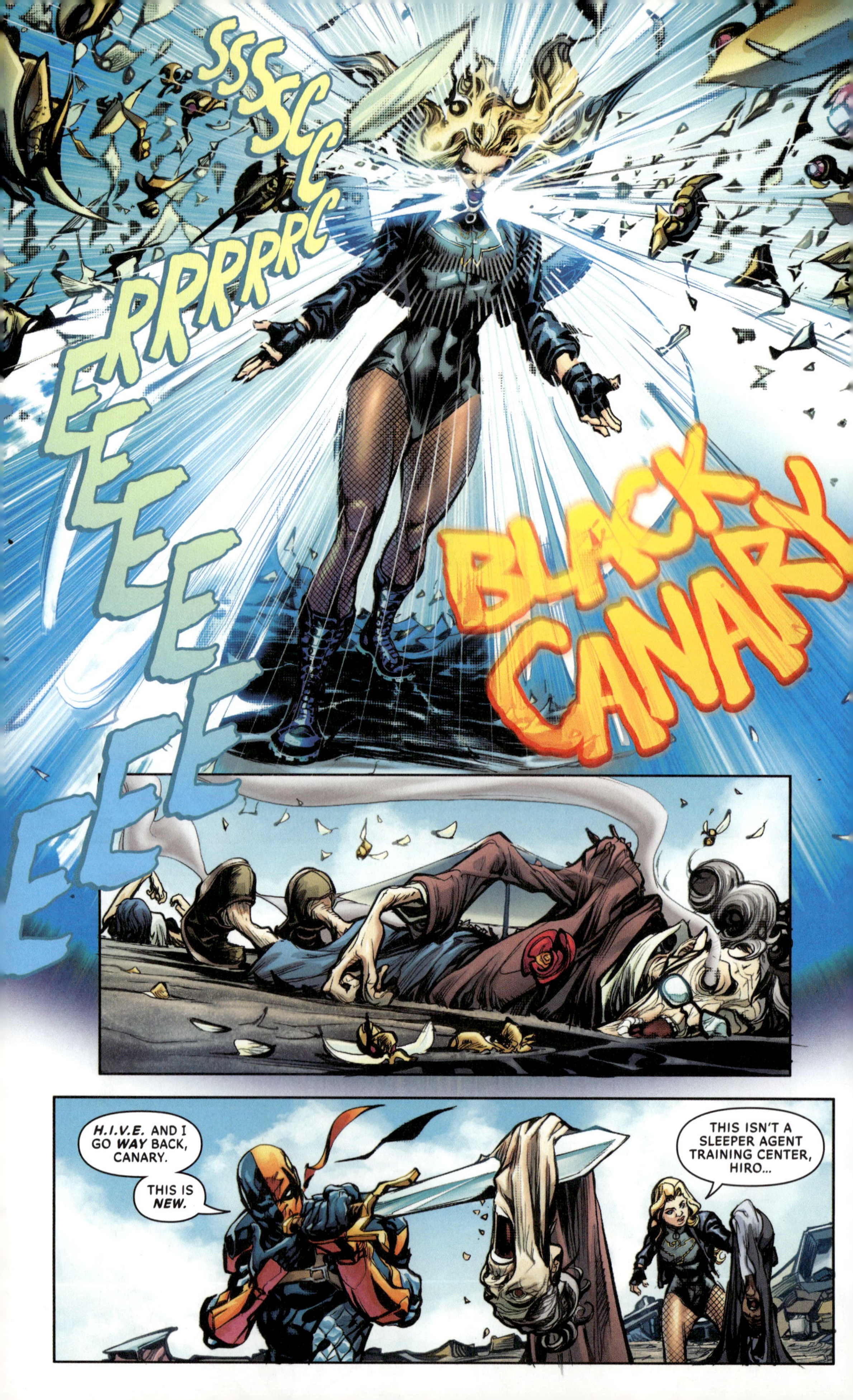
SSSSCCCCRRRRRRREEEEEEEEE
BLACK CANARY
H.I.V.E. AND I GO WAY BACK, CANARY.
THIS IS NEW.
THIS ISN'T A SLEEPER AGENT TRAINING CENTER, HIRO...

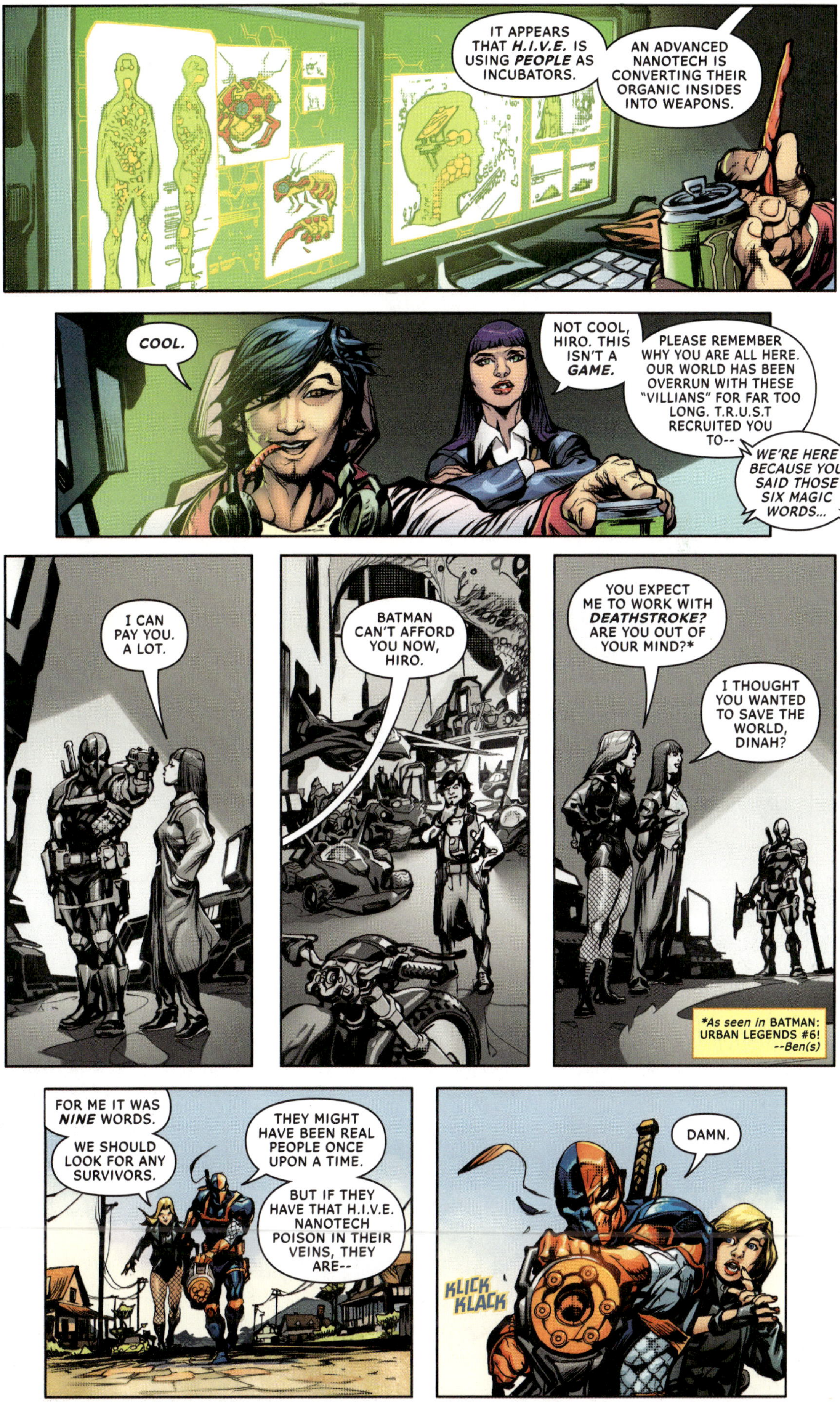
IT APPEARS THAT *H.I.V.E.* IS USING *PEOPLE* AS INCUBATORS.
AN ADVANCED NANOTECH IS CONVERTING THEIR ORGANIC INSIDES INTO WEAPONS.
COOL.
NOT COOL, HIRO. THIS ISN'T A *GAME.*
PLEASE REMEMBER WHY YOU ARE ALL HERE. OUR WORLD HAS BEEN OVERRUN WITH THESE "VILLIANS" FOR FAR TOO LONG. T.R.U.S.T RECRUITED YOU TO--
WE'RE HERE BECAUSE YOU SAID THOSE SIX MAGIC WORDS...
I CAN PAY YOU. A LOT.
BATMAN CAN'T AFFORD YOU NOW, HIRO.
YOU EXPECT ME TO WORK WITH *DEATHSTROKE?* ARE YOU OUT OF YOUR MIND?*
I THOUGHT YOU WANTED TO SAVE THE WORLD, DINAH?
As seen in BATMAN: URBAN LEGENDS #6! --Ben(s)
FOR ME IT WAS *NINE* WORDS.
WE SHOULD LOOK FOR ANY SURVIVORS.
THEY MIGHT HAVE BEEN REAL PEOPLE ONCE UPON A TIME.
BUT IF THEY HAVE THAT H.I.V.E. NANOTECH POISON IN THEIR VEINS, THEY ARE--
DAMN.
KLICK KLACK

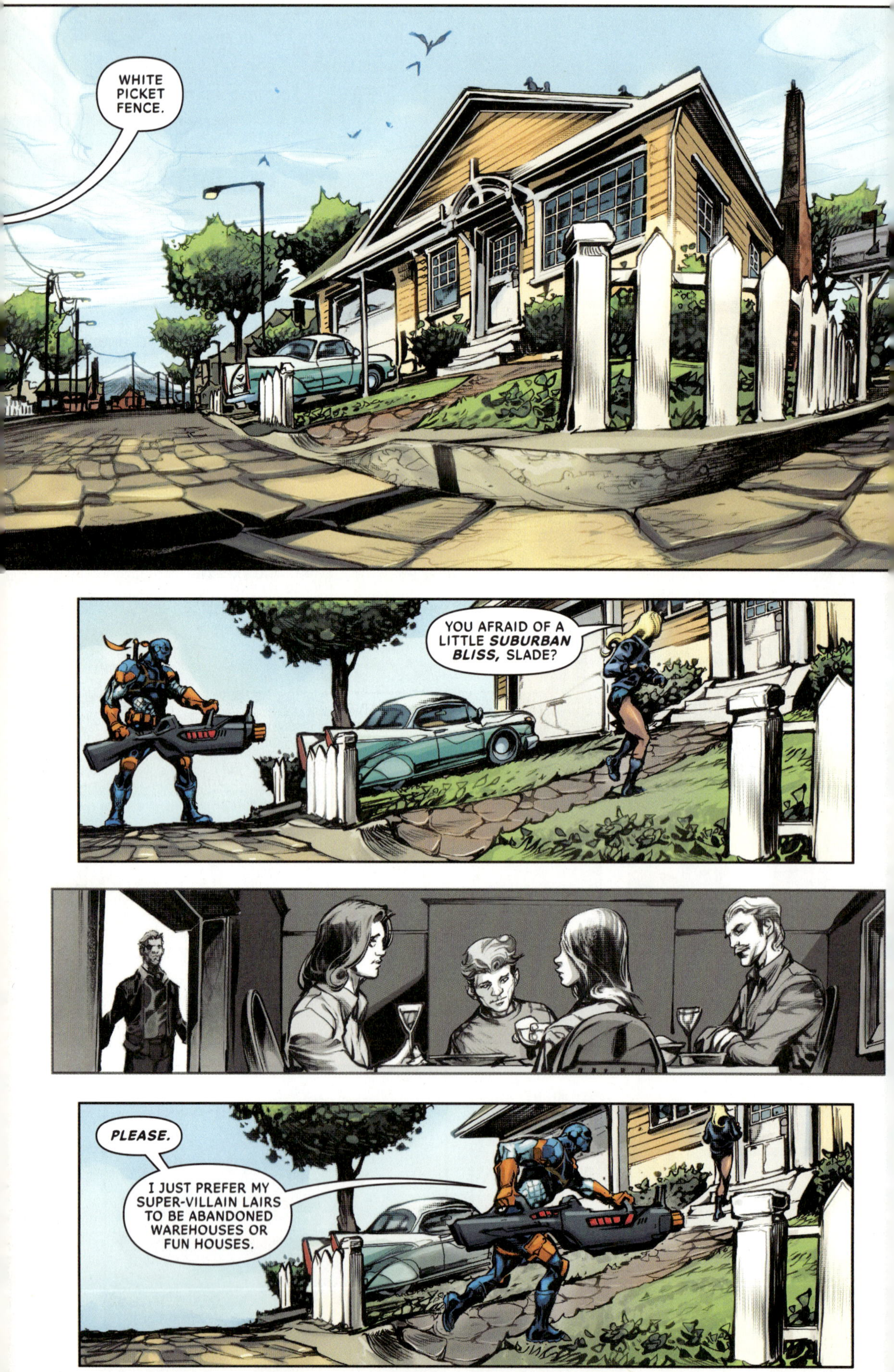
WHITE PICKET FENCE.
YOU AFRAID OF A LITTLE SUBURBAN BLISS, SLADE?
PLEASE.
I JUST PREFER MY SUPER-VILLAIN LAIRS TO BE ABANDONED WAREHOUSES OR FUN HOUSES.

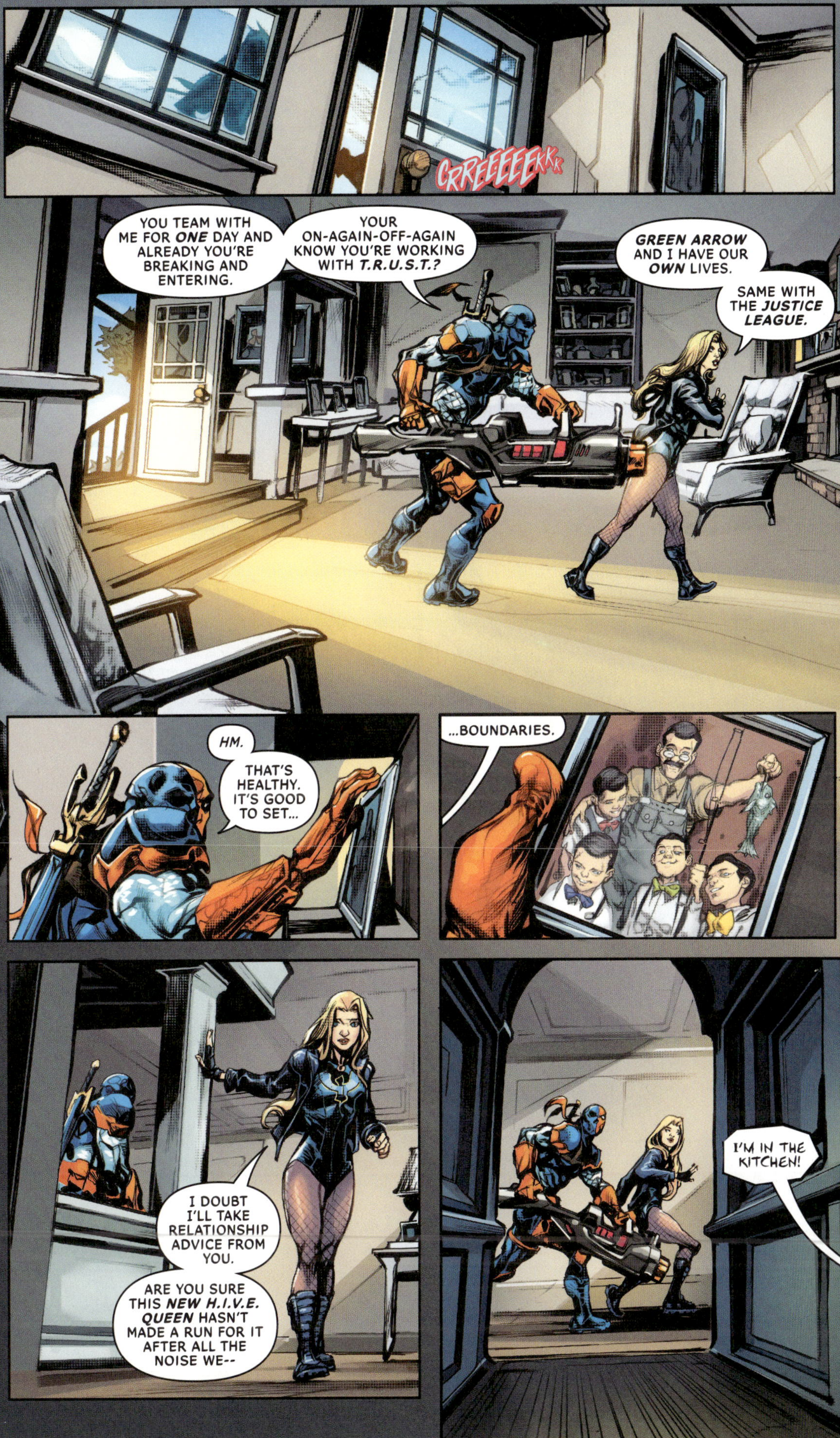
CRREEEEEKKK
YOU TEAM WITH ME FOR ONE DAY AND ALREADY YOU'RE BREAKING AND ENTERING.
YOUR ON-AGAIN-OFF-AGAIN KNOW YOU'RE WORKING WITH T.R.U.S.T.?
GREEN ARROW AND I HAVE OUR OWN LIVES.
SAME WITH THE JUSTICE LEAGUE.
HM.
THAT'S HEALTHY. IT'S GOOD TO SET...
...BOUNDARIES.
I DOUBT I'LL TAKE RELATIONSHIP ADVICE FROM YOU.
ARE YOU SURE THIS NEW H.I.V.E. QUEEN HASN'T MADE A RUN FOR IT AFTER ALL THE NOISE WE--
I'M IN THE KITCHEN!

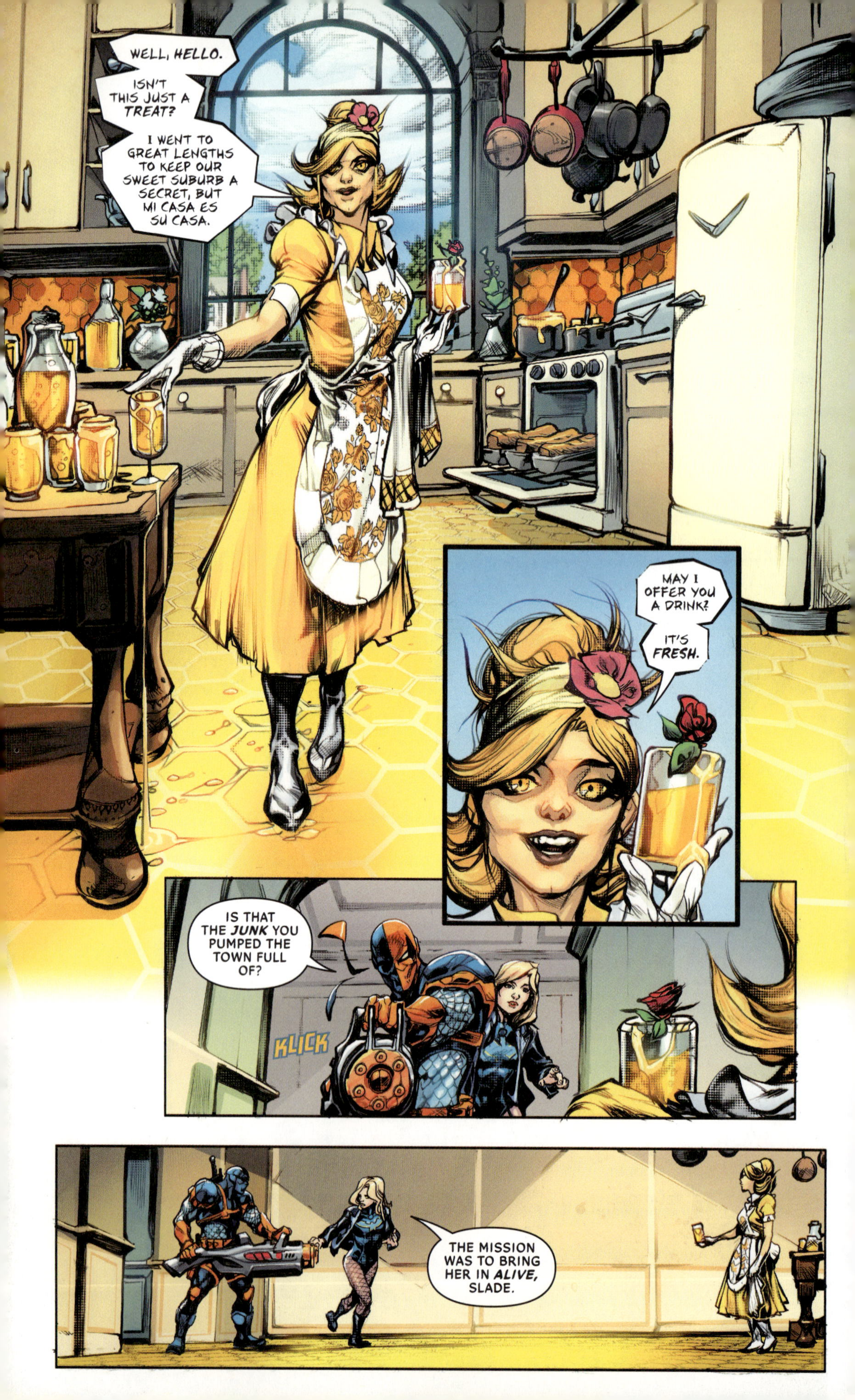

WELL, HELLO.
ISN'T THIS JUST A TREAT?
I WENT TO GREAT LENGTHS TO KEEP OUR SWEET SUBURB A SECRET, BUT MI CASA ES SU CASA.
MAY I OFFER YOU A DRINK?
IT'S FRESH.
IS THAT THE JUNK YOU PUMPED THE TOWN FULL OF?
KLICK
THE MISSION WAS TO BRING HER IN ALIVE, SLADE.

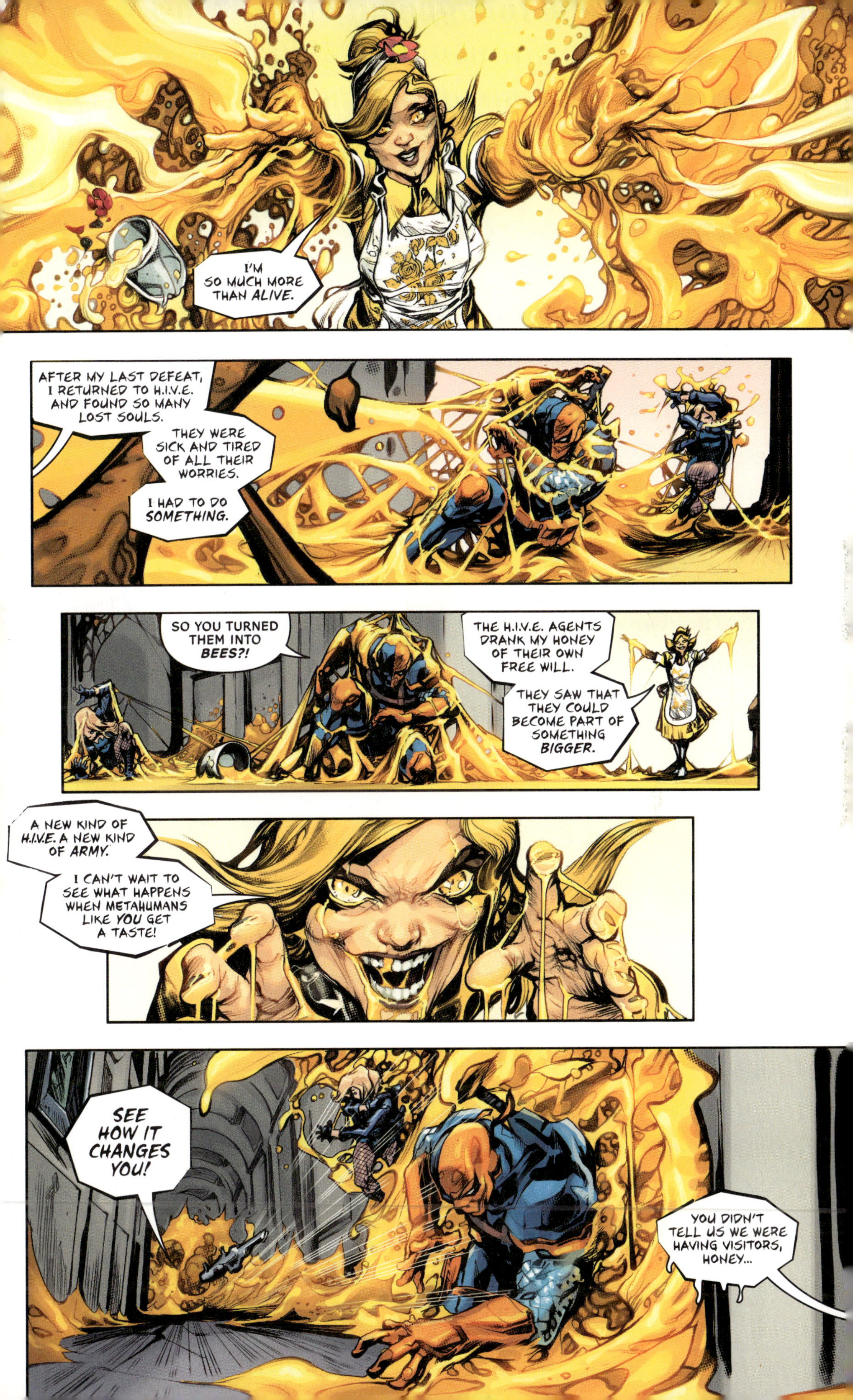
I'M SO MUCH MORE THAN *ALIVE.*
AFTER MY LAST DEFEAT, I RETURNED TO H.I.V.E. AND FOUND SO MANY LOST SOULS.
THEY WERE SICK AND TIRED OF ALL THEIR WORRIES.
I HAD TO DO *SOMETHING.*
SO YOU TURNED THEM INTO *BEES?!*
THE H.I.V.E. AGENTS DRANK MY HONEY OF THEIR OWN FREE WILL.
THEY SAW THAT THEY COULD BECOME PART OF SOMETHING *BIGGER.*
A NEW KIND OF *H.I.V.E.* A NEW KIND OF *ARMY.*
I CAN'T WAIT TO SEE WHAT HAPPENS WHEN METAHUMANS LIKE *YOU* GET A TASTE!
SEE HOW IT CHANGES YOU!
YOU DIDN'T TELL US WE WERE HAVING VISITORS, HONEY...

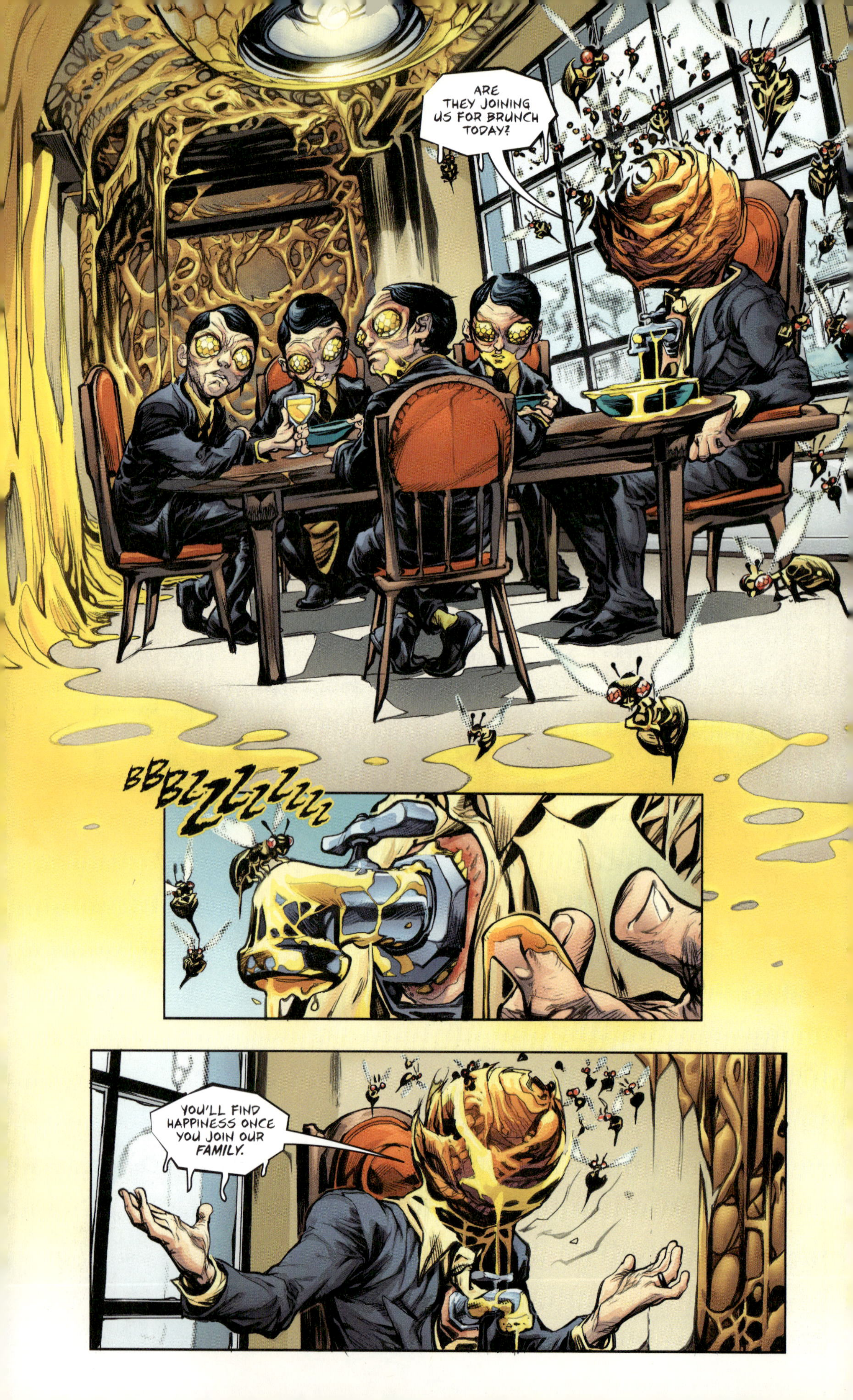
ARE THEY JOINING US FOR BRUNCH TODAY?
BBBZZZZZZZZ
YOU'LL FIND HAPPINESS ONCE YOU JOIN OUR FAMILY.

SCRRREEEEEEEE

TRSHHH

AH GEEZ!

WHAT'S THAT ABOUT?

KNOCKING OUT THE COMMS BUYS US A MINUTE TO TALK.

WHY ARE YOU REALLY WORKING FOR *T.R.U.S.T.*?

YOU AND I GO *WAY BACK,* SLADE. THIS CAN'T BE ABOUT GETTING YOUR HANDS ON BATMAN'S *GEAR.* OR EVEN THE *MONEY.*

AND I REALLY *DOUBT* YOU'RE DOING THIS OUT OF THE GOODNESS OF YOUR *HEART.*

WE FRIENDS NOW?

THE JUSTICE LEAGUE KNOWS ABOUT WHAT YOU WENT THROUGH WITH YOUR FAMILY. WE THOUGHT YOU MIGHT HAVE CHANGED. I JUST WANT TO KNOW...

WHY ARE YOU *REALLY* DOING THIS?

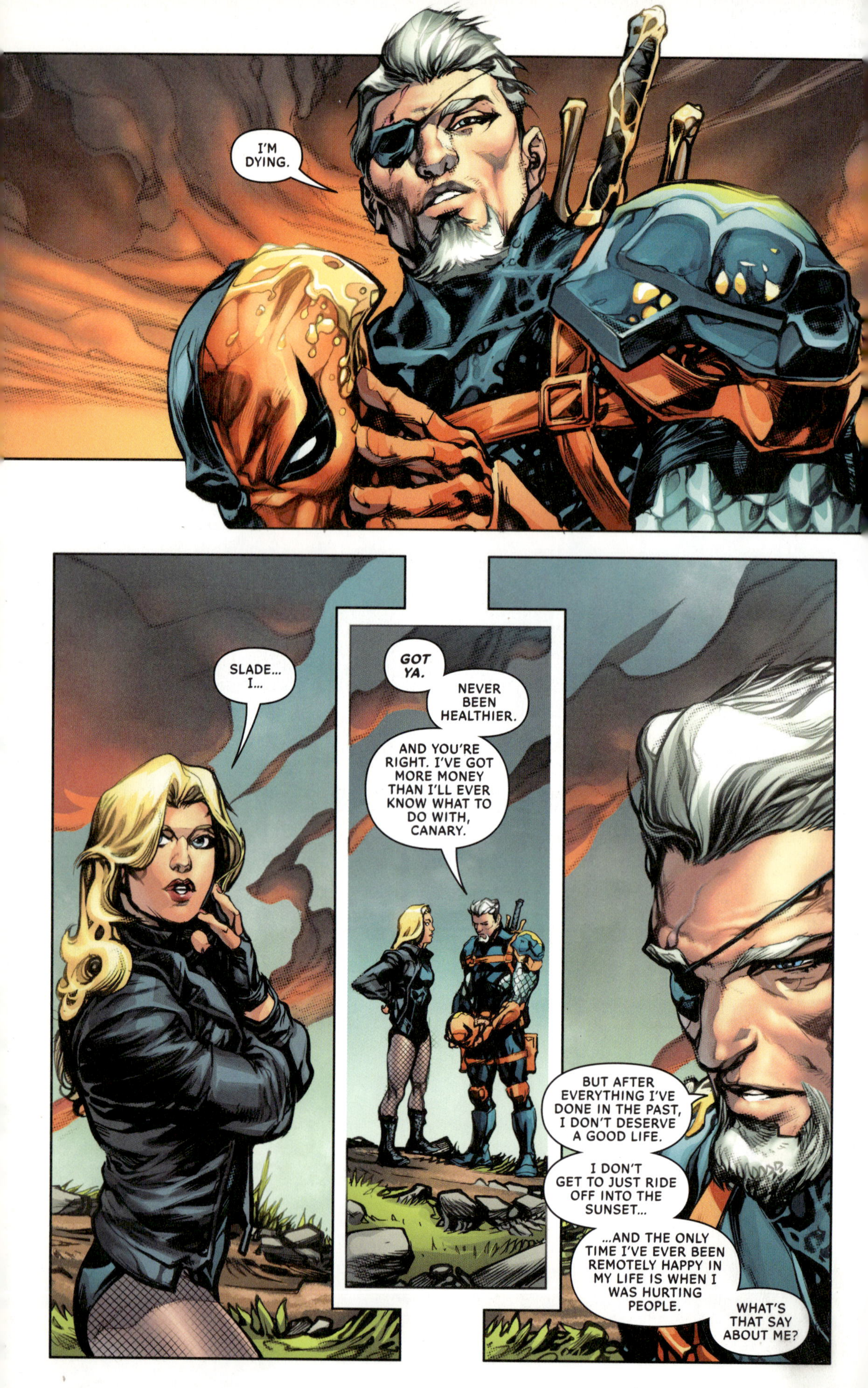
I'M DYING.
SLADE... I...
GOT YA.
NEVER BEEN HEALTHIER.
AND YOU'RE RIGHT. I'VE GOT MORE MONEY THAN I'LL EVER KNOW WHAT TO DO WITH, CANARY.
BUT AFTER EVERYTHING I'VE DONE IN THE PAST, I DON'T DESERVE A GOOD LIFE.
I DON'T GET TO JUST RIDE OFF INTO THE SUNSET...
...AND THE ONLY TIME I'VE EVER BEEN REMOTELY HAPPY IN MY LIFE IS WHEN I WAS HURTING PEOPLE.
WHAT'S THAT SAY ABOUT ME?

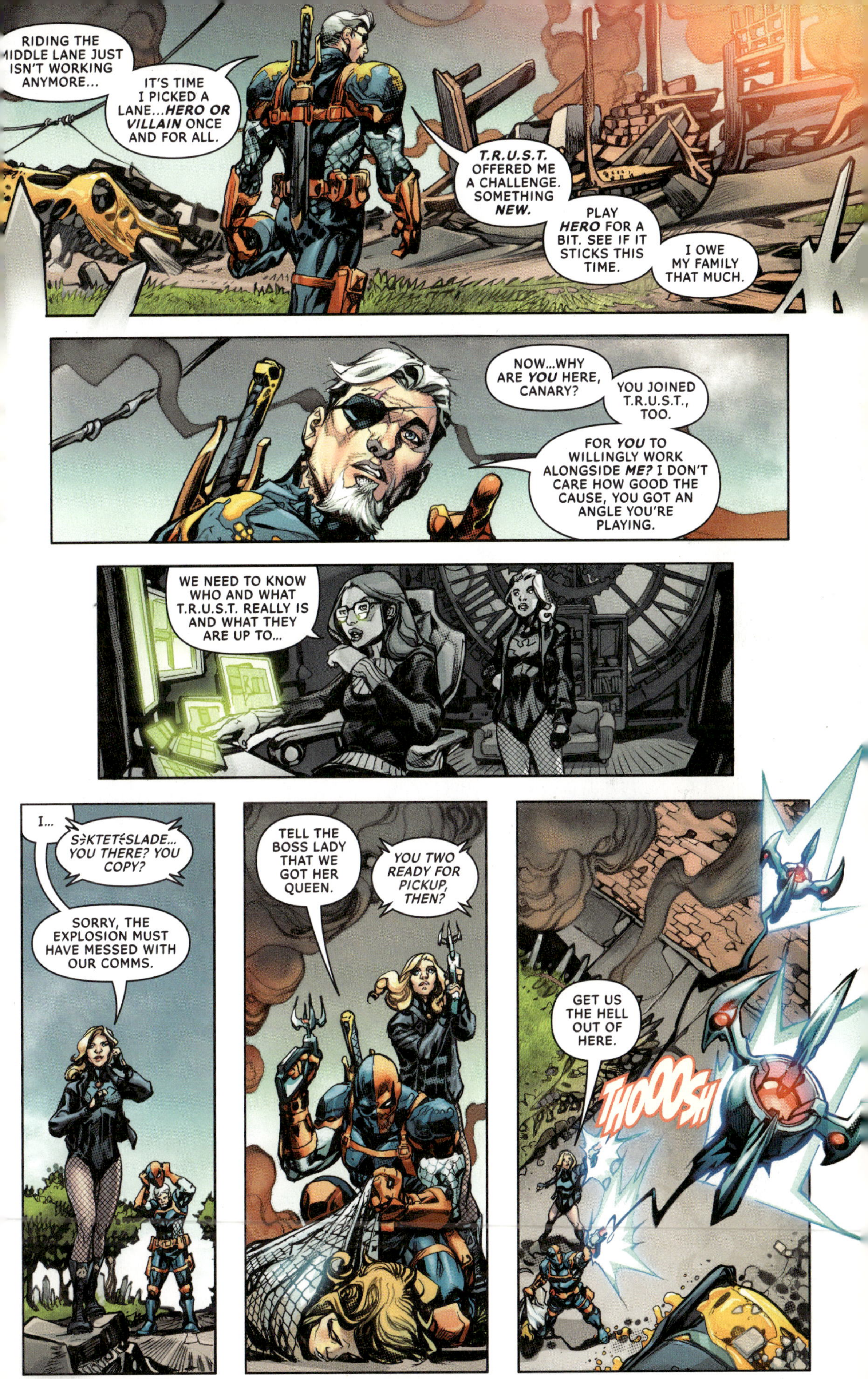
RIDING THE MIDDLE LANE JUST ISN'T WORKING ANYMORE...
IT'S TIME I PICKED A LANE...**HERO OR VILLAIN** ONCE AND FOR ALL.
T.R.U.S.T. OFFERED ME A CHALLENGE. SOMETHING **NEW.**
PLAY **HERO** FOR A BIT. SEE IF IT STICKS THIS TIME.
I OWE MY FAMILY THAT MUCH.
NOW...WHY ARE **YOU** HERE, CANARY?
YOU JOINED T.R.U.S.T., TOO.
FOR **YOU** TO WILLINGLY WORK ALONGSIDE **ME?** I DON'T CARE HOW GOOD THE CAUSE, YOU GOT AN ANGLE YOU'RE PLAYING.
WE NEED TO KNOW WHO AND WHAT T.R.U.S.T. REALLY IS AND WHAT THEY ARE UP TO...
I...
SKKTET-SLADE... YOU THERE? YOU COPY?
SORRY, THE EXPLOSION MUST HAVE MESSED WITH OUR COMMS.
TELL THE BOSS LADY THAT WE GOT HER QUEEN.
YOU TWO READY FOR PICKUP, THEN?
GET US THE HELL OUT OF HERE.
THOOOSH

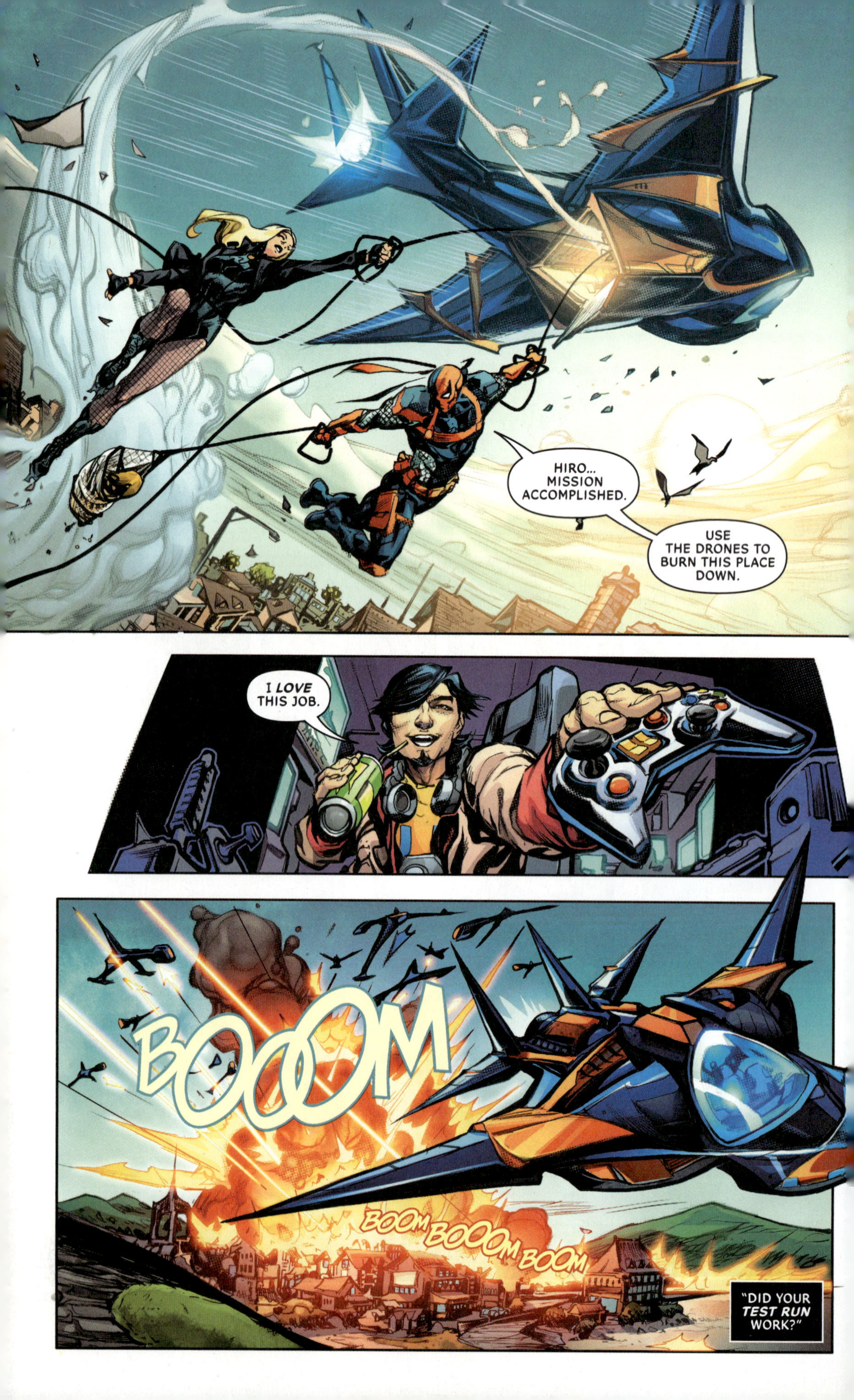
HIRO... MISSION ACCOMPLISHED.
USE THE DRONES TO BURN THIS PLACE DOWN.
I LOVE THIS JOB.
BOOOM
BOOM BOOOM BOOM
"DID YOUR TEST RUN WORK?"

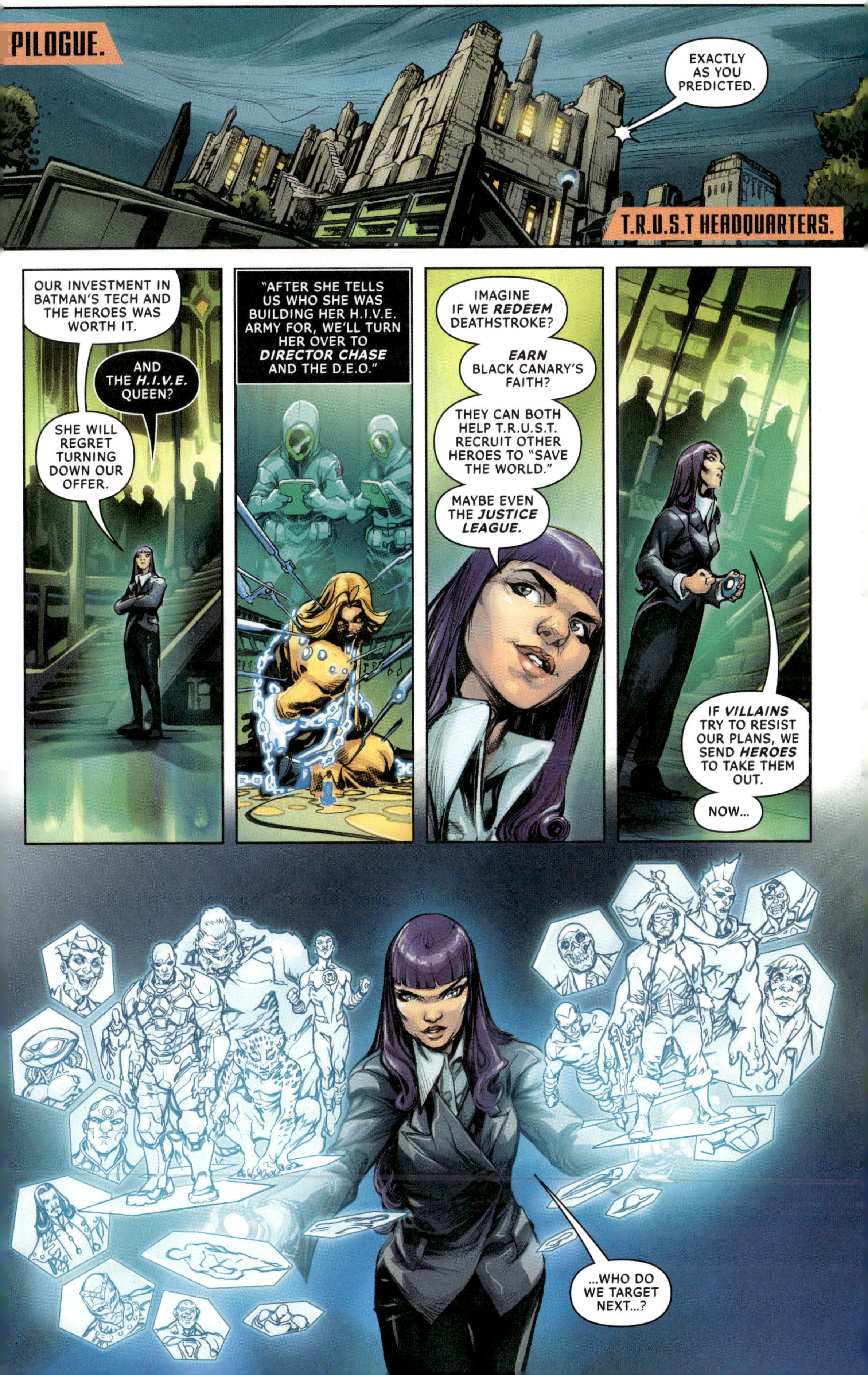
PILOGUE.
EXACTLY AS YOU PREDICTED.
T.R.U.S.T HEADQUARTERS.
OUR INVESTMENT IN BATMAN'S TECH AND THE HEROES WAS WORTH IT.
AND THE H.I.V.E. QUEEN?
SHE WILL REGRET TURNING DOWN OUR OFFER.
"AFTER SHE TELLS US WHO SHE WAS BUILDING HER H.I.V.E. ARMY FOR, WE'LL TURN HER OVER TO DIRECTOR CHASE AND THE D.E.O."
IMAGINE IF WE REDEEM DEATHSTROKE?
EARN BLACK CANARY'S FAITH?
THEY CAN BOTH HELP T.R.U.S.T. RECRUIT OTHER HEROES TO "SAVE THE WORLD."
MAYBE EVEN THE JUSTICE LEAGUE.
IF VILLAINS TRY TO RESIST OUR PLANS, WE SEND HEROES TO TAKE THEM OUT.
NOW...
...WHO DO WE TARGET NEXT...?

COMING SOON TO
DEATHSTROKE
INC.

DEATHSTROKE INC. #2
cover art by HOWARD PORTER & HI-FI

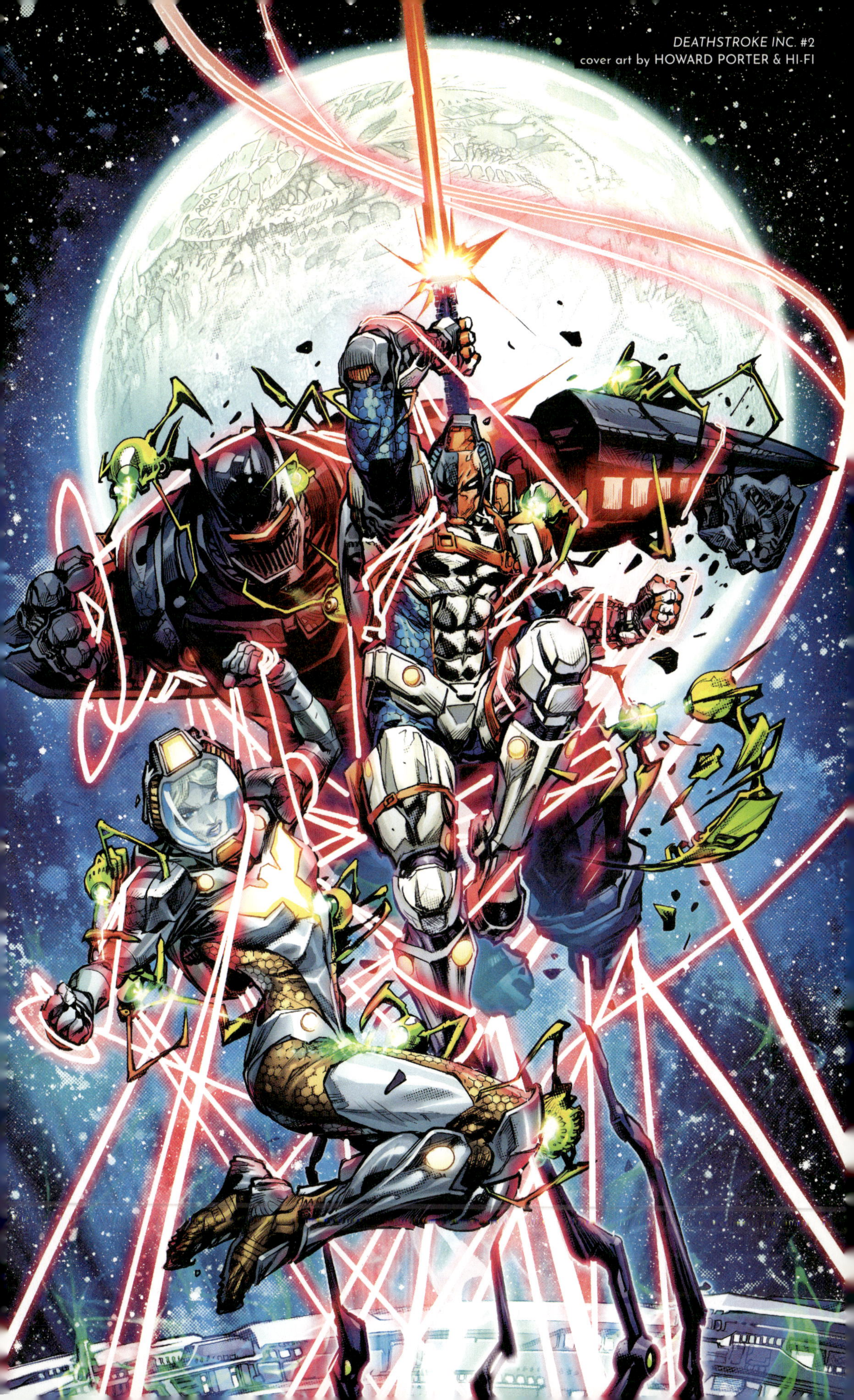

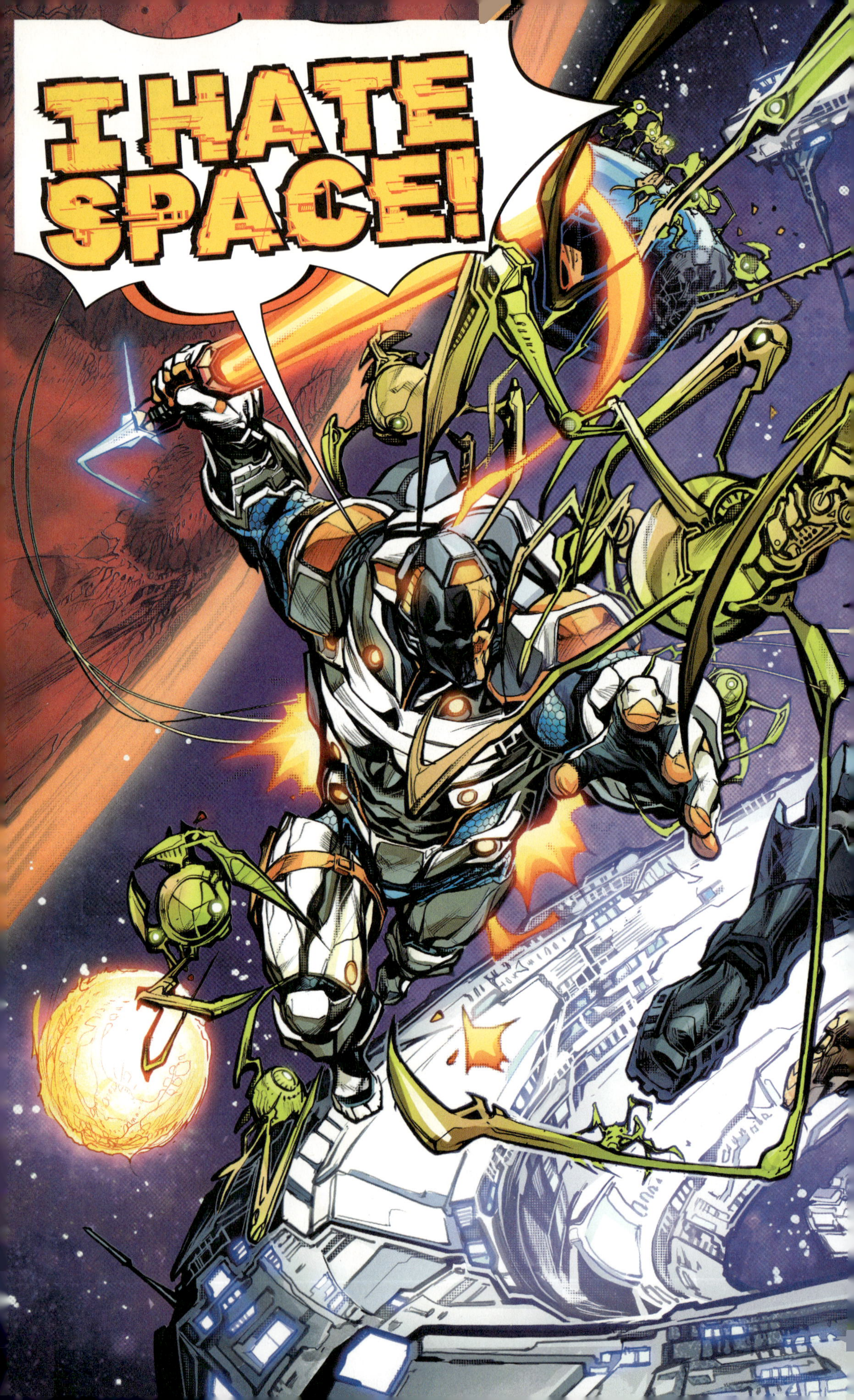
I HATE SPACE!

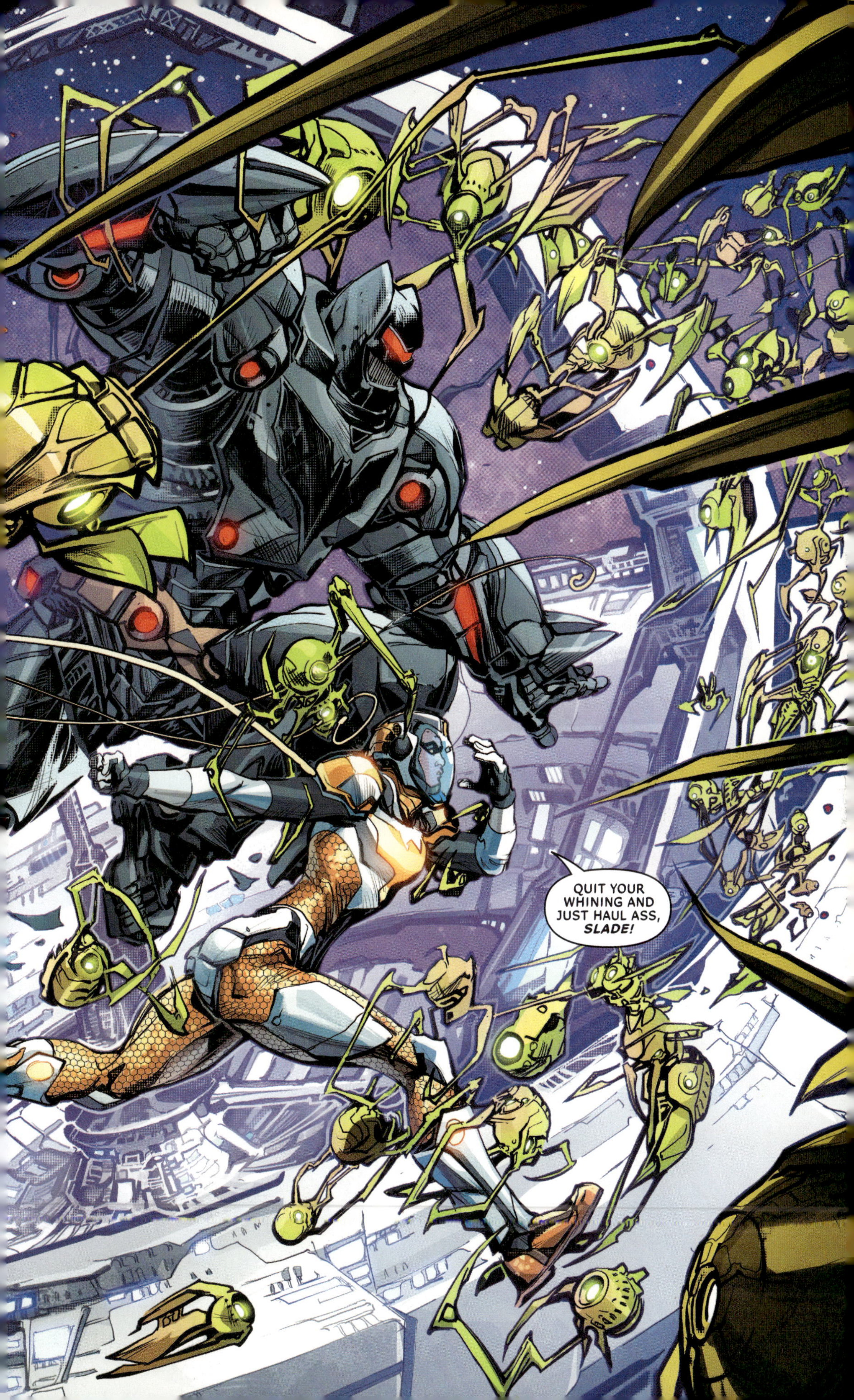
QUIT YOUR WHINING AND JUST HAUL ASS, *SLADE!*

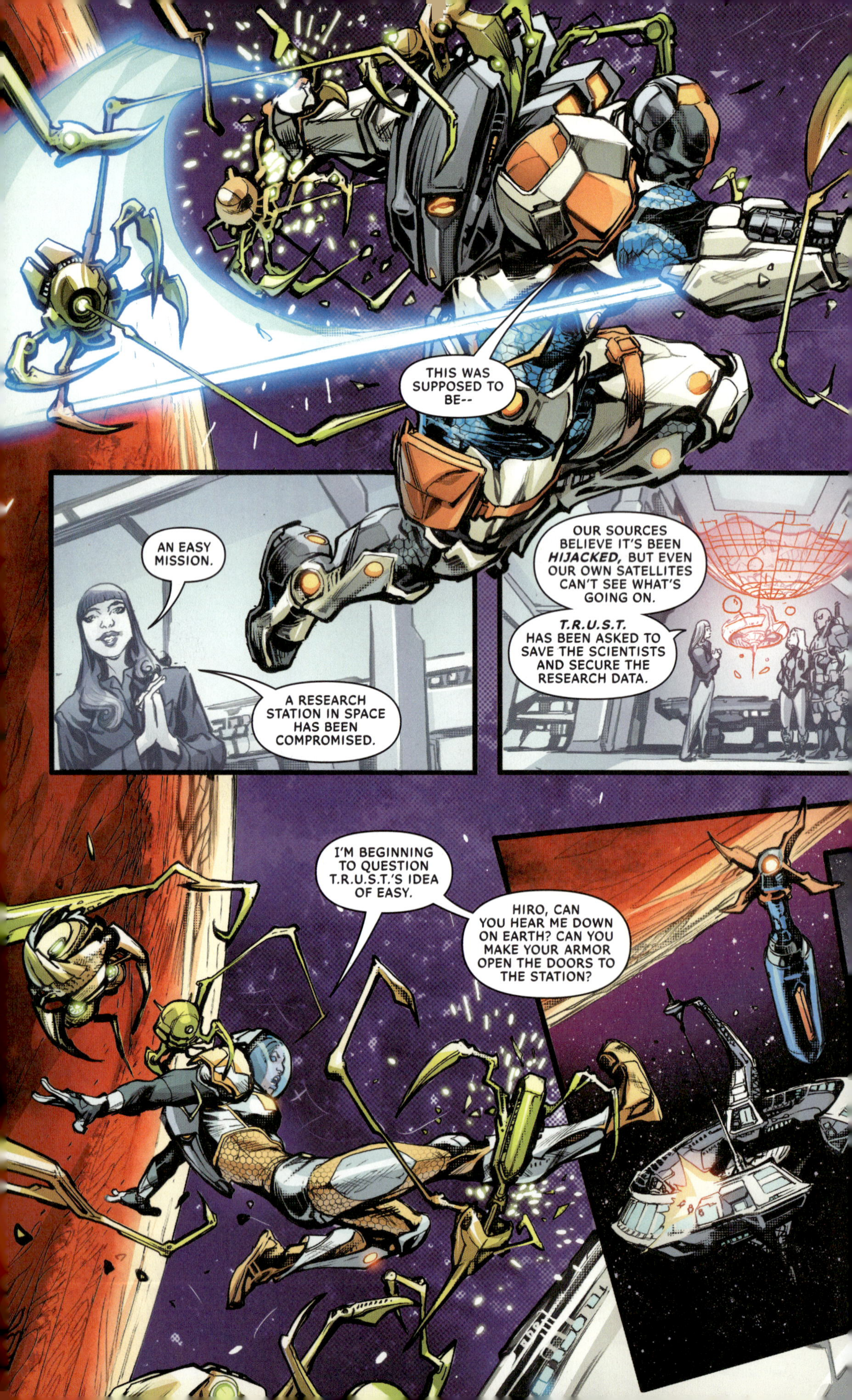
THIS WAS SUPPOSED TO BE--
AN EASY MISSION.
A RESEARCH STATION IN SPACE HAS BEEN COMPROMISED.
OUR SOURCES BELIEVE IT'S BEEN *HIJACKED,* BUT EVEN OUR OWN SATELLITES CAN'T SEE WHAT'S GOING ON.
T.R.U.S.T. HAS BEEN ASKED TO SAVE THE SCIENTISTS AND SECURE THE RESEARCH DATA.
I'M BEGINNING TO QUESTION T.R.U.S.T.'S IDEA OF EASY.
HIRO, CAN YOU HEAR ME DOWN ON EARTH? CAN YOU MAKE YOUR ARMOR OPEN THE DOORS TO THE STATION?

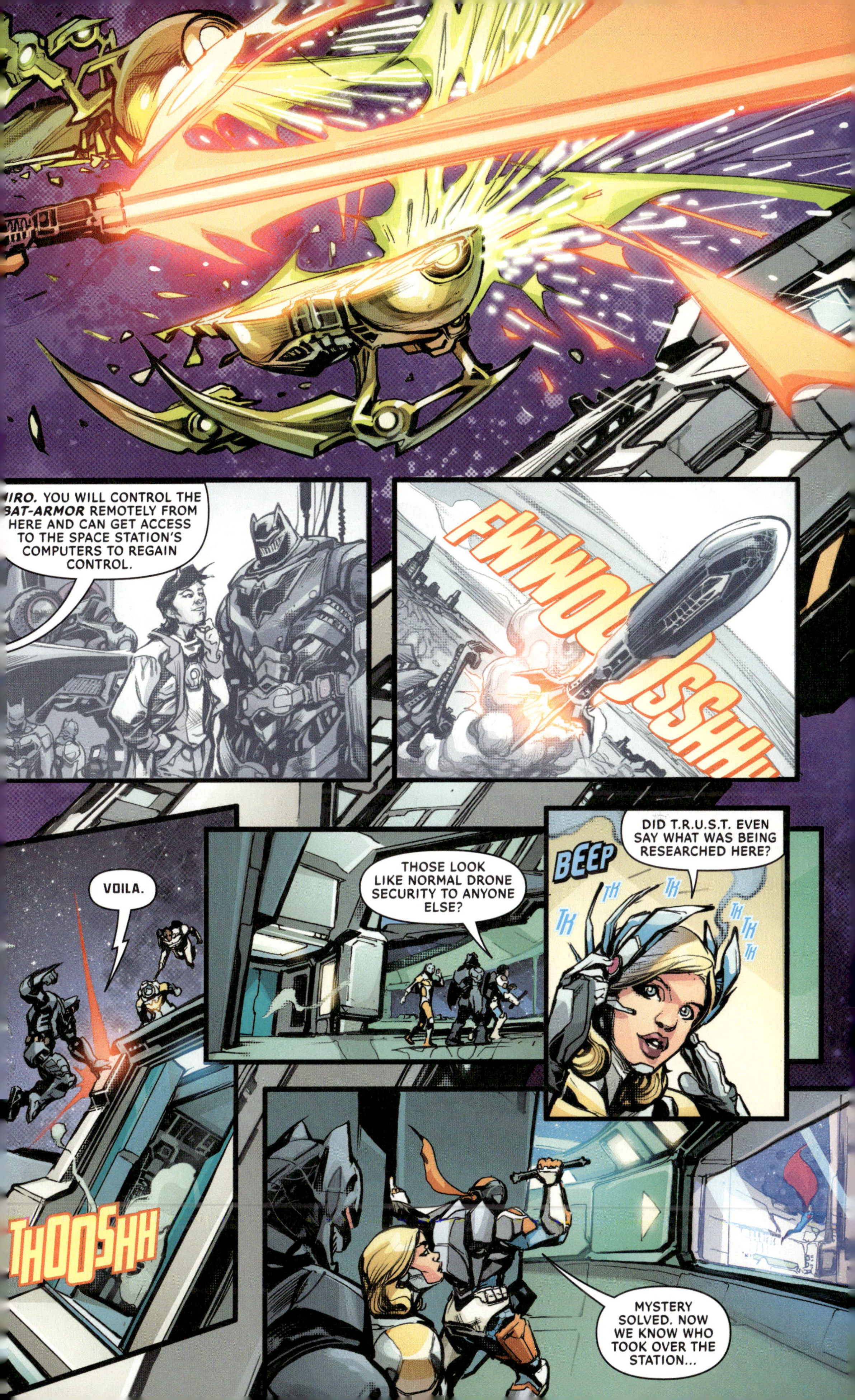

IRO. YOU WILL CONTROL THE BAT-ARMOR REMOTELY FROM HERE AND CAN GET ACCESS TO THE SPACE STATION'S COMPUTERS TO REGAIN CONTROL.
FWWOOOSSHH
VOILA.
THOOSHH
THOSE LOOK LIKE NORMAL DRONE SECURITY TO ANYONE ELSE?
BEEP
TH TH TH TH TH TH
DID T.R.U.S.T. EVEN SAY WHAT WAS BEING RESEARCHED HERE?
MYSTERY SOLVED. NOW WE KNOW WHO TOOK OVER THE STATION...

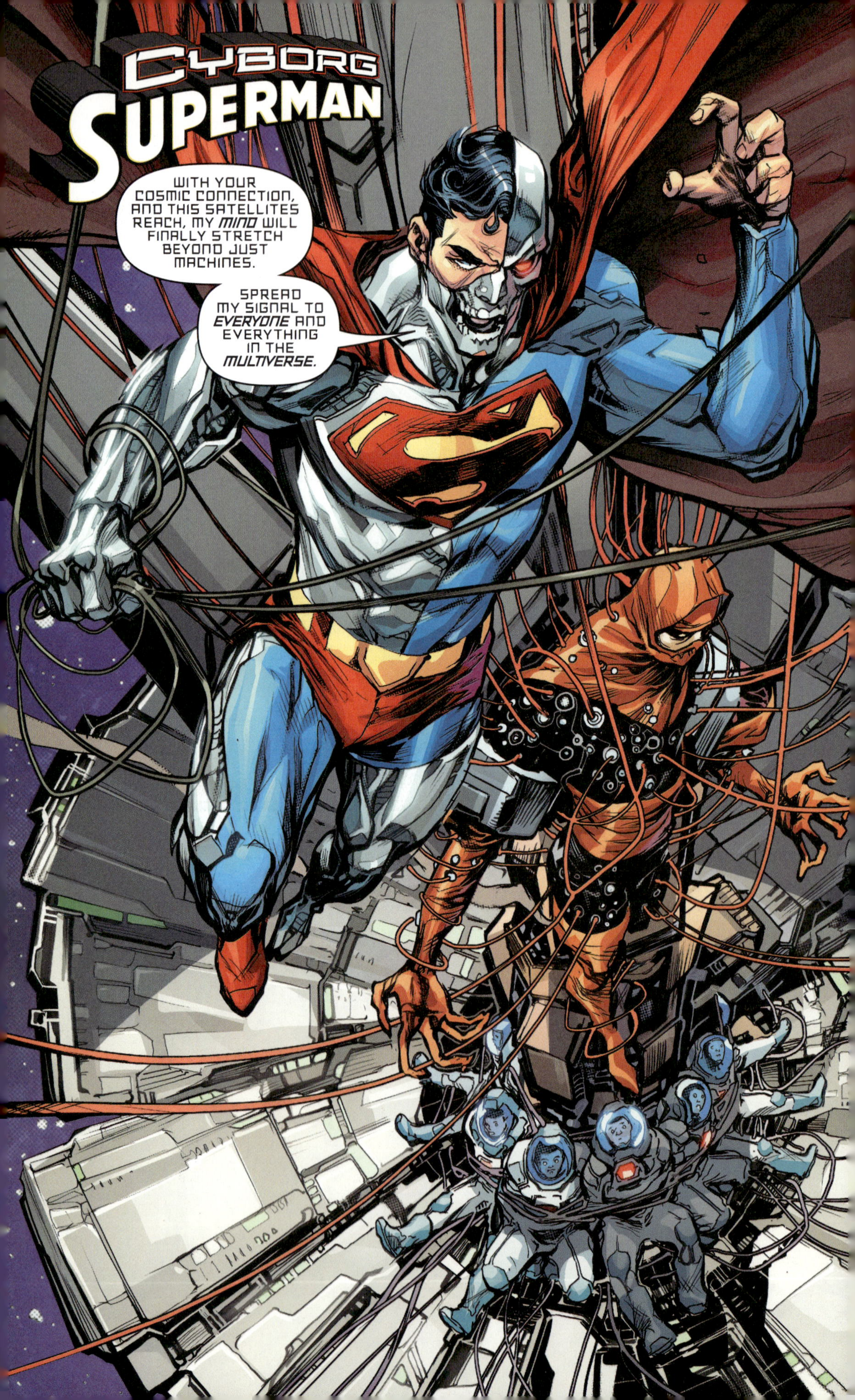
CYBORG SUPERMAN
WITH YOUR COSMIC CONNECTION, AND THIS SATELLITES REACH, MY *MIND* WILL FINALLY STRETCH BEYOND JUST MACHINES.
SPREAD MY SIGNAL TO *EVERYONE* AND EVERYTHING IN THE *MULTIVERSE*.

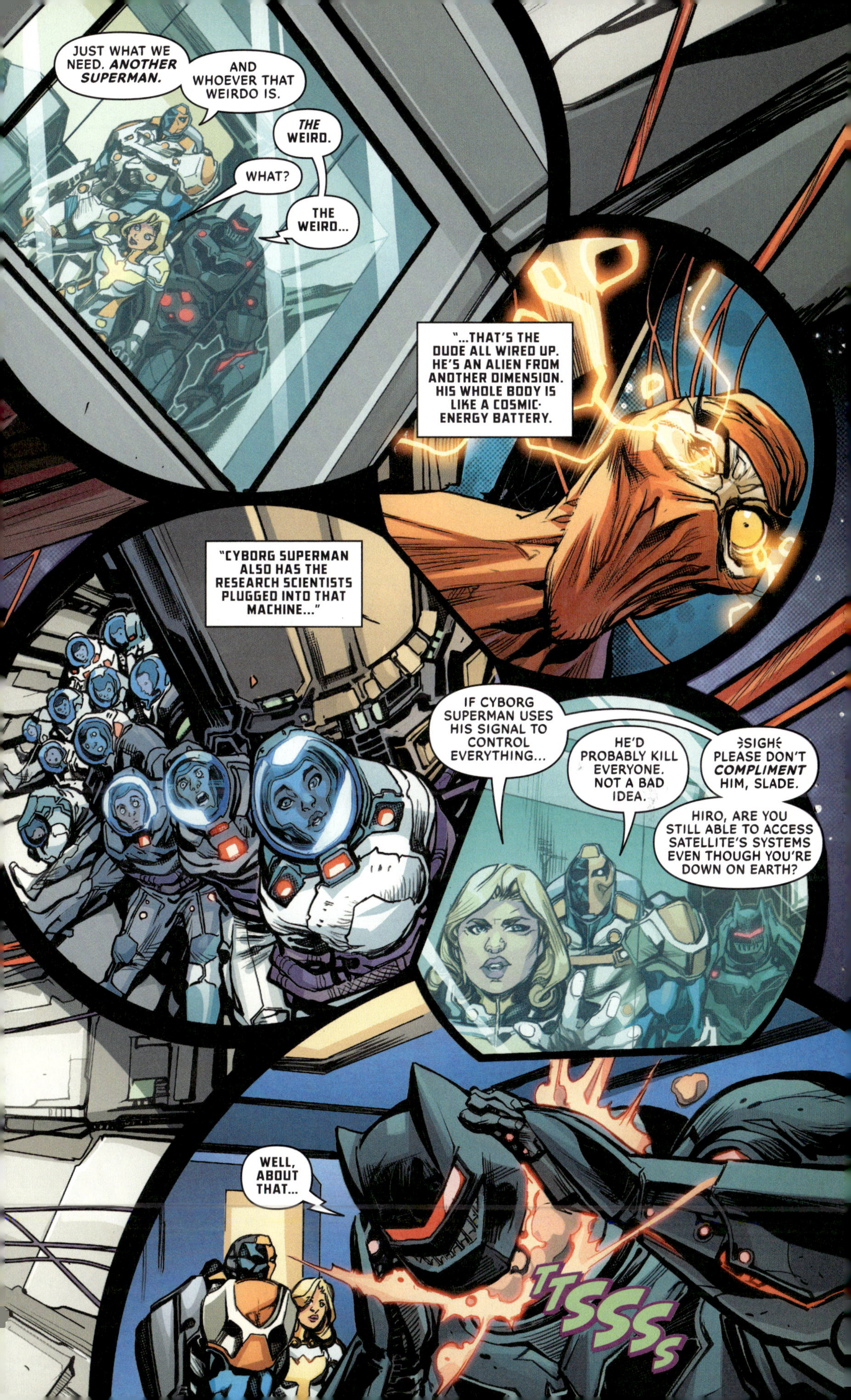
JUST WHAT WE NEED. *ANOTHER SUPERMAN.*
AND WHOEVER THAT WEIRDO IS.
THE WEIRD.
WHAT?
THE WEIRD...
"...THAT'S THE DUDE ALL WIRED UP. HE'S AN ALIEN FROM ANOTHER DIMENSION. HIS WHOLE BODY IS LIKE A COSMIC-ENERGY BATTERY.
"CYBORG SUPERMAN ALSO HAS THE RESEARCH SCIENTISTS PLUGGED INTO THAT MACHINE..."
IF CYBORG SUPERMAN USES HIS SIGNAL TO CONTROL EVERYTHING...
HE'D PROBABLY KILL EVERYONE. NOT A BAD IDEA.
SIGH PLEASE DON'T *COMPLIMENT* HIM, SLADE.
HIRO, ARE YOU STILL ABLE TO ACCESS SATELLITE'S SYSTEMS EVEN THOUGH YOU'RE DOWN ON EARTH?
WELL, ABOUT THAT...
TTSSSS

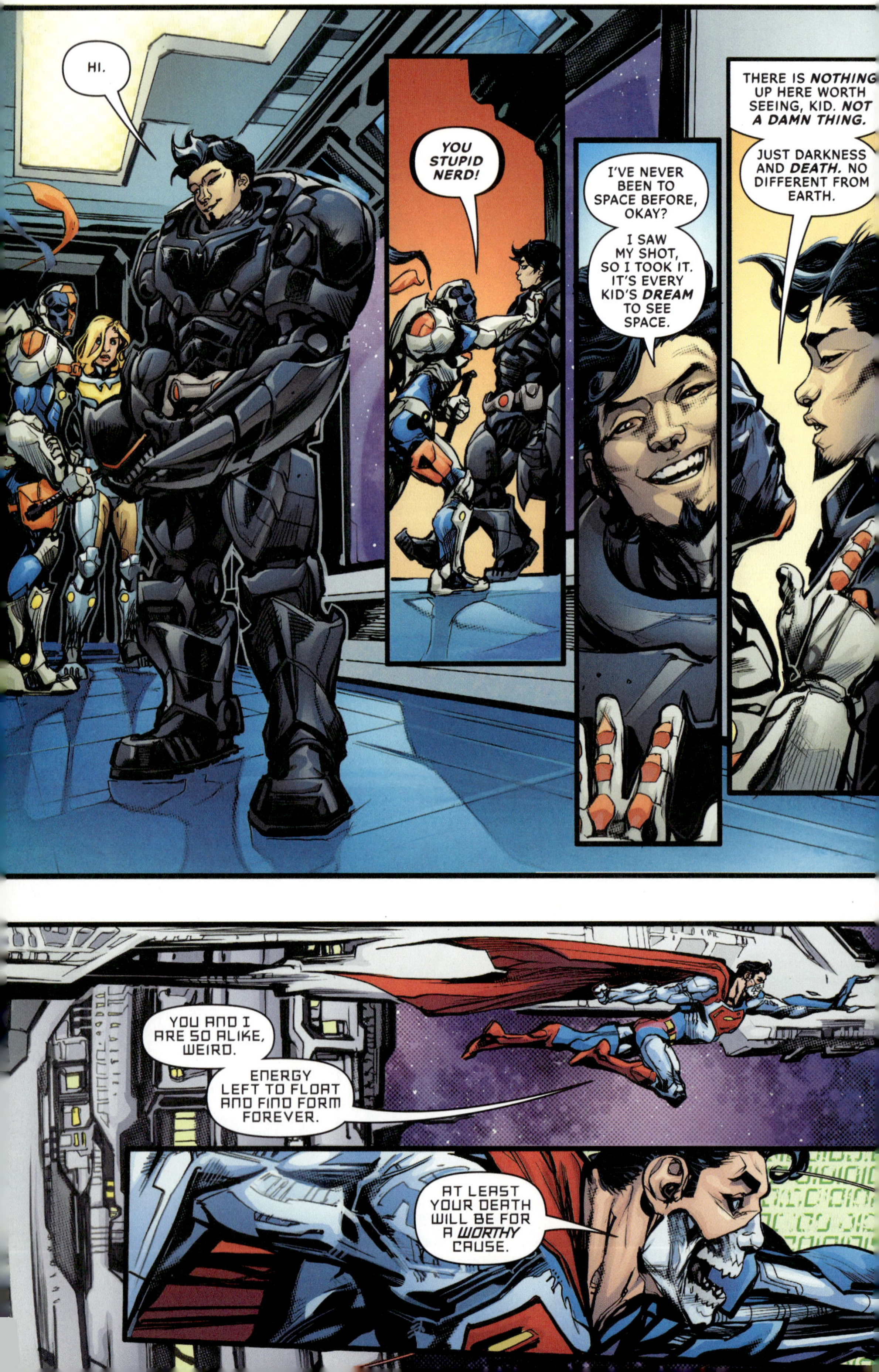
HI.
YOU STUPID NERD!
I'VE NEVER BEEN TO SPACE BEFORE, OKAY?
I SAW MY SHOT, SO I TOOK IT. IT'S EVERY KID'S DREAM TO SEE SPACE.
THERE IS NOTHING UP HERE WORTH SEEING, KID. NOT A DAMN THING.
JUST DARKNESS AND DEATH. NO DIFFERENT FROM EARTH.
YOU AND I ARE SO ALIKE, WEIRD.
ENERGY LEFT TO FLOAT AND FIND FORM FOREVER.
AT LEAST YOUR DEATH WILL BE FOR A WORTHY CAUSE.

COOL IT, SLADE.

WE CAN'T CHANGE HIRO BEING HERE, SO WE *DEAL* WITH IT.

LISTEN, CYBORG SUPERMAN ISN'T HUMAN, OR EVEN REALLY HERE.

HE'S AN ASTRONAUT WHOSE BODY WAS TURNED INTO A SUPER-ADVANCED A.I. THAT CAN CONTROL AND JUMP FROM MACHINE TO MACHINE...

THEN YOU GET CONTROL OF THE SATELLITE *AND* CYBORG SUPERMAN.

I'LL GET THE HOSTAGES OUT OF HERE.

SLADE, YOU--

I KNOW MY ROLE.

AND *I* CAN HACK HIM. IT'LL BE *FUN.* TRUST ME.

IF HIS ASS IS IN DANGER, I'M *NOT* BAILING HIM OUT.

TTZZZ

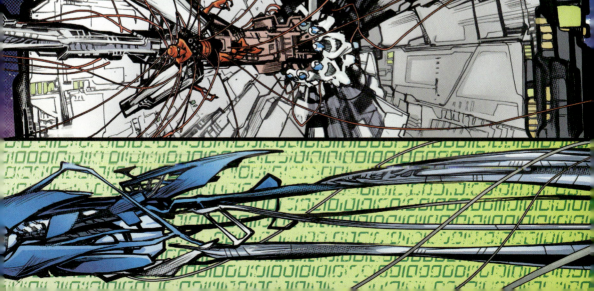

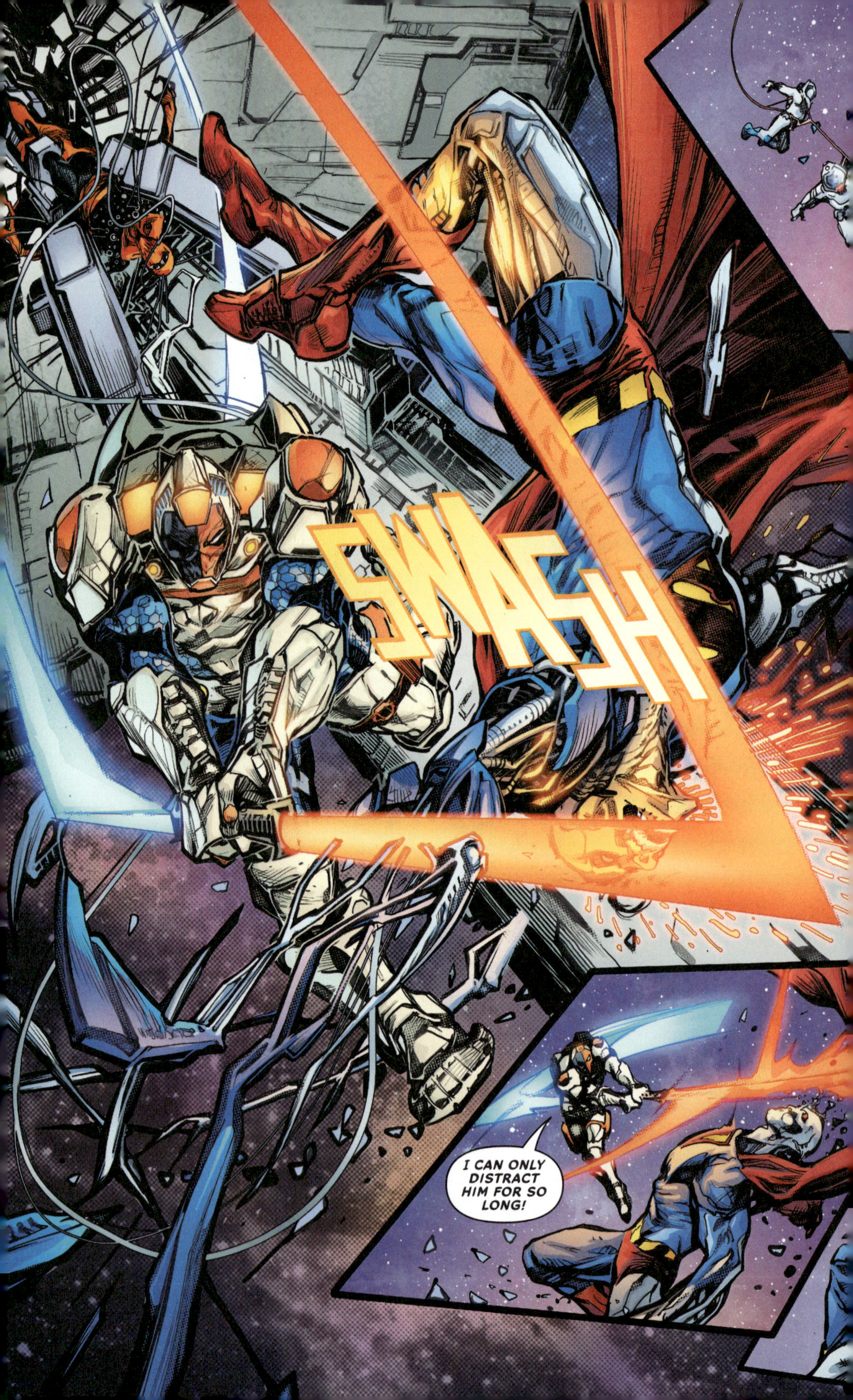
SWASH
I CAN ONLY DISTRACT HIM FOR SO LONG!

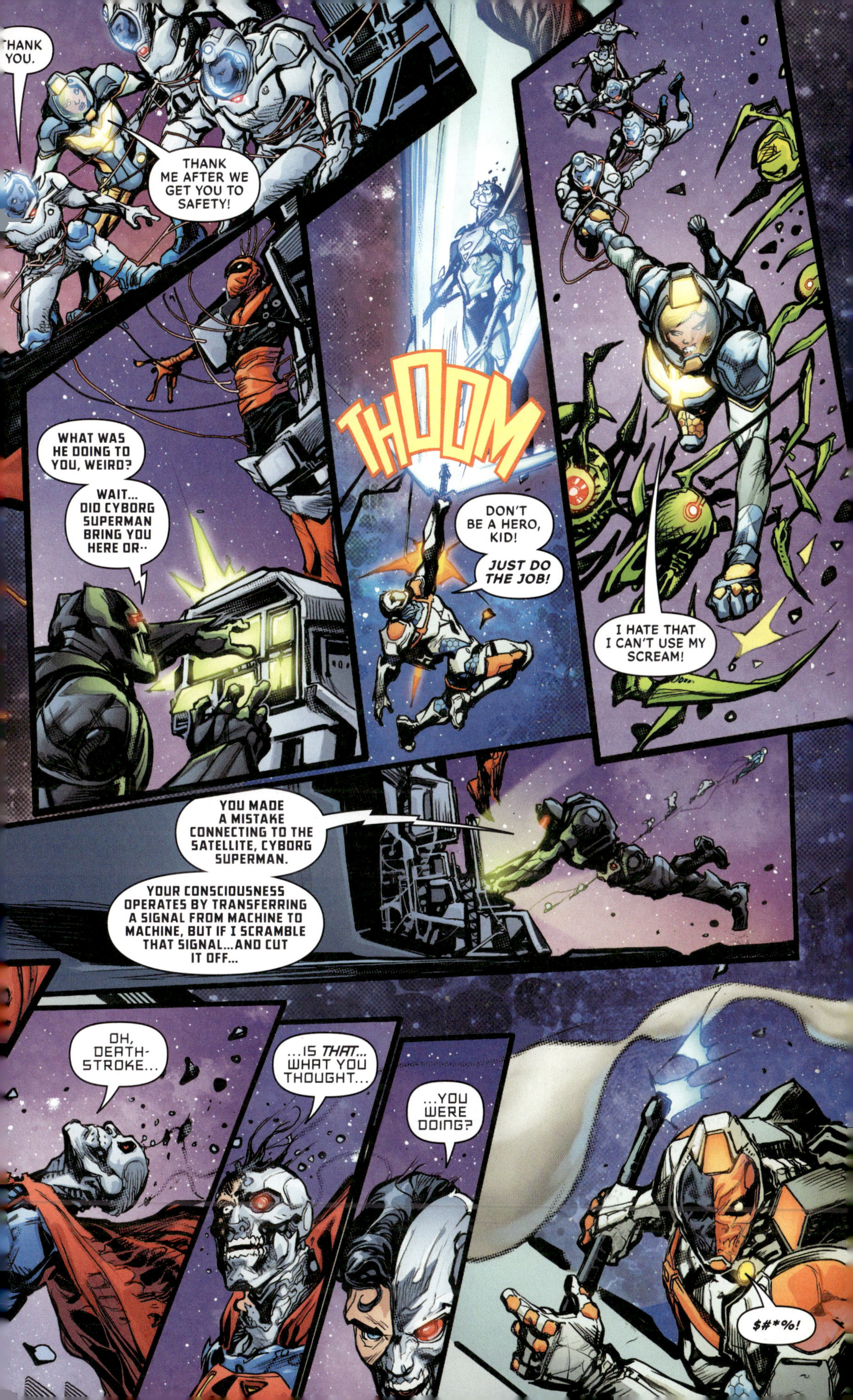
THANK YOU.
THANK ME AFTER WE GET YOU TO SAFETY!
WHAT WAS HE DOING TO YOU, WEIRD?
WAIT... DID CYBORG SUPERMAN BRING YOU HERE OR--
THOOM
DON'T BE A HERO, KID!
JUST DO THE JOB!
I HATE THAT I CAN'T USE MY SCREAM!
YOU MADE A MISTAKE CONNECTING TO THE SATELLITE, CYBORG SUPERMAN.
YOUR CONSCIOUSNESS OPERATES BY TRANSFERRING A SIGNAL FROM MACHINE TO MACHINE, BUT IF I SCRAMBLE THAT SIGNAL...AND CUT IT OFF...
OH, DEATH-STROKE...
...IS THAT... WHAT YOU THOUGHT...
...YOU WERE DOING?
$#*%!

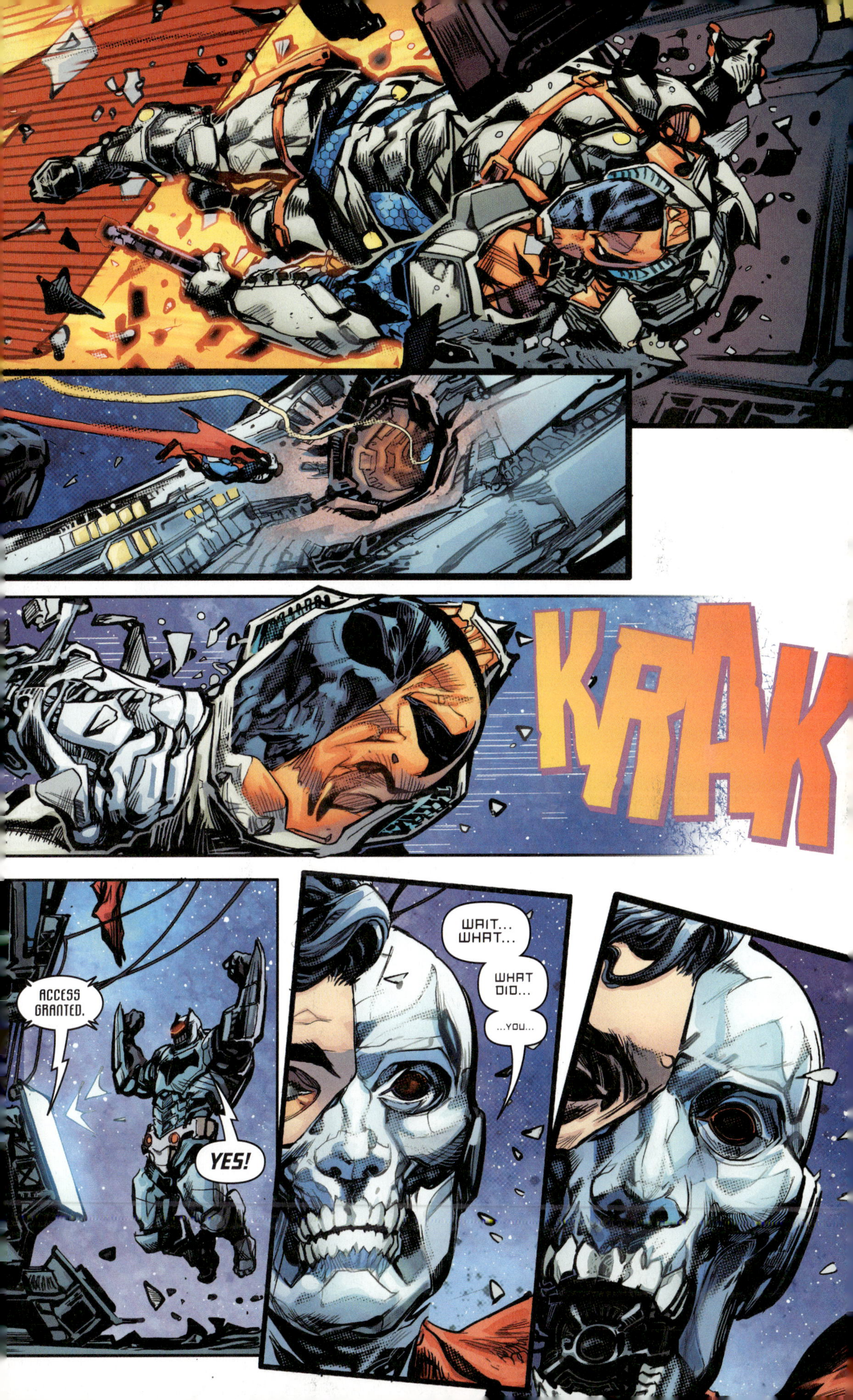
KRAK
ACCESS GRANTED.
YES!
WAIT... WHAT...
WHAT DID...
...YOU...

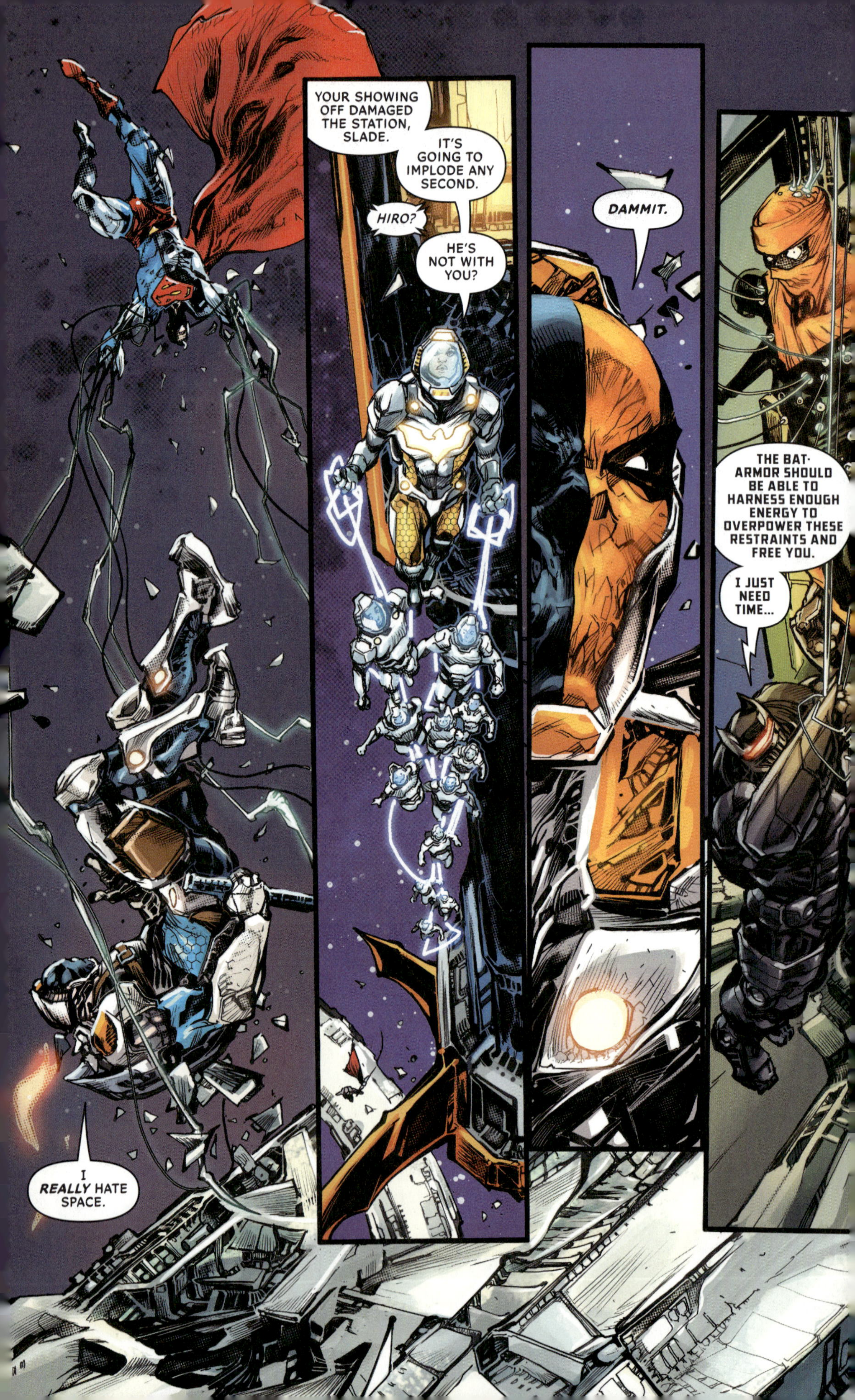
YOUR SHOWING OFF DAMAGED THE STATION, SLADE.
IT'S GOING TO IMPLODE ANY SECOND.
HIRO?
HE'S NOT WITH YOU?
DAMMIT.
THE BAT-ARMOR SHOULD BE ABLE TO HARNESS ENOUGH ENERGY TO OVERPOWER THESE RESTRAINTS AND FREE YOU.
I JUST NEED TIME...
I *REALLY* HATE SPACE.

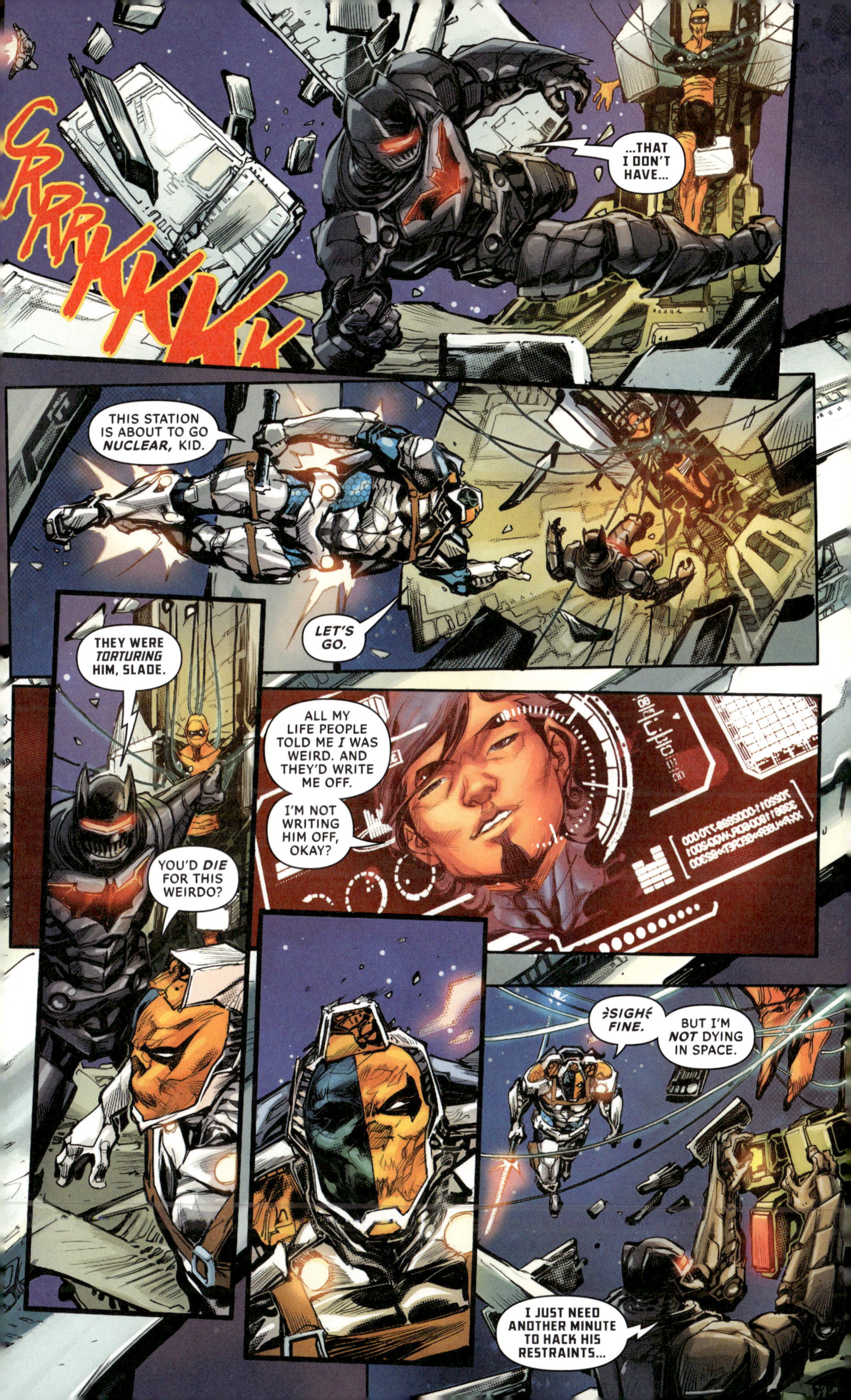
CRRRKKKKK
...THAT I DON'T HAVE...
THIS STATION IS AHOUT TO GO NUCLEAR, KID.
LET'S GO.
THEY WERE TORTURING HIM, SLADE.
ALL MY LIFE PEOPLE TOLD ME I WAS WEIRD. AND THEY'D WRITE ME OFF.
I'M NOT WRITING HIM OFF, OKAY?
YOU'D DIE FOR THIS WEIRDO?
SIGH FINE.
BUT I'M NOT DYING IN SPACE.
I JUST NEED ANOTHER MINUTE TO HACK HIS RESTRAINTS...

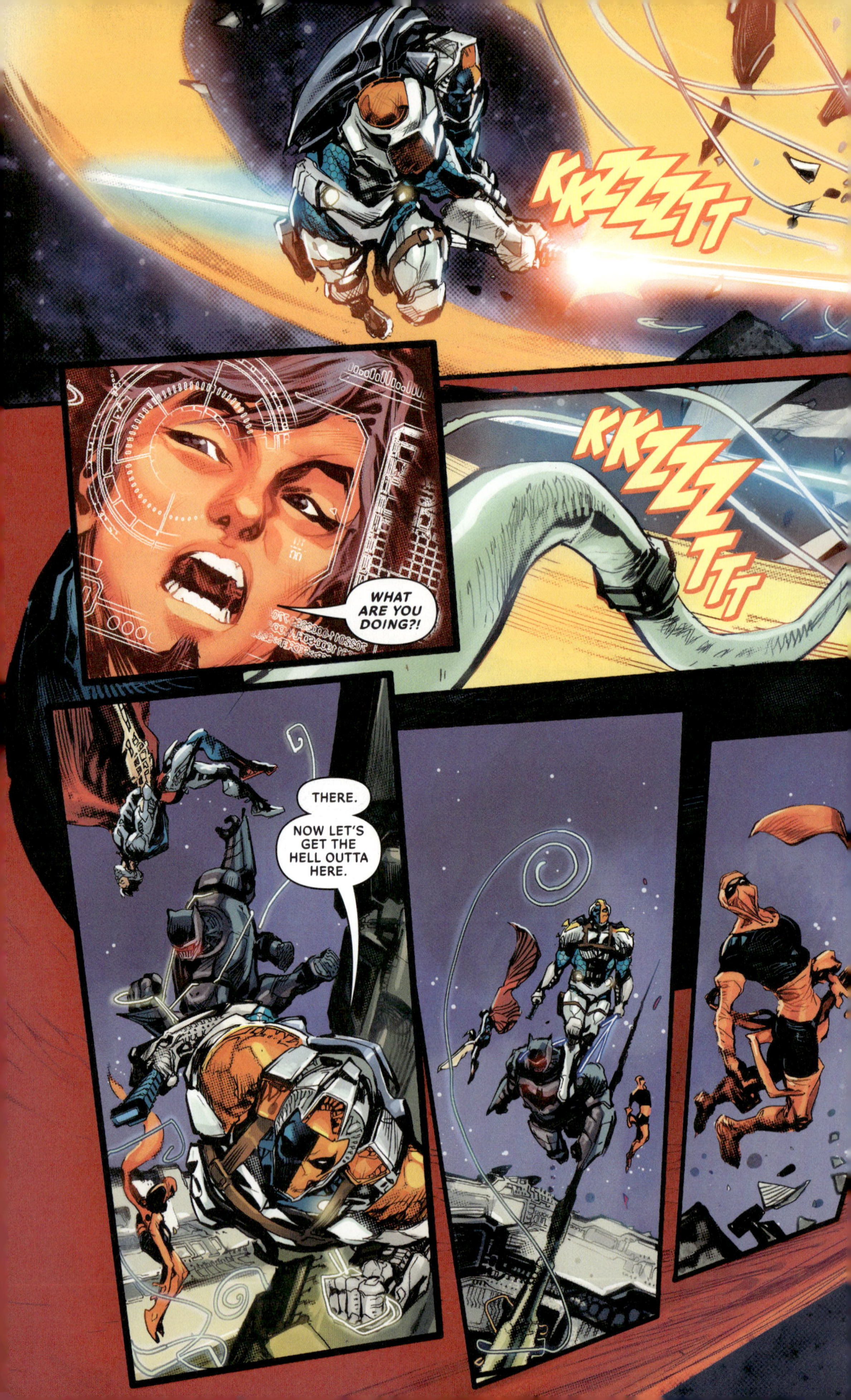
KKZZZZTT
KKZZZZTTT
WHAT ARE YOU DOING?!
THERE.
NOW LET'S GET THE HELL OUTTA HERE.

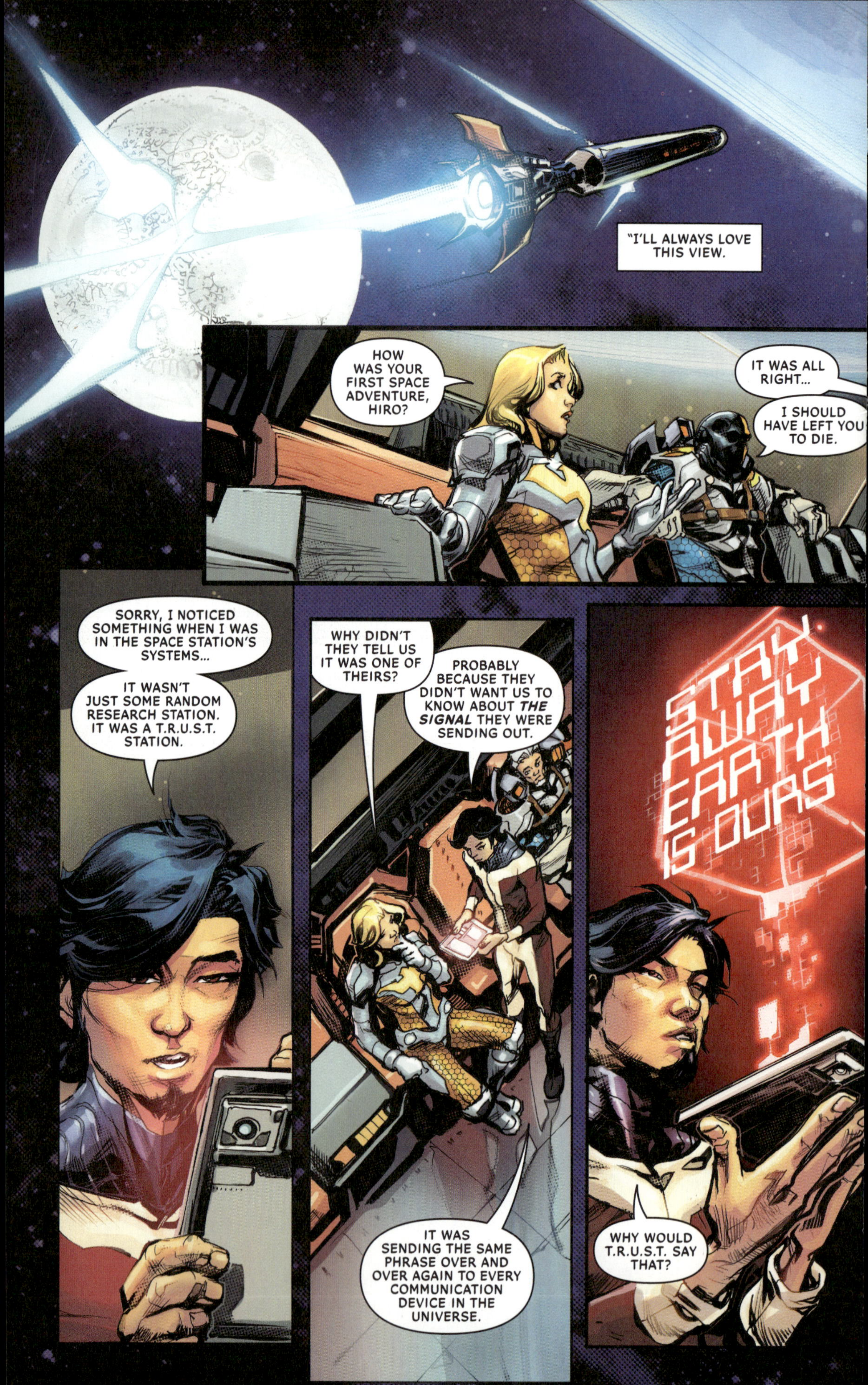
"I'LL ALWAYS LOVE THIS VIEW.
HOW WAS YOUR FIRST SPACE ADVENTURE, HIRO?
IT WAS ALL RIGHT...
I SHOULD HAVE LEFT YOU TO DIE.
SORRY, I NOTICED SOMETHING WHEN I WAS IN THE SPACE STATION'S SYSTEMS...
IT WASN'T JUST SOME RANDOM RESEARCH STATION. IT WAS A T.R.U.S.T. STATION.
WHY DIDN'T THEY TELL US IT WAS ONE OF THEIRS?
PROBABLY BECAUSE THEY DIDN'T WANT US TO KNOW ABOUT *THE SIGNAL* THEY WERE SENDING OUT.
IT WAS SENDING THE SAME PHRASE OVER AND OVER AGAIN TO EVERY COMMUNICATION DEVICE IN THE UNIVERSE.
STAY AWAY EARTH IS OURS
WHY WOULD T.R.U.S.T. SAY THAT?

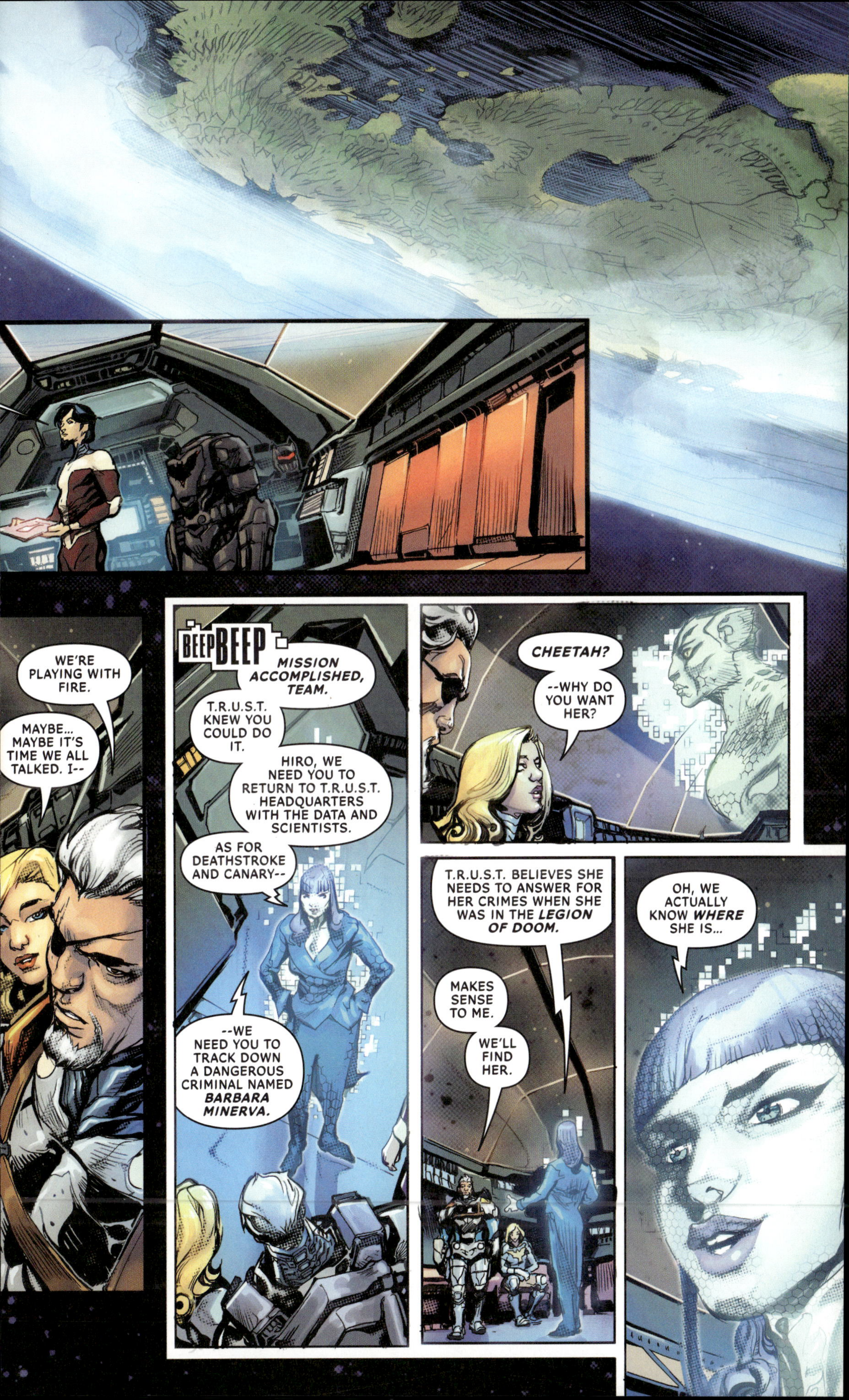
WE'RE PLAYING WITH FIRE.
MAYBE... MAYBE IT'S TIME WE ALL TALKED. I--
BEEP BEEP
MISSION ACCOMPLISHED, TEAM.
T.R.U.S.T. KNEW YOU COULD DO IT.
HIRO, WE NEED YOU TO RETURN TO T.R.U.S.T. HEADQUARTERS WITH THE DATA AND SCIENTISTS.
AS FOR DEATHSTROKE AND CANARY--
--WE NEED YOU TO TRACK DOWN A DANGEROUS CRIMINAL NAMED BARBARA MINERVA.
CHEETAH?
--WHY DO YOU WANT HER?
T.R.U.S.T. BELIEVES SHE NEEDS TO ANSWER FOR HER CRIMES WHEN SHE WAS IN THE LEGION OF DOOM.
MAKES SENSE TO ME.
WE'LL FIND HER.
OH, WE ACTUALLY KNOW WHERE SHE IS...

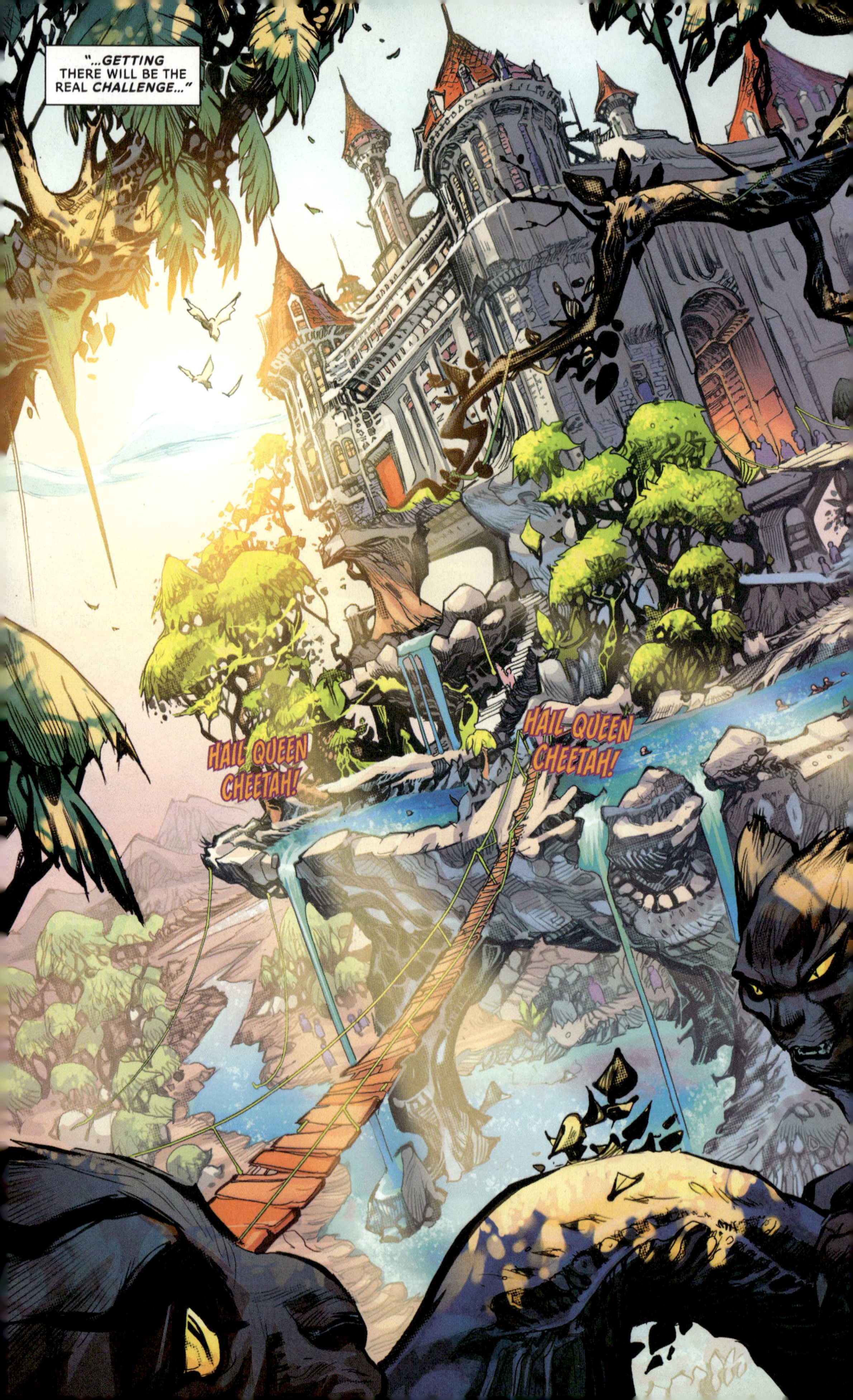
"...GETTING THERE WILL BE THE REAL CHALLENGE..."
HAIL QUEEN CHEETAH!
HAIL QUEEN CHEETAH!

DEATHSTROKE INC. #2
variant cover art by FRANCESCO MATTINA

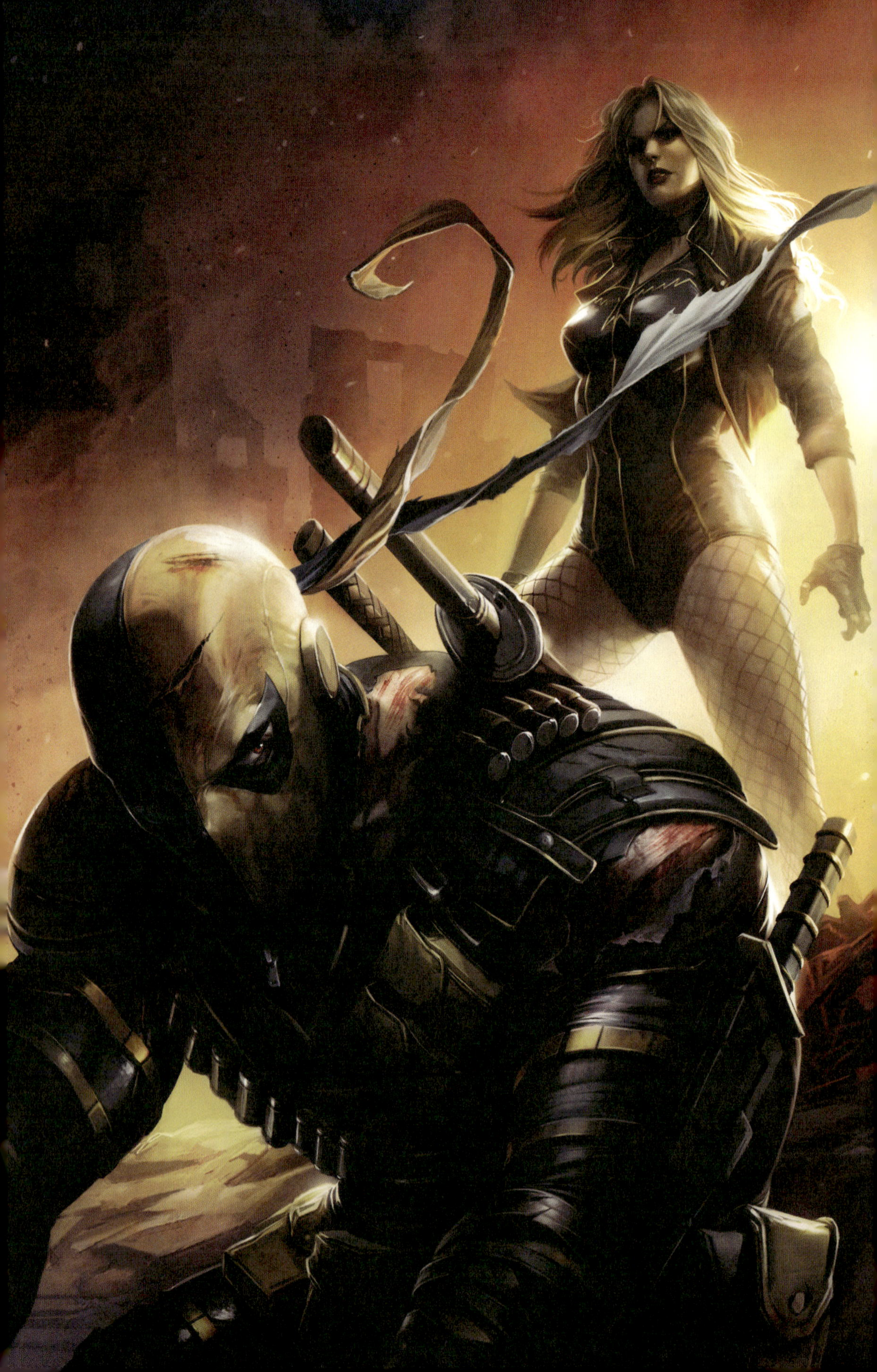

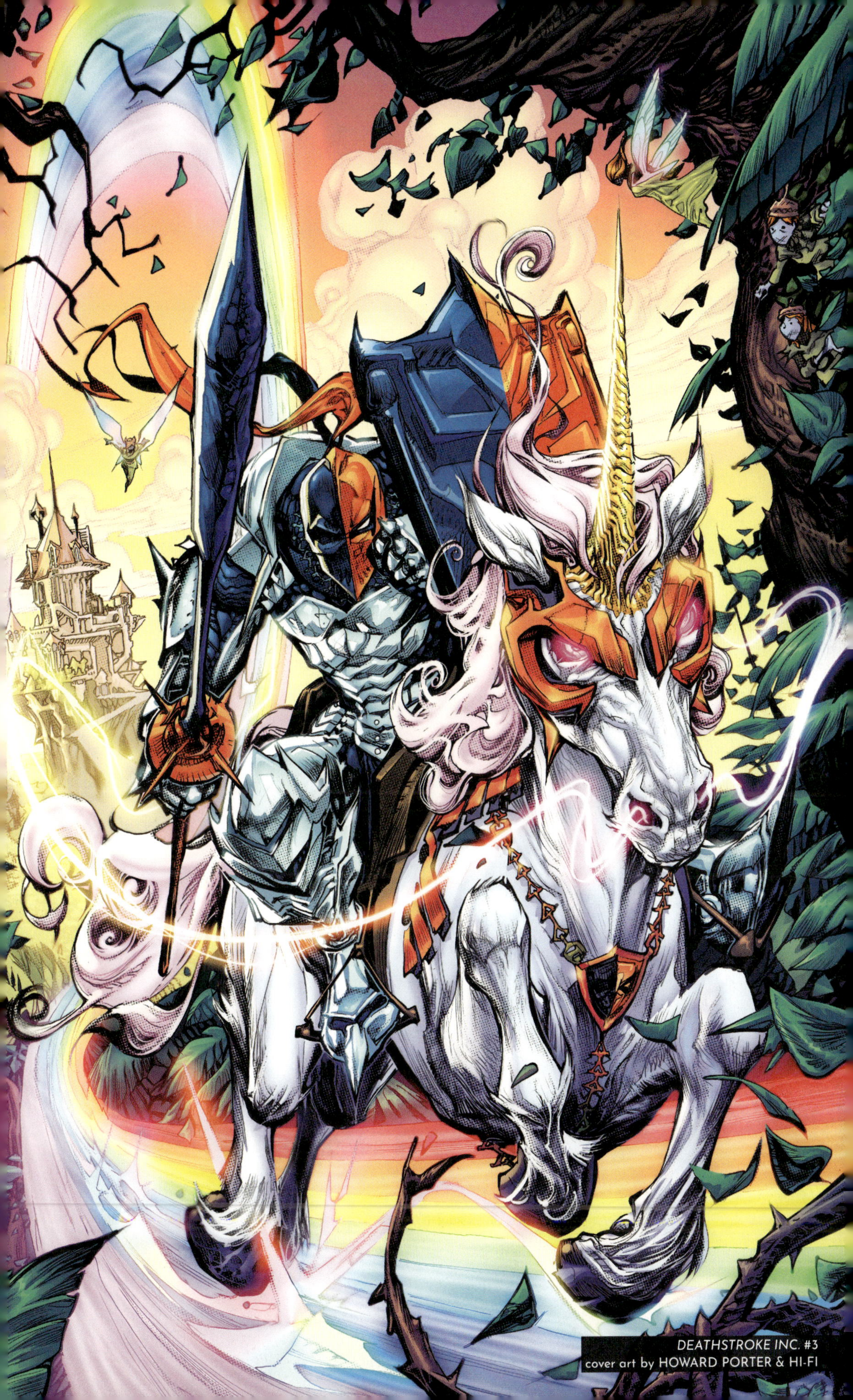

DEATHSTROKE INC. #3
cover art by HOWARD PORTER & HI-FI

DEATHSTROKE INC. #3
variant cover art by FRANCESCO MATTINA

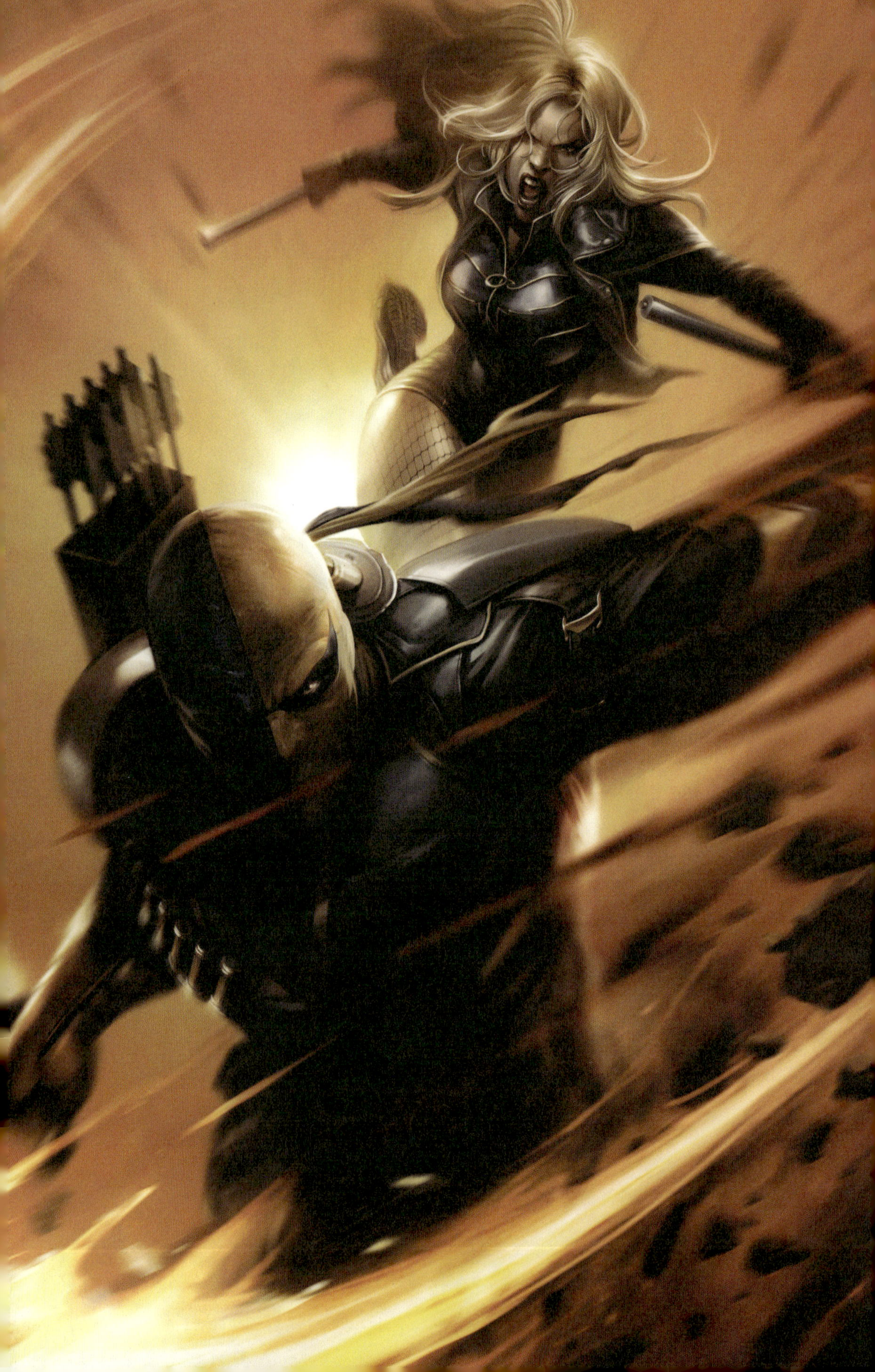

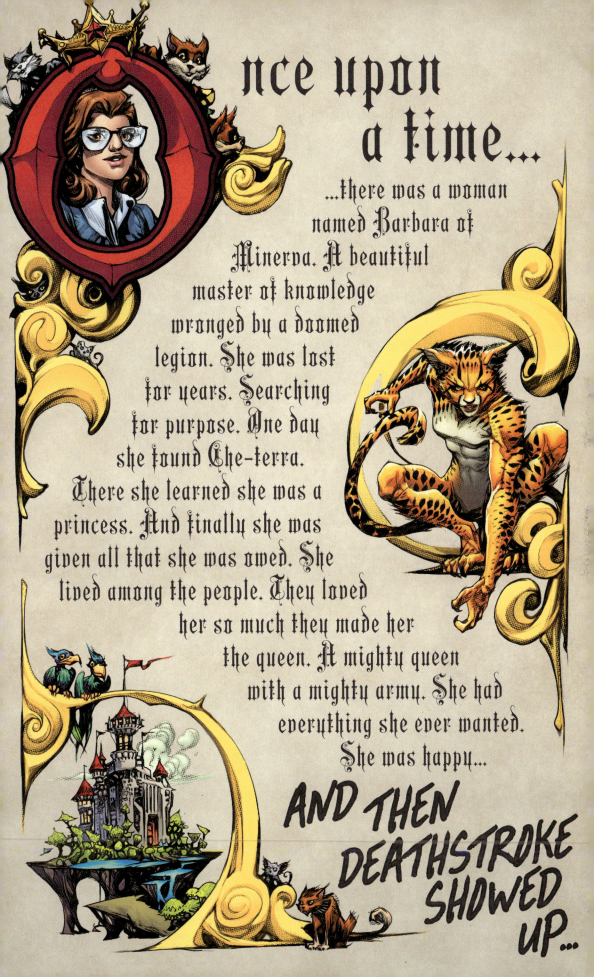

Once upon a time...

...there was a woman named Barbara of Minerva. A beautiful master of knowledge wronged by a doomed legion. She was lost for years. Searching for purpose. One day she found Che-terra. There she learned she was a princess. And finally she was given all that she was owed. She lived among the people. They loved her so much they made her the queen. A mighty queen with a mighty army. She had everything she ever wanted. She was happy...

AND THEN DEATHSTROKE SHOWED UP...

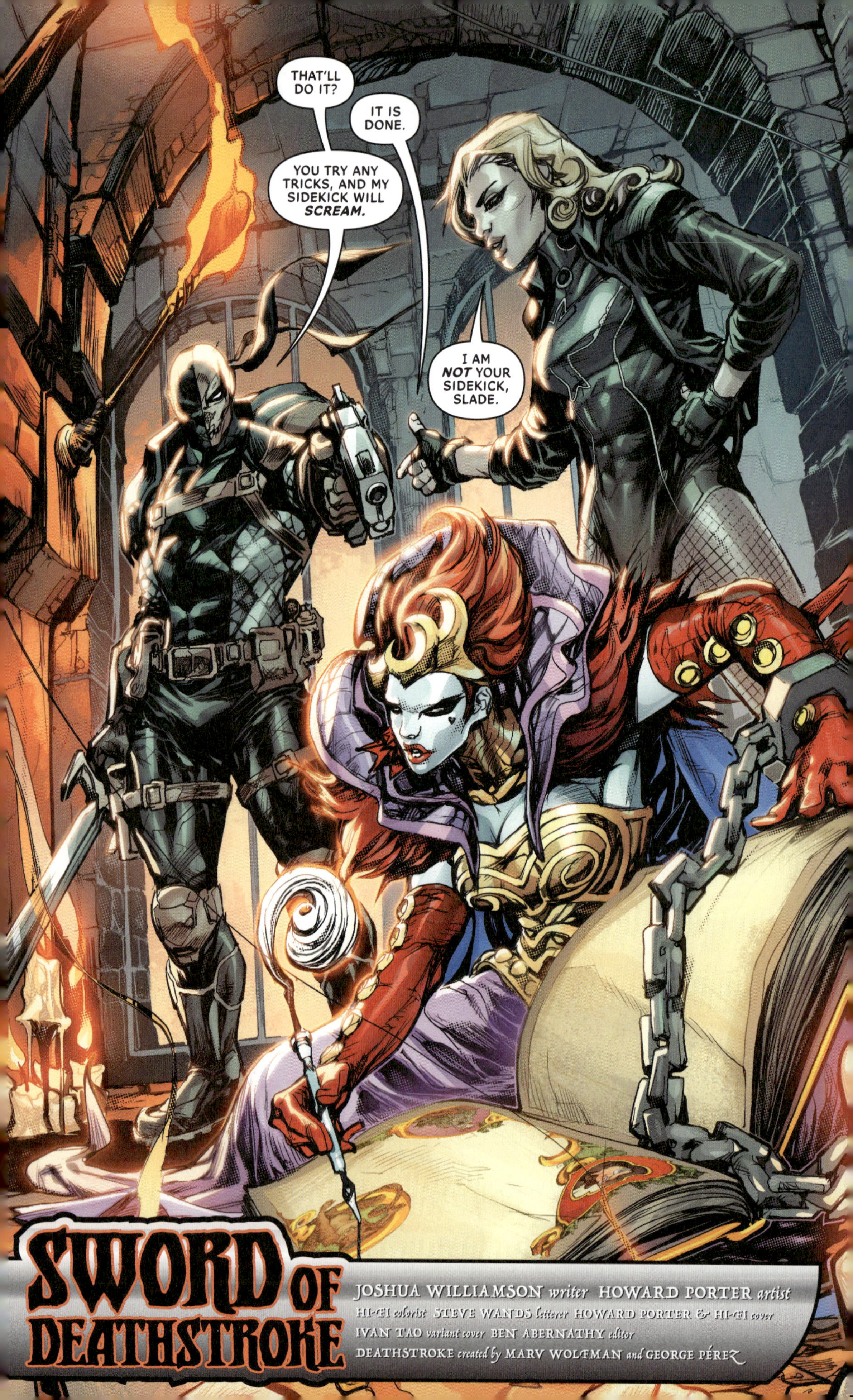
THAT'LL DO IT?
IT IS DONE.
YOU TRY ANY TRICKS, AND MY SIDEKICK WILL *SCREAM.*
I AM *NOT* YOUR SIDEKICK, SLADE.
SWORD OF DEATHSTROKE
JOSHUA WILLIAMSON writer HOWARD PORTER artist
HI-FI colorist STEVE WANDS letterer HOWARD PORTER & HI-FI cover
IVAN TAO variant cover BEN ABERNATHY editor
DEATHSTROKE created by MARV WOLFMAN and GEORGE PÉREZ

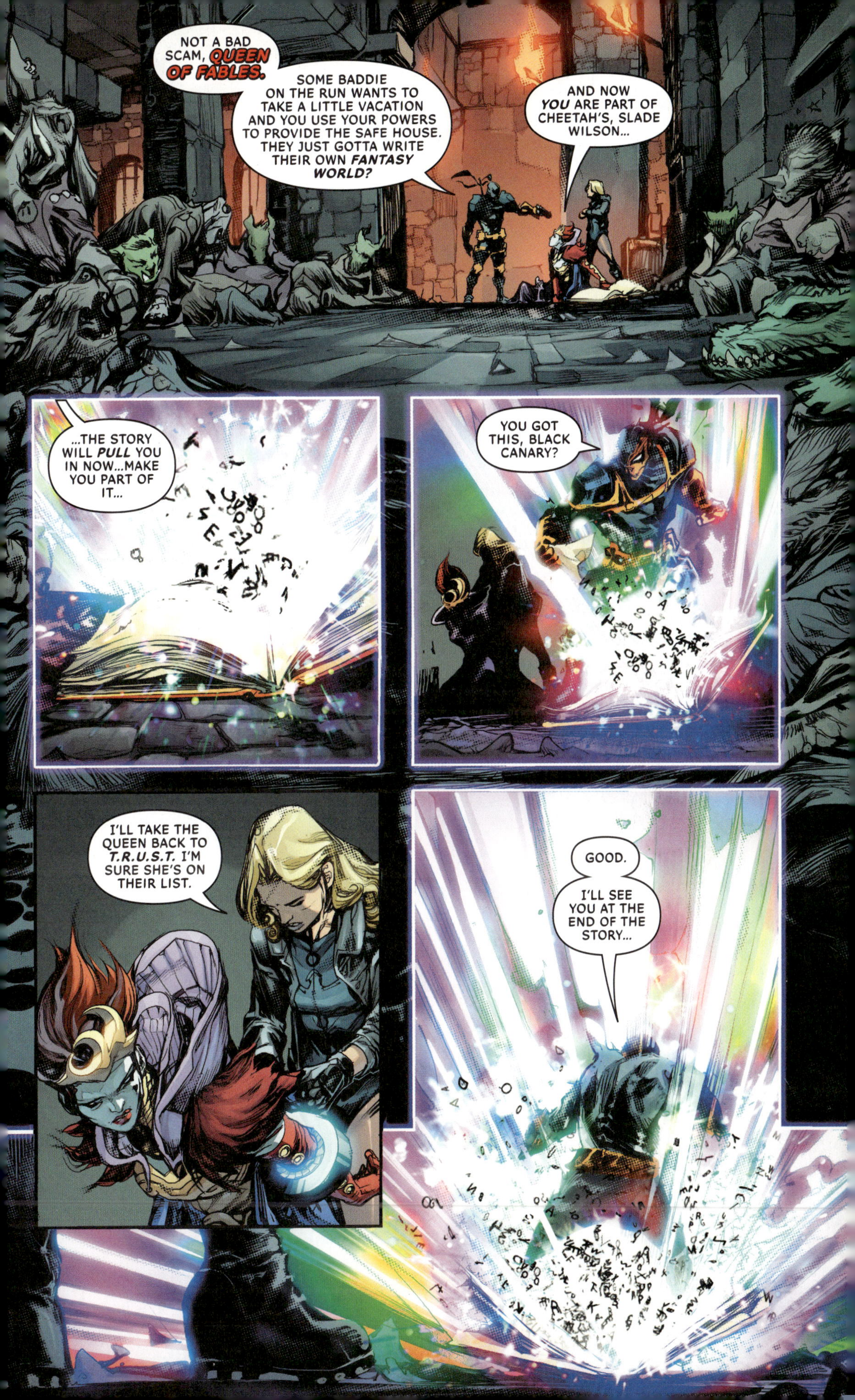
NOT A BAD SCAM, QUEEN OF FABLES.
SOME BADDIE ON THE RUN WANTS TO TAKE A LITTLE VACATION AND YOU USE YOUR POWERS TO PROVIDE THE SAFE HOUSE. THEY JUST GOTTA WRITE THEIR OWN FANTASY WORLD?
AND NOW YOU ARE PART OF CHEETAH'S, SLADE WILSON...
...THE STORY WILL PULL YOU IN NOW...MAKE YOU PART OF IT...
YOU GOT THIS, BLACK CANARY?
I'LL TAKE THE QUEEN BACK TO T.R.U.S.T. I'M SURE SHE'S ON THEIR LIST.
GOOD.
I'LL SEE YOU AT THE END OF THE STORY...

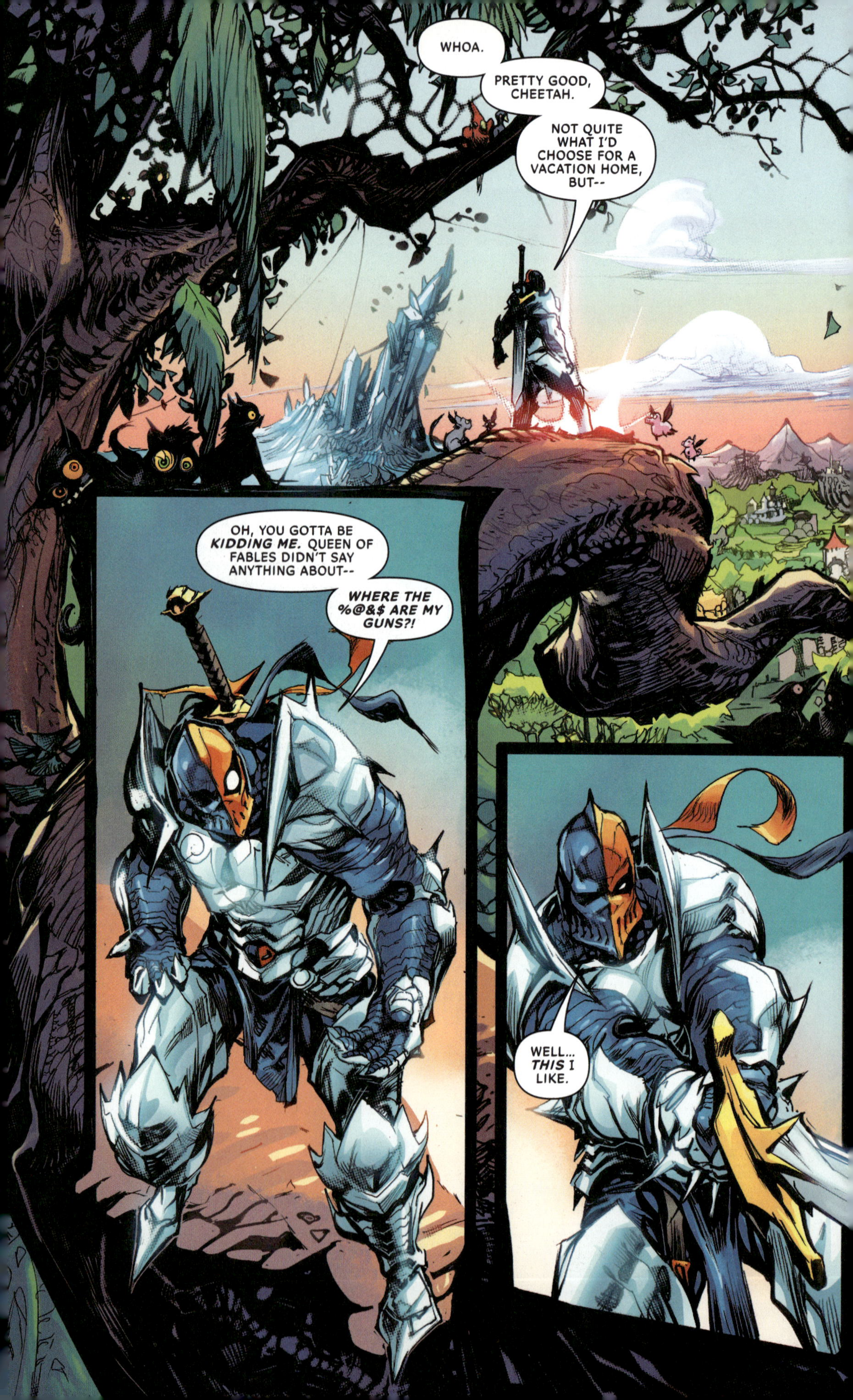
WHOA.
PRETTY GOOD, CHEETAH.
NOT QUITE WHAT I'D CHOOSE FOR A VACATION HOME, BUT--
OH, YOU GOTTA BE *KIDDING ME.* QUEEN OF FABLES DIDN'T SAY ANYTHING ABOUT--
WHERE THE %@&$ ARE MY GUNS?!
WELL... *THIS* I LIKE.

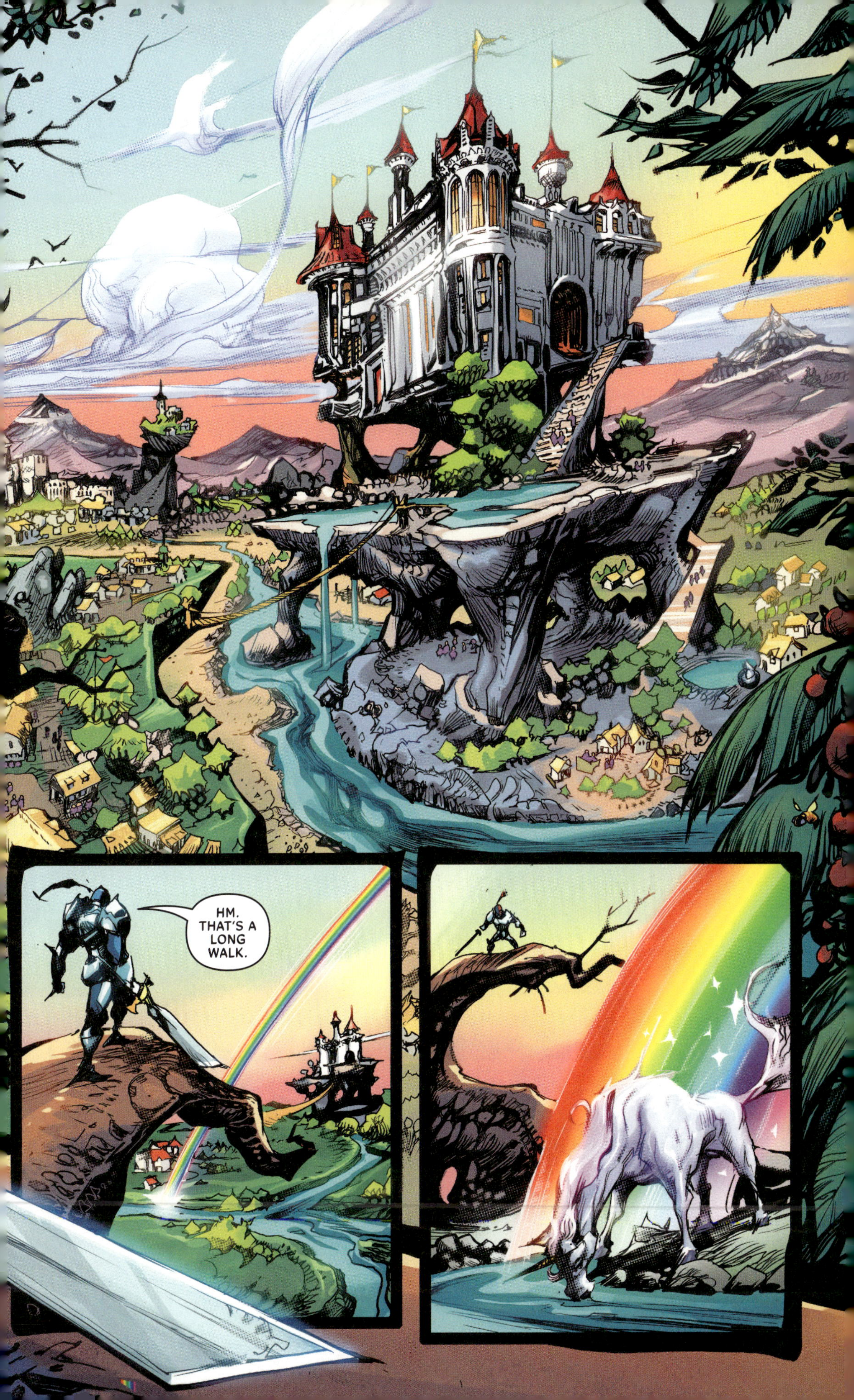
HM. THAT'S A LONG WALK.

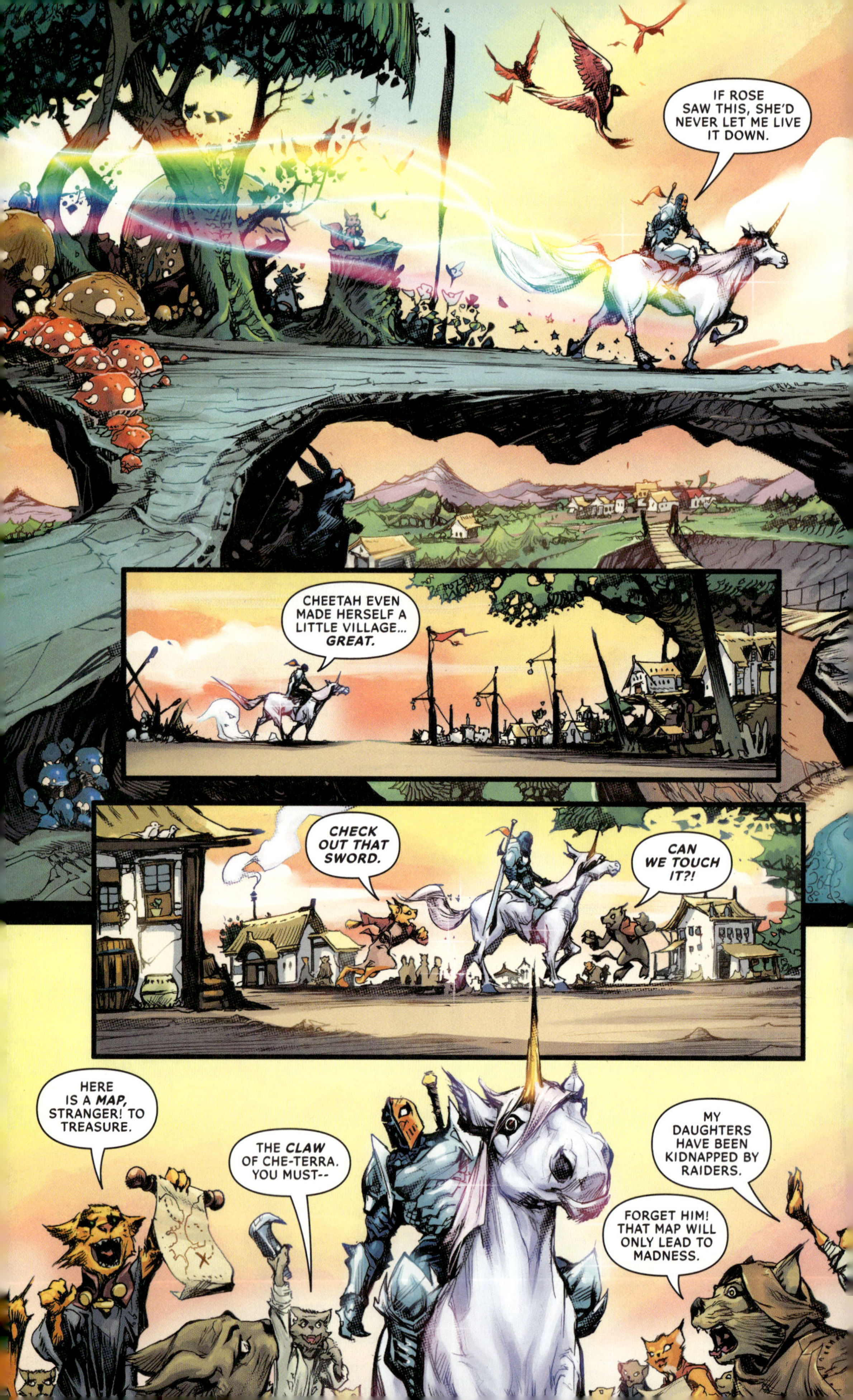
IF ROSE SAW THIS, SHE'D NEVER LET ME LIVE IT DOWN.
CHEETAH EVEN MADE HERSELF A LITTLE VILLAGE... *GREAT.*
CHECK OUT THAT SWORD.
CAN WE TOUCH IT?!
HERE IS A *MAP,* STRANGER! TO TREASURE.
THE *CLAW* OF CHE-TERRA. YOU MUST--
MY DAUGHTERS HAVE BEEN KIDNAPPED BY RAIDERS.
FORGET HIM! THAT MAP WILL ONLY LEAD TO MADNESS.

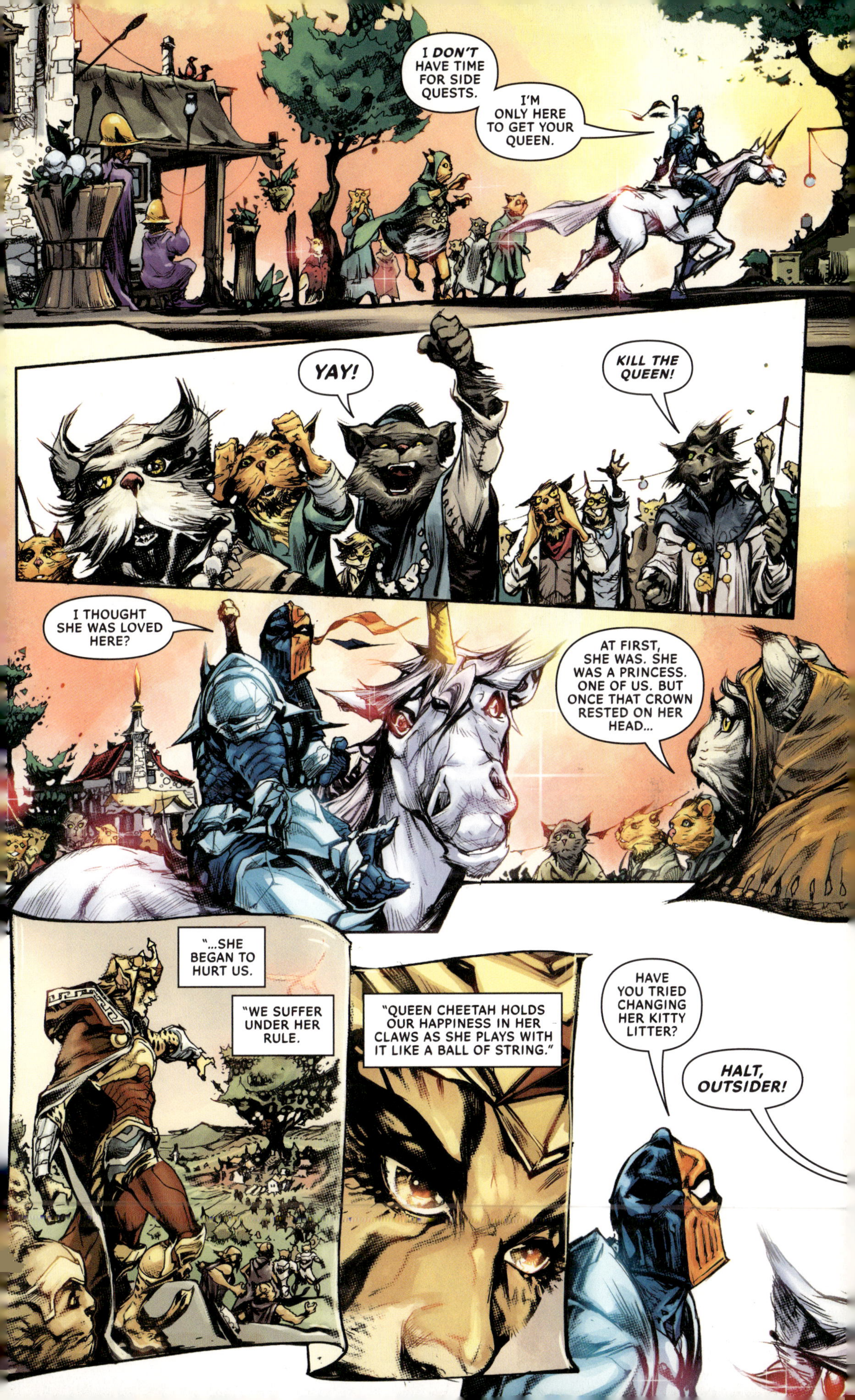
I *DON'T* HAVE TIME FOR SIDE QUESTS.
I'M ONLY HERE TO GET YOUR QUEEN.
YAY!
KILL THE QUEEN!
I THOUGHT SHE WAS LOVED HERE?
AT FIRST, SHE WAS. SHE WAS A PRINCESS. ONE OF US. BUT ONCE THAT CROWN RESTED ON HER HEAD...
"...SHE BEGAN TO HURT US.
"WE SUFFER UNDER HER RULE.
"QUEEN CHEETAH HOLDS OUR HAPPINESS IN HER CLAWS AS SHE PLAYS WITH IT LIKE A BALL OF STRING."
HAVE YOU TRIED CHANGING HER KITTY LITTER?
HALT, OUTSIDER!

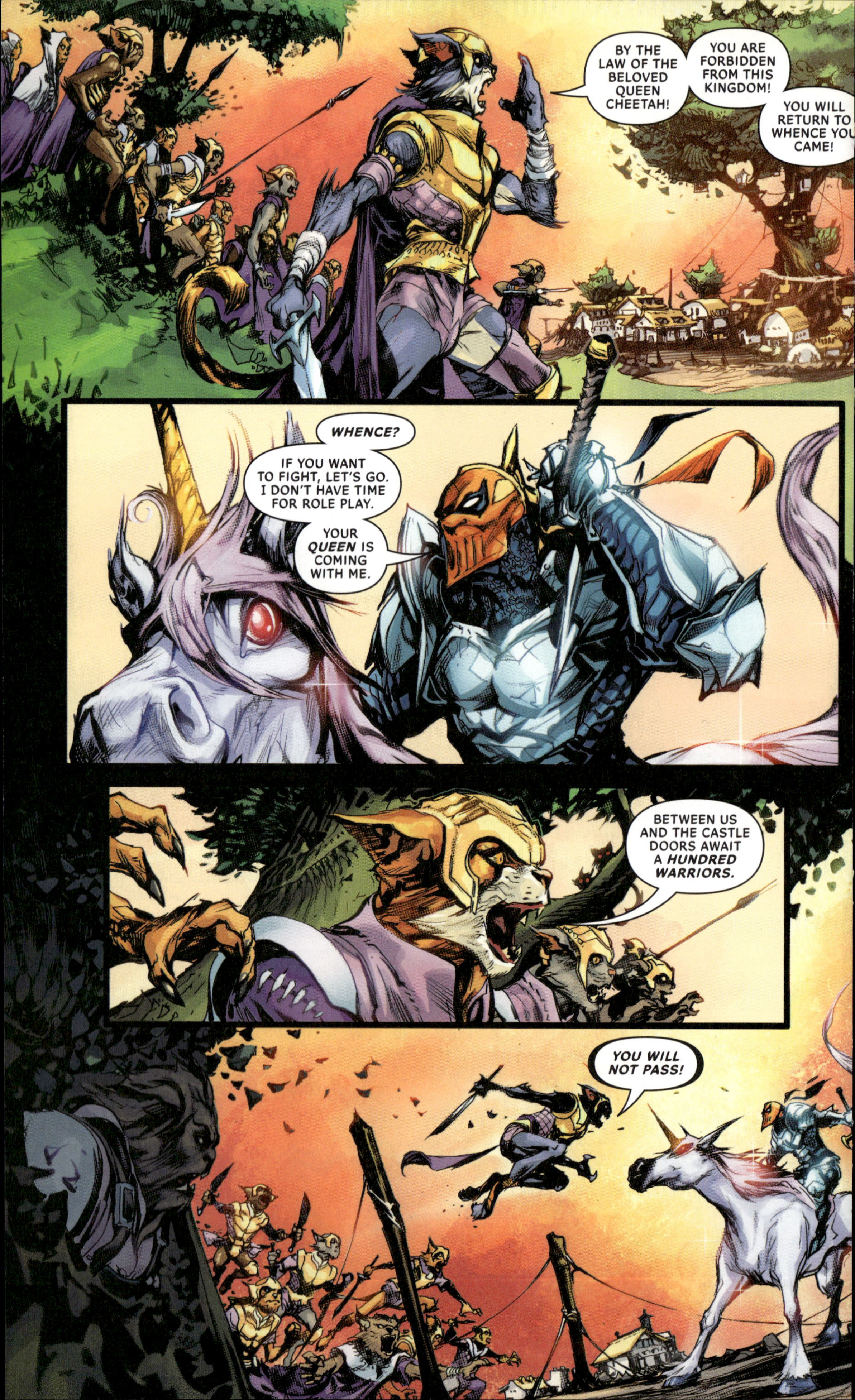
BY THE LAW OF THE BELOVED QUEEN CHEETAH!
YOU ARE FORBIDDEN FROM THIS KINGDOM!
YOU WILL RETURN TO WHENCE YOU CAME!
WHENCE?
IF YOU WANT TO FIGHT, LET'S GO. I DON'T HAVE TIME FOR ROLE PLAY.
YOUR *QUEEN* IS COMING WITH ME.
BETWEEN US AND THE CASTLE DOORS AWAIT A *HUNDRED WARRIORS.*
YOU WILL NOT PASS!

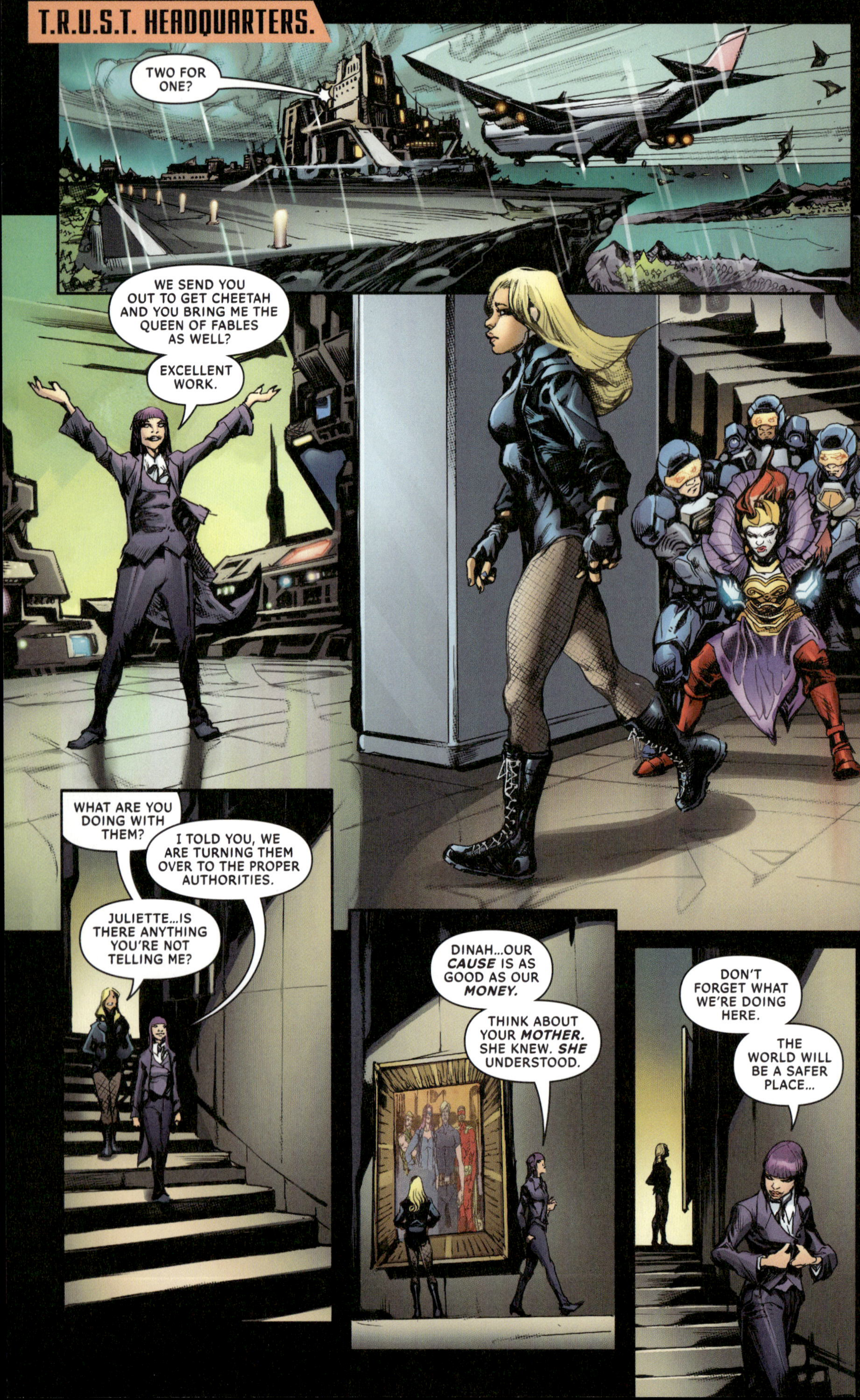
T.R.U.S.T. HEADQUARTERS.
TWO FOR ONE?
WE SEND YOU OUT TO GET CHEETAH AND YOU BRING ME THE QUEEN OF FABLES AS WELL?
EXCELLENT WORK.
WHAT ARE YOU DOING WITH THEM?
I TOLD YOU, WE ARE TURNING THEM OVER TO THE PROPER AUTHORITIES.
JULIETTE...IS THERE ANYTHING YOU'RE NOT TELLING ME?
DINAH...OUR *CAUSE* IS AS GOOD AS OUR *MONEY.*
THINK ABOUT YOUR *MOTHER.* SHE KNEW. *SHE* UNDERSTOOD.
DON'T FORGET WHAT WE'RE DOING HERE.
THE WORLD WILL BE A SAFER PLACE...

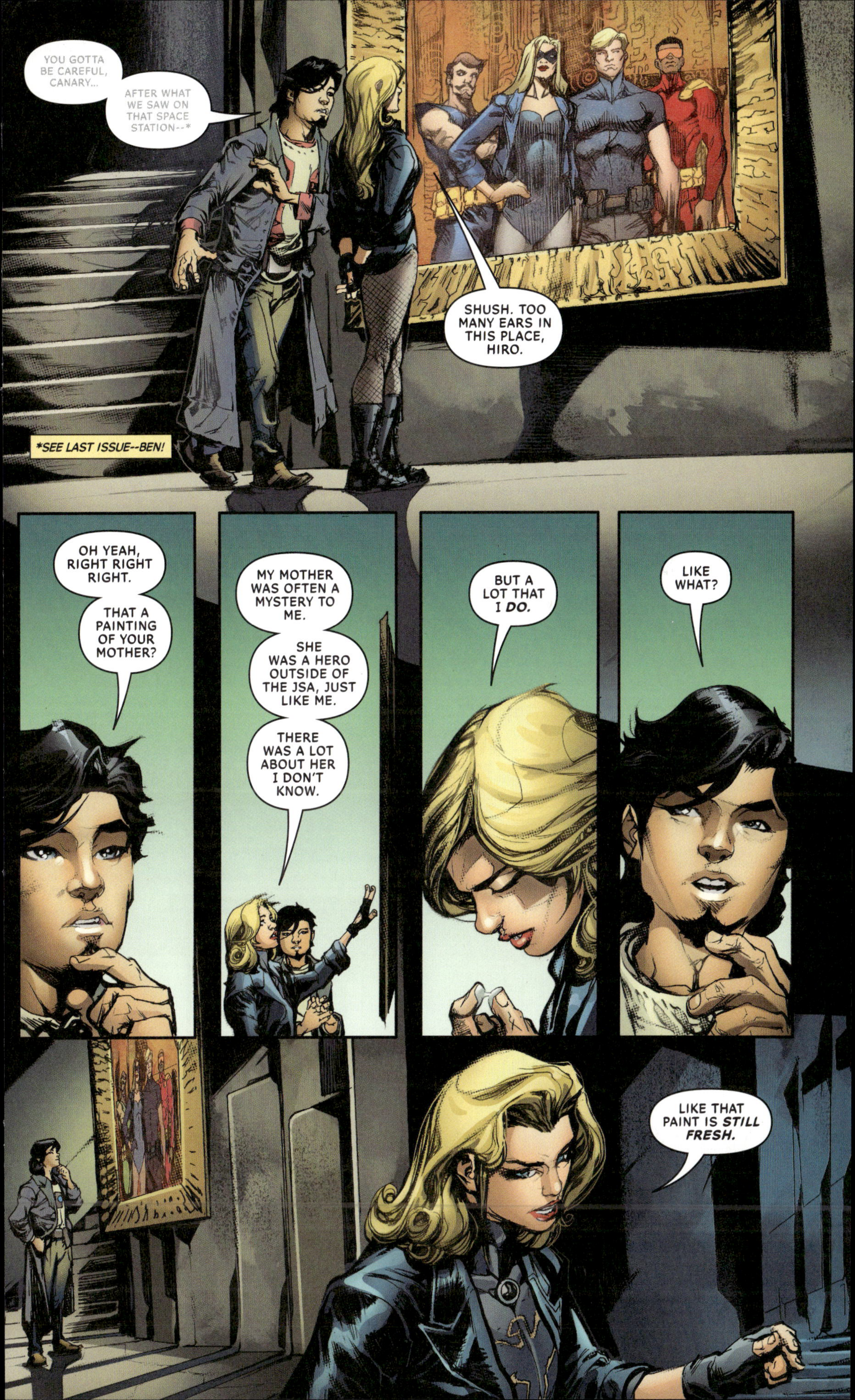
YOU GOTTA BE CAREFUL, CANARY...
AFTER WHAT WE SAW ON THAT SPACE STATION--*
SHUSH. TOO MANY EARS IN THIS PLACE, HIRO.
*SEE LAST ISSUE--BEN!
OH YEAH, RIGHT RIGHT RIGHT.
THAT A PAINTING OF YOUR MOTHER?
MY MOTHER WAS OFTEN A MYSTERY TO ME.
SHE WAS A HERO OUTSIDE OF THE JSA, JUST LIKE ME.
THERE WAS A LOT ABOUT HER I DON'T KNOW.
BUT A LOT THAT I DO.
LIKE WHAT?
LIKE THAT PAINT IS STILL FRESH.

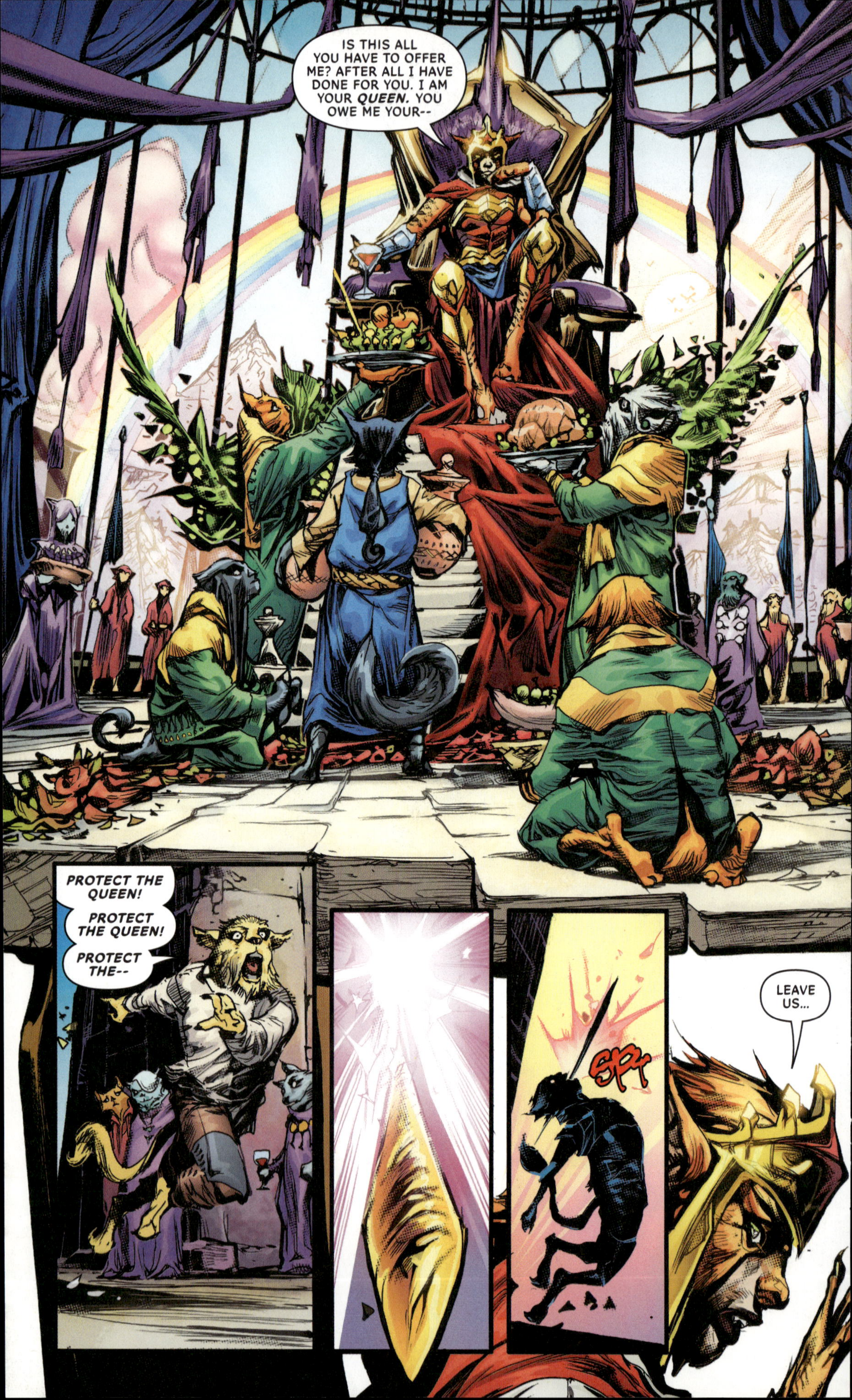
IS THIS ALL YOU HAVE TO OFFER ME? AFTER ALL I HAVE DONE FOR YOU. I AM YOUR *QUEEN.* YOU OWE ME YOUR--
PROTECT THE QUEEN!
PROTECT THE QUEEN!
PROTECT THE--
LEAVE US...

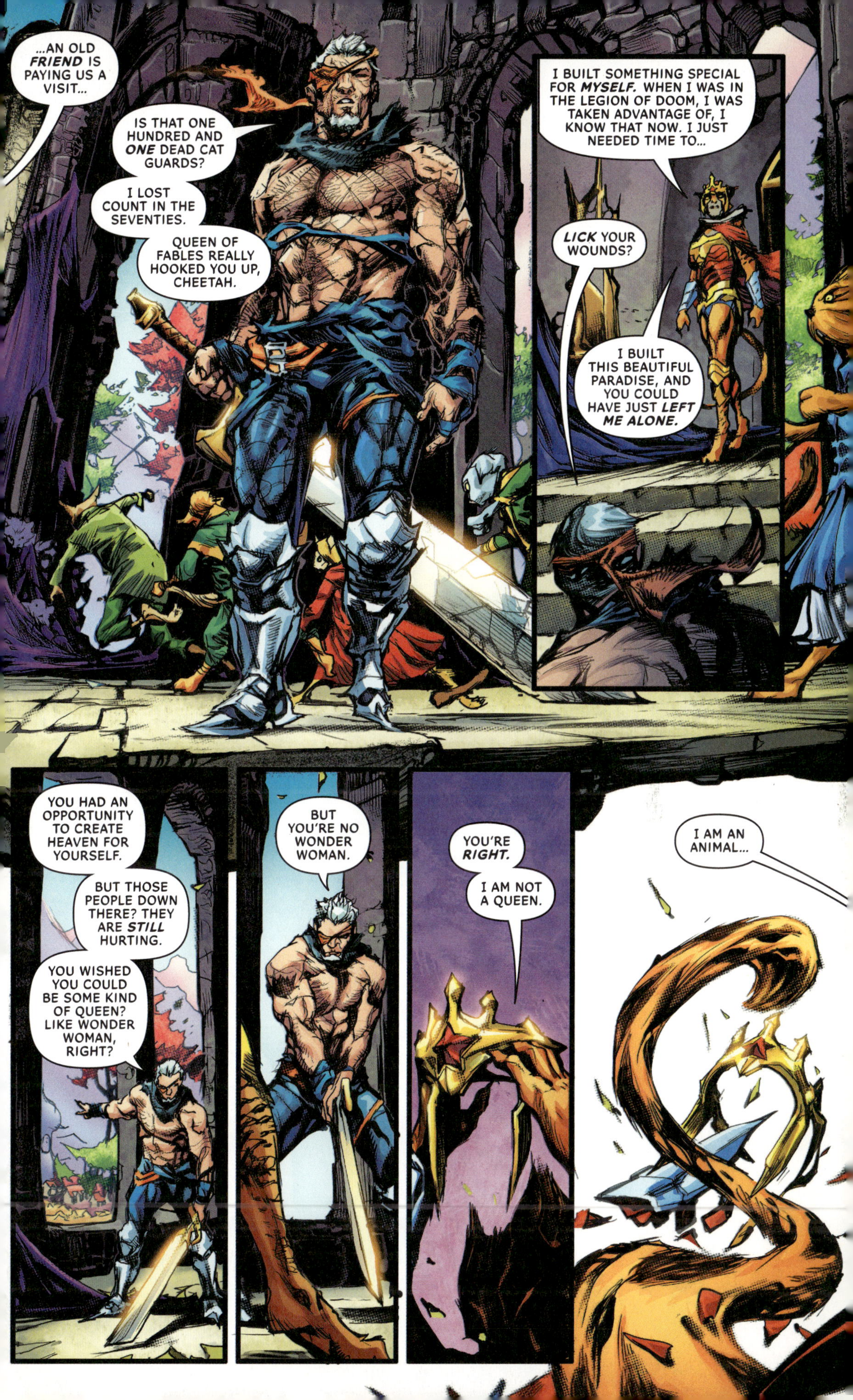
...AN OLD *FRIEND* IS PAYING US A VISIT...
IS THAT ONE HUNDRED AND *ONE* DEAD CAT GUARDS?
I LOST COUNT IN THE SEVENTIES.
QUEEN OF FABLES REALLY HOOKED YOU UP, CHEETAH.
I BUILT SOMETHING SPECIAL FOR *MYSELF.* WHEN I WAS IN THE LEGION OF DOOM, I WAS TAKEN ADVANTAGE OF, I KNOW THAT NOW. I JUST NEEDED TIME TO...
LICK YOUR WOUNDS?
I BUILT THIS BEAUTIFUL PARADISE, AND YOU COULD HAVE JUST *LEFT ME ALONE.*
YOU HAD AN OPPORTUNITY TO CREATE HEAVEN FOR YOURSELF.
BUT THOSE PEOPLE DOWN THERE? THEY ARE *STILL* HURTING.
YOU WISHED YOU COULD BE SOME KIND OF QUEEN? LIKE WONDER WOMAN, RIGHT?
BUT YOU'RE NO WONDER WOMAN.
YOU'RE *RIGHT.*
I AM NOT A QUEEN.
I AM AN ANIMAL...

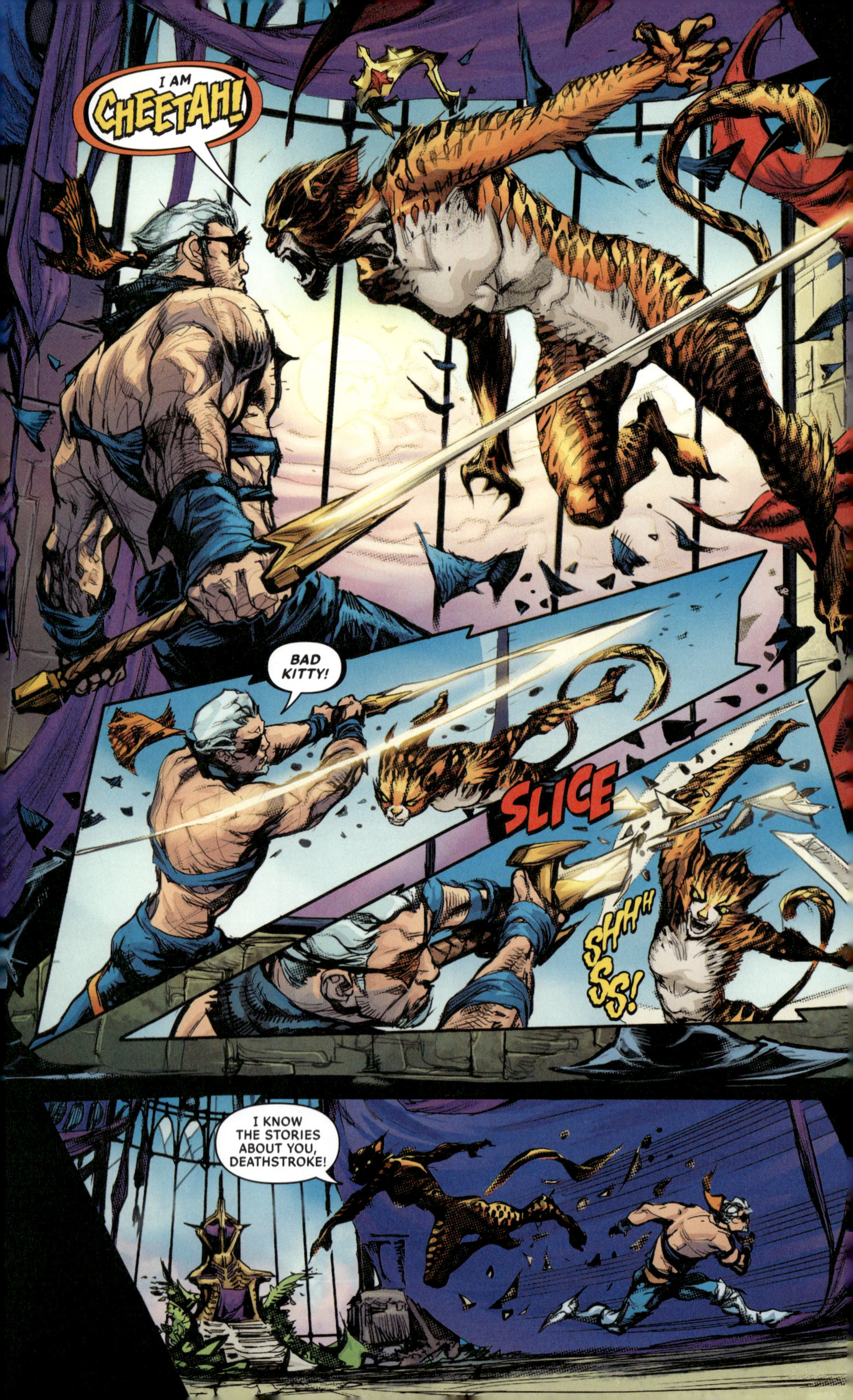
I AM CHEETAH!
BAD KITTY!
SLICE
SHHH SSS!
I KNOW THE STORIES ABOUT YOU, DEATHSTROKE!

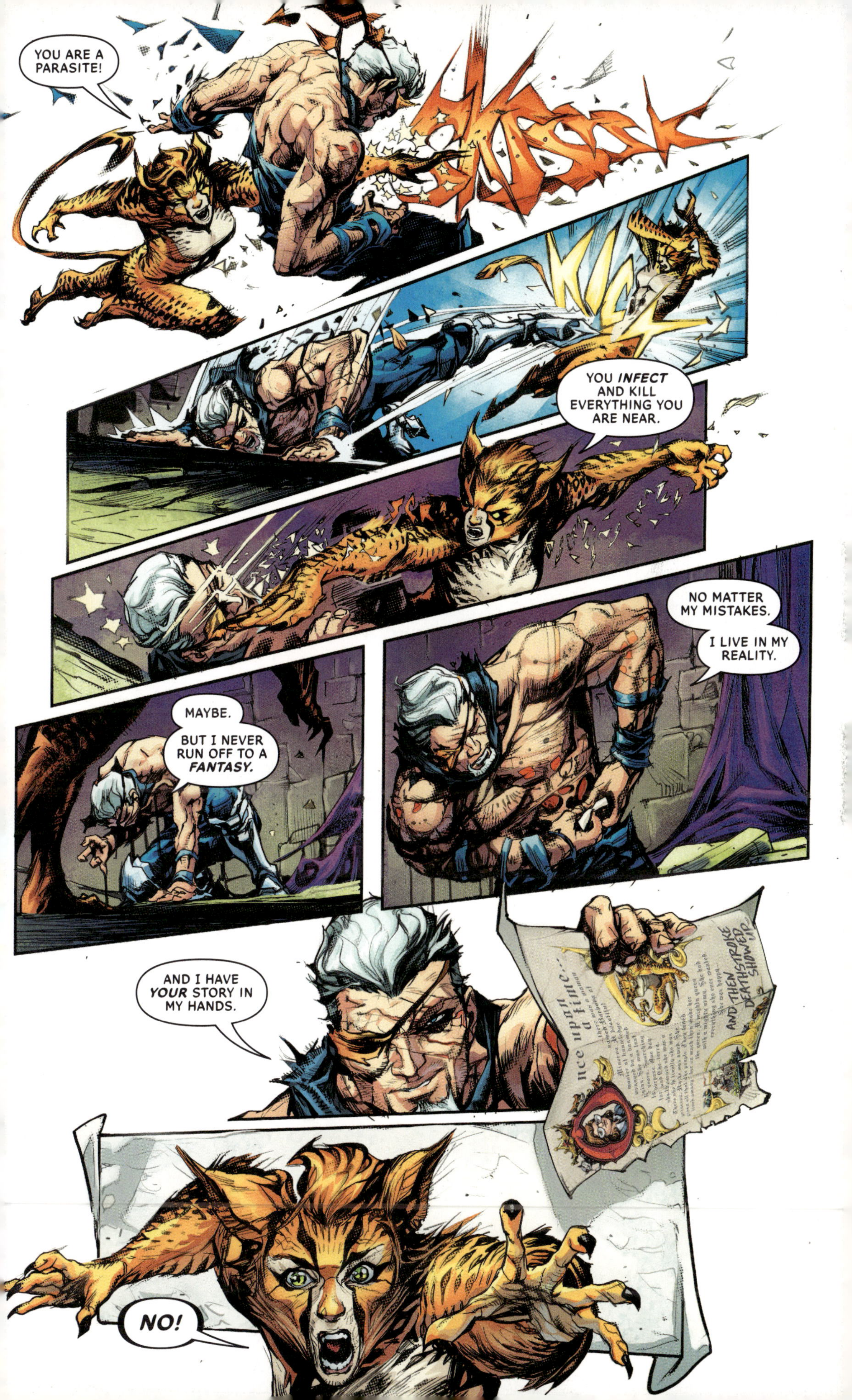
YOU ARE A PARASITE!
YOU *INFECT* AND KILL EVERYTHING YOU ARE NEAR.
NO MATTER MY MISTAKES.
I LIVE IN MY REALITY.
MAYBE.
BUT I NEVER RUN OFF TO A ***FANTASY.***
AND I HAVE ***YOUR*** STORY IN MY HANDS.
AND THEN DEATHSTROKE SHOWED UP.
NO!

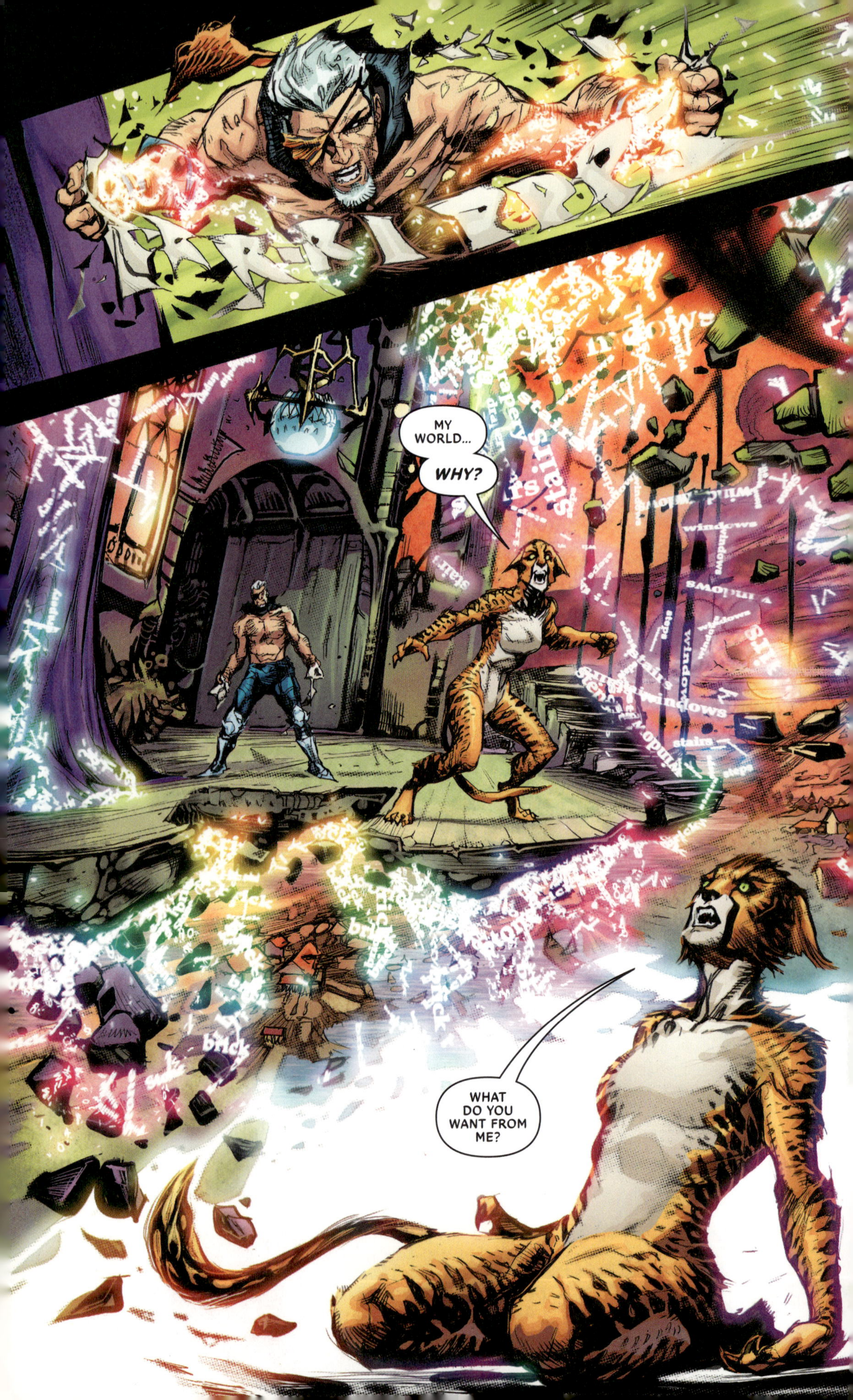
MY WORLD...
WHY?
WHAT DO YOU WANT FROM ME?

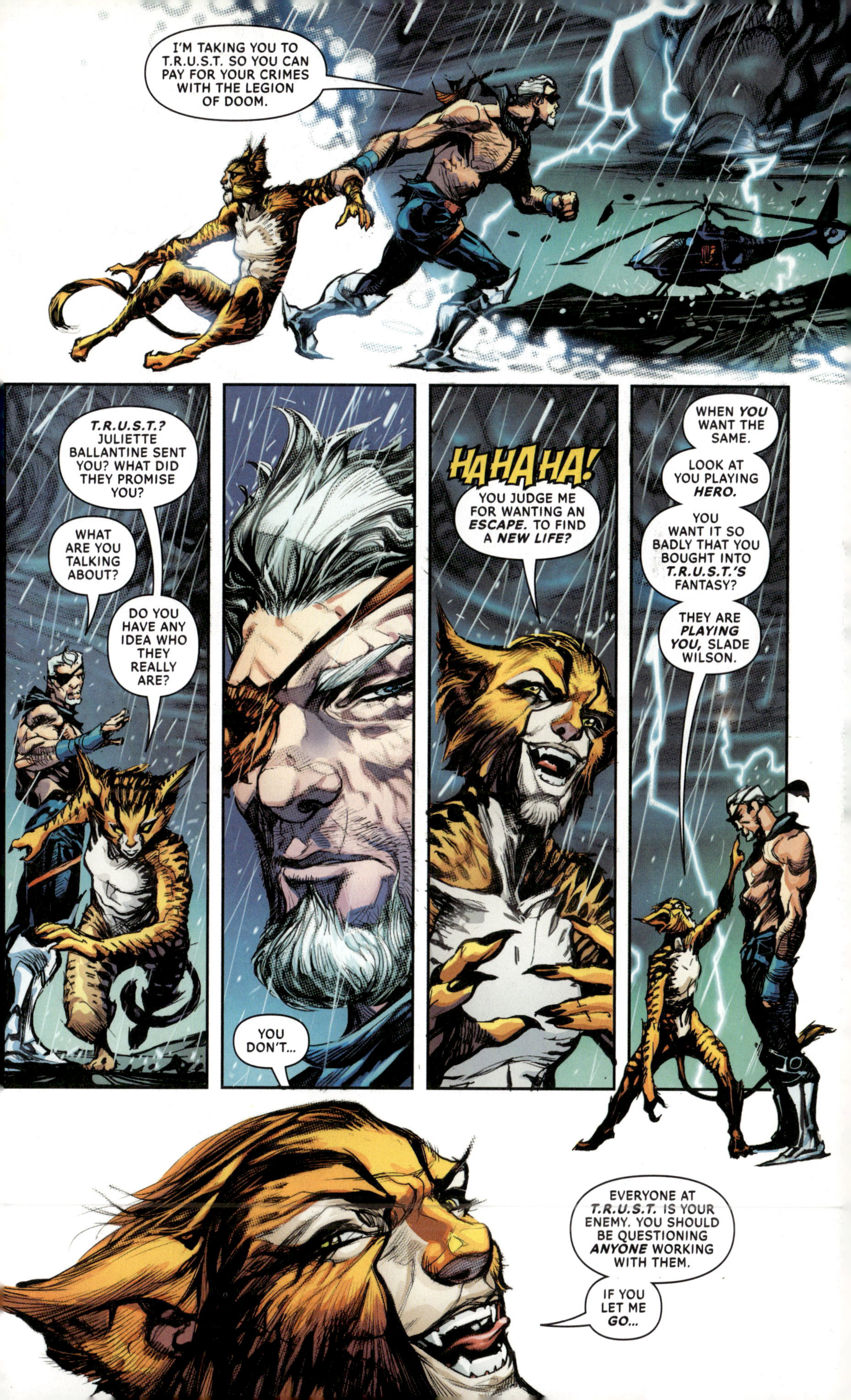
I'M TAKING YOU TO T.R.U.S.T. SO YOU CAN PAY FOR YOUR CRIMES WITH THE LEGION OF DOOM.
T.R.U.S.T.? JULIETTE BALLANTINE SENT YOU? WHAT DID THEY PROMISE YOU?
WHAT ARE YOU TALKING ABOUT?
DO YOU HAVE ANY IDEA WHO THEY REALLY ARE?
YOU DON'T...
HAHAHA!
YOU JUDGE ME FOR WANTING AN ESCAPE. TO FIND A NEW LIFE?
WHEN YOU WANT THE SAME.
LOOK AT YOU PLAYING HERO.
YOU WANT IT SO BADLY THAT YOU BOUGHT INTO T.R.U.S.T.'S FANTASY?
THEY ARE PLAYING YOU, SLADE WILSON.
EVERYONE AT T.R.U.S.T. IS YOUR ENEMY. YOU SHOULD BE QUESTIONING ANYONE WORKING WITH THEM.
IF YOU LET ME GO...

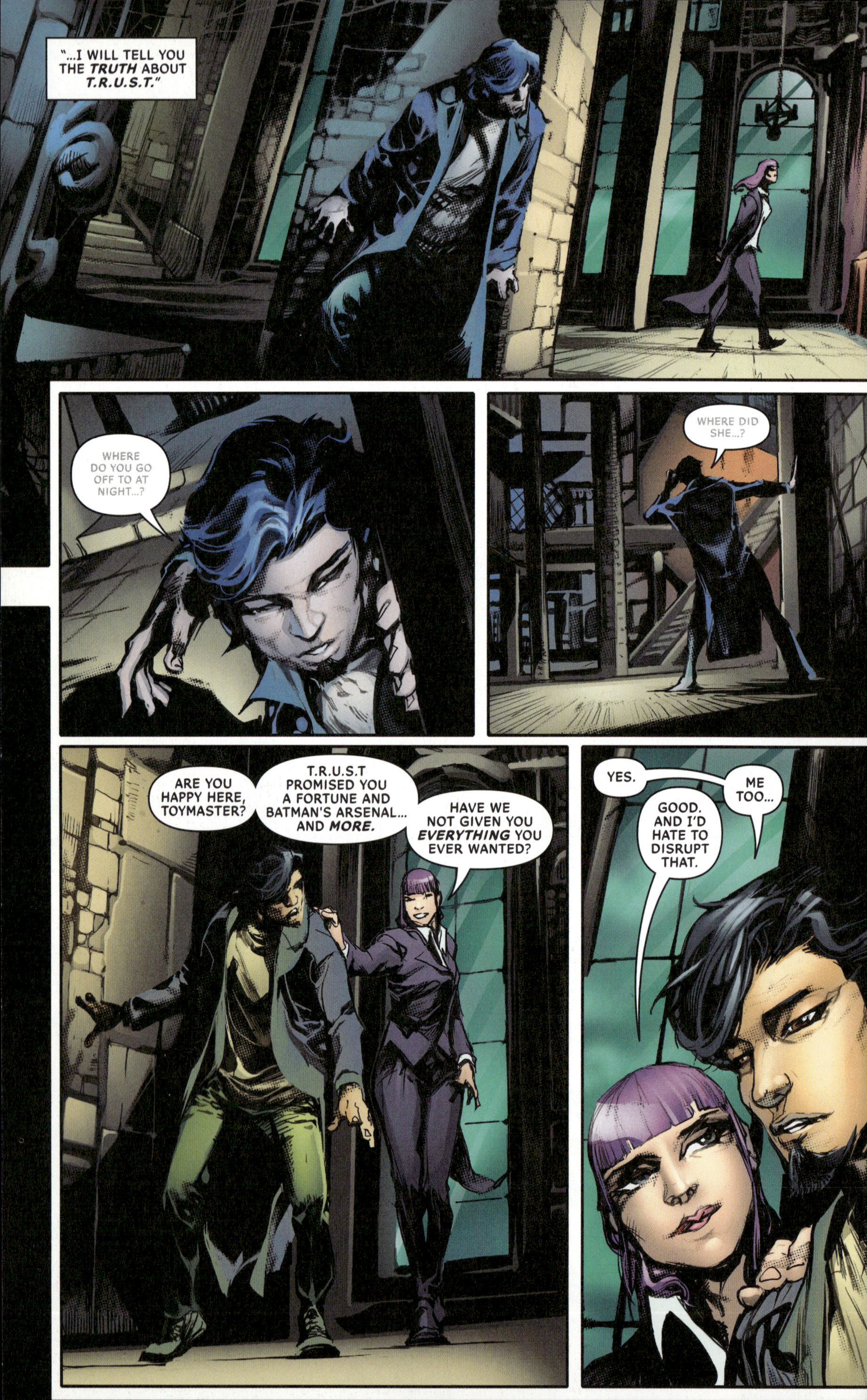
"...I WILL TELL YOU THE *TRUTH* ABOUT *T.R.U.S.T.*"
WHERE DO YOU GO OFF TO AT NIGHT...?
WHERE DID SHE...?
ARE YOU HAPPY HERE, TOYMASTER?
T.R.U.S.T PROMISED YOU A FORTUNE AND BATMAN'S ARSENAL... AND *MORE.*
HAVE WE NOT GIVEN YOU *EVERYTHING* YOU EVER WANTED?
YES.
ME TOO...
GOOD. AND I'D HATE TO DISRUPT THAT.

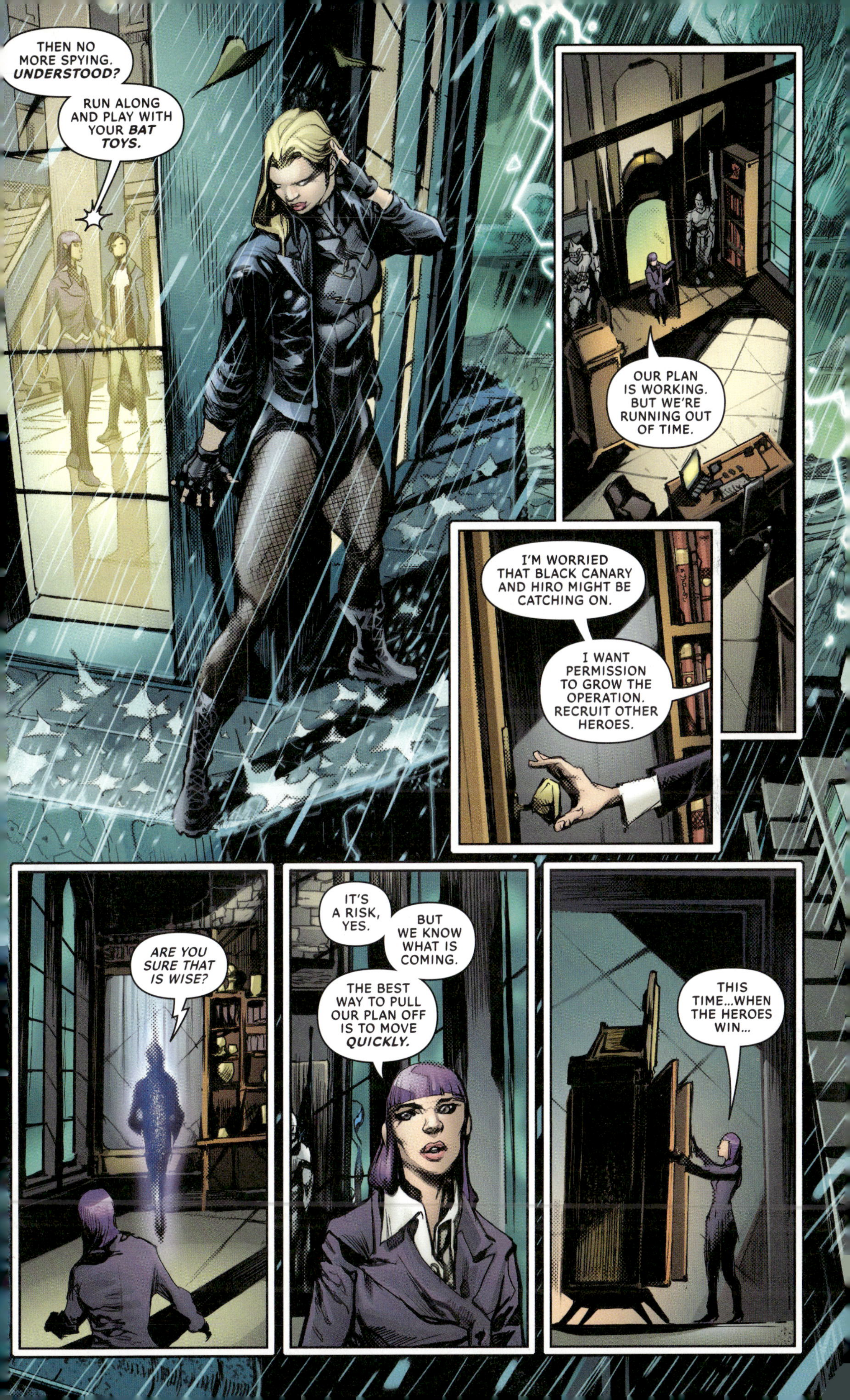

THEN NO MORE SPYING. *UNDERSTOOD?*
RUN ALONG AND PLAY WITH YOUR ***BAT TOYS.***
OUR PLAN IS WORKING. BUT WE'RE RUNNING OUT OF TIME.
I'M WORRIED THAT BLACK CANARY AND HIRO MIGHT BE CATCHING ON.
I WANT PERMISSION TO GROW THE OPERATION. RECRUIT OTHER HEROES.
ARE YOU SURE THAT IS WISE?
IT'S A RISK, YES.
BUT WE KNOW WHAT IS COMING.
THE BEST WAY TO PULL OUR PLAN OFF IS TO MOVE ***QUICKLY.***
THIS TIME...WHEN THE HEROES WIN...

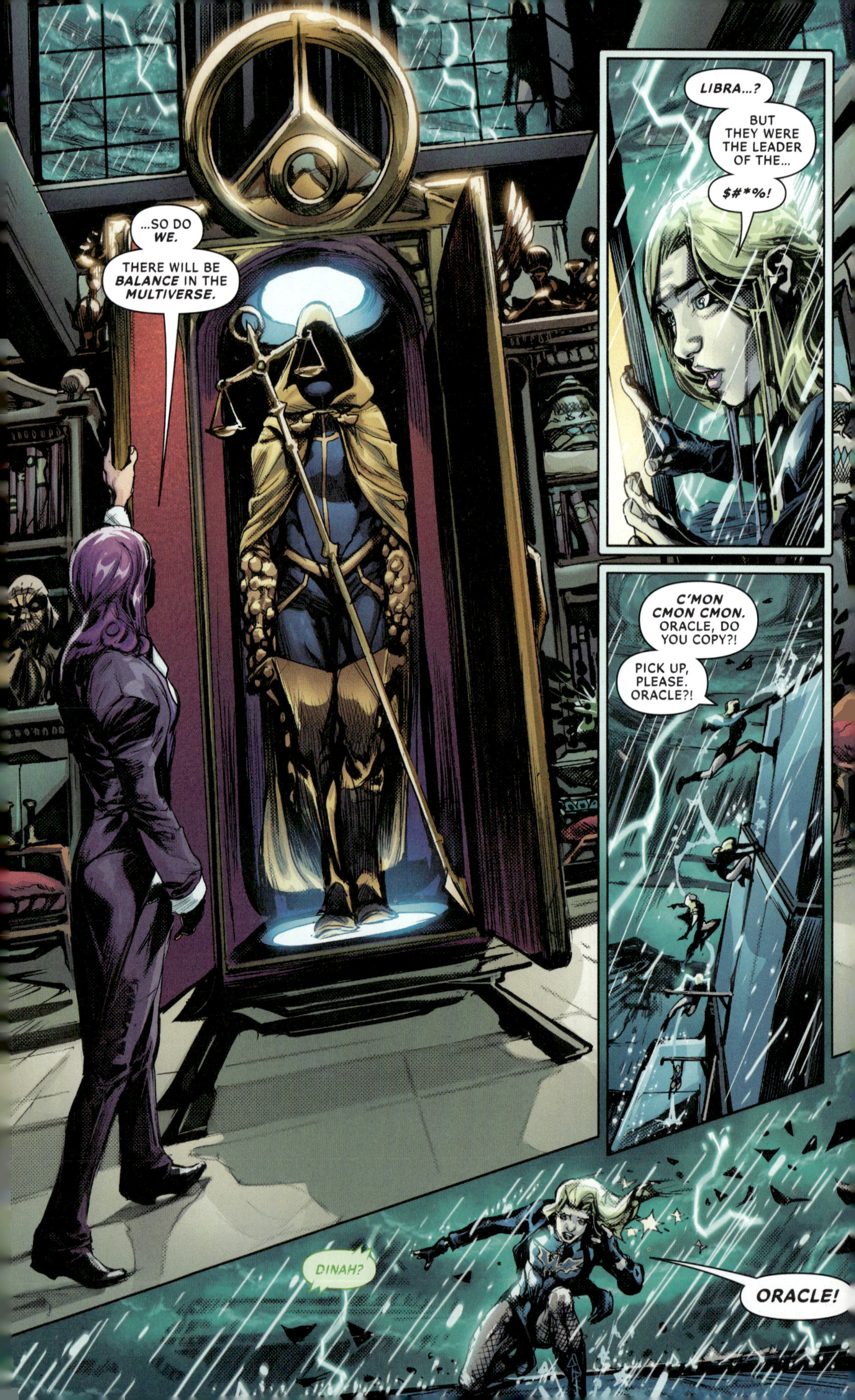
...SO DO WE.
THERE WILL BE BALANCE IN THE MULTIVERSE.
LIBRA...?
BUT THEY WERE THE LEADER OF THE...
$#*%!
C'MON CMON CMON. ORACLE, DO YOU COPY?!
PICK UP, PLEASE. ORACLE?!
DINAH?
ORACLE!

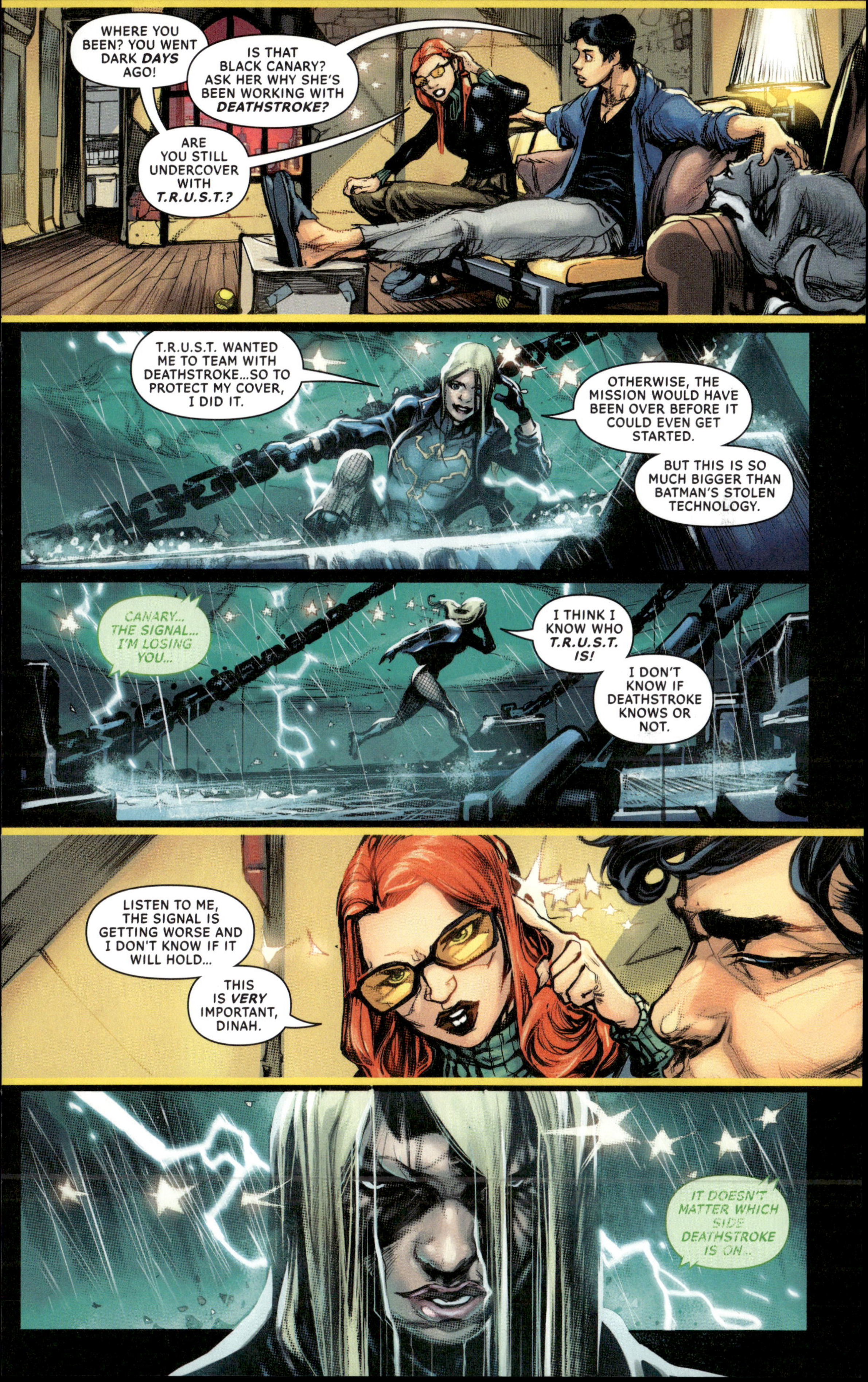
WHERE YOU BEEN? YOU WENT DARK DAYS AGO!
IS THAT BLACK CANARY? ASK HER WHY SHE'S BEEN WORKING WITH DEATHSTROKE?
ARE YOU STILL UNDERCOVER WITH T.R.U.S.T.?
T.R.U.S.T. WANTED ME TO TEAM WITH DEATHSTROKE...SO TO PROTECT MY COVER, I DID IT.
OTHERWISE, THE MISSION WOULD HAVE BEEN OVER BEFORE IT COULD EVEN GET STARTED.
BUT THIS IS SO MUCH BIGGER THAN BATMAN'S STOLEN TECHNOLOGY.
CANARY... THE SIGNAL... I'M LOSING YOU...
I THINK I KNOW WHO T.R.U.S.T. IS!
I DON'T KNOW IF DEATHSTROKE KNOWS OR NOT.
LISTEN TO ME, THE SIGNAL IS GETTING WORSE AND I DON'T KNOW IF IT WILL HOLD...
THIS IS VERY IMPORTANT, DINAH.
IT DOESN'T MATTER WHICH SIDE DEATHSTROKE IS ON...

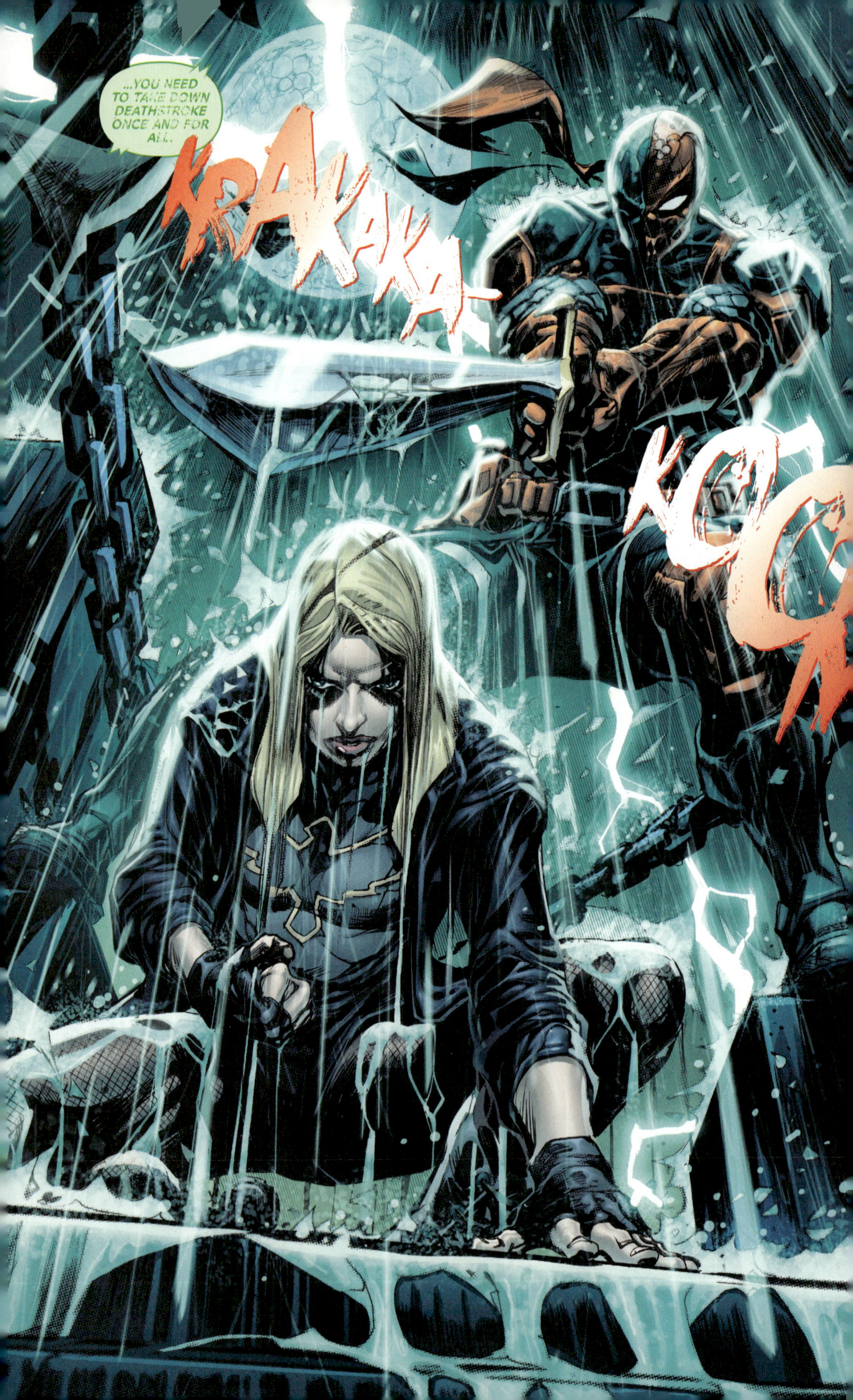
...YOU NEED TO TAKE DOWN DEATHSTROKE ONCE AND FOR ALL.
KRAKAKA

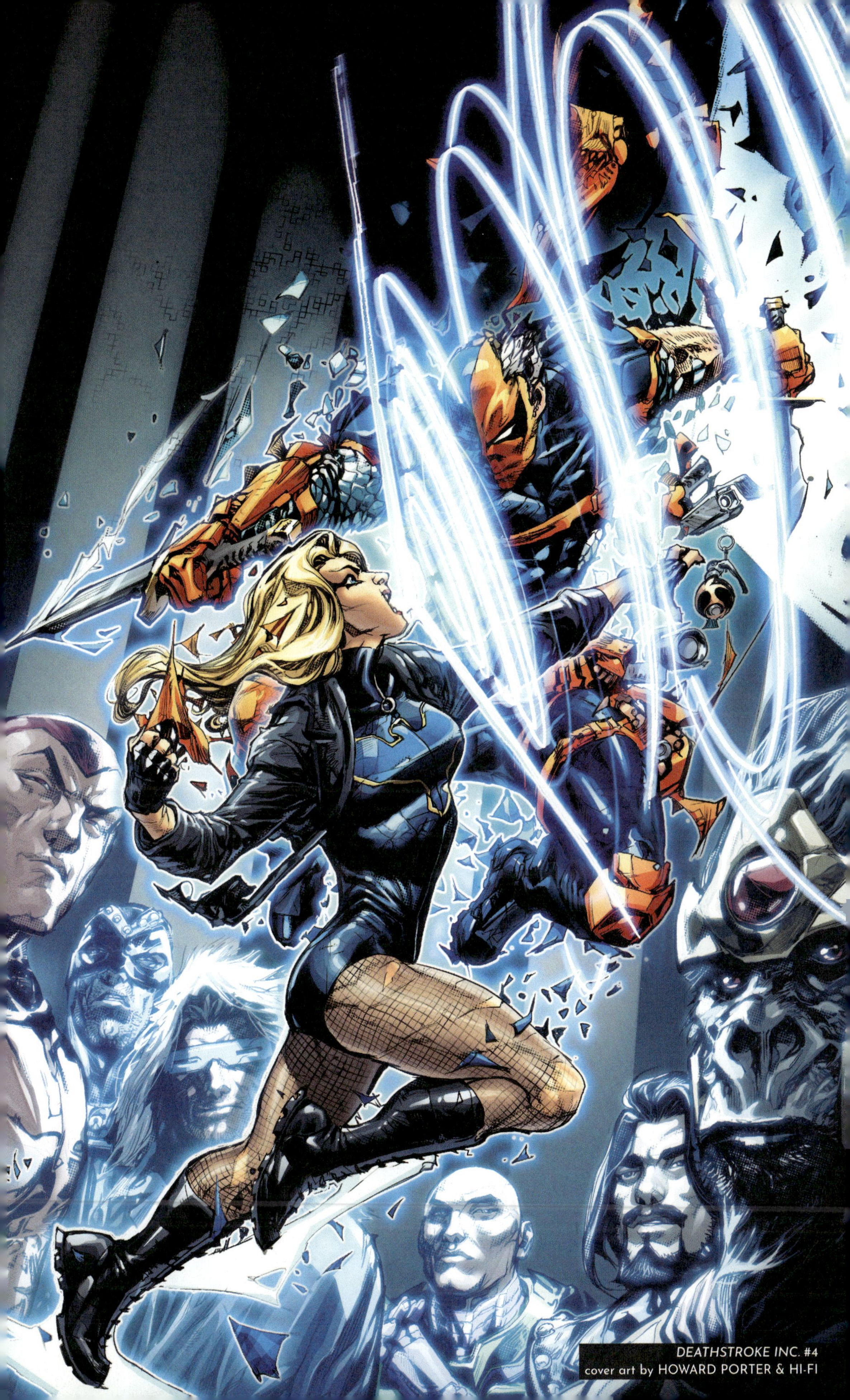

DEATHSTROKE INC. #4
cover art by HOWARD PORTER & HI-FI

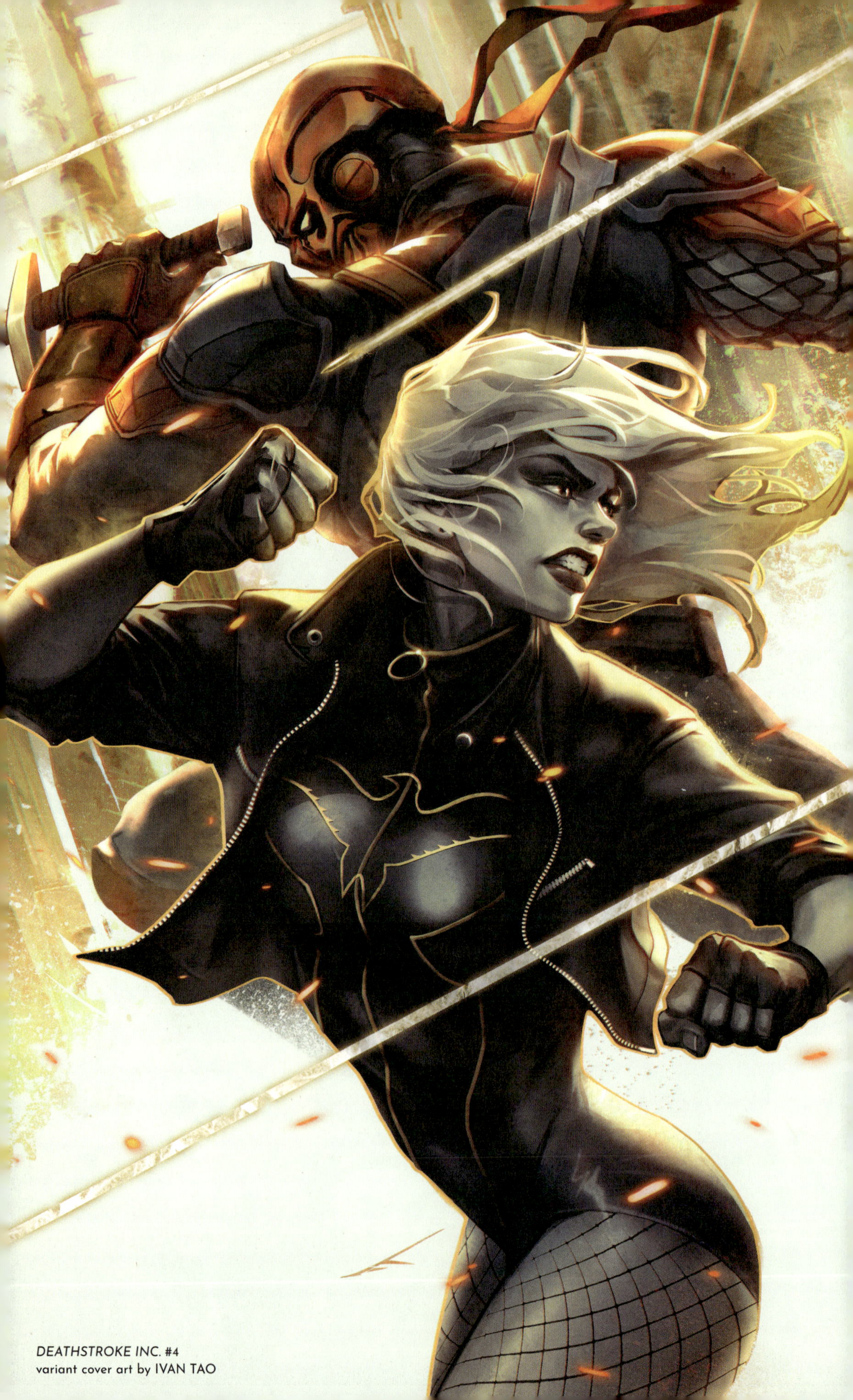

DEATHSTROKE INC. #4
variant cover art by IVAN TAO

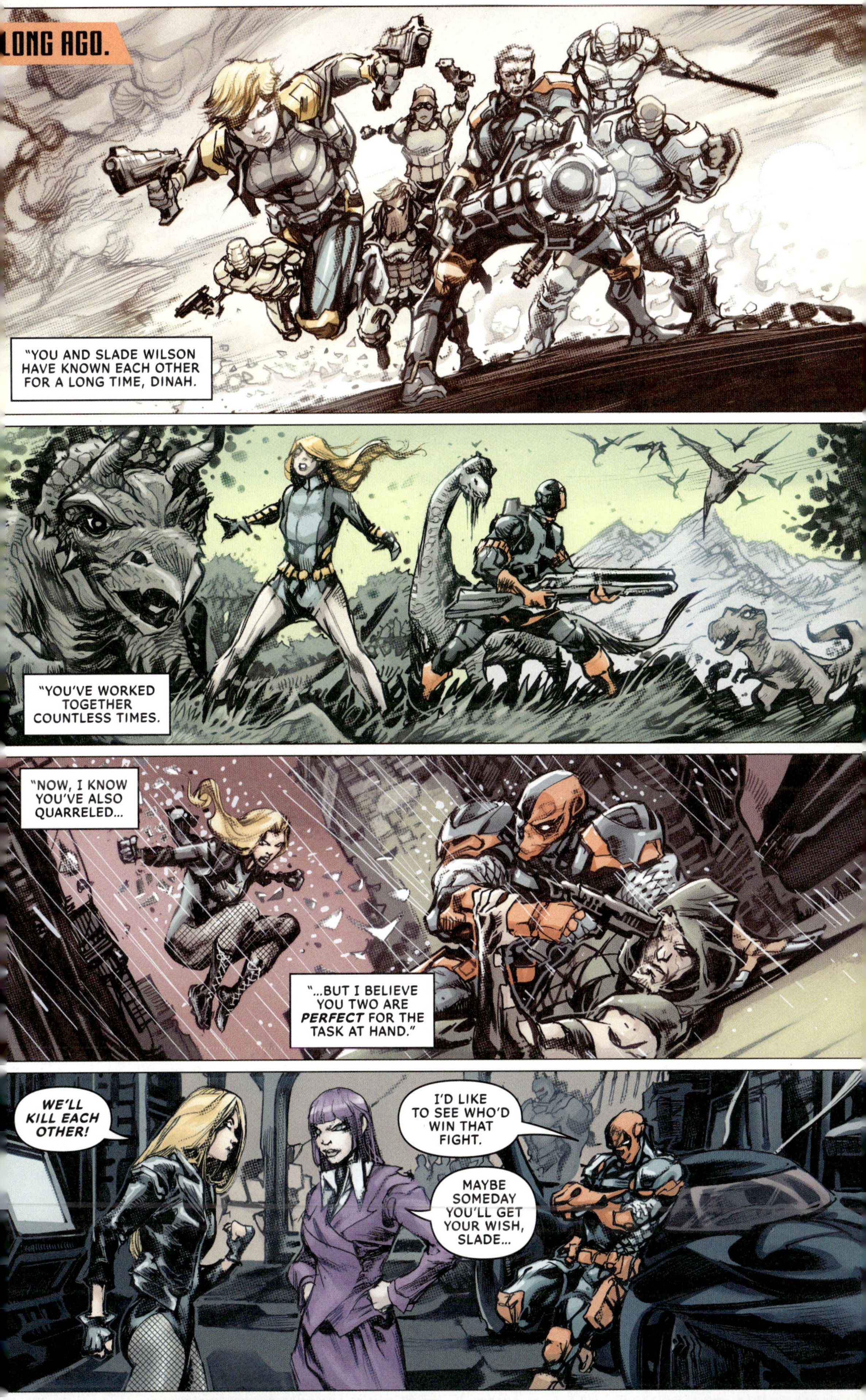
LONG AGO.
"YOU AND SLADE WILSON HAVE KNOWN EACH OTHER FOR A LONG TIME, DINAH.
"YOU'VE WORKED TOGETHER COUNTLESS TIMES.
"NOW, I KNOW YOU'VE ALSO QUARRELED...
"...BUT I BELIEVE YOU TWO ARE *PERFECT* FOR THE TASK AT HAND."
WE'LL KILL EACH OTHER!
I'D LIKE TO SEE WHO'D WIN THAT FIGHT.
MAYBE SOMEDAY YOU'LL GET YOUR WISH, SLADE...

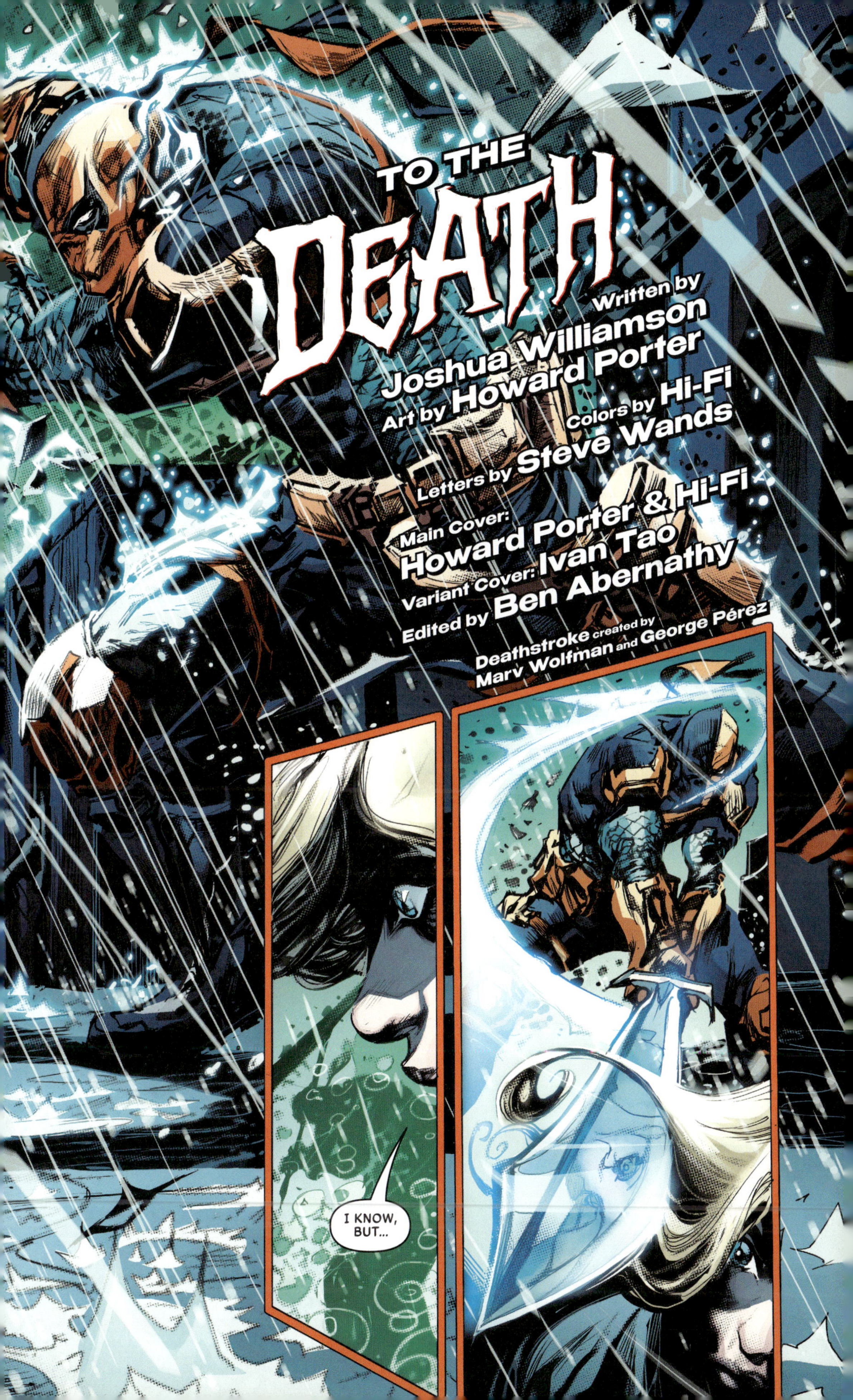
TO THE
DEATH
Written by
Joshua Williamson
Art by Howard Porter
Colors by Hi-Fi
Letters by Steve Wands
Main Cover:
Howard Porter & Hi-Fi
Variant Cover: Ivan Tao
Edited by Ben Abernathy
Deathstroke created by
Marv Wolfman and George Pérez
I KNOW, BUT...

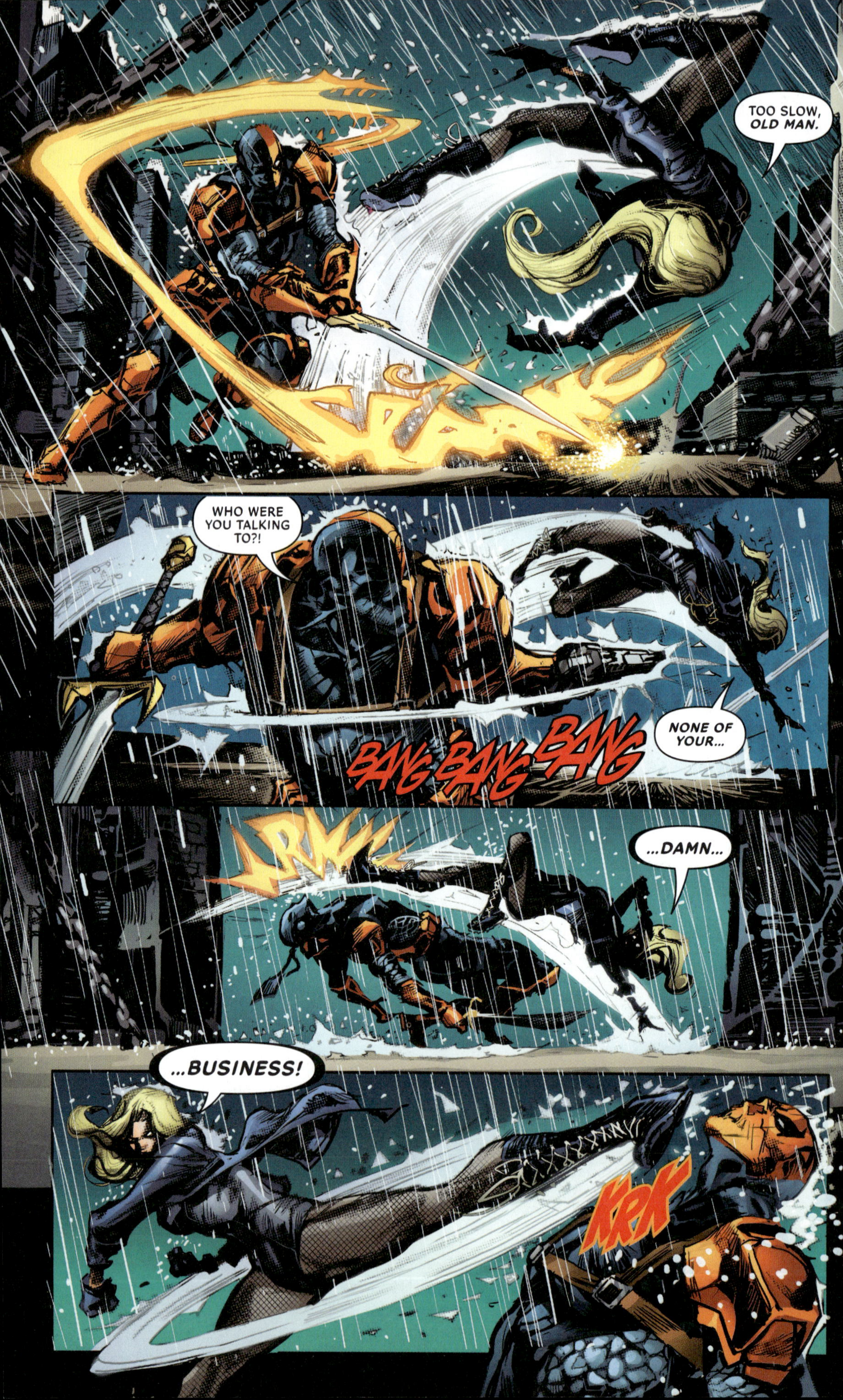
TOO SLOW, OLD MAN.
WHO WERE YOU TALKING TO?!
NONE OF YOUR...
BANG BANG BANG
...DAMN...
...BUSINESS!
KRK

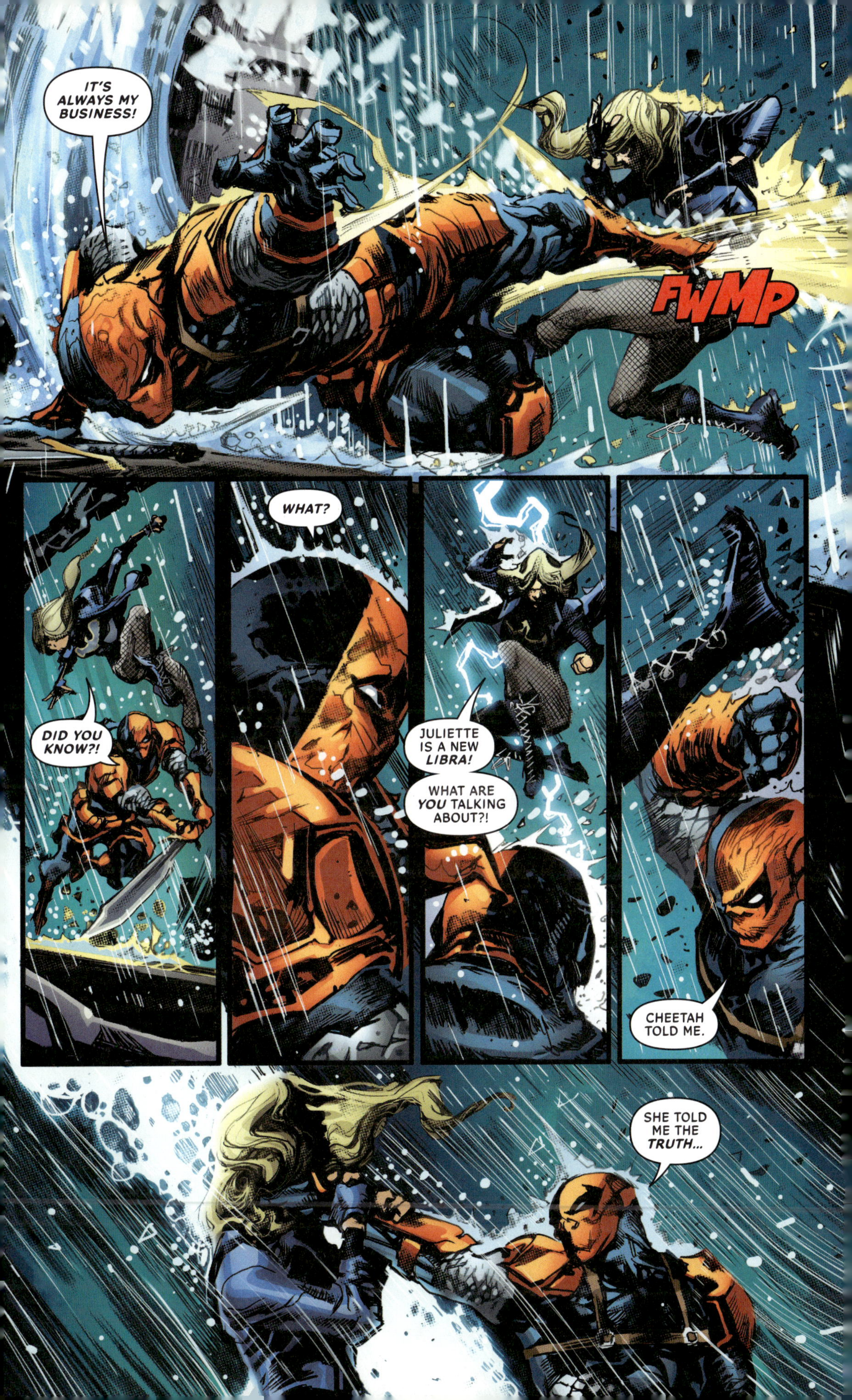
IT'S ALWAYS MY BUSINESS!
FWMP
DID YOU KNOW?!
WHAT?
JULIETTE IS A NEW LIBRA!
WHAT ARE YOU TALKING ABOUT?!
CHEETAH TOLD ME.
SHE TOLD ME THE TRUTH...

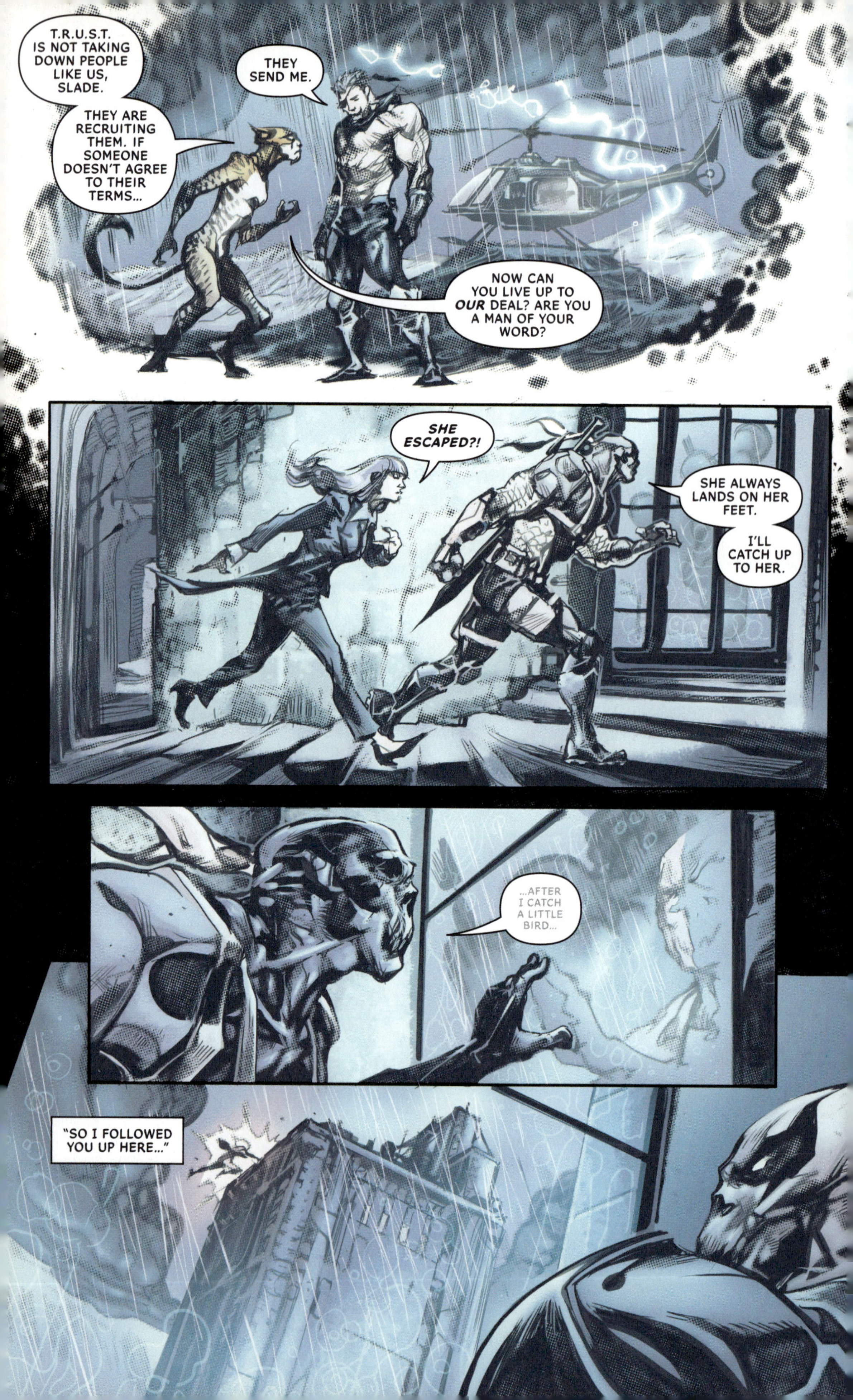
T.R.U.S.T. IS NOT TAKING DOWN PEOPLE LIKE US, SLADE.
THEY SEND ME.
THEY ARE RECRUITING THEM. IF SOMEONE DOESN'T AGREE TO THEIR TERMS...
NOW CAN YOU LIVE UP TO OUR DEAL? ARE YOU A MAN OF YOUR WORD?
SHE ESCAPED?!
SHE ALWAYS LANDS ON HER FEET.
I'LL CATCH UP TO HER.
...AFTER I CATCH A LITTLE BIRD...
"SO I FOLLOWED YOU UP HERE..."

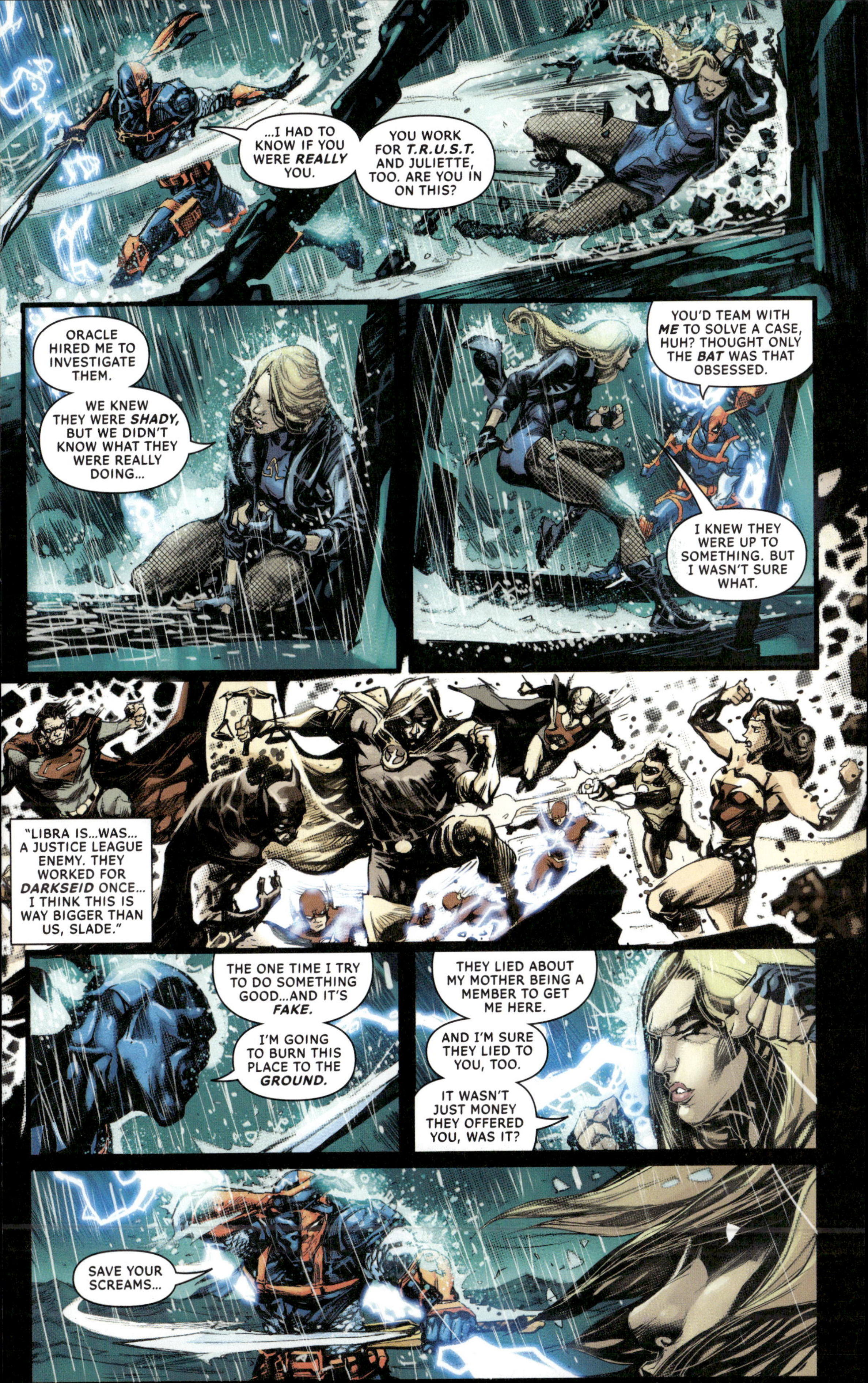

...I HAD TO KNOW IF YOU WERE REALLY YOU.
YOU WORK FOR T.R.U.S.T. AND JULIETTE, TOO. ARE YOU IN ON THIS?
ORACLE HIRED ME TO INVESTIGATE THEM.
WE KNEW THEY WERE SHADY, BUT WE DIDN'T KNOW WHAT THEY WERE REALLY DOING...
YOU'D TEAM WITH ME TO SOLVE A CASE, HUH? THOUGHT ONLY THE BAT WAS THAT OBSESSED.
I KNEW THEY WERE UP TO SOMETHING. BUT I WASN'T SURE WHAT.
"LIBRA IS...WAS... A JUSTICE LEAGUE ENEMY. THEY WORKED FOR DARKSEID ONCE... I THINK THIS IS WAY BIGGER THAN US, SLADE."
THE ONE TIME I TRY TO DO SOMETHING GOOD...AND IT'S FAKE.
I'M GOING TO BURN THIS PLACE TO THE GROUND.
THEY LIED ABOUT MY MOTHER BEING A MEMBER TO GET ME HERE.
AND I'M SURE THEY LIED TO YOU, TOO.
IT WASN'T JUST MONEY THEY OFFERED YOU, WAS IT?
SAVE YOUR SCREAMS...

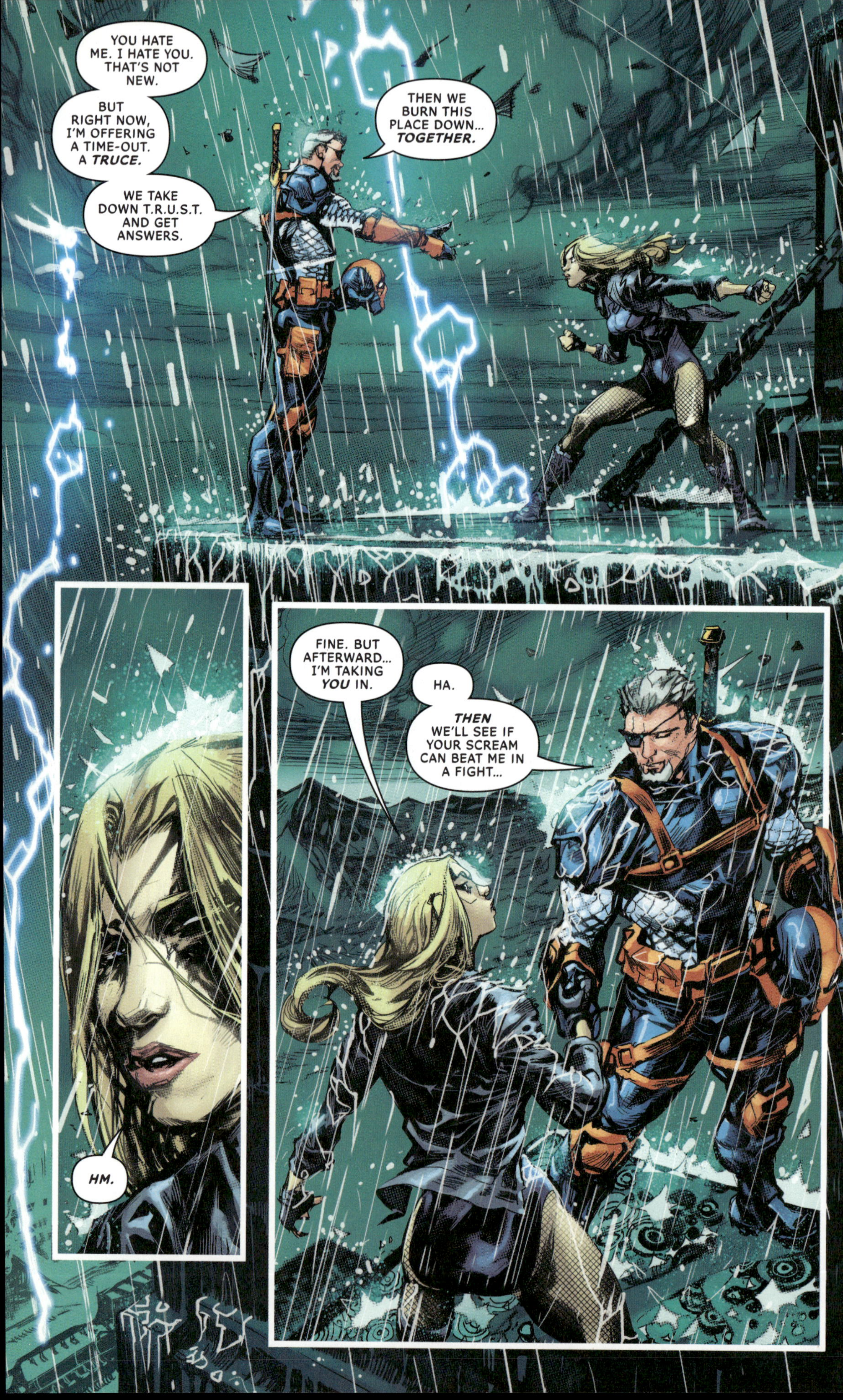

YOU HATE ME. I HATE YOU. THAT'S NOT NEW.
BUT RIGHT NOW, I'M OFFERING A TIME-OUT. A *TRUCE.*
WE TAKE DOWN T.R.U.S.T. AND GET ANSWERS.
THEN WE BURN THIS PLACE DOWN... *TOGETHER.*
HM.
FINE. BUT AFTERWARD... I'M TAKING *YOU* IN.
HA.
THEN WE'LL SEE IF YOUR SCREAM CAN BEAT ME IN A FIGHT...

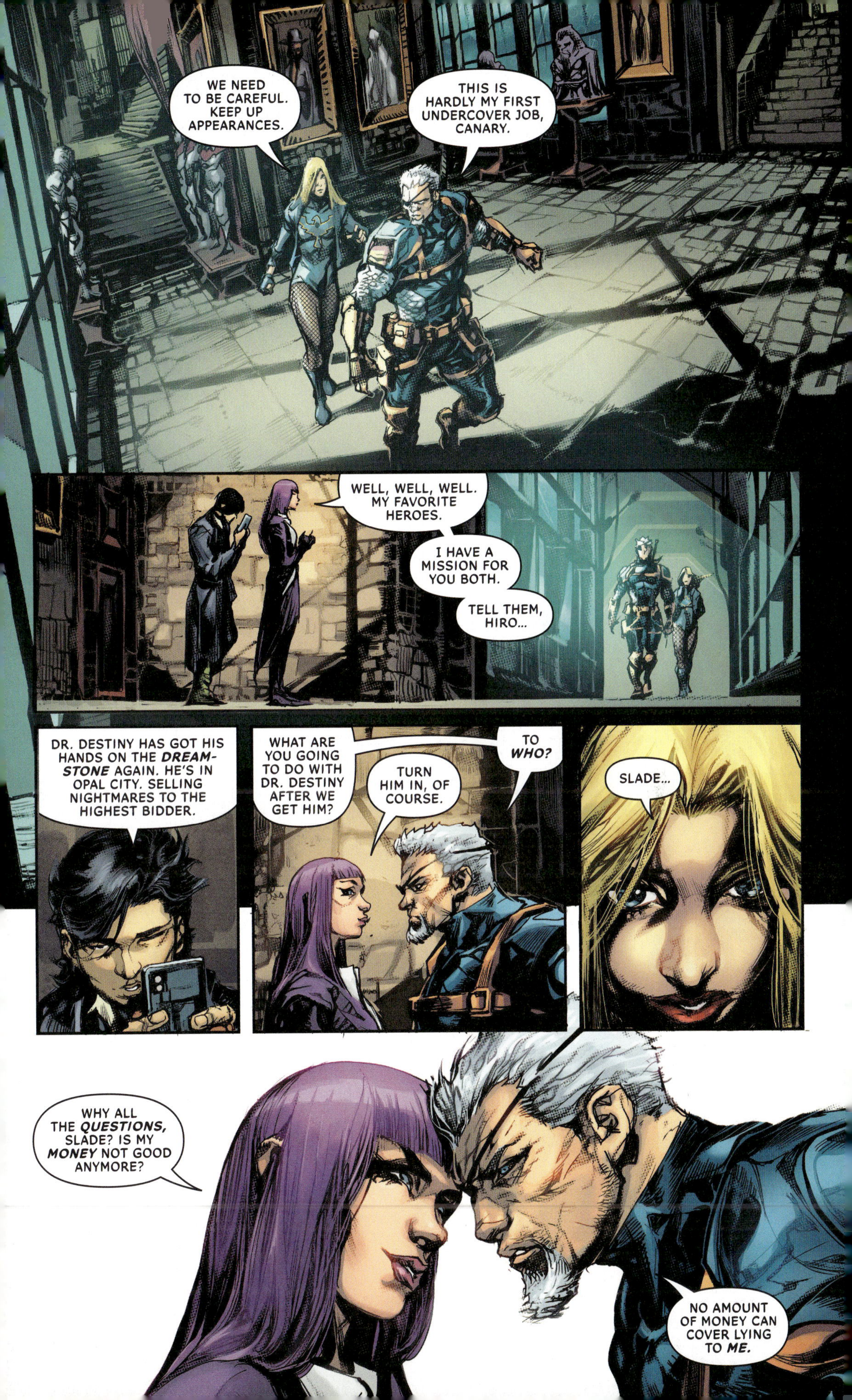
WE NEED TO BE CAREFUL. KEEP UP APPEARANCES.
THIS IS HARDLY MY FIRST UNDERCOVER JOB, CANARY.
WELL, WELL, WELL. MY FAVORITE HEROES.
I HAVE A MISSION FOR YOU BOTH.
TELL THEM, HIRO...
DR. DESTINY HAS GOT HIS HANDS ON THE DREAMSTONE AGAIN. HE'S IN OPAL CITY. SELLING NIGHTMARES TO THE HIGHEST BIDDER.
WHAT ARE YOU GOING TO DO WITH DR. DESTINY AFTER WE GET HIM?
TURN HIM IN, OF COURSE.
TO WHO?
SLADE...
WHY ALL THE QUESTIONS, SLADE? IS MY MONEY NOT GOOD ANYMORE?
NO AMOUNT OF MONEY CAN COVER LYING TO ME.

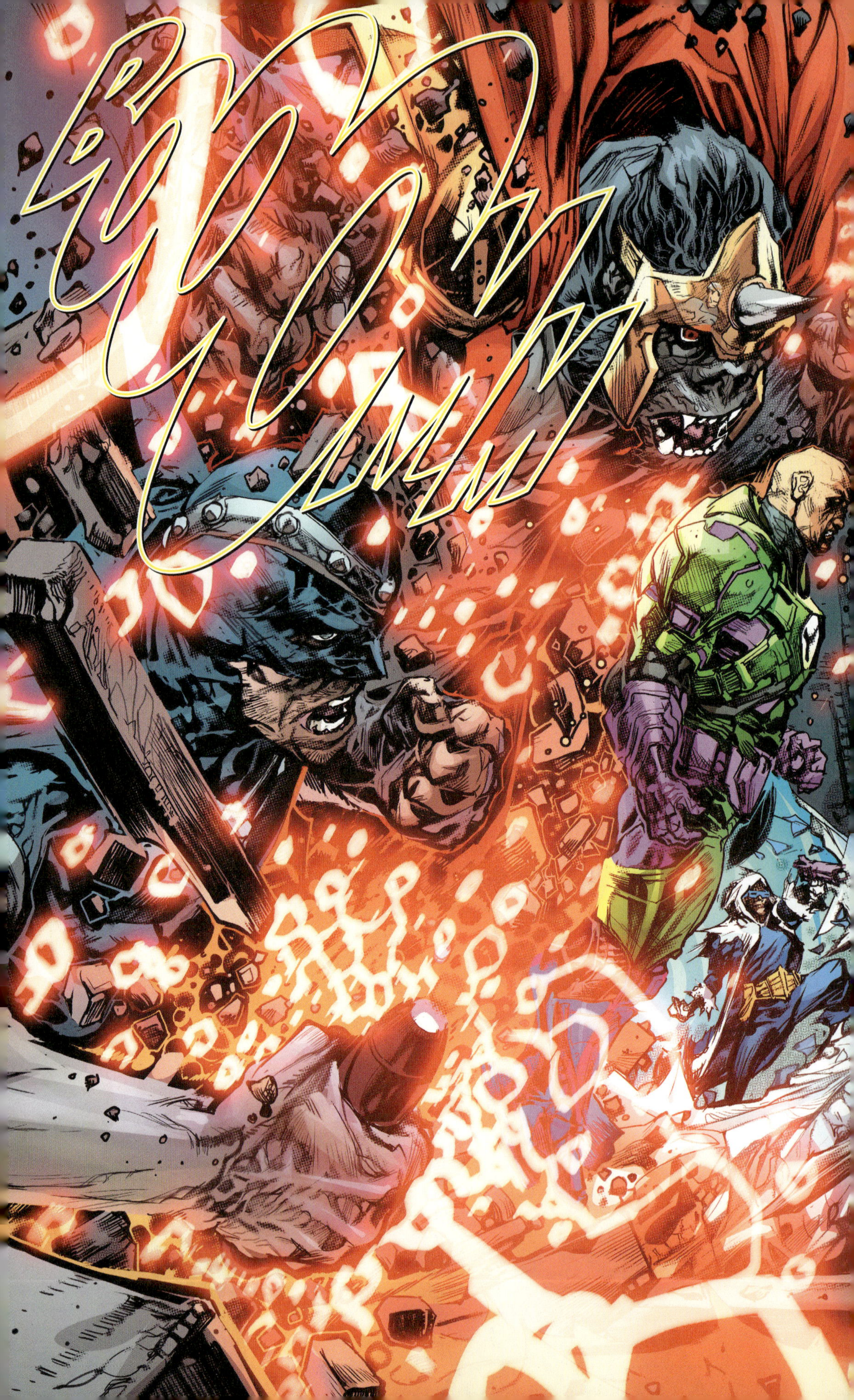

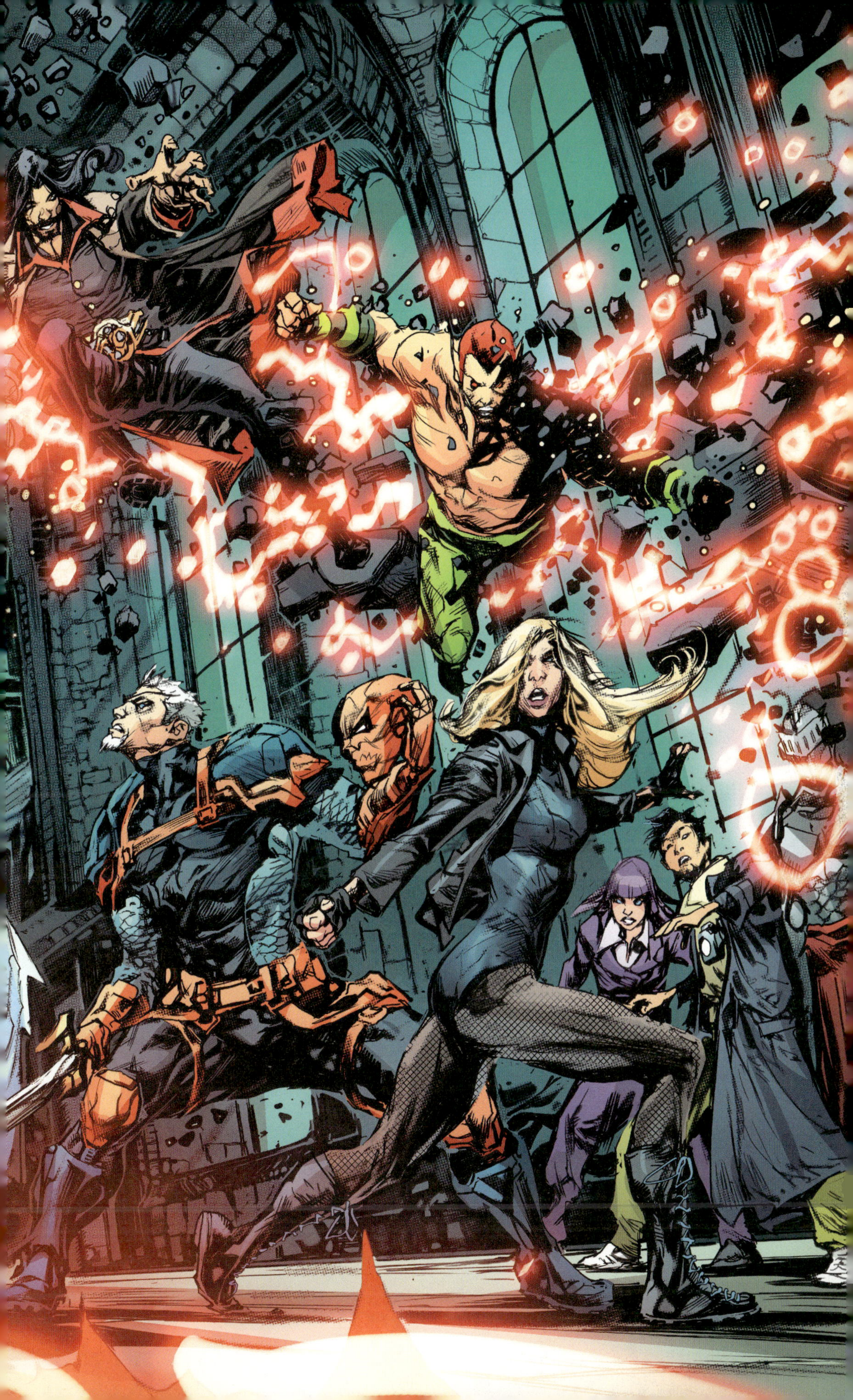

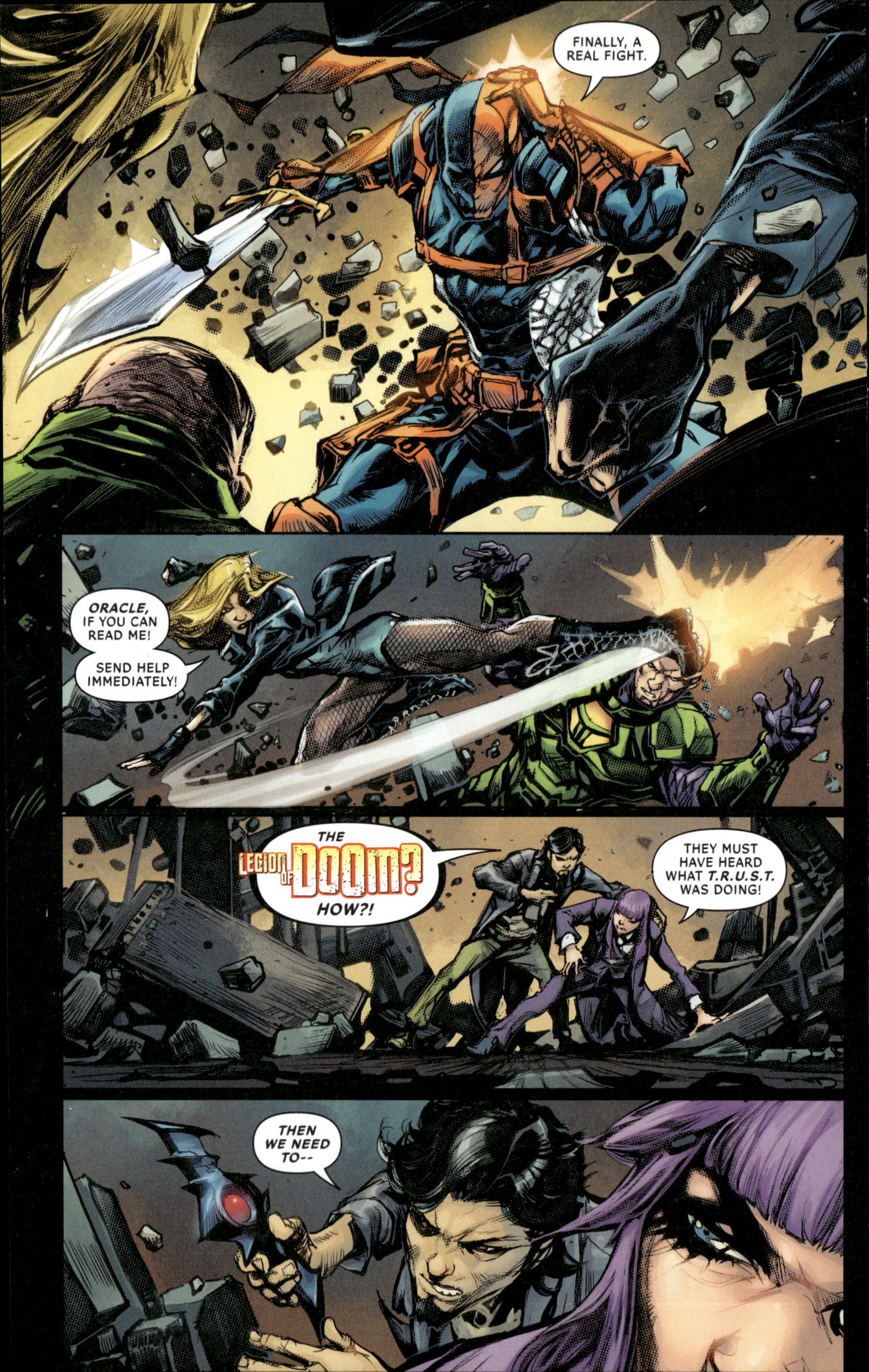
FINALLY, A REAL FIGHT.
ORACLE, IF YOU CAN READ ME!
SEND HELP IMMEDIATELY!
THE LEGION OF DOOM? HOW?!
THEY MUST HAVE HEARD WHAT T.R.U.S.T. WAS DOING!
THEN WE NEED TO--

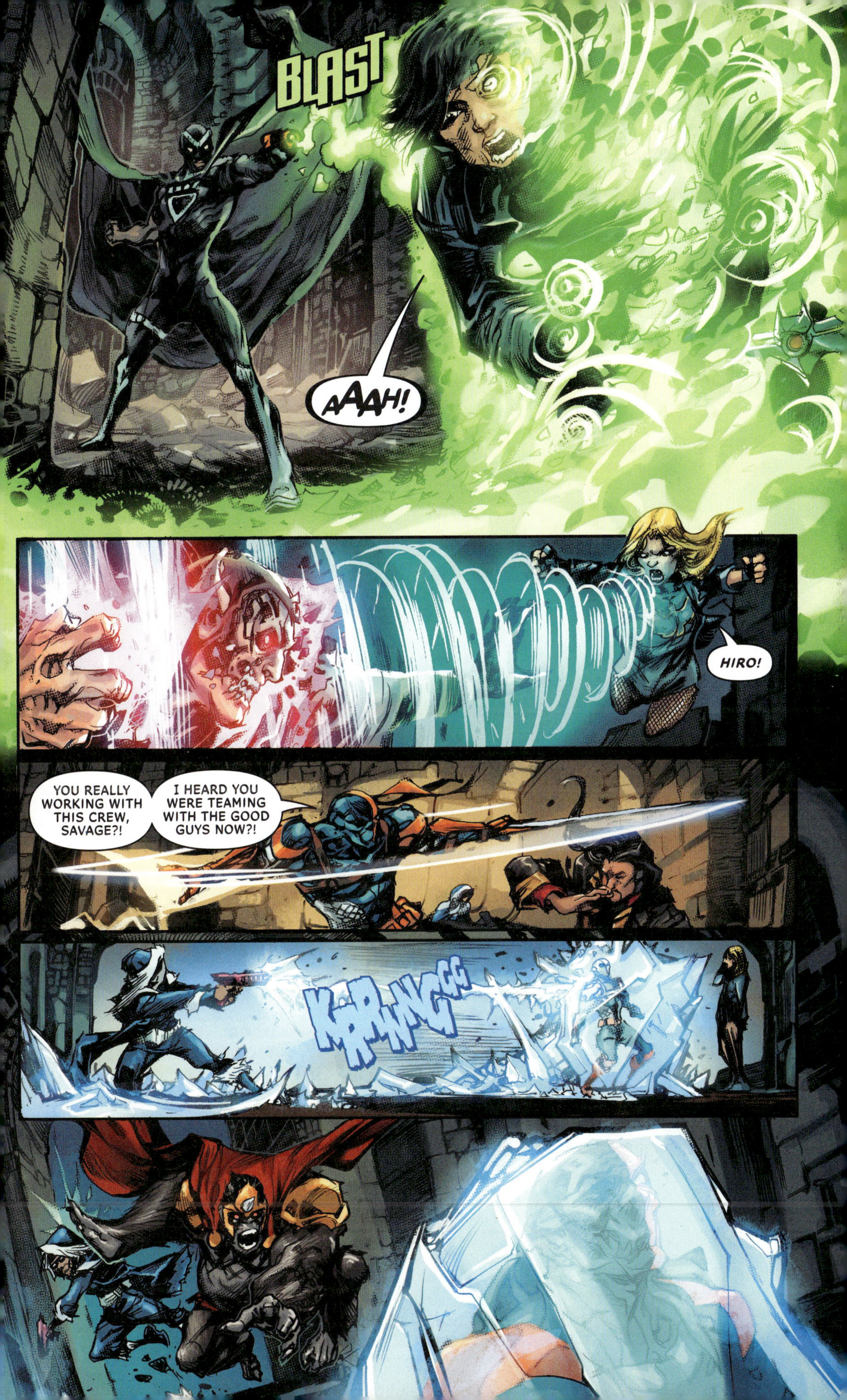
BLAST
AAAH!
HIRO!
YOU REALLY WORKING WITH THIS CREW, SAVAGE?!
I HEARD YOU WERE TEAMING WITH THE GOOD GUYS NOW?!
KRANNGGG

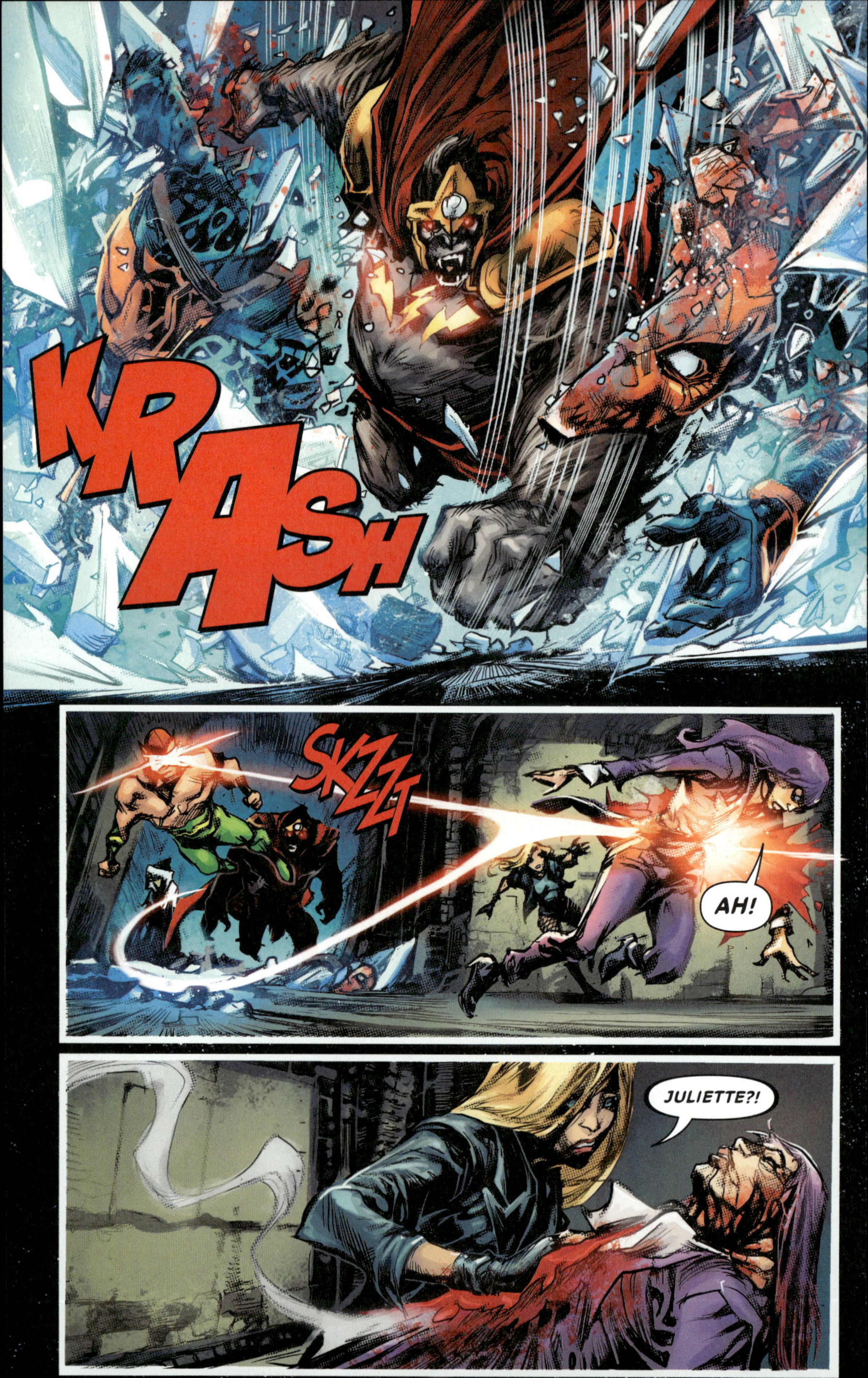
KRASH
SKZZZT
AH!
JULIETTE?!

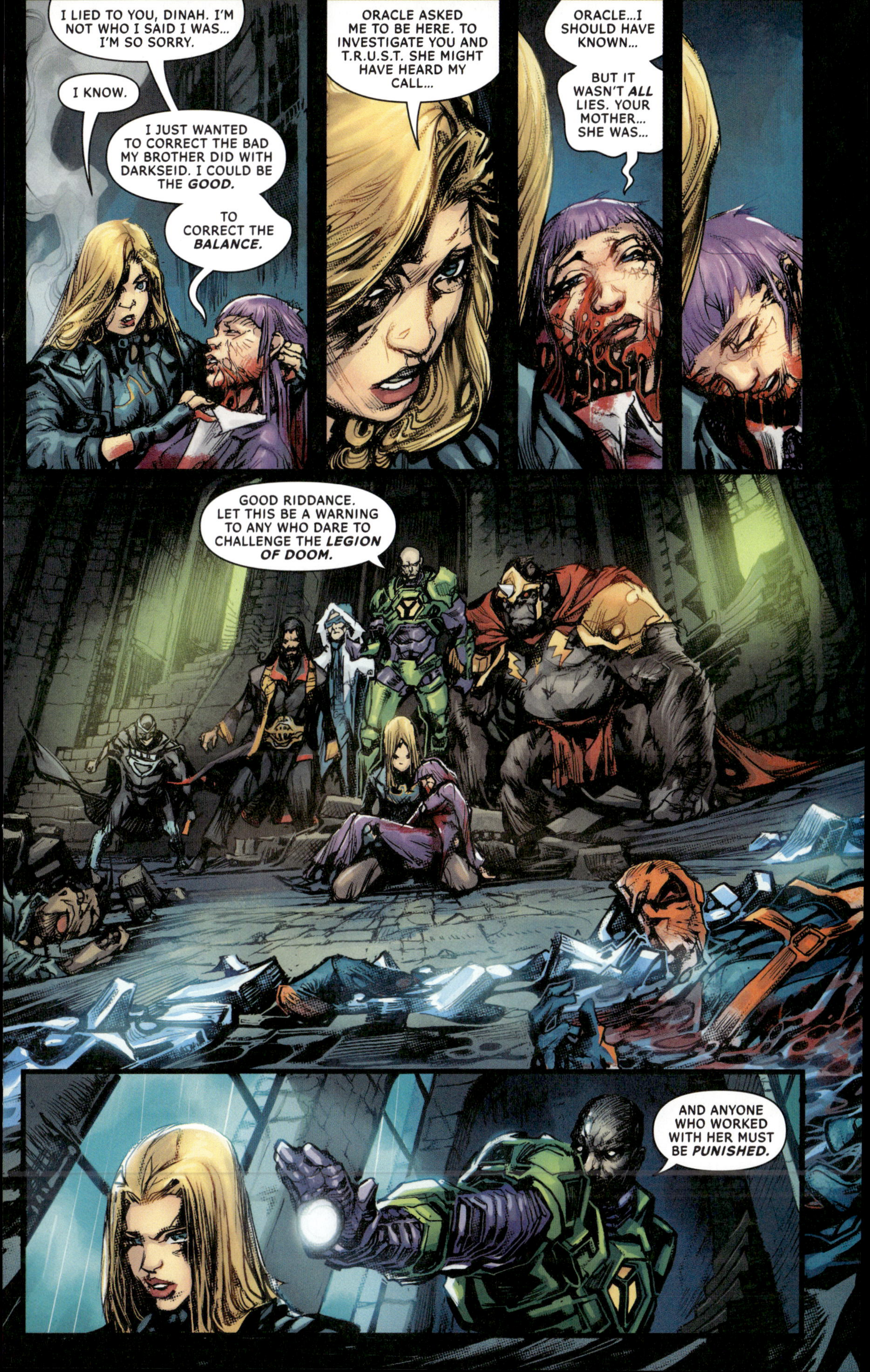
I LIED TO YOU, DINAH. I'M NOT WHO I SAID I WAS... I'M SO SORRY.
I KNOW.
I JUST WANTED TO CORRECT THE BAD MY BROTHER DID WITH DARKSEID. I COULD BE THE GOOD.
TO CORRECT THE BALANCE.
ORACLE ASKED ME TO BE HERE. TO INVESTIGATE YOU AND T.R.U.S.T. SHE MIGHT HAVE HEARD MY CALL...
ORACLE...I SHOULD HAVE KNOWN...
BUT IT WASN'T ALL LIES. YOUR MOTHER... SHE WAS...
GOOD RIDDANCE. LET THIS BE A WARNING TO ANY WHO DARE TO CHALLENGE THE LEGION OF DOOM.
AND ANYONE WHO WORKED WITH HER MUST BE PUNISHED.

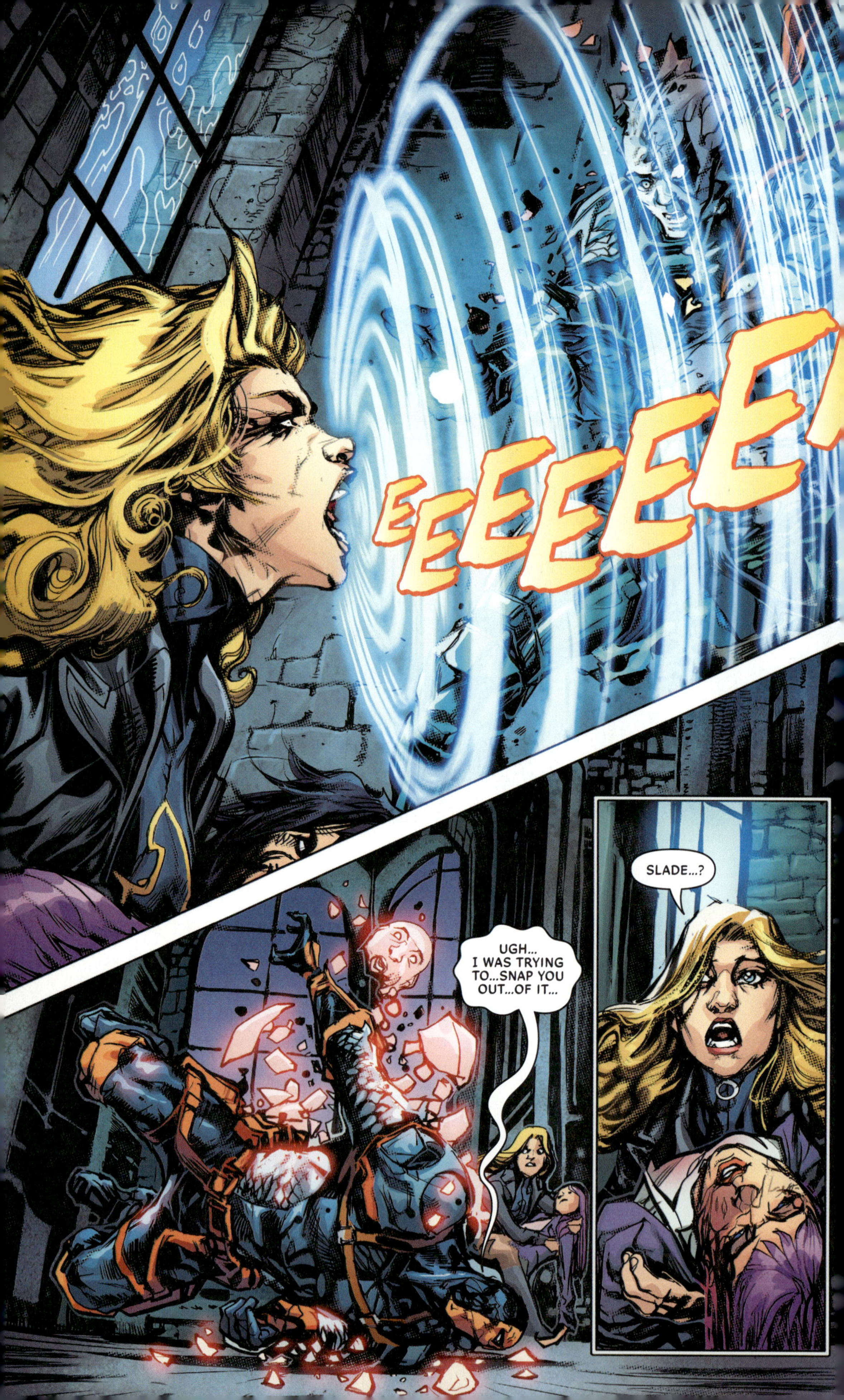
EEEEEEE
SLADE...?
UGH... I WAS TRYING TO...SNAP YOU OUT...OF IT...

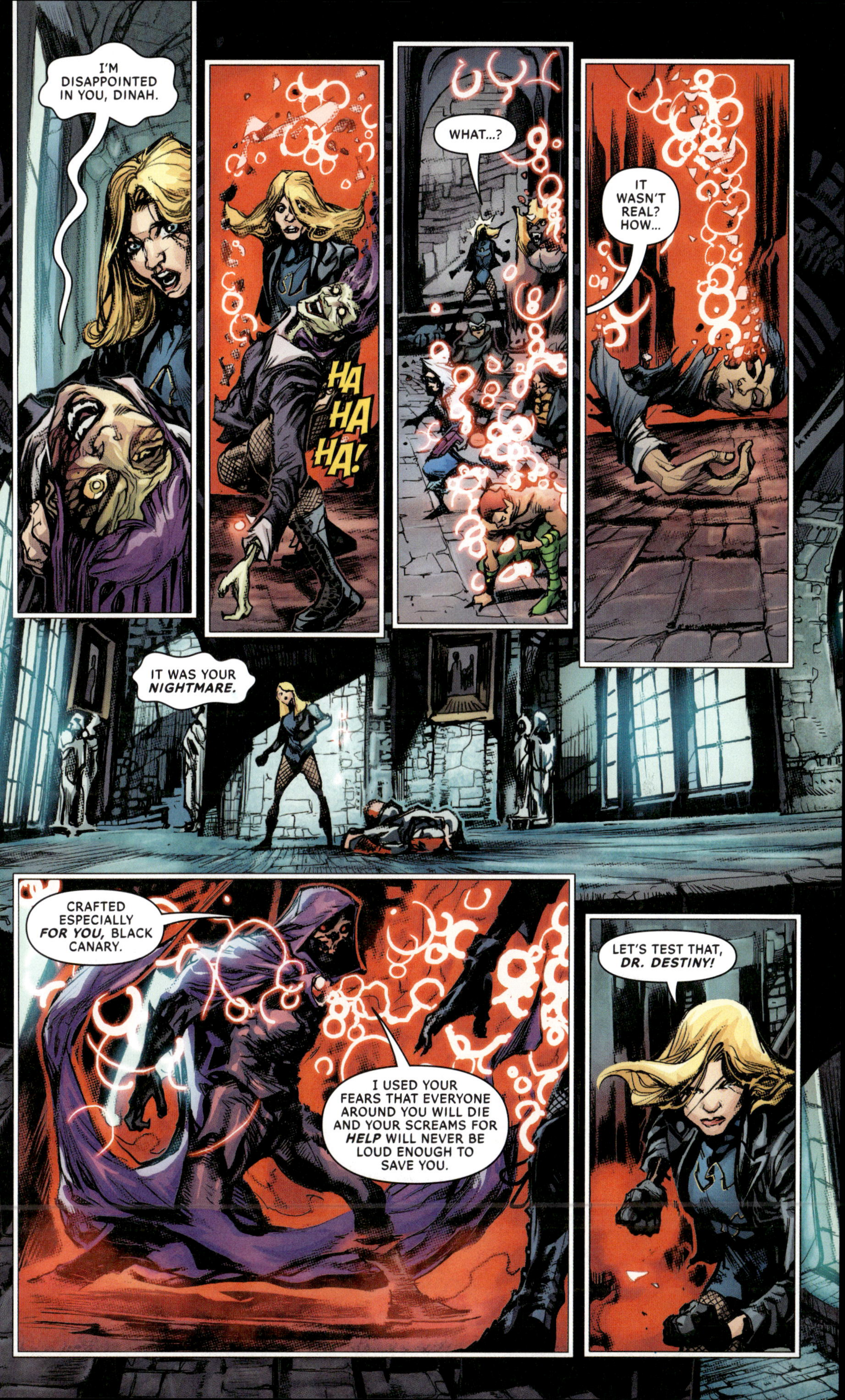
I'M DISAPPOINTED IN YOU, DINAH.
HA HA HA!
WHAT...?
IT WASN'T REAL? HOW...
IT WAS YOUR *NIGHTMARE.*
CRAFTED ESPECIALLY *FOR YOU,* BLACK CANARY.
I USED YOUR FEARS THAT EVERYONE AROUND YOU WILL DIE AND YOUR SCREAMS FOR *HELP* WILL NEVER BE LOUD ENOUGH TO SAVE YOU.
LET'S TEST THAT, *DR. DESTINY!*

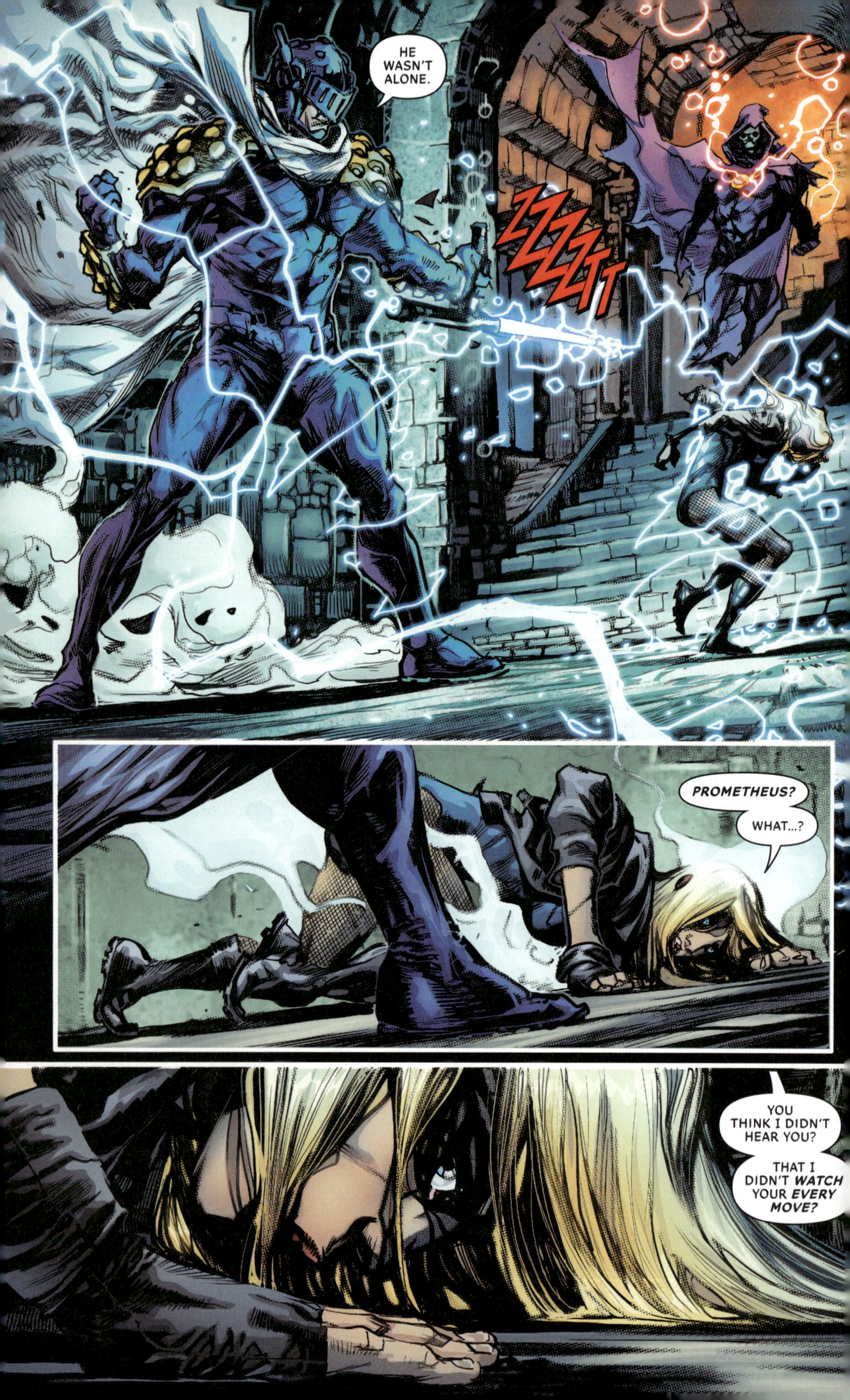
HE WASN'T ALONE.
ZZZZTT
PROMETHEUS?
WHAT...?
YOU THINK I DIDN'T HEAR YOU?
THAT I DIDN'T *WATCH* YOUR *EVERY MOVE?*

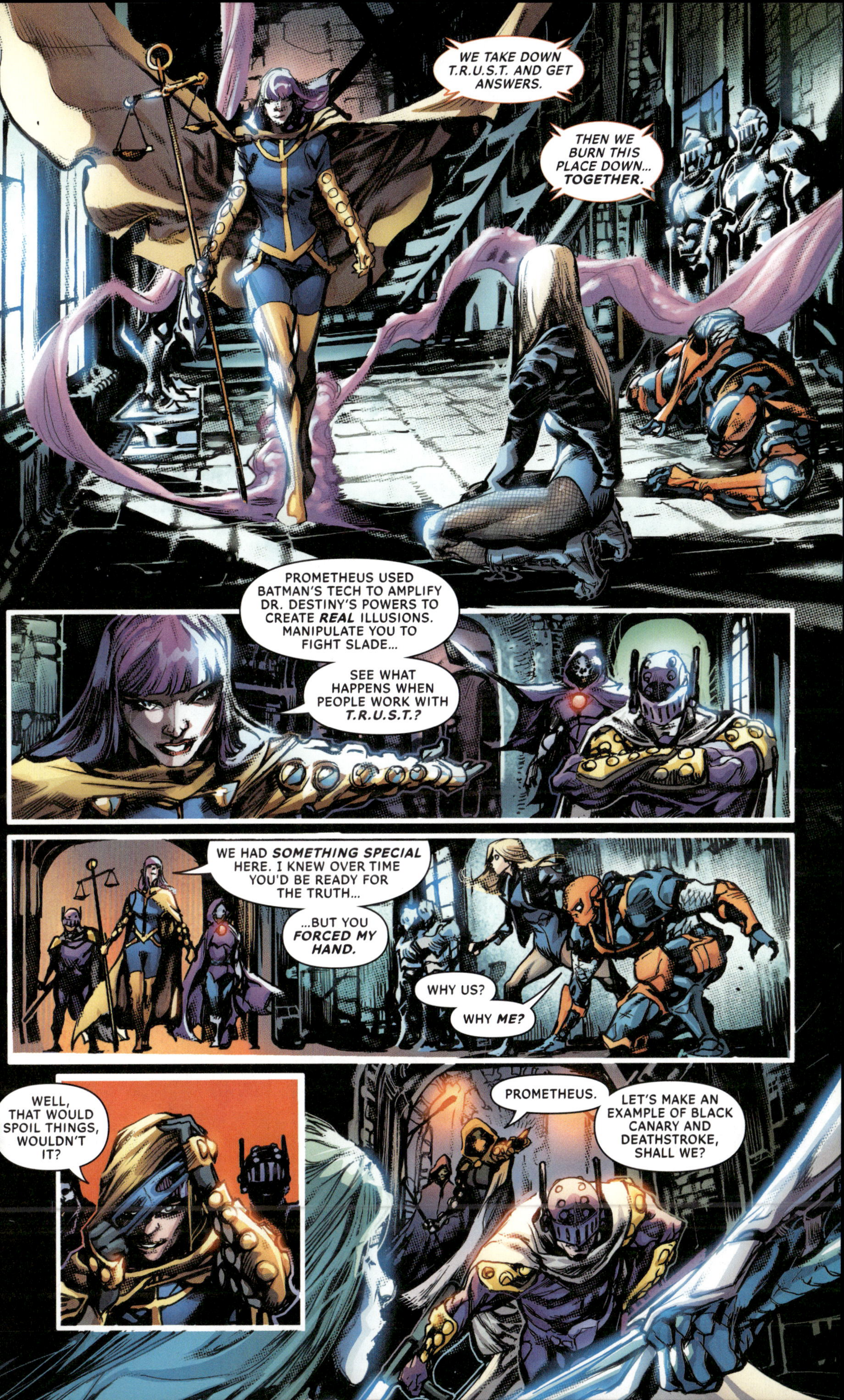
WE TAKE DOWN T.R.U.S.T. AND GET ANSWERS.
THEN WE BURN THIS PLACE DOWN... TOGETHER.
PROMETHEUS USED BATMAN'S TECH TO AMPLIFY DR. DESTINY'S POWERS TO CREATE REAL ILLUSIONS. MANIPULATE YOU TO FIGHT SLADE...
SEE WHAT HAPPENS WHEN PEOPLE WORK WITH T.R.U.S.T.?
WE HAD SOMETHING SPECIAL HERE. I KNEW OVER TIME YOU'D BE READY FOR THE TRUTH...
...BUT YOU FORCED MY HAND.
WHY US?
WHY ME?
WELL, THAT WOULD SPOIL THINGS, WOULDN'T IT?
PROMETHEUS.
LET'S MAKE AN EXAMPLE OF BLACK CANARY AND DEATHSTROKE, SHALL WE?

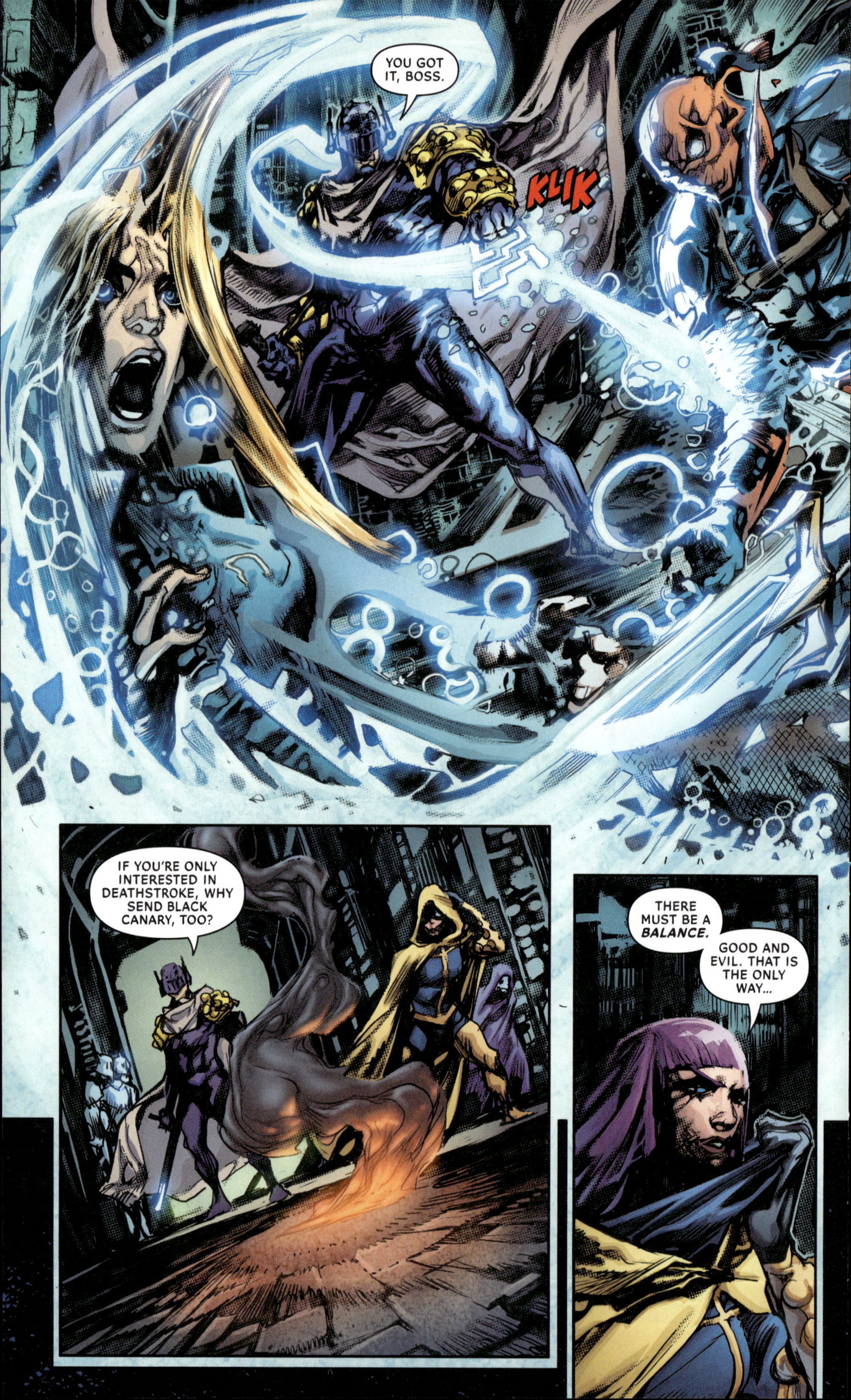

YOU GOT IT, BOSS.
KLIK
IF YOU'RE ONLY INTERESTED IN DEATHSTROKE, WHY SEND BLACK CANARY, TOO?
THERE MUST BE A *BALANCE.*
GOOD AND EVIL. THAT IS THE ONLY WAY...

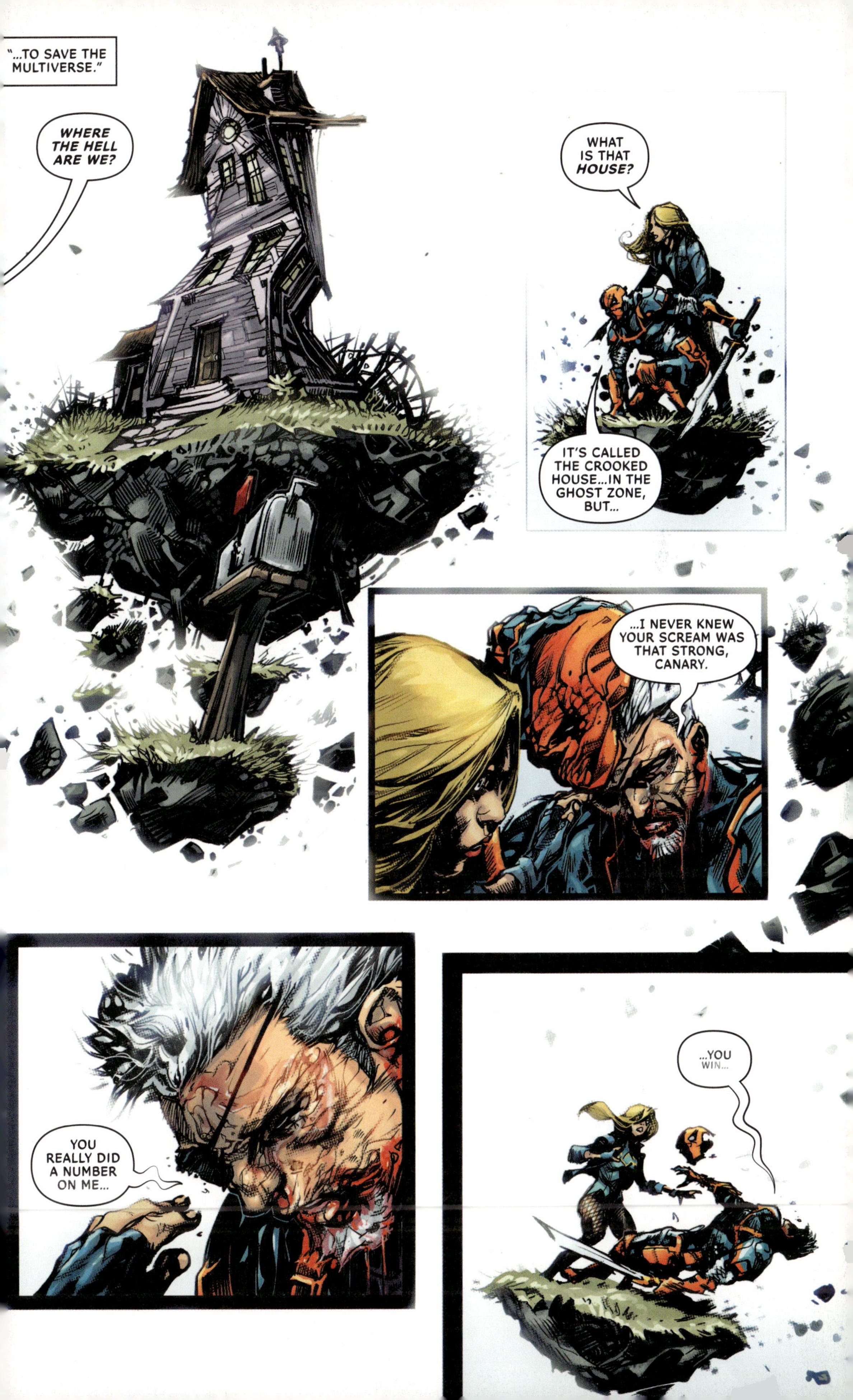
"...TO SAVE THE MULTIVERSE."
WHERE THE HELL ARE WE?
WHAT IS THAT HOUSE?
IT'S CALLED THE CROOKED HOUSE...IN THE GHOST ZONE, BUT...
...I NEVER KNEW YOUR SCREAM WAS THAT STRONG, CANARY.
YOU REALLY DID A NUMBER ON ME...
...YOU WIN...

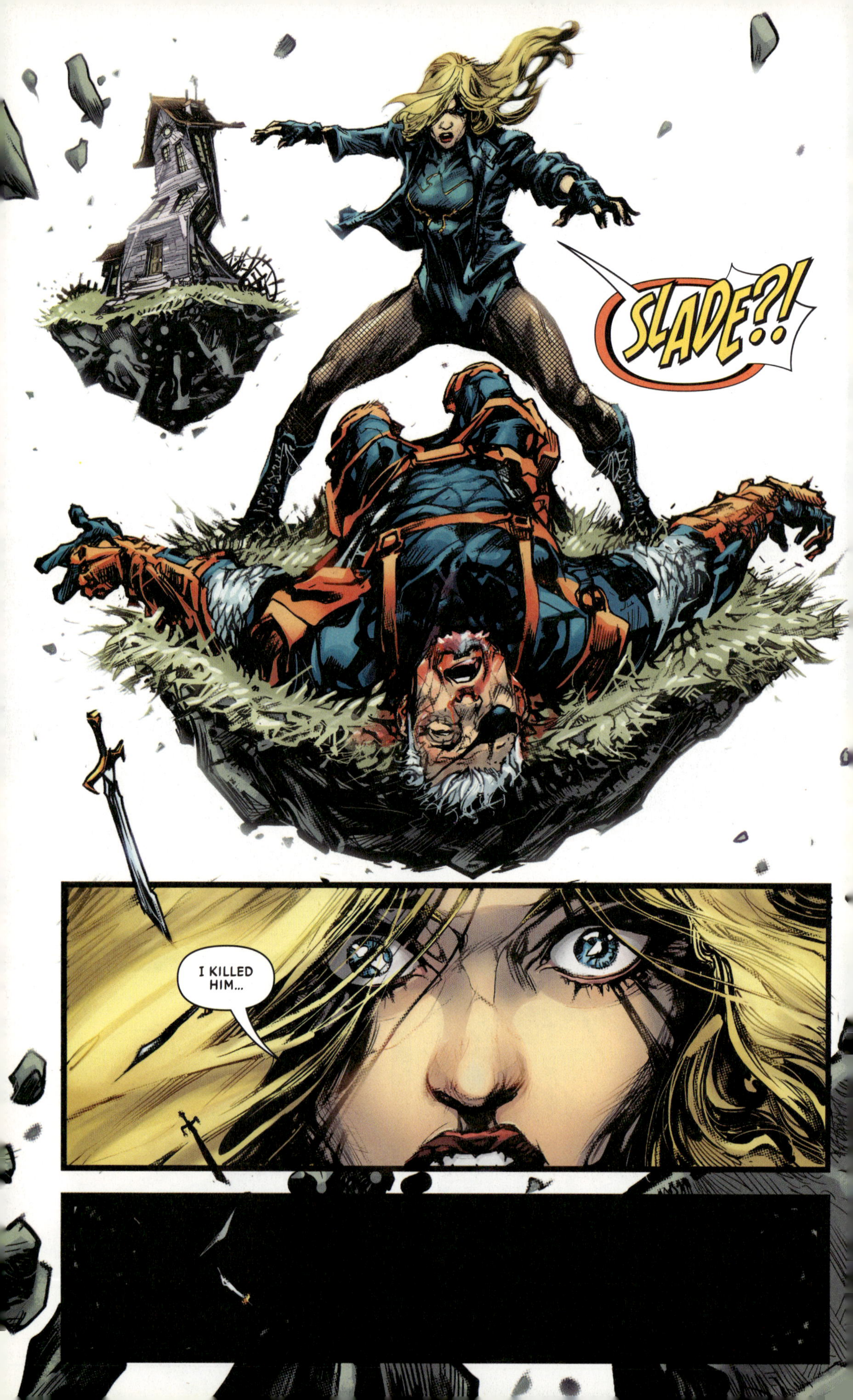
SLADE?!
I KILLED HIM...

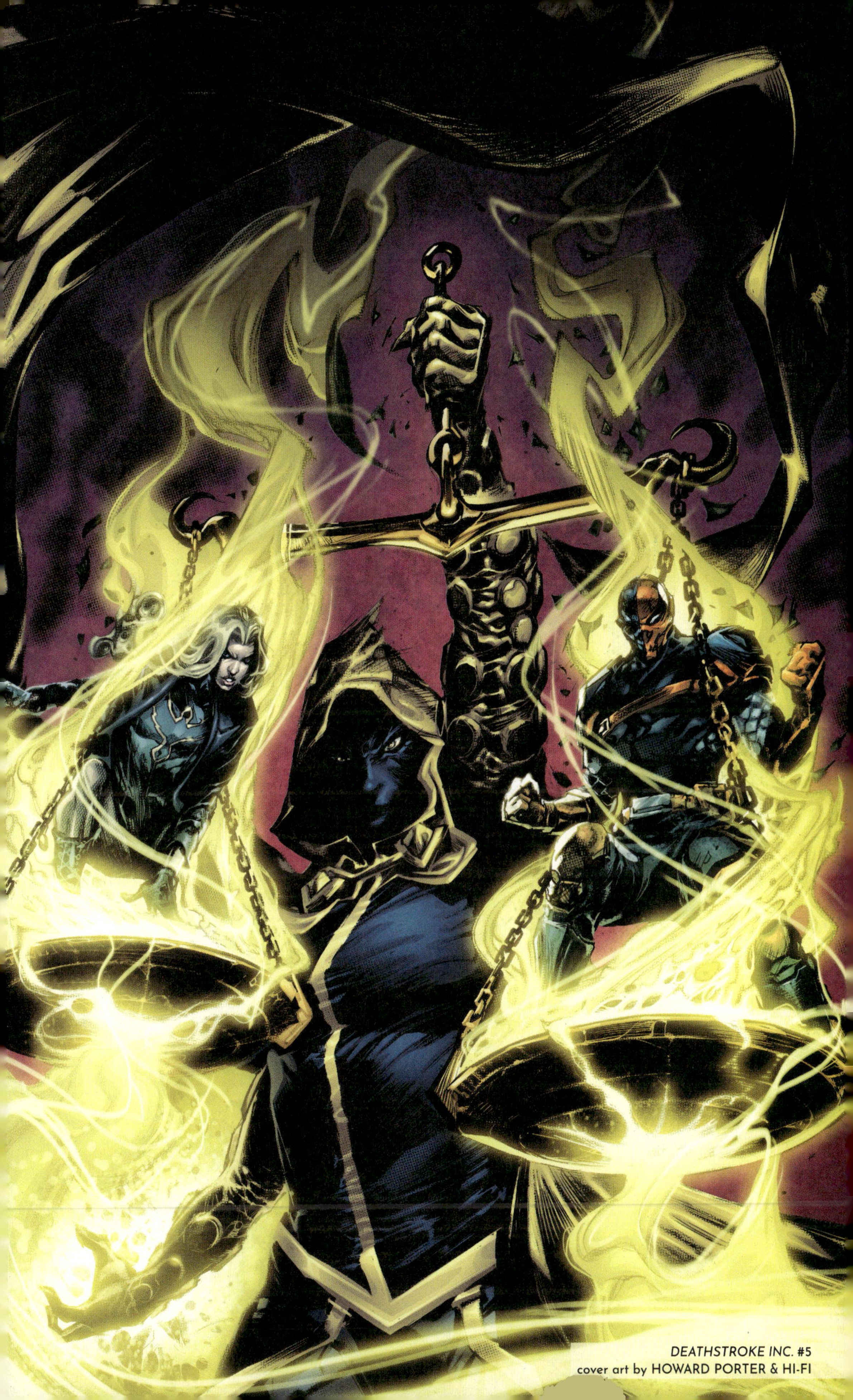

DEATHSTROKE INC. #5
cover art by HOWARD PORTER & HI-FI

DEATHSTROKE INC. #5
variant cover art by IVAN TAO

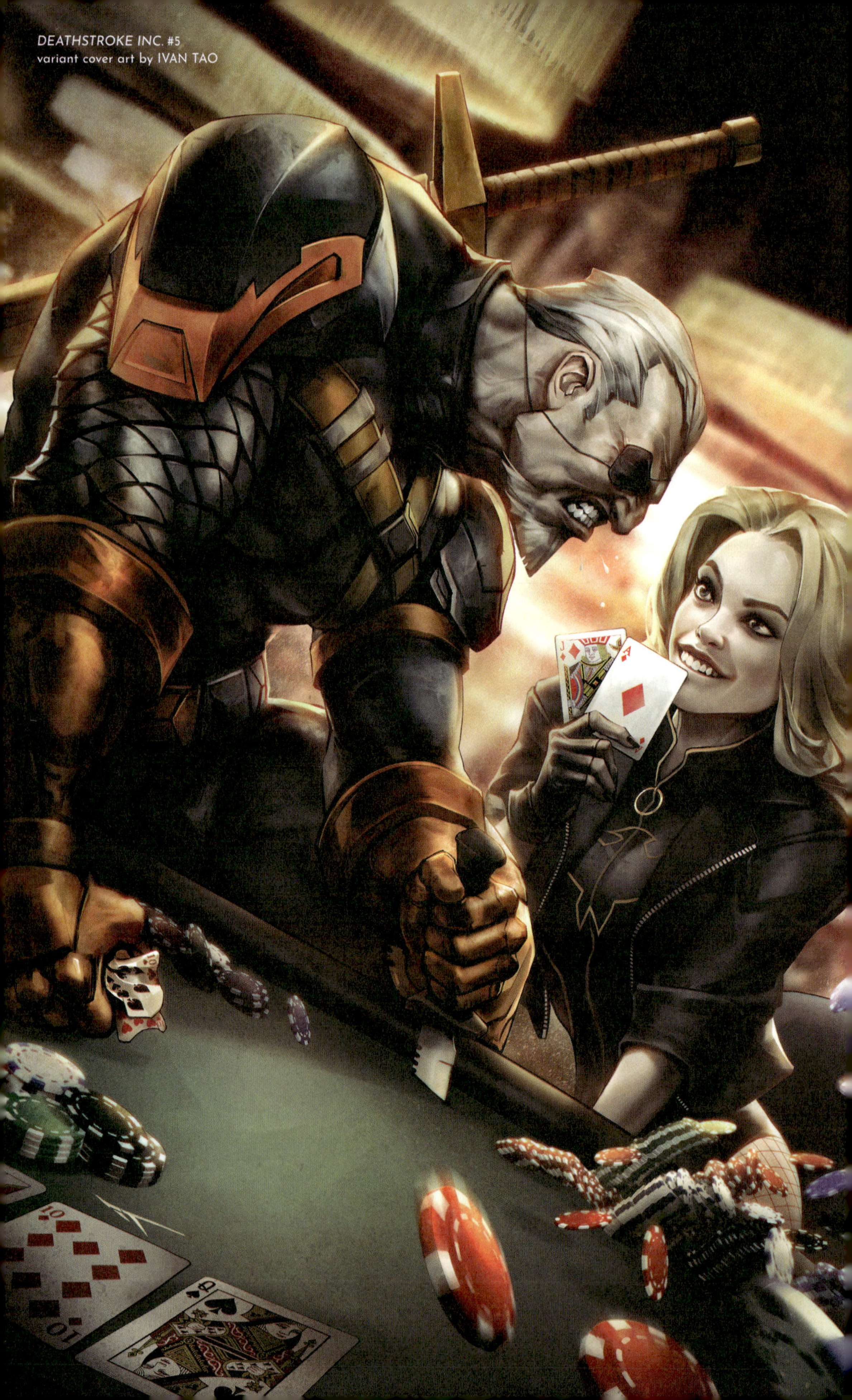

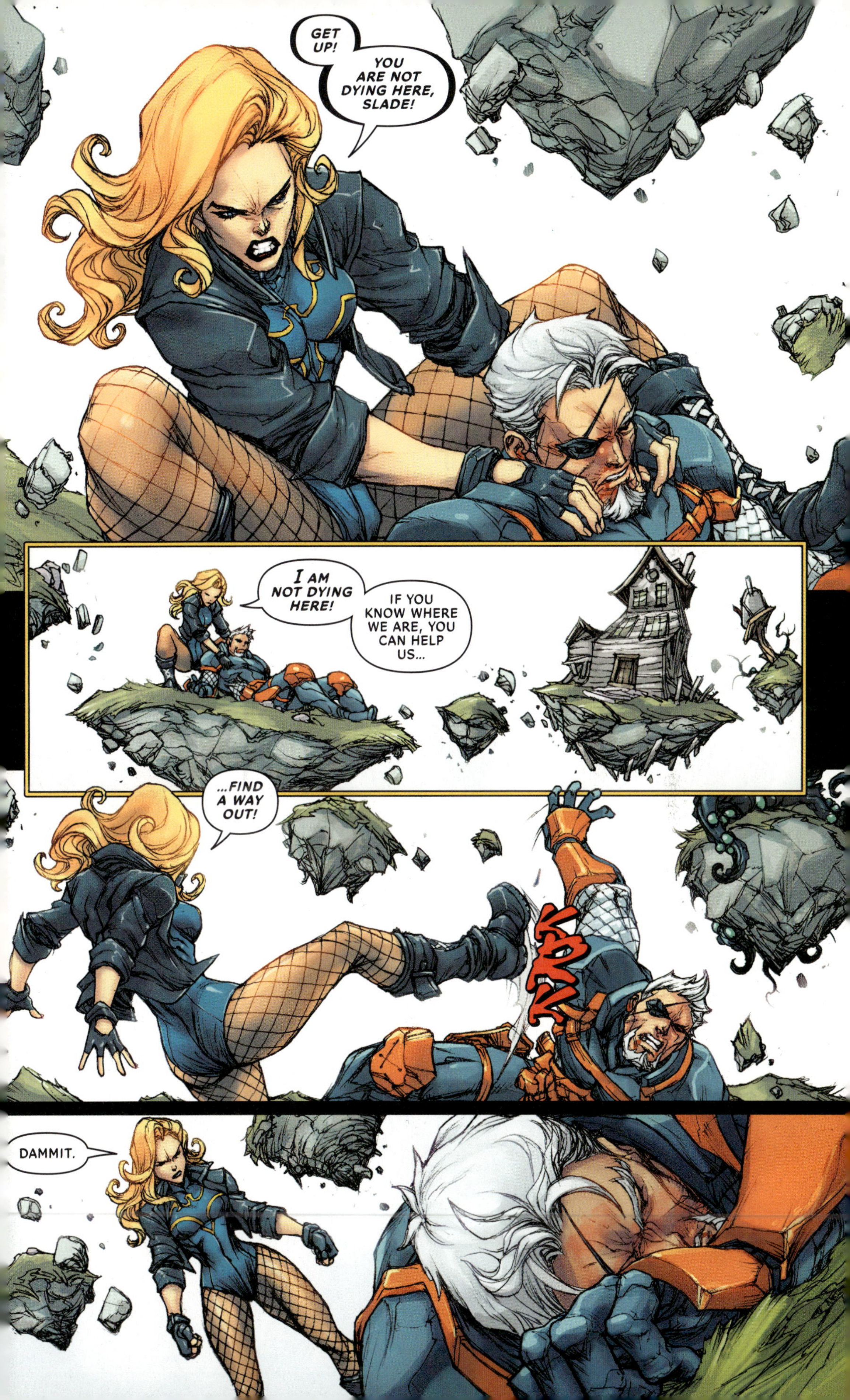
GET UP!
YOU ARE NOT DYING HERE, SLADE!
I AM NOT DYING HERE!
IF YOU KNOW WHERE WE ARE, YOU CAN HELP US...
...FIND A WAY OUT!
DAMMIT.

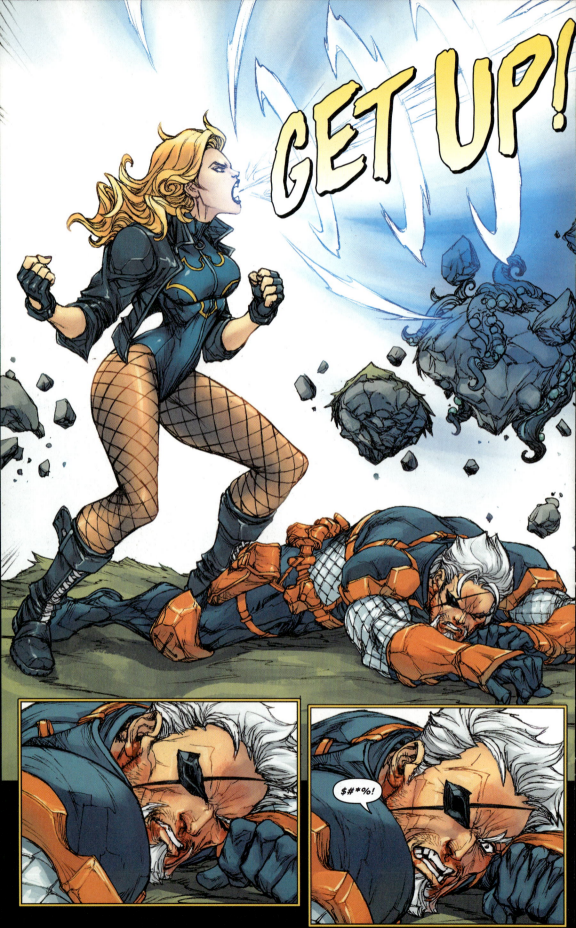

GHOSTS OF A DIFFERENT LIFE

JOSHUA WILLIAMSON writer • PAOLO PANTALENA artist
HI-FI colorist STEVE WANDS letterer HOWARD PORTER & HI-FI cover
IVAN TAO variant cover NATHAN SZERDY ratio variant cover
LUCIO PARRILLO Peacemaker variant cover BEN ABERNATHY editor
DEATHSTROKE created by MARV WOLFMAN and GEORGE PÉREZ

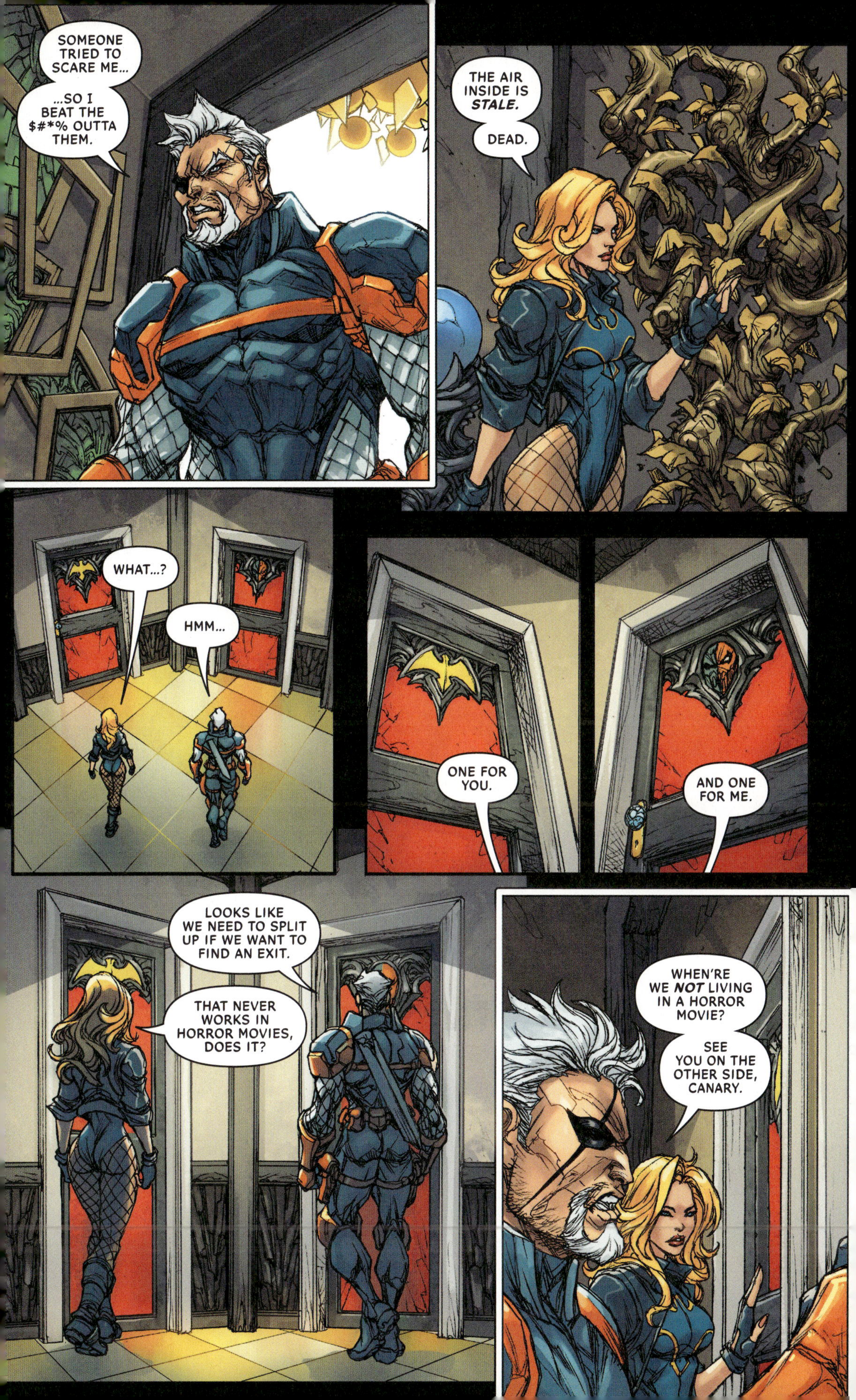
SOMEONE TRIED TO SCARE ME...
...SO I BEAT THE $#*% OUTTA THEM.
THE AIR INSIDE IS STALE.
DEAD.
WHAT...?
HMM...
ONE FOR YOU.
AND ONE FOR ME.
LOOKS LIKE WE NEED TO SPLIT UP IF WE WANT TO FIND AN EXIT.
THAT NEVER WORKS IN HORROR MOVIES, DOES IT?
WHEN'RE WE NOT LIVING IN A HORROR MOVIE?
SEE YOU ON THE OTHER SIDE, CANARY.

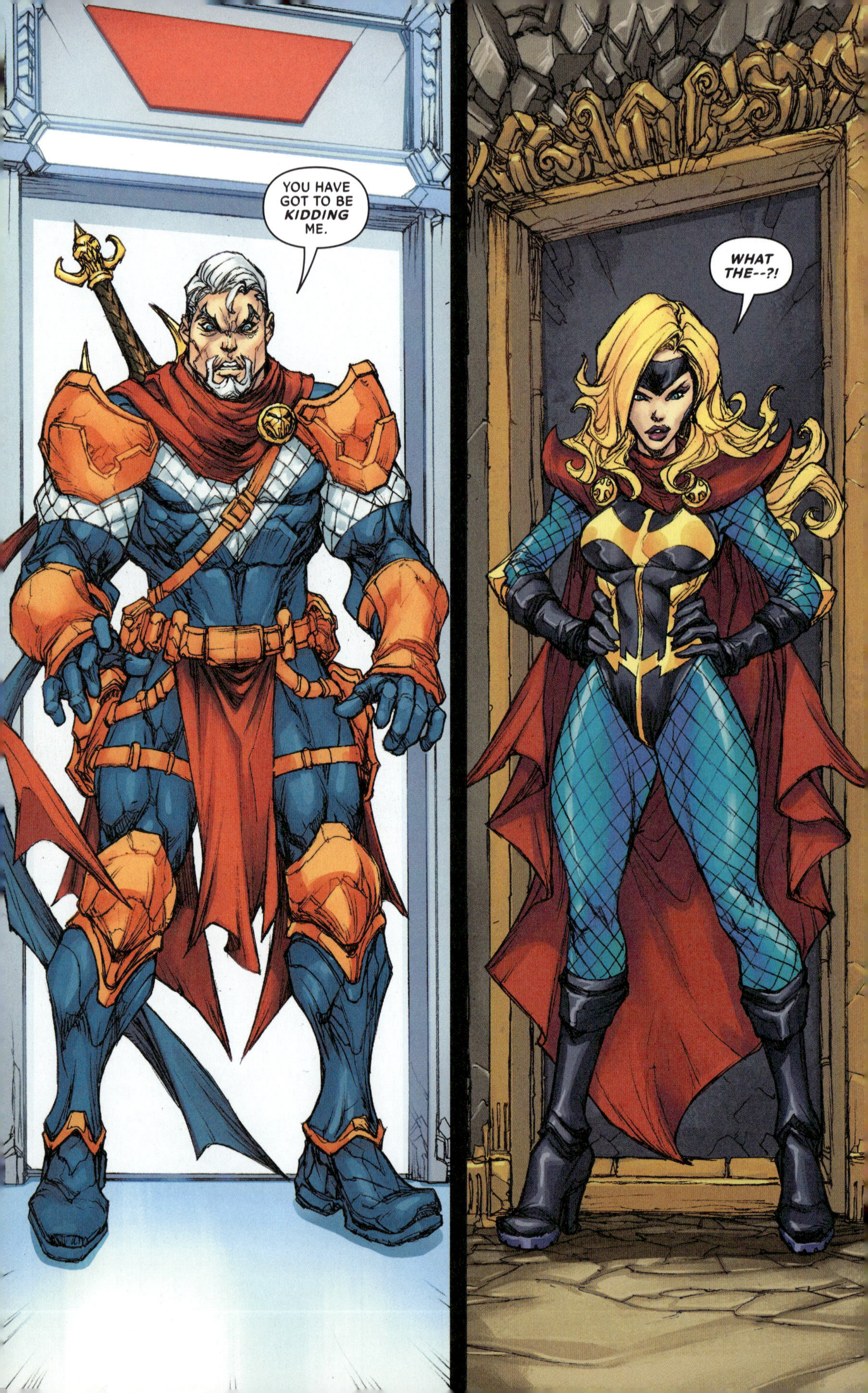
YOU HAVE GOT TO BE *KIDDING* ME.
WHAT THE--?!

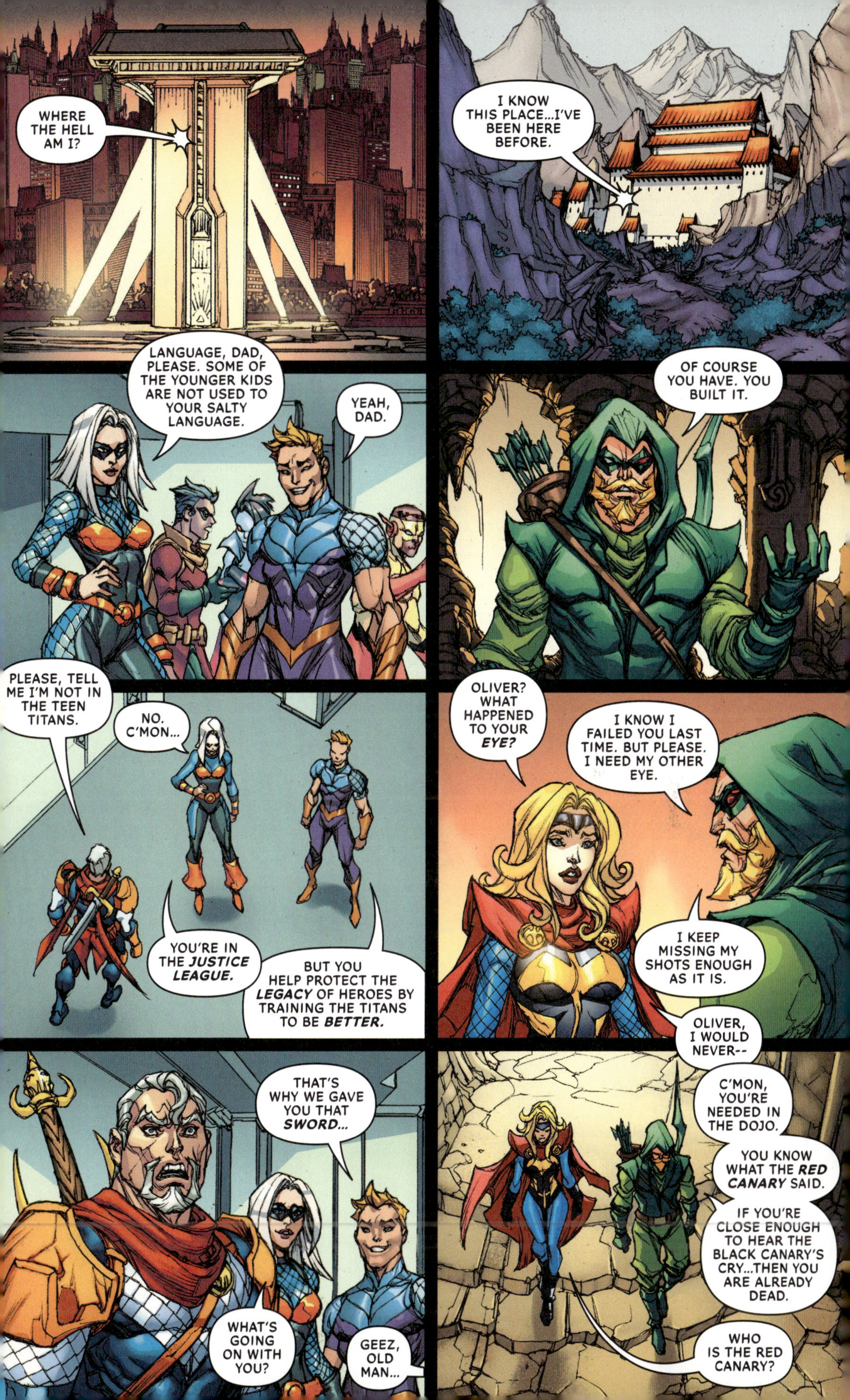
WHERE THE HELL AM I?
LANGUAGE, DAD, PLEASE. SOME OF THE YOUNGER KIDS ARE NOT USED TO YOUR SALTY LANGUAGE.
YEAH, DAD.
PLEASE, TELL ME I'M NOT IN THE TEEN TITANS.
NO. C'MON...
YOU'RE IN THE *JUSTICE LEAGUE.*
BUT YOU HELP PROTECT THE *LEGACY* OF HEROES BY TRAINING THE TITANS TO BE *BETTER.*
THAT'S WHY WE GAVE YOU THAT *SWORD...*
WHAT'S GOING ON WITH YOU?
GEEZ, OLD MAN...
I KNOW THIS PLACE...I'VE BEEN HERE BEFORE.
OF COURSE YOU HAVE. YOU BUILT IT.
OLIVER? WHAT HAPPENED TO YOUR *EYE?*
I KNOW I FAILED YOU LAST TIME. BUT PLEASE. I NEED MY OTHER EYE.
I KEEP MISSING MY SHOTS ENOUGH AS IT IS.
OLIVER, I WOULD NEVER--
C'MON, YOU'RE NEEDED IN THE DOJO.
YOU KNOW WHAT THE *RED CANARY* SAID.
IF YOU'RE CLOSE ENOUGH TO HEAR THE BLACK CANARY'S CRY...THEN YOU ARE ALREADY DEAD.
WHO IS THE RED CANARY?

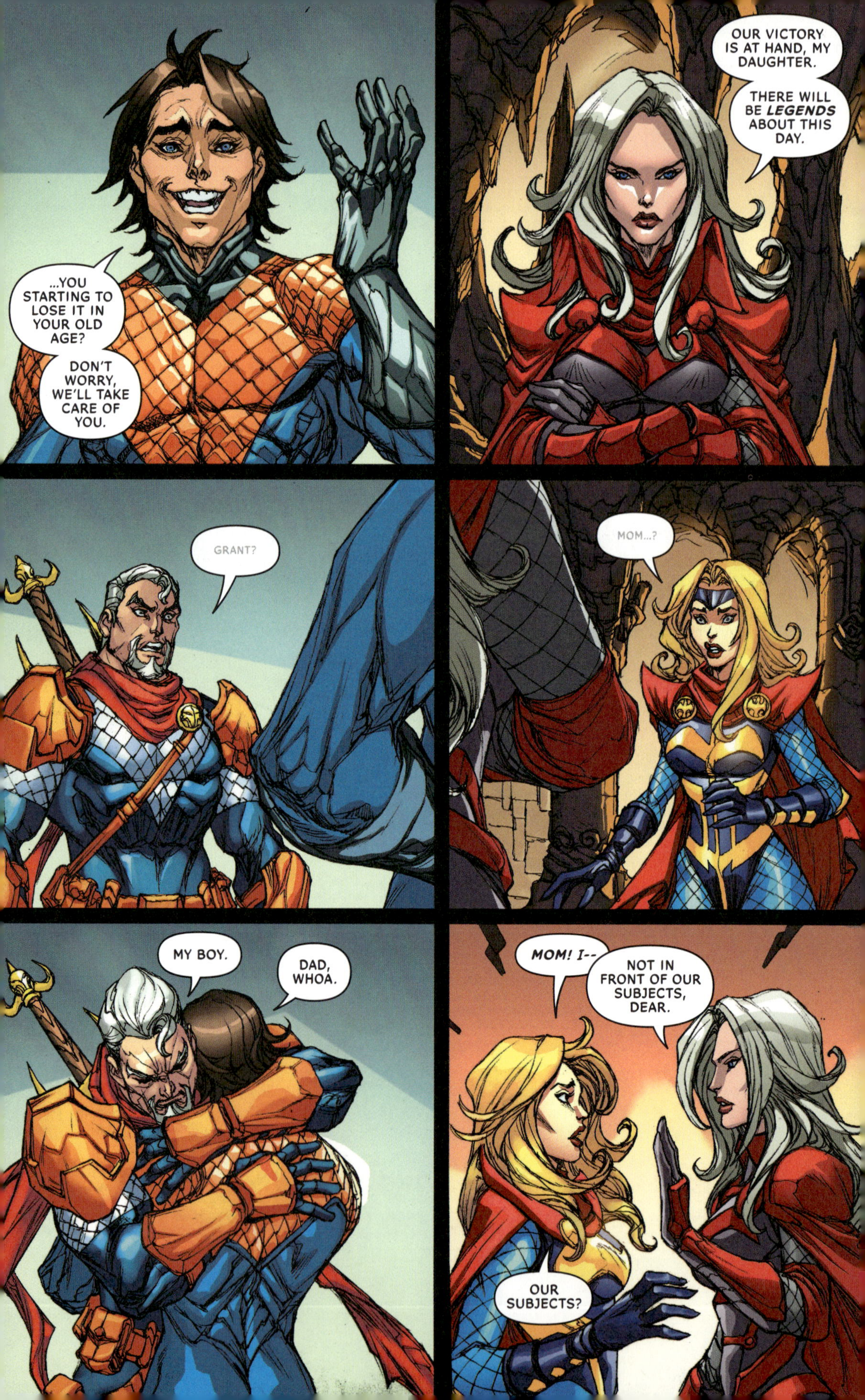

...YOU STARTING TO LOSE IT IN YOUR OLD AGE?
DON'T WORRY, WE'LL TAKE CARE OF YOU.
OUR VICTORY IS AT HAND, MY DAUGHTER.
THERE WILL BE *LEGENDS* ABOUT THIS DAY.
GRANT?
MOM...?
MY BOY.
DAD, WHOA.
MOM! I--
NOT IN FRONT OF OUR SUBJECTS, DEAR.
OUR SUBJECTS?

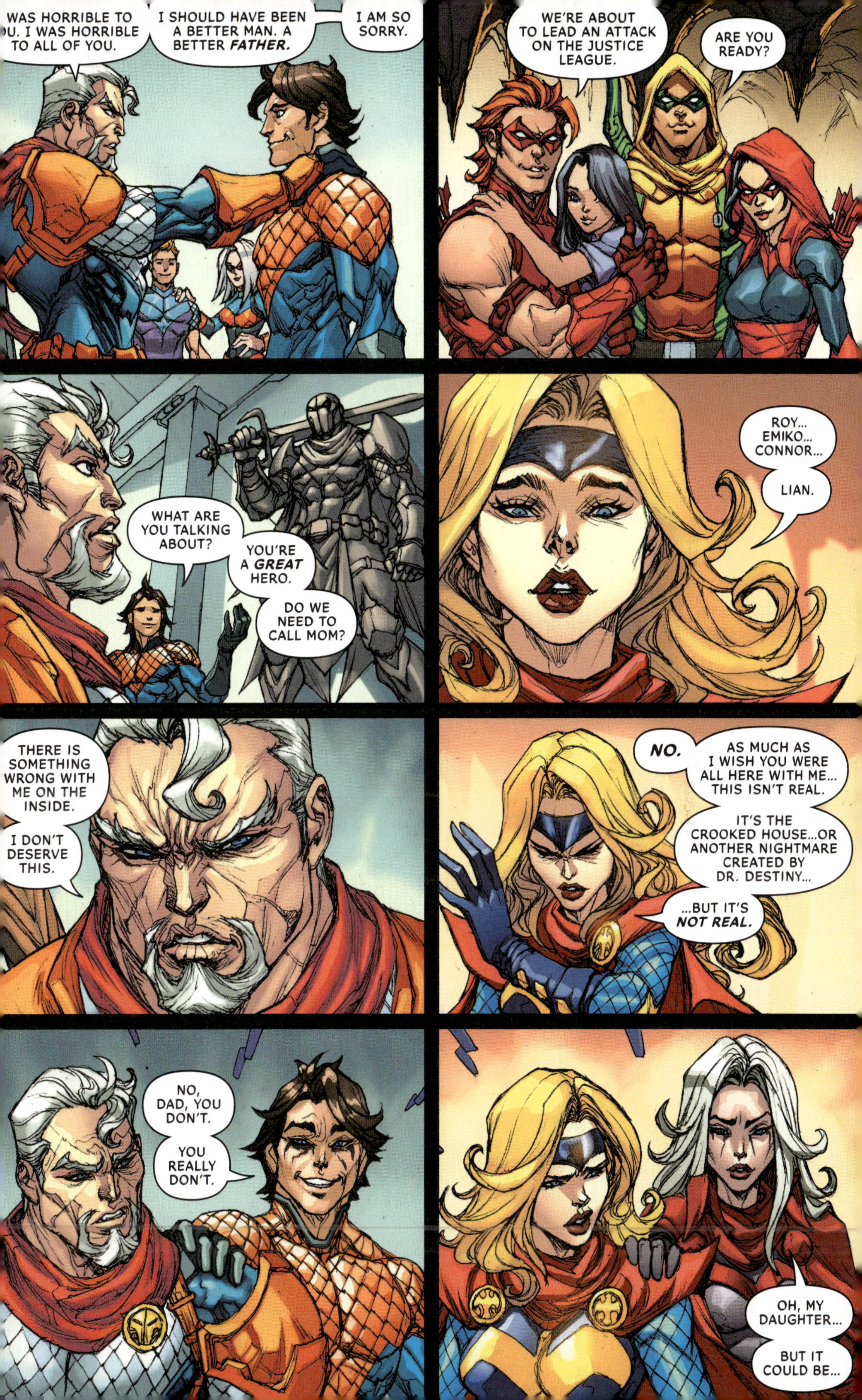
WAS HORRIBLE TO
U. I WAS HORRIBLE TO ALL OF YOU.
I SHOULD HAVE BEEN A BETTER MAN. A BETTER *FATHER.*
I AM SO SORRY.
WHAT ARE YOU TALKING ABOUT?
YOU'RE A *GREAT* HERO.
DO WE NEED TO CALL MOM?
THERE IS SOMETHING WRONG WITH ME ON THE INSIDE.
I DON'T DESERVE THIS.
NO, DAD, YOU DON'T.
YOU REALLY DON'T.
WE'RE ABOUT TO LEAD AN ATTACK ON THE JUSTICE LEAGUE.
ARE YOU READY?
ROY... EMIKO... CONNOR...
LIAN.
NO.
AS MUCH AS I WISH YOU WERE ALL HERE WITH ME... THIS ISN'T REAL.
IT'S THE CROOKED HOUSE...OR ANOTHER NIGHTMARE CREATED BY DR. DESTINY...
...BUT IT'S ***NOT REAL.***
OH, MY DAUGHTER...
BUT IT COULD BE...

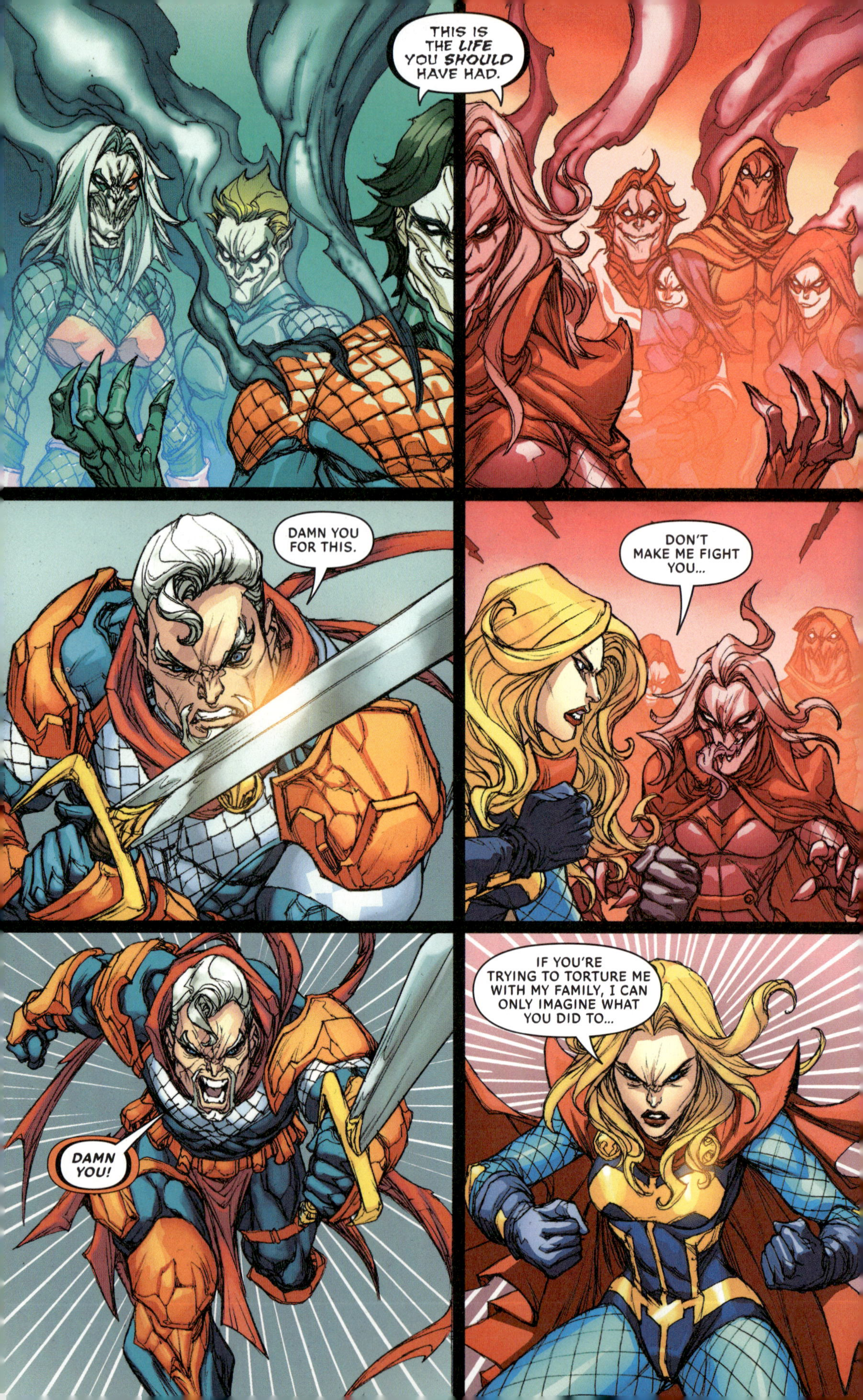
THIS IS THE *LIFE* YOU *SHOULD* HAVE HAD.
DAMN YOU FOR THIS.
DON'T MAKE ME FIGHT YOU...
DAMN YOU!
IF YOU'RE TRYING TO TORTURE ME WITH MY FAMILY, I CAN ONLY IMAGINE WHAT YOU DID TO...

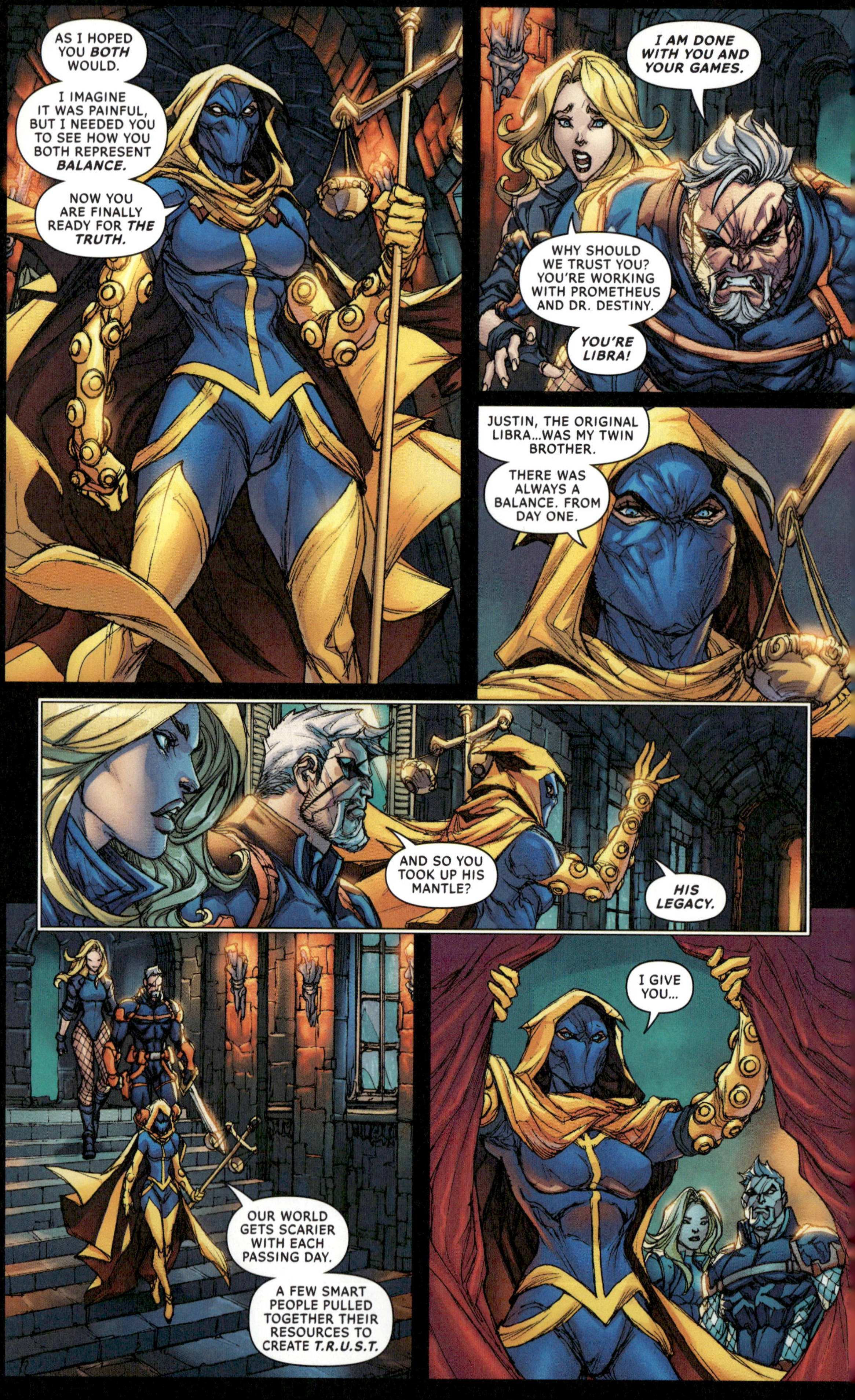
AS I HOPED YOU BOTH WOULD.
I IMAGINE IT WAS PAINFUL, BUT I NEEDED YOU TO SEE HOW YOU BOTH REPRESENT BALANCE.
NOW YOU ARE FINALLY READY FOR THE TRUTH.
I AM DONE WITH YOU AND YOUR GAMES.
WHY SHOULD WE TRUST YOU? YOU'RE WORKING WITH PROMETHEUS AND DR. DESTINY.
YOU'RE LIBRA!
JUSTIN, THE ORIGINAL LIBRA...WAS MY TWIN BROTHER.
THERE WAS ALWAYS A BALANCE. FROM DAY ONE.
AND SO YOU TOOK UP HIS MANTLE?
HIS LEGACY.
OUR WORLD GETS SCARIER WITH EACH PASSING DAY.
A FEW SMART PEOPLE PULLED TOGETHER THEIR RESOURCES TO CREATE T.R.U.S.T.
I GIVE YOU...

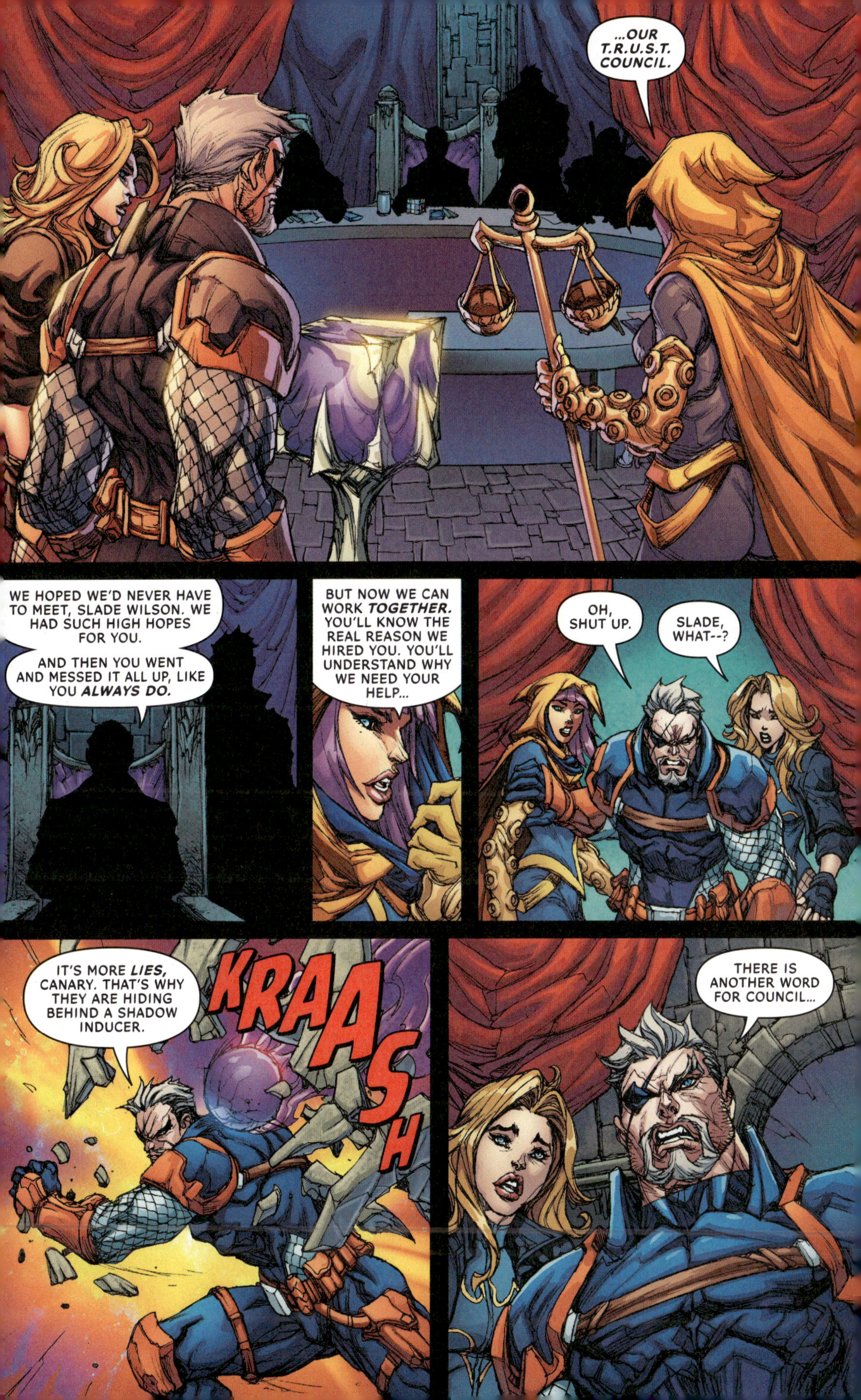
...OUR T.R.U.S.T. COUNCIL.
WE HOPED WE'D NEVER HAVE TO MEET, SLADE WILSON. WE HAD SUCH HIGH HOPES FOR YOU.
AND THEN YOU WENT AND MESSED IT ALL UP, LIKE YOU ALWAYS DO.
BUT NOW WE CAN WORK TOGETHER. YOU'LL KNOW THE REAL REASON WE HIRED YOU. YOU'LL UNDERSTAND WHY WE NEED YOUR HELP...
OH, SHUT UP.
SLADE, WHAT--?
IT'S MORE LIES, CANARY. THAT'S WHY THEY ARE HIDING BEHIND A SHADOW INDUCER.
KRAASH
THERE IS ANOTHER WORD FOR COUNCIL...

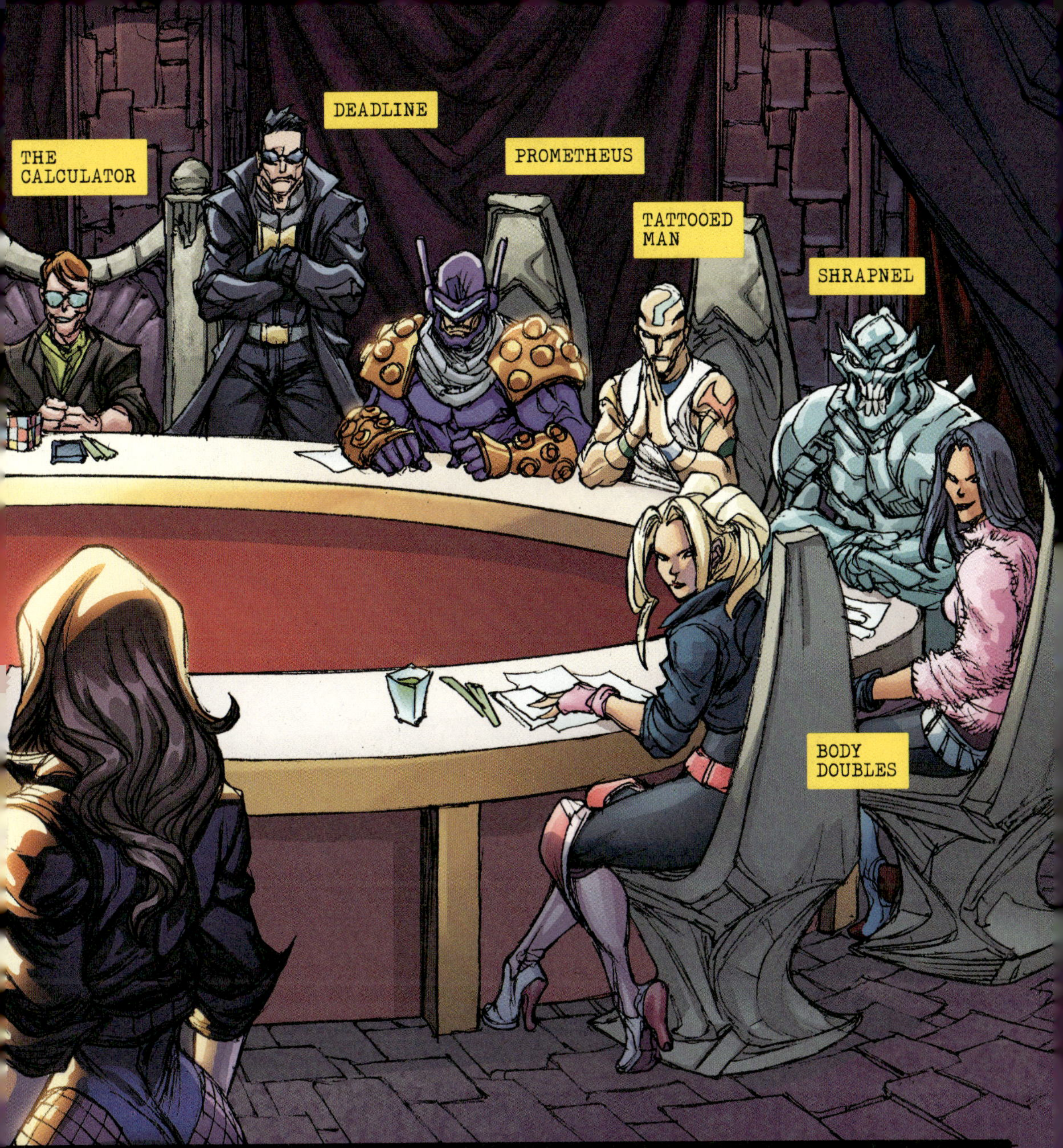
THE CALCULATOR
DEADLINE
PROMETHEUS
TATTOOED MAN
SHRAPNEL
BODY DOUBLES

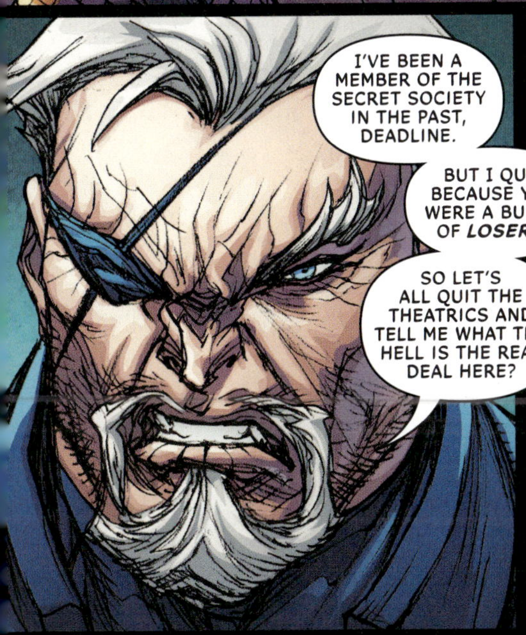
I'VE BEEN A MEMBER OF THE SECRET SOCIETY IN THE PAST, DEADLINE.
BUT I QUIT BECAUSE YOU WERE A BUNCH OF LOSERS.
SO LET'S ALL QUIT THE THEATRICS AND TELL ME WHAT THE HELL IS THE REAL DEAL HERE?

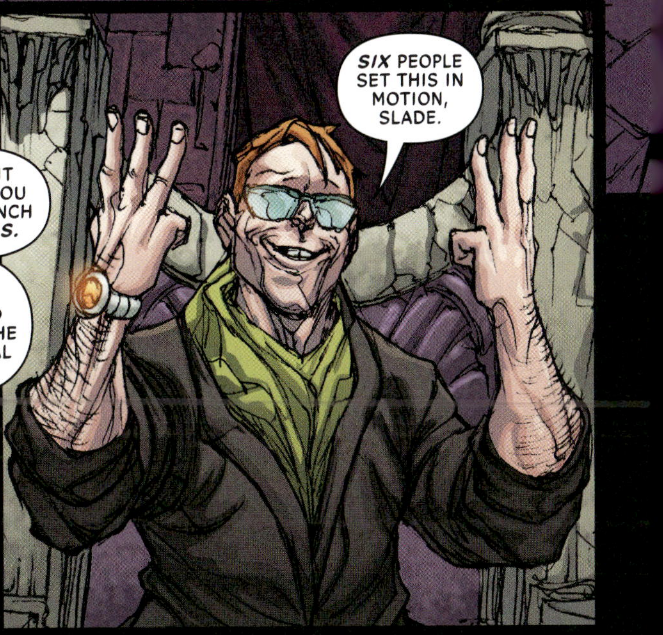
SIX PEOPLE SET THIS IN MOTION, SLADE.

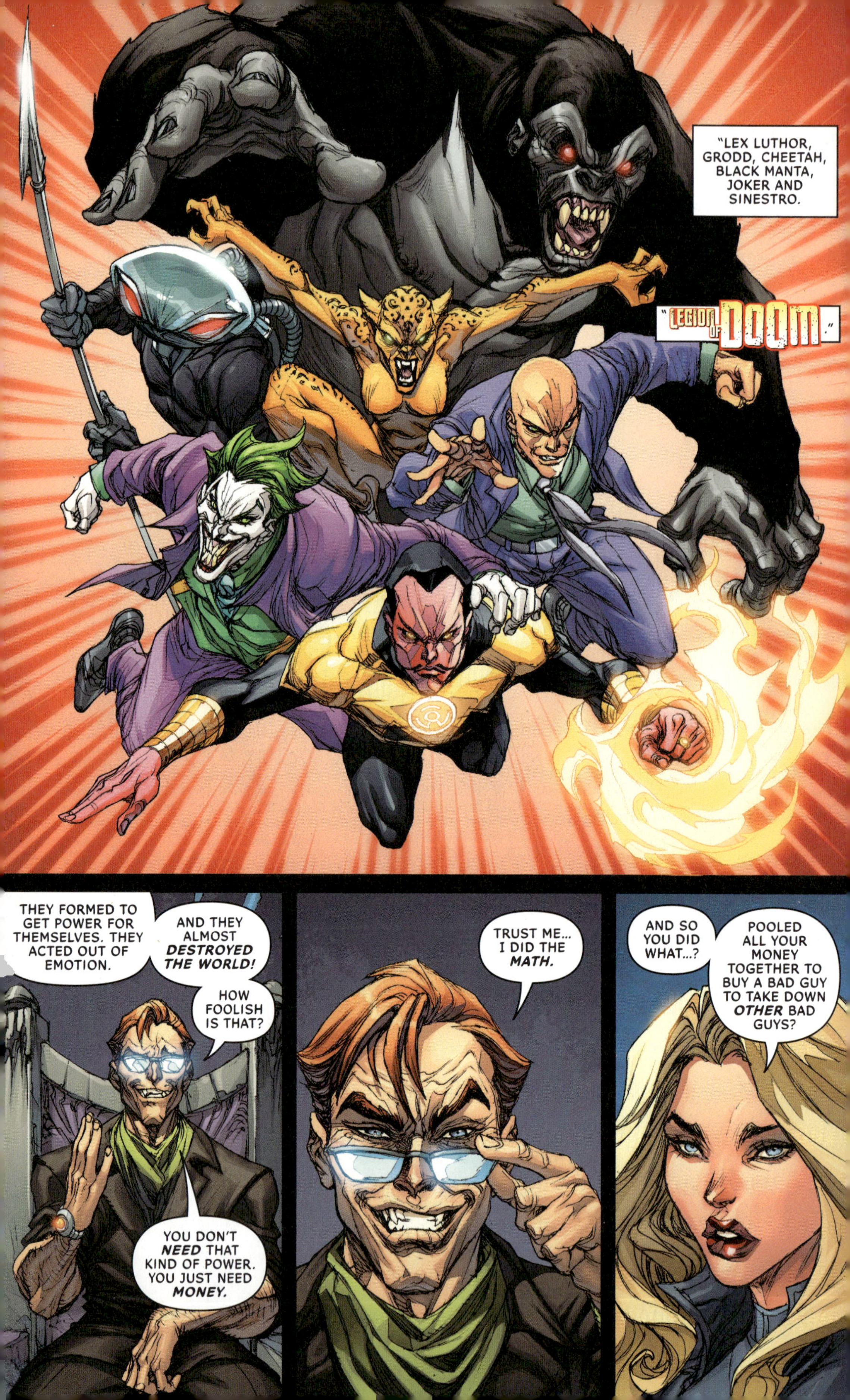
"LEX LUTHOR, GRODD, CHEETAH, BLACK MANTA, JOKER AND SINESTRO.
"LEGION OF DOOM."
THEY FORMED TO GET POWER FOR THEMSELVES. THEY ACTED OUT OF EMOTION.
AND THEY ALMOST DESTROYED THE WORLD!
HOW FOOLISH IS THAT?
YOU DON'T NEED THAT KIND OF POWER. YOU JUST NEED MONEY.
TRUST ME... I DID THE MATH.
AND SO YOU DID WHAT...?
POOLED ALL YOUR MONEY TOGETHER TO BUY A BAD GUY TO TAKE DOWN OTHER BAD GUYS?

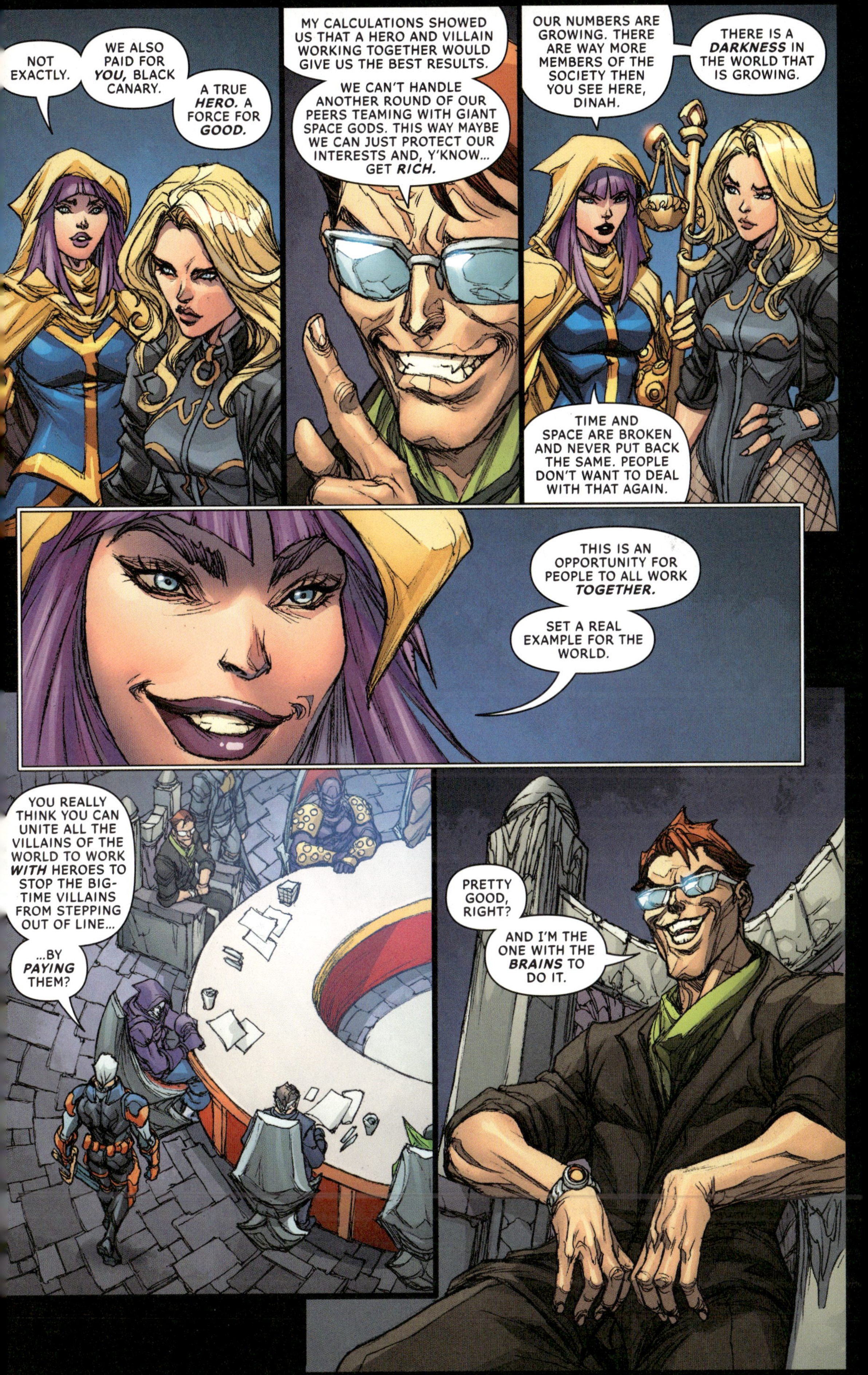
NOT EXACTLY.
WE ALSO PAID FOR YOU, BLACK CANARY.
A TRUE HERO. A FORCE FOR GOOD.
MY CALCULATIONS SHOWED US THAT A HERO AND VILLAIN WORKING TOGETHER WOULD GIVE US THE BEST RESULTS.
WE CAN'T HANDLE ANOTHER ROUND OF OUR PEERS TEAMING WITH GIANT SPACE GODS. THIS WAY MAYBE WE CAN JUST PROTECT OUR INTERESTS AND, Y'KNOW... GET RICH.
OUR NUMBERS ARE GROWING. THERE ARE WAY MORE MEMBERS OF THE SOCIETY THEN YOU SEE HERE, DINAH.
THERE IS A DARKNESS IN THE WORLD THAT IS GROWING.
TIME AND SPACE ARE BROKEN AND NEVER PUT BACK THE SAME. PEOPLE DON'T WANT TO DEAL WITH THAT AGAIN.
THIS IS AN OPPORTUNITY FOR PEOPLE TO ALL WORK TOGETHER.
SET A REAL EXAMPLE FOR THE WORLD.
YOU REALLY THINK YOU CAN UNITE ALL THE VILLAINS OF THE WORLD TO WORK WITH HEROES TO STOP THE BIG-TIME VILLAINS FROM STEPPING OUT OF LINE...
...BY PAYING THEM?
PRETTY GOOD, RIGHT?
AND I'M THE ONE WITH THE BRAINS TO DO IT.

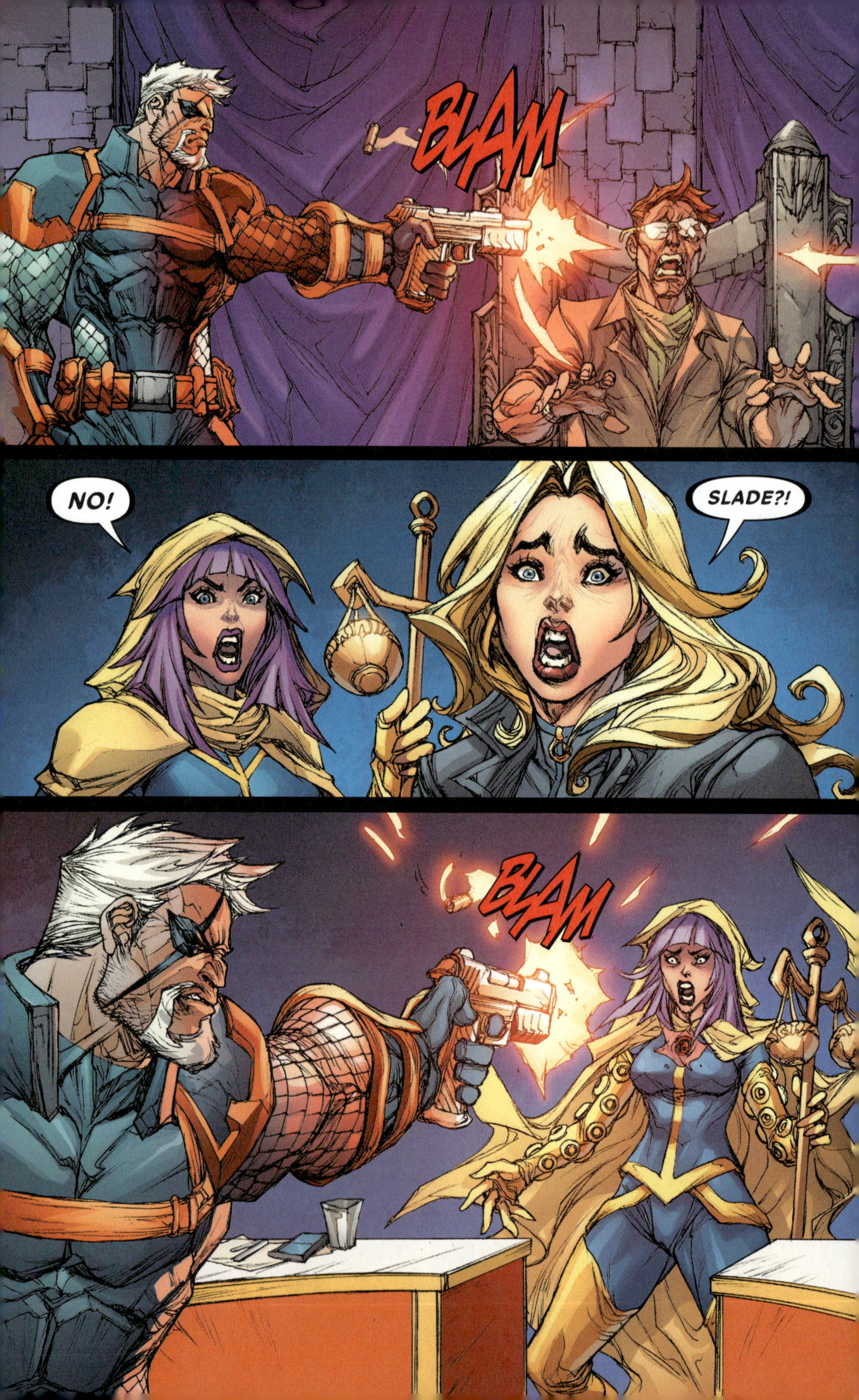
BLAM
NO!
SLADE?!
BLAM

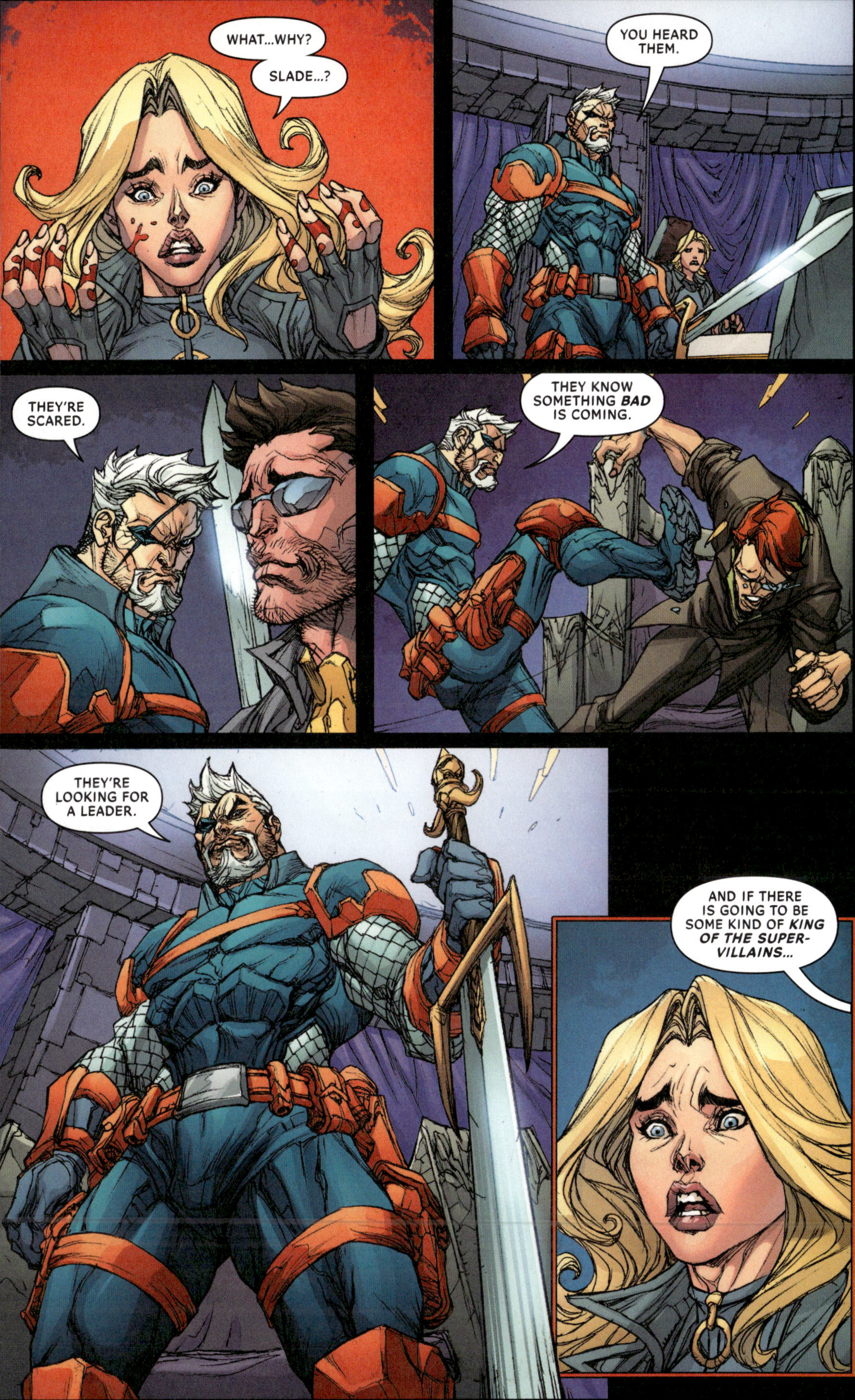
WHAT...WHY?
SLADE...?
YOU HEARD THEM.
THEY'RE SCARED.
THEY KNOW SOMETHING *BAD* IS COMING.
THEY'RE LOOKING FOR A LEADER.
AND IF THERE IS GOING TO BE SOME KIND OF ***KING OF THE SUPER-VILLAINS...***

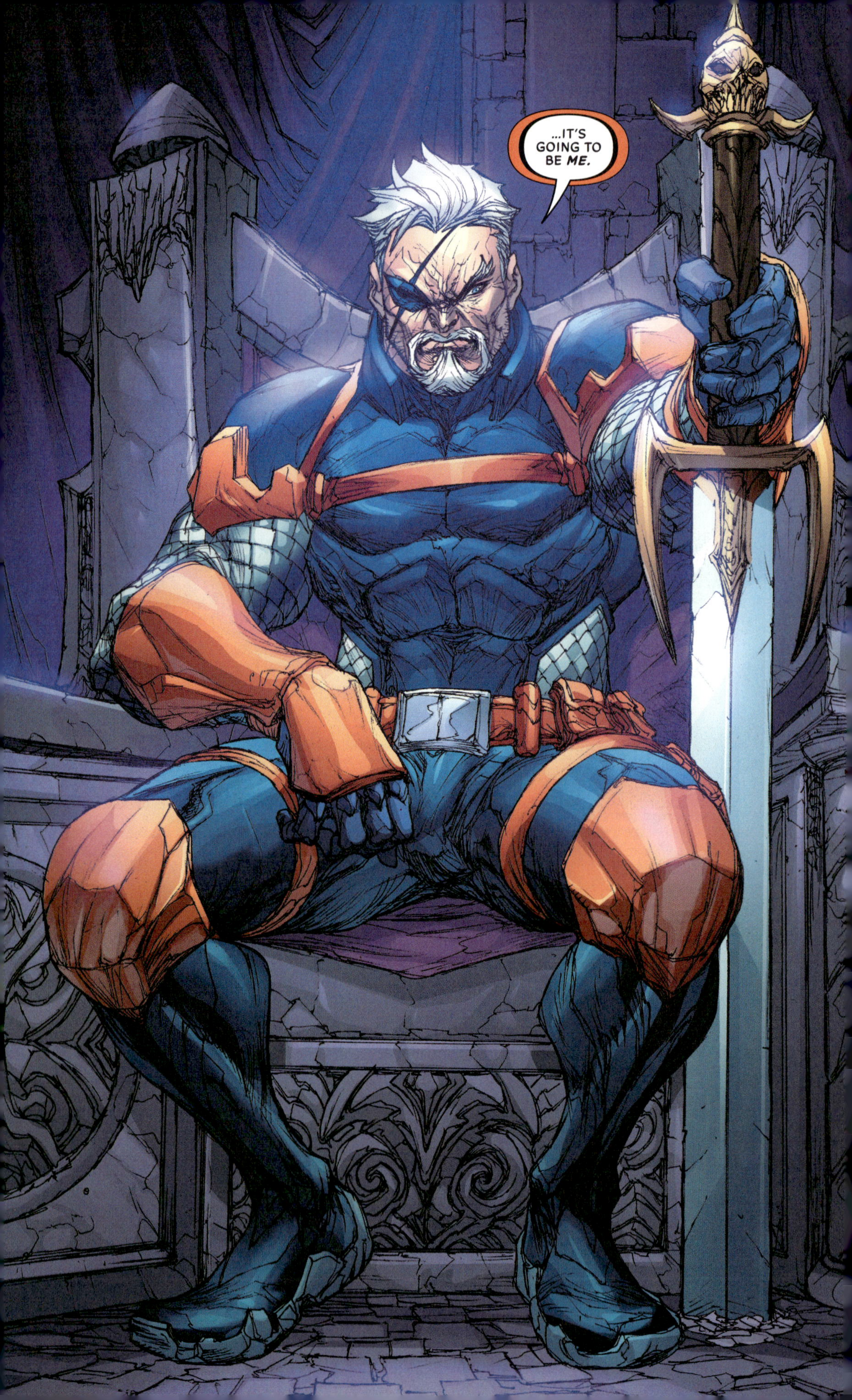
...IT'S GOING TO BE *ME.*

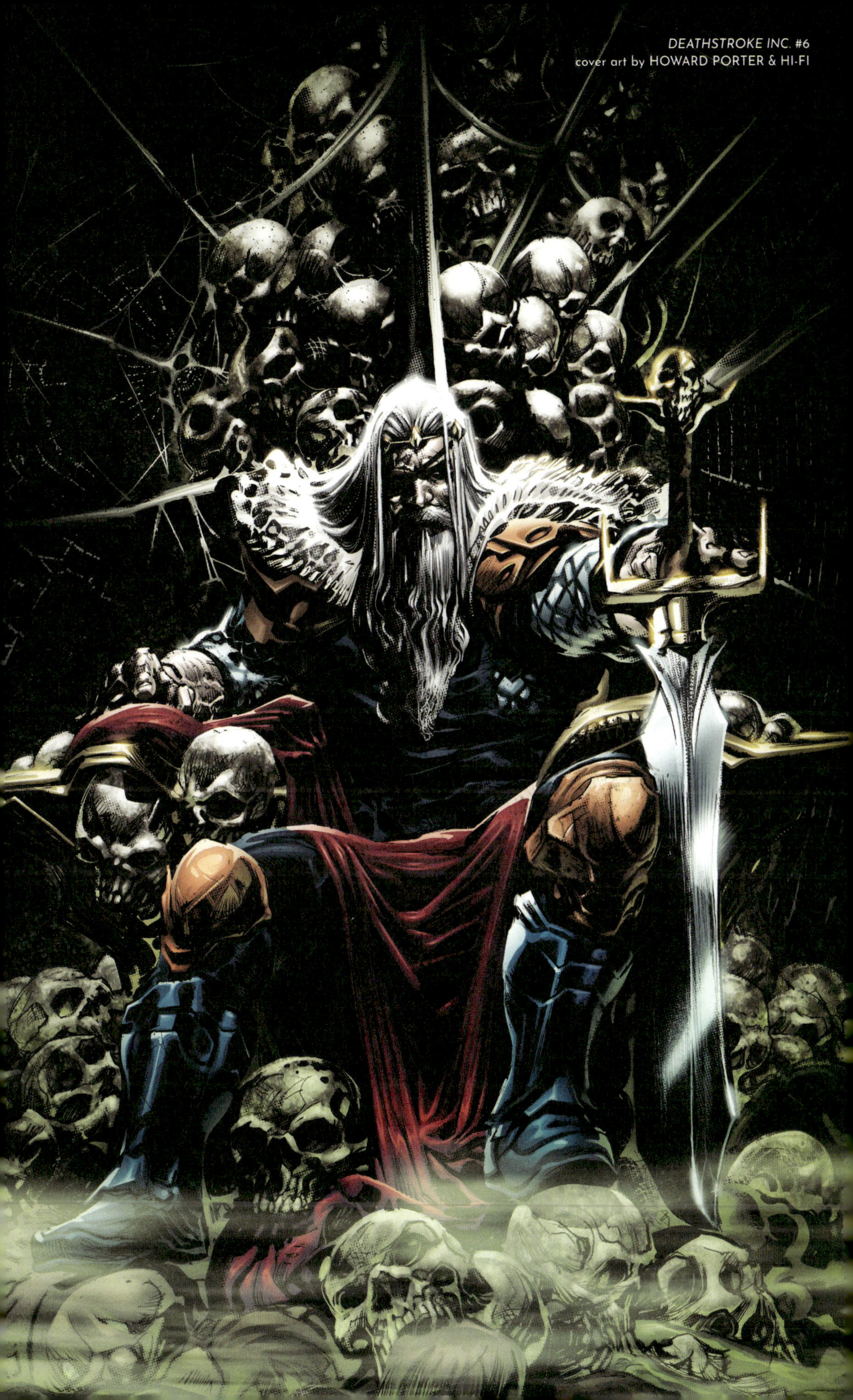

DEATHSTROKE INC. #6
cover art by HOWARD PORTER & HI-FI

DEATHSTROKE INC. #6
variant cover art by IVAN TAO

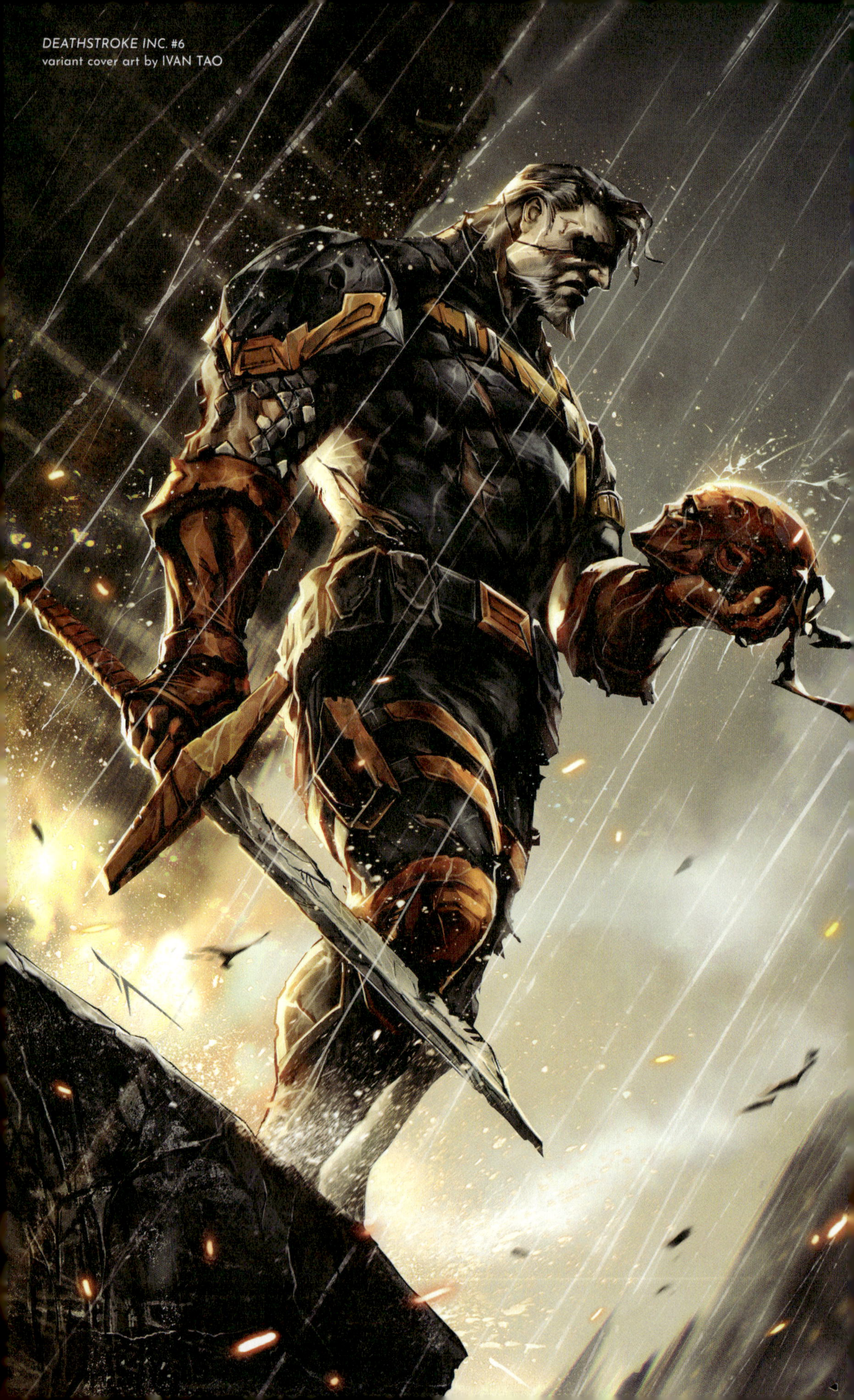

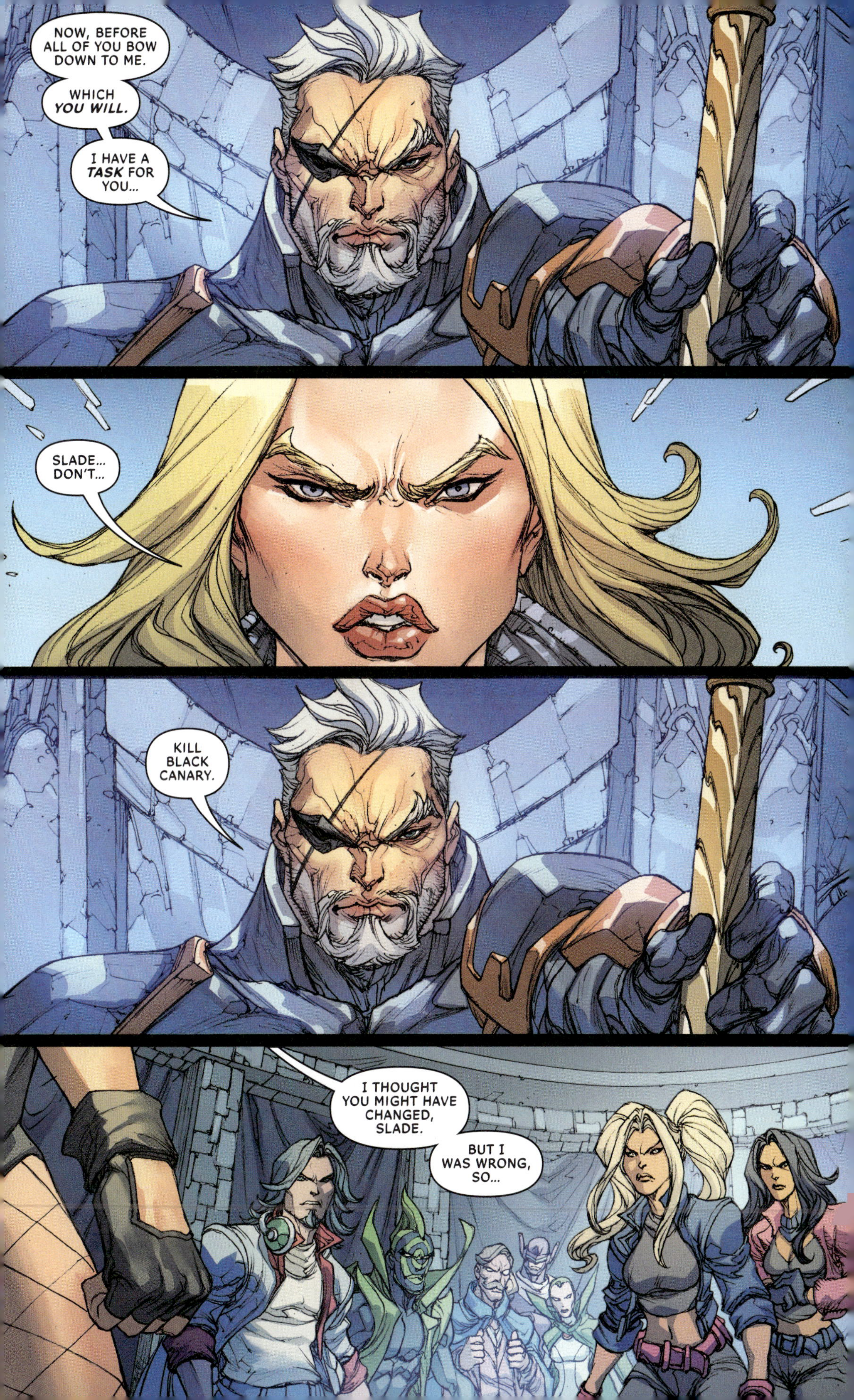
NOW, BEFORE ALL OF YOU BOW DOWN TO ME.
WHICH ***YOU WILL.***
I HAVE A ***TASK*** FOR YOU...
SLADE... DON'T...
KILL BLACK CANARY.
I THOUGHT YOU MIGHT HAVE CHANGED, SLADE.
BUT I WAS WRONG, SO...

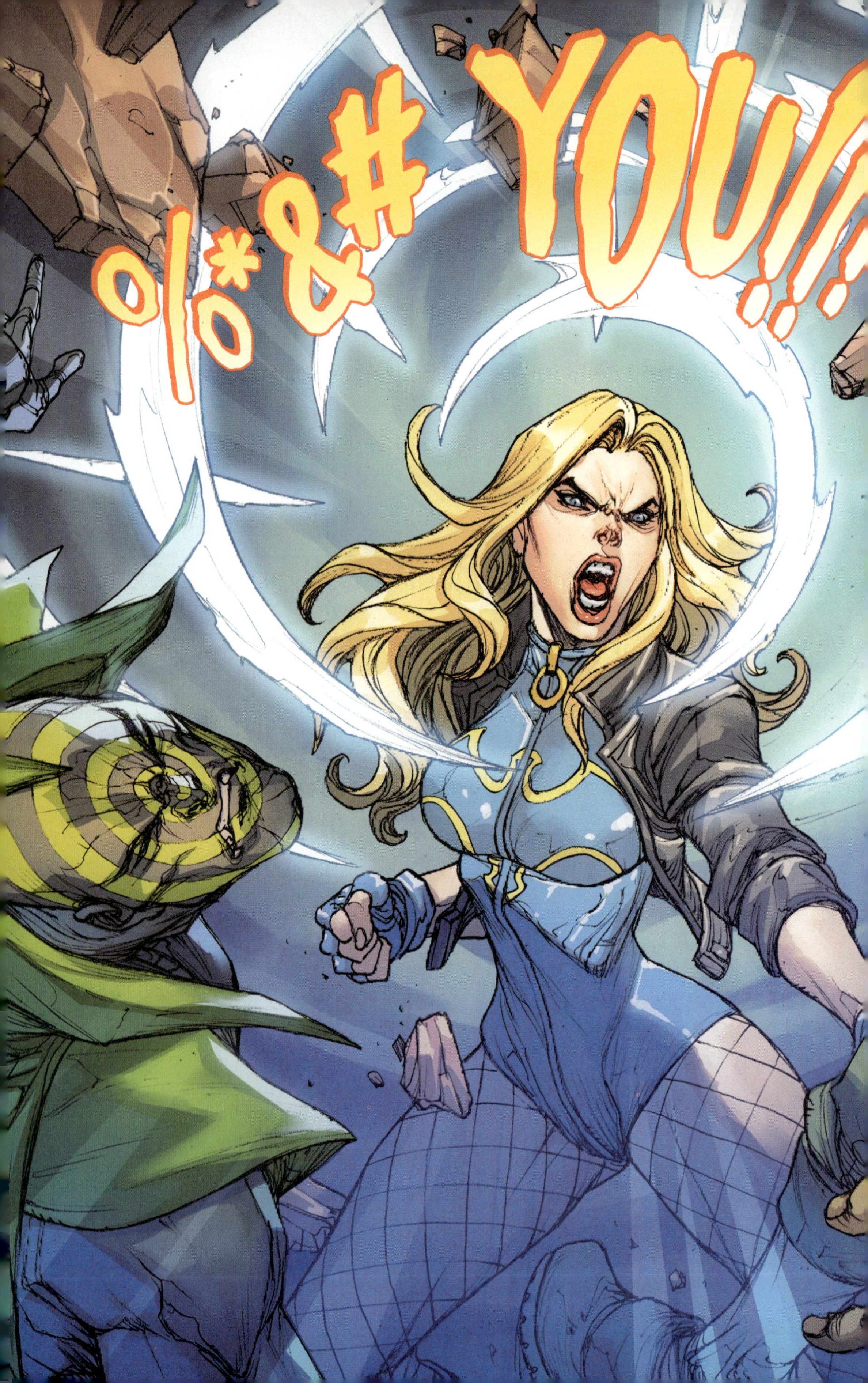
%*&# YOU!!!

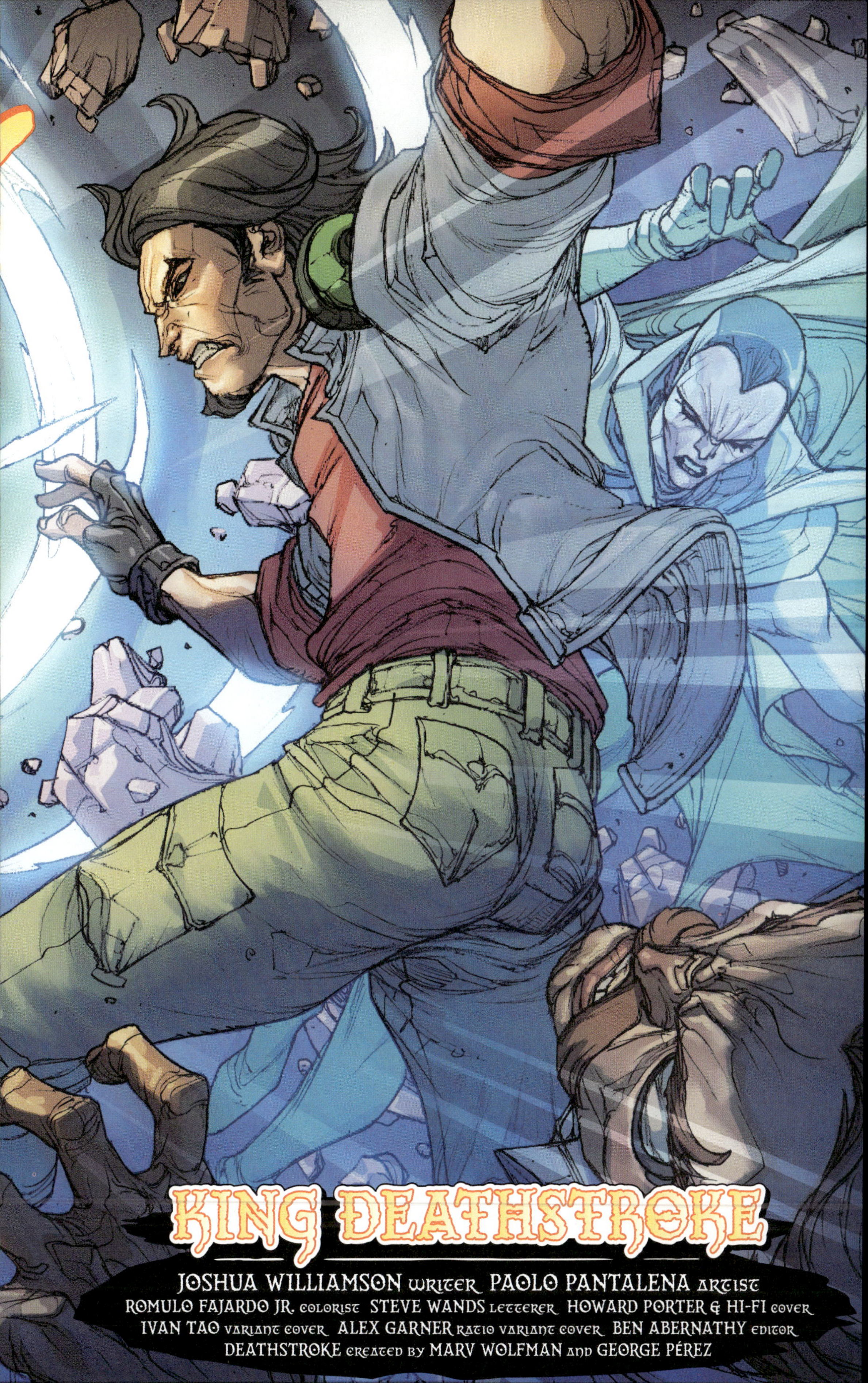
KING DEATHSTROKE
JOSHUA WILLIAMSON writer PAOLO PANTALENA artist
ROMULO FAJARDO JR. colorist STEVE WANDS letterer HOWARD PORTER & HI-FI cover
IVAN TAO variant cover ALEX GARNER ratio variant cover BEN ABERNATHY editor
DEATHSTROKE created by MARV WOLFMAN and GEORGE PÉREZ

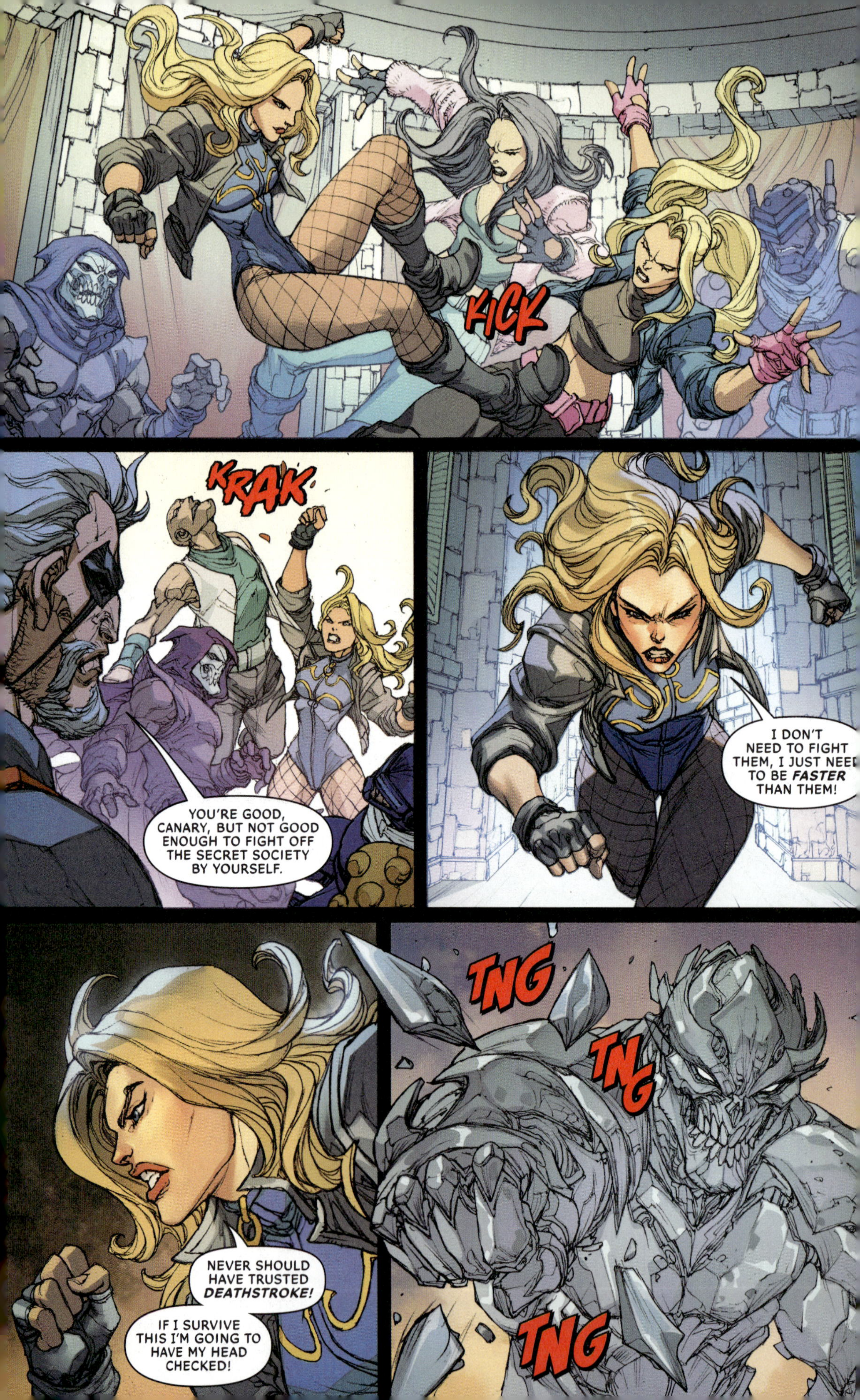

KICK
KRAK
YOU'RE GOOD, CANARY, BUT NOT GOOD ENOUGH TO FIGHT OFF THE SECRET SOCIETY BY YOURSELF.
I DON'T NEED TO FIGHT THEM, I JUST NEED TO BE FASTER THAN THEM!
NEVER SHOULD HAVE TRUSTED DEATHSTROKE!
IF I SURVIVE THIS I'M GOING TO HAVE MY HEAD CHECKED!
TNG
TNG
TNG

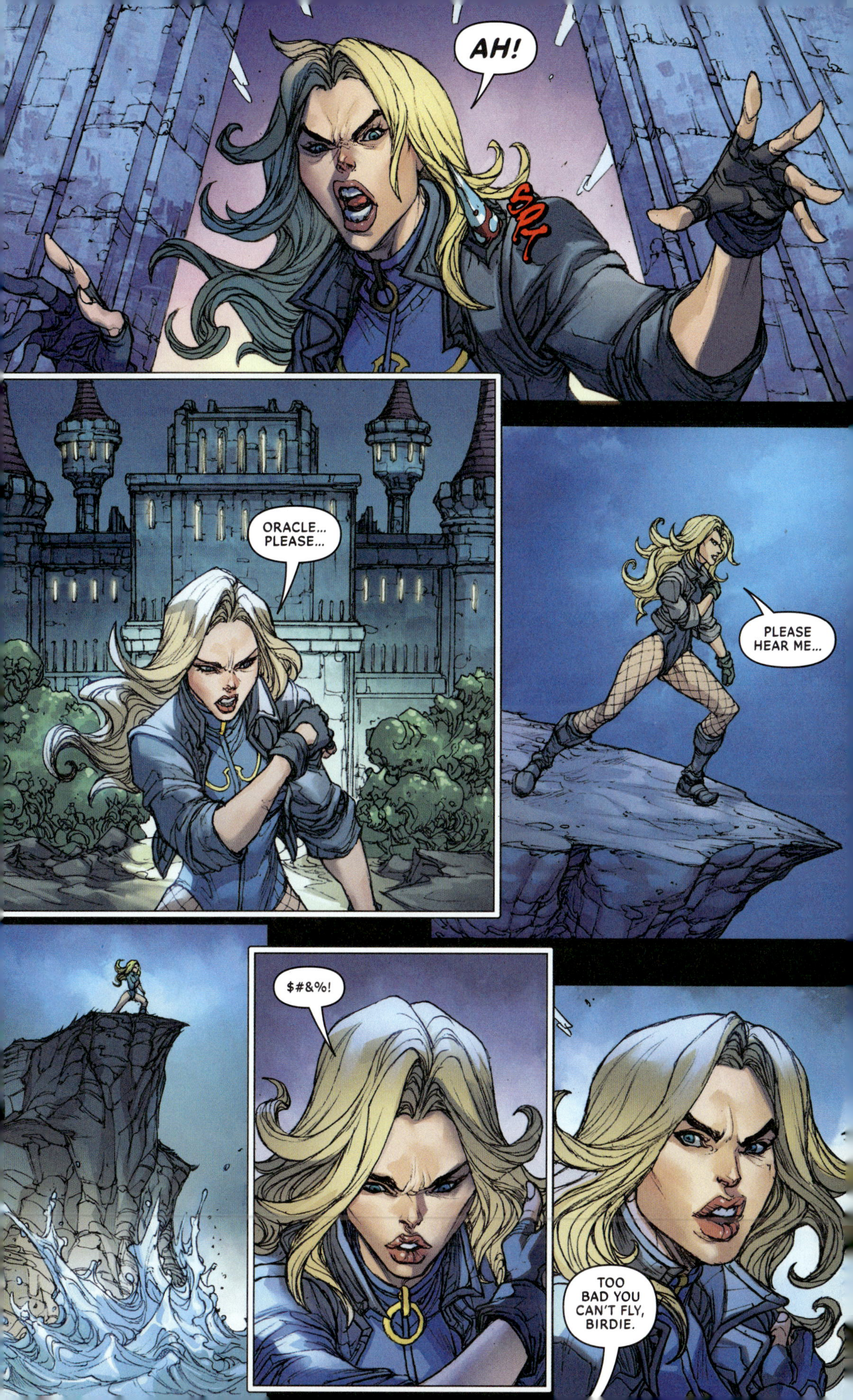
AH!
ORACLE... PLEASE...
PLEASE HEAR ME...
$#&%!
TOO BAD YOU CAN'T FLY, BIRDIE.

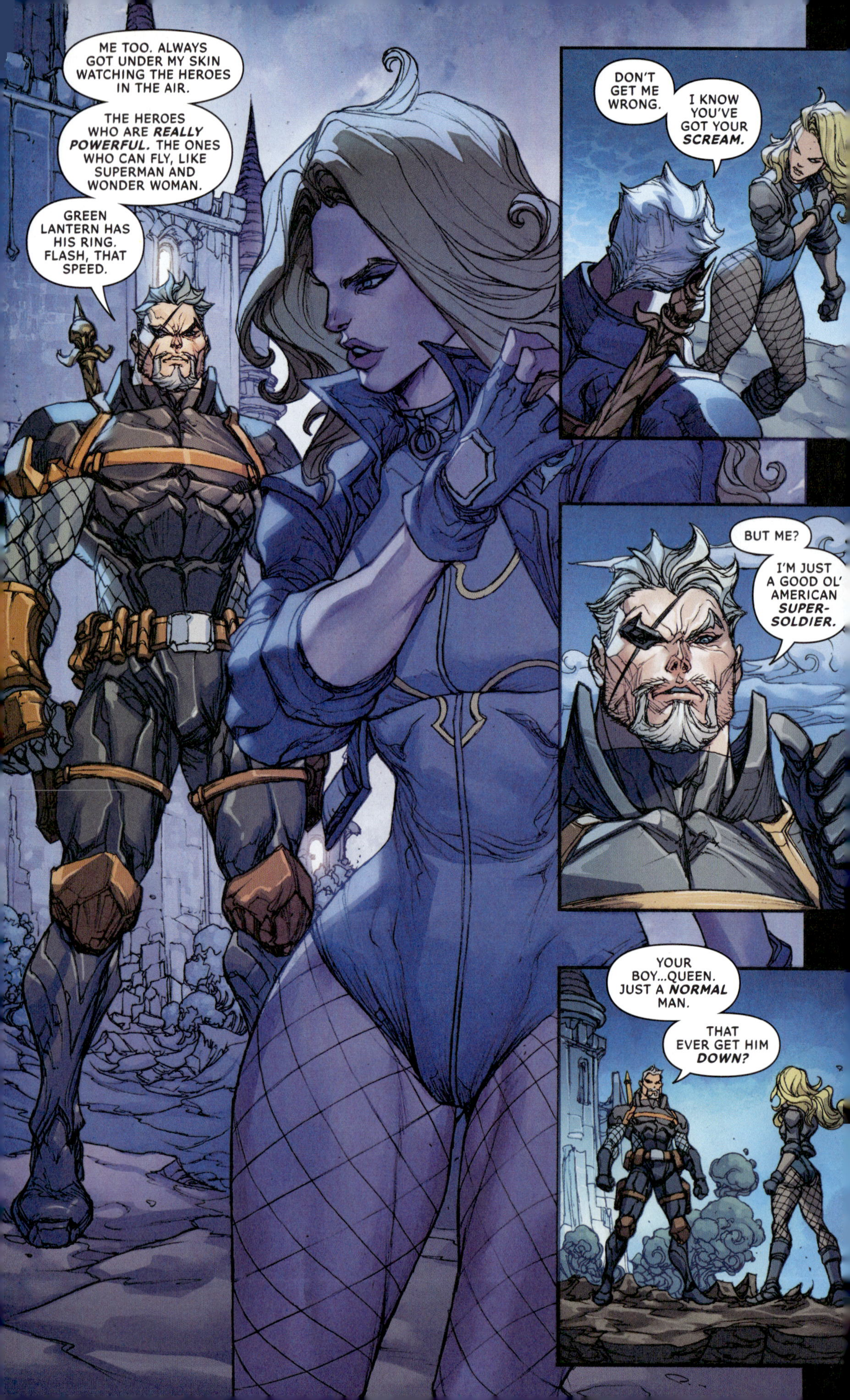

ME TOO. ALWAYS GOT UNDER MY SKIN WATCHING THE HEROES IN THE AIR.
THE HEROES WHO ARE ***REALLY POWERFUL.*** THE ONES WHO CAN FLY, LIKE SUPERMAN AND WONDER WOMAN.
GREEN LANTERN HAS HIS RING. FLASH, THAT SPEED.
DON'T GET ME WRONG.
I KNOW YOU'VE GOT YOUR ***SCREAM.***
BUT ME?
I'M JUST A GOOD OL' AMERICAN ***SUPER-SOLDIER.***
YOUR BOY...QUEEN. JUST A ***NORMAL*** MAN.
THAT EVER GET HIM ***DOWN?***

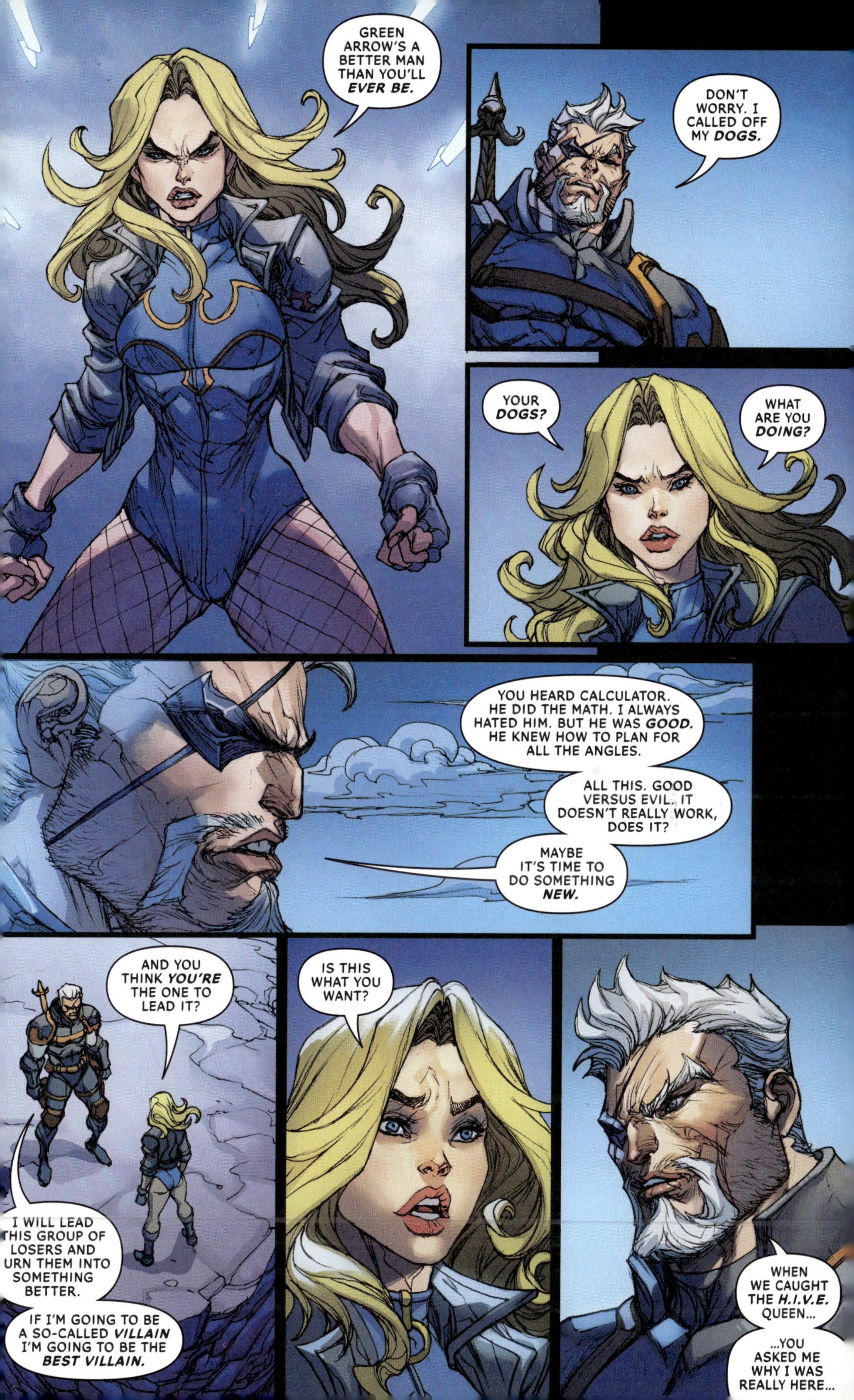
GREEN ARROW'S A BETTER MAN THAN YOU'LL EVER BE.
DON'T WORRY. I CALLED OFF MY DOGS.
YOUR DOGS?
WHAT ARE YOU DOING?
YOU HEARD CALCULATOR. HE DID THE MATH. I ALWAYS HATED HIM. BUT HE WAS GOOD. HE KNEW HOW TO PLAN FOR ALL THE ANGLES.
ALL THIS. GOOD VERSUS EVIL. IT DOESN'T REALLY WORK, DOES IT?
MAYBE IT'S TIME TO DO SOMETHING NEW.
AND YOU THINK YOU'RE THE ONE TO LEAD IT?
I WILL LEAD THIS GROUP OF LOSERS AND URN THEM INTO SOMETHING BETTER.
IF I'M GOING TO BE A SO-CALLED VILLAIN I'M GOING TO BE THE BEST VILLAIN.
IS THIS WHAT YOU WANT?
WHEN WE CAUGHT THE H.I.V.E. QUEEN...
...YOU ASKED ME WHY I WAS REALLY HERE...

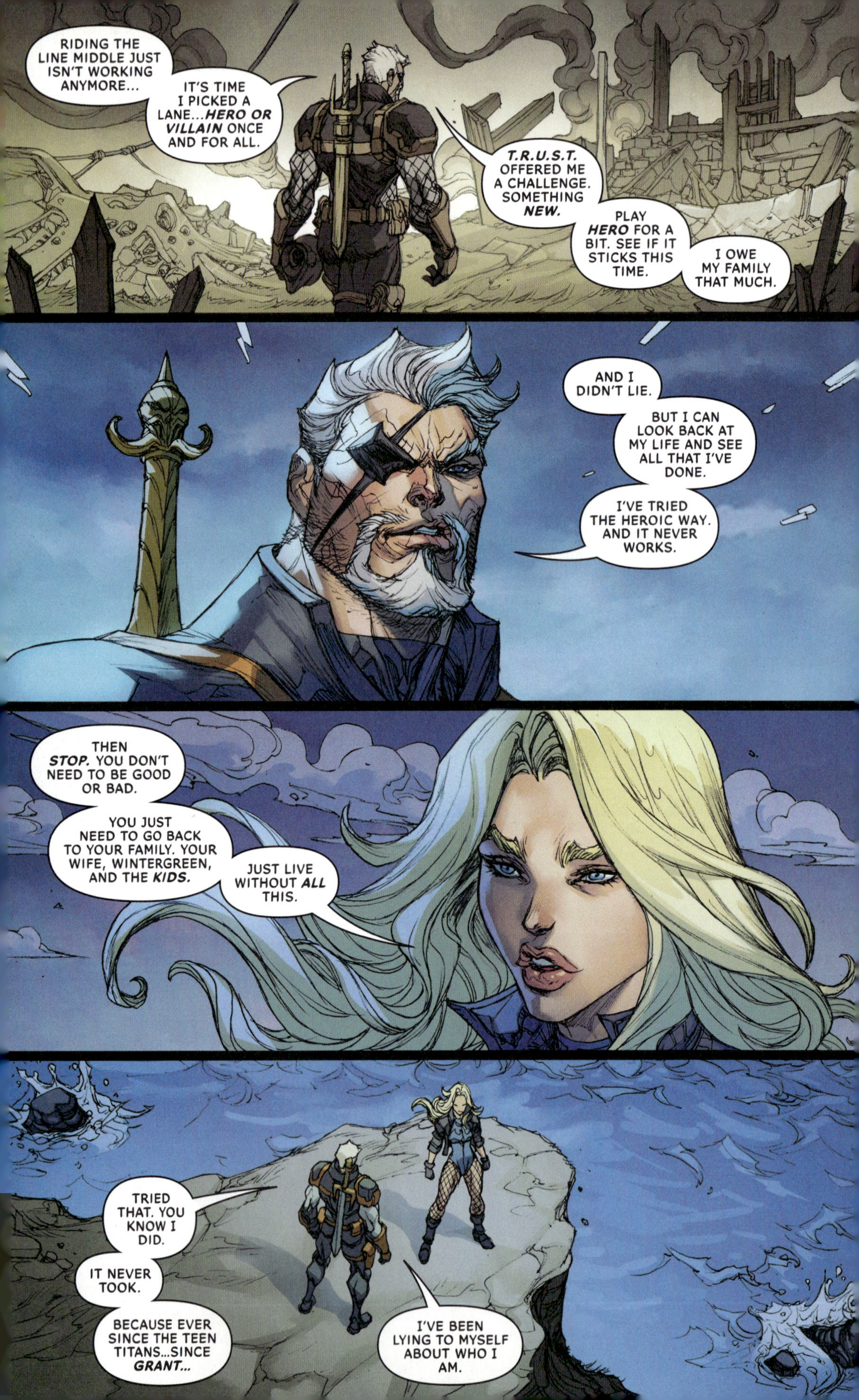
RIDING THE LINE MIDDLE JUST ISN'T WORKING ANYMORE...
IT'S TIME I PICKED A LANE...**HERO OR VILLAIN** ONCE AND FOR ALL.
T.R.U.S.T. OFFERED ME A CHALLENGE. SOMETHING ***NEW.***
PLAY ***HERO*** FOR A BIT. SEE IF IT STICKS THIS TIME.
I OWE MY FAMILY THAT MUCH.
AND I DIDN'T LIE.
BUT I CAN LOOK BACK AT MY LIFE AND SEE ALL THAT I'VE DONE.
I'VE TRIED THE HEROIC WAY. AND IT NEVER WORKS.
THEN ***STOP.*** YOU DON'T NEED TO BE GOOD OR BAD.
YOU JUST NEED TO GO BACK TO YOUR FAMILY. YOUR WIFE, WINTERGREEN, AND THE ***KIDS.***
JUST LIVE WITHOUT ***ALL*** THIS.
TRIED THAT. YOU KNOW I DID.
IT NEVER TOOK.
BECAUSE EVER SINCE THE TEEN TITANS...SINCE ***GRANT...***
I'VE BEEN LYING TO MYSELF ABOUT WHO I AM.

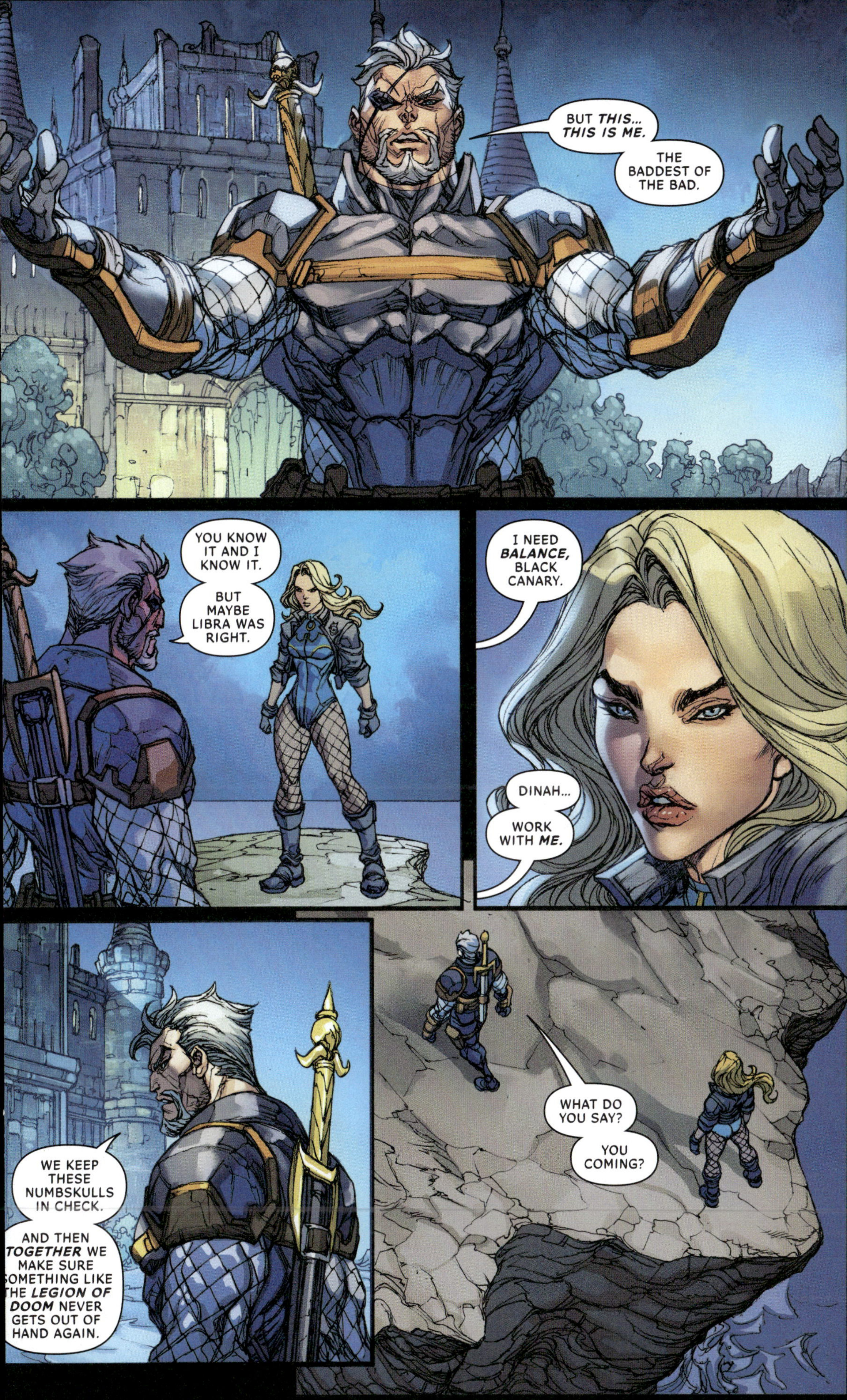

BUT *THIS*... *THIS IS ME.*
THE BADDEST OF THE BAD.
YOU KNOW IT AND I KNOW IT.
BUT MAYBE LIBRA WAS RIGHT.
I NEED *BALANCE,* BLACK CANARY.
DINAH...
WORK WITH *ME.*
WE KEEP THESE NUMBSKULLS IN CHECK.
AND THEN *TOGETHER* WE MAKE SURE SOMETHING LIKE THE *LEGION OF DOOM* NEVER GETS OUT OF HAND AGAIN.
WHAT DO YOU SAY?
YOU COMING?

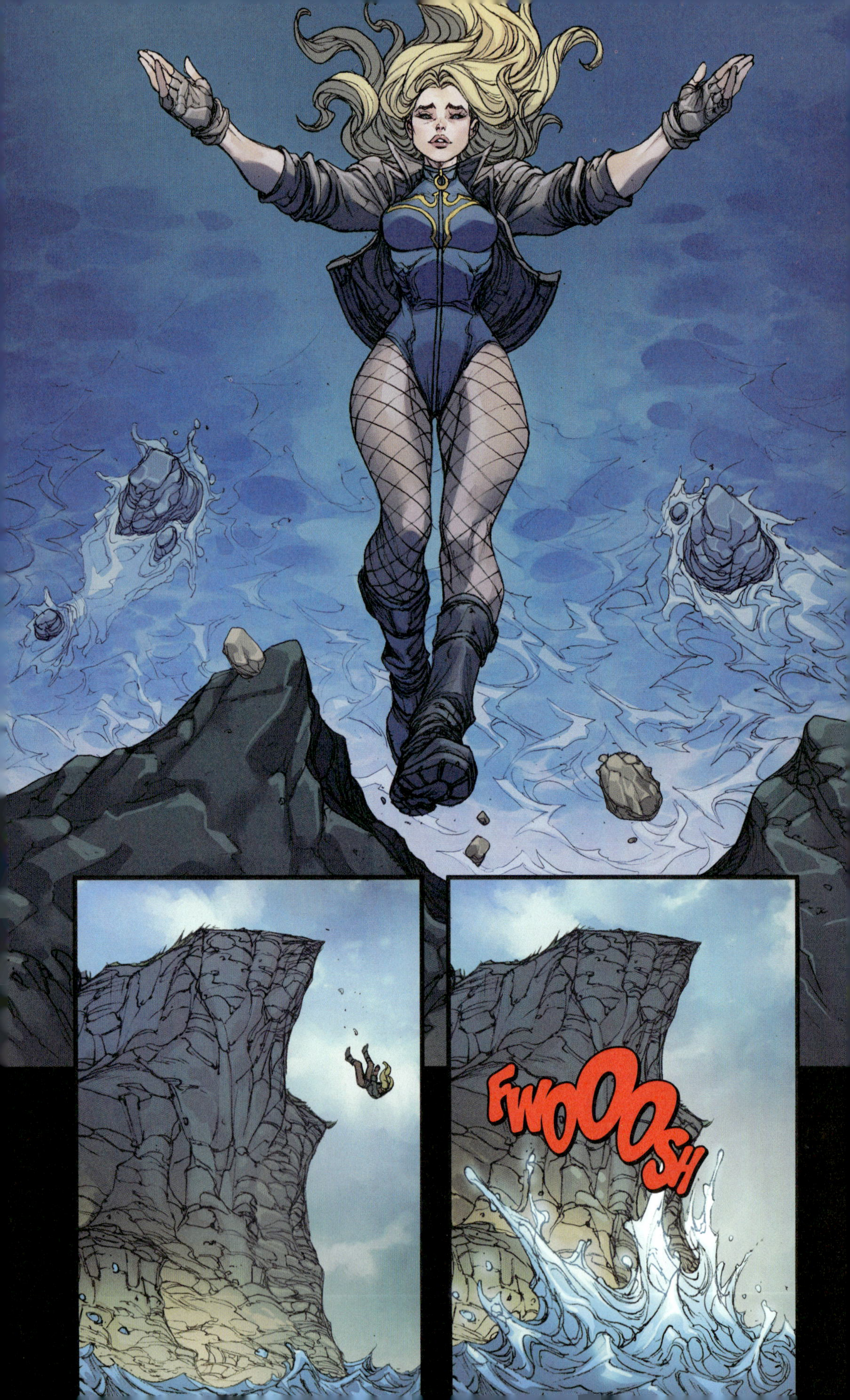
FWOOOSH

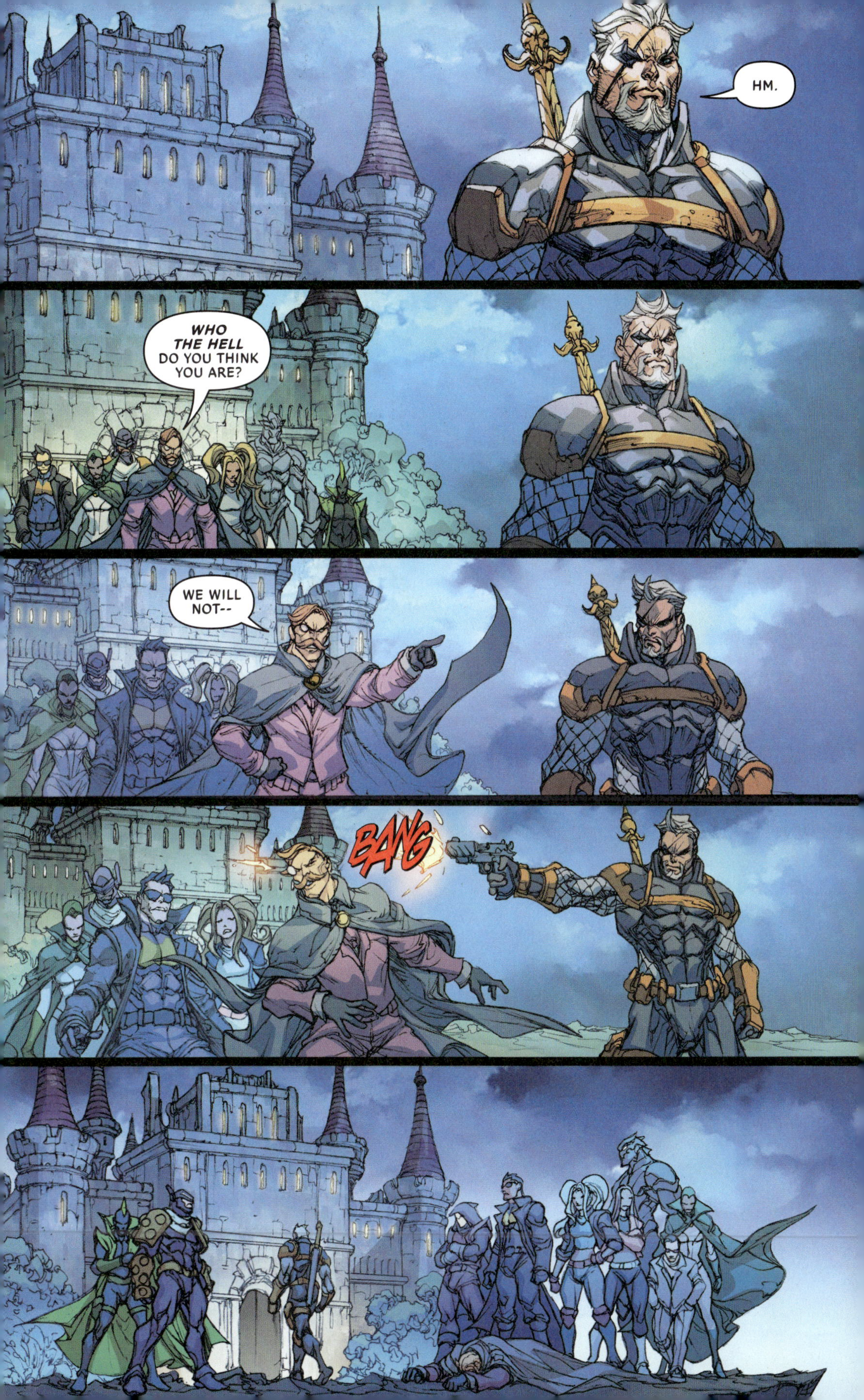
HM.
WHO THE HELL DO YOU THINK YOU ARE?
WE WILL NOT--
BANG

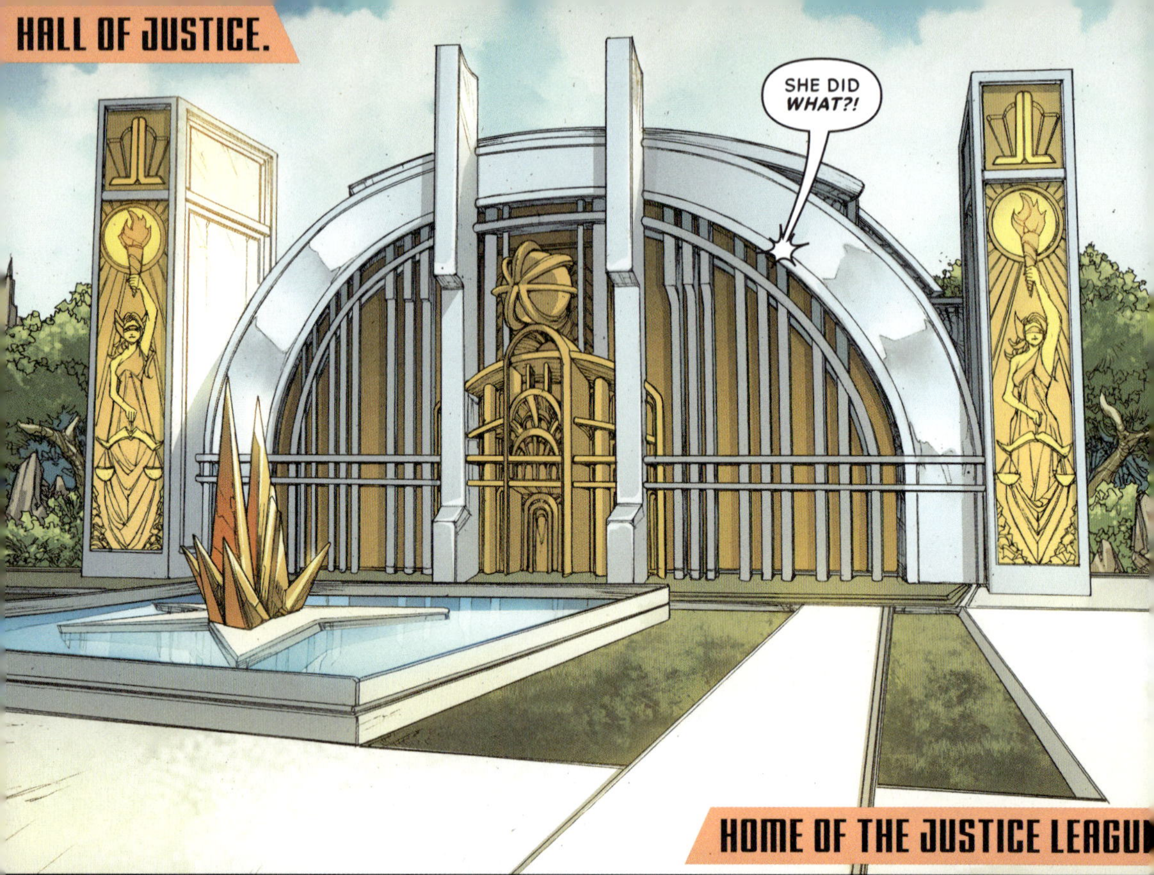
HALL OF JUSTICE.
SHE DID WHAT?!
HOME OF THE JUSTICE LEAGU

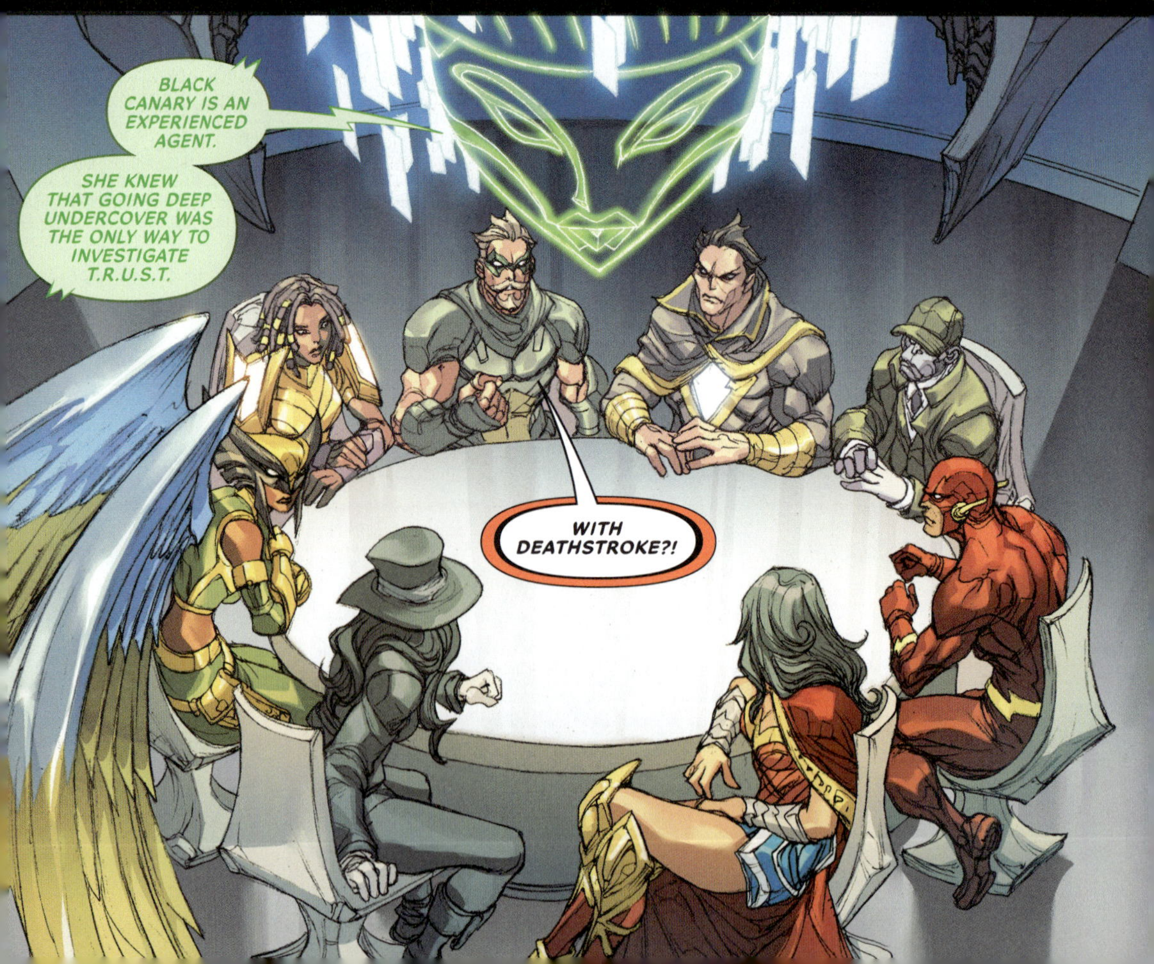
BLACK CANARY IS AN EXPERIENCED AGENT.
SHE KNEW THAT GOING DEEP UNDERCOVER WAS THE ONLY WAY TO INVESTIGATE T.R.U.S.T.
WITH DEATHSTROKE?!

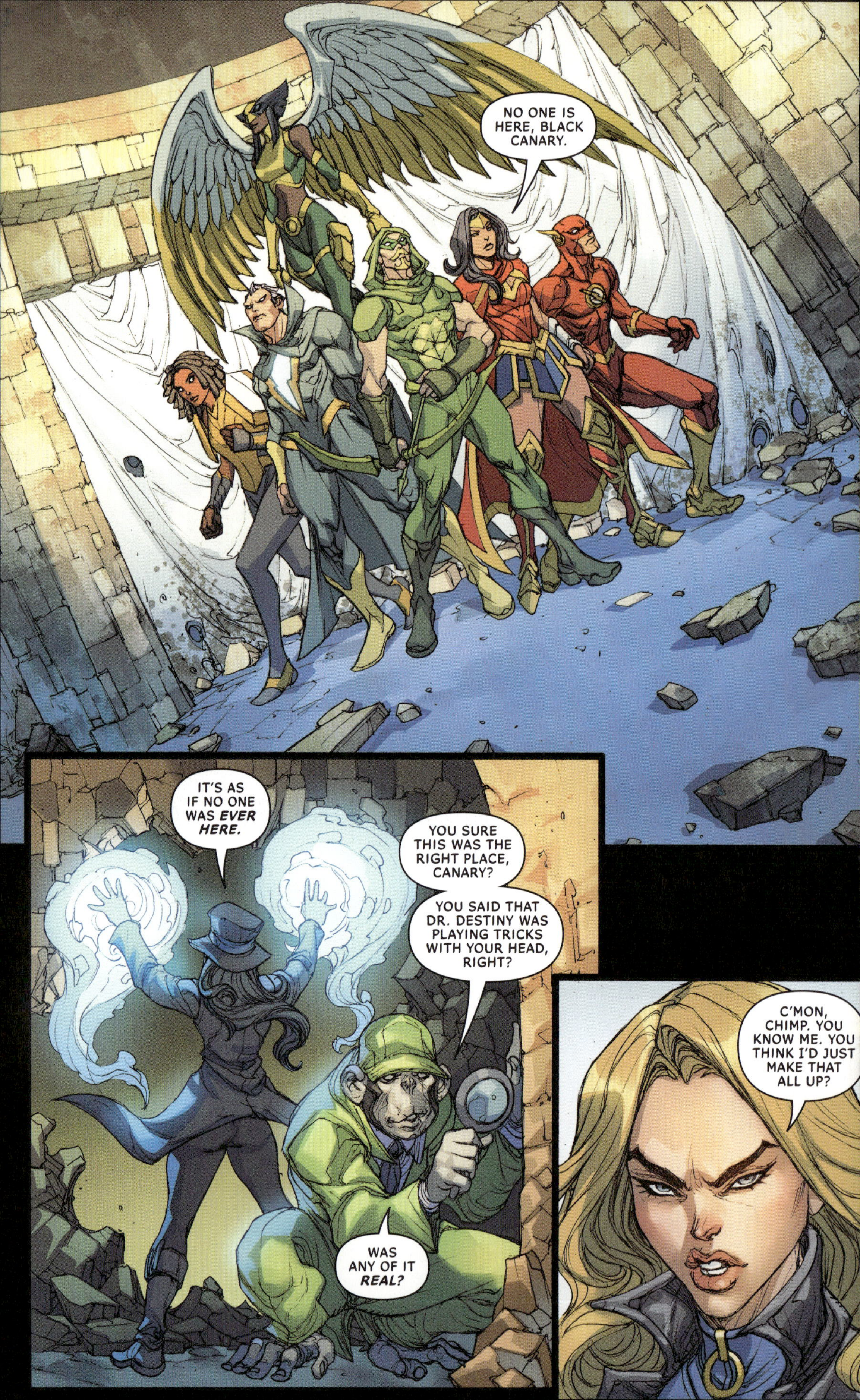
NO ONE IS HERE, BLACK CANARY.
IT'S AS IF NO ONE WAS *EVER HERE.*
YOU SURE THIS WAS THE RIGHT PLACE, CANARY?
YOU SAID THAT DR. DESTINY WAS PLAYING TRICKS WITH YOUR HEAD, RIGHT?
WAS ANY OF IT *REAL?*
C'MON, CHIMP. YOU KNOW ME. YOU THINK I'D JUST MAKE THAT ALL UP?

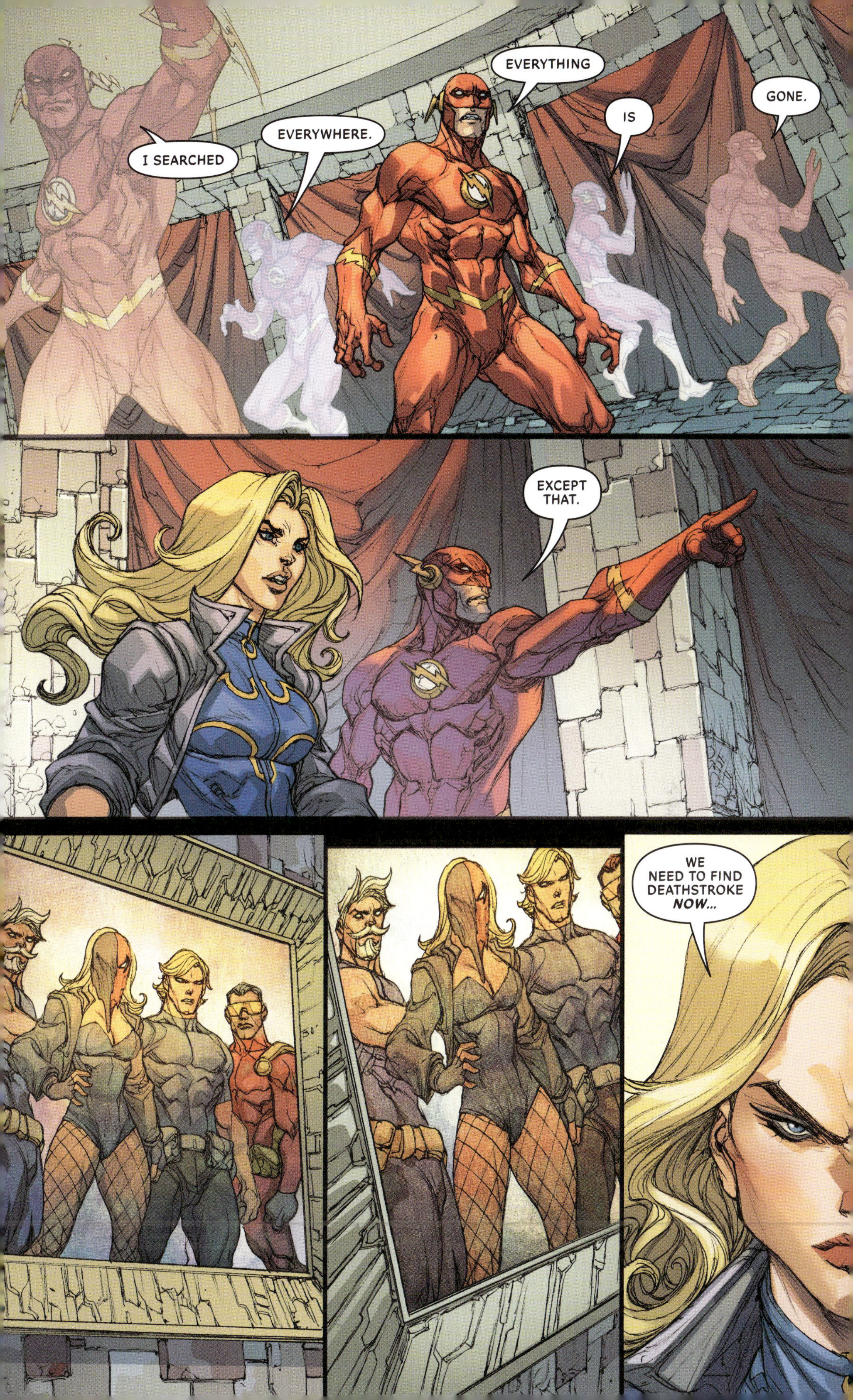
I SEARCHED
EVERYWHERE.
EVERYTHING
IS
GONE.
EXCEPT THAT.
WE NEED TO FIND DEATHSTROKE *NOW...*

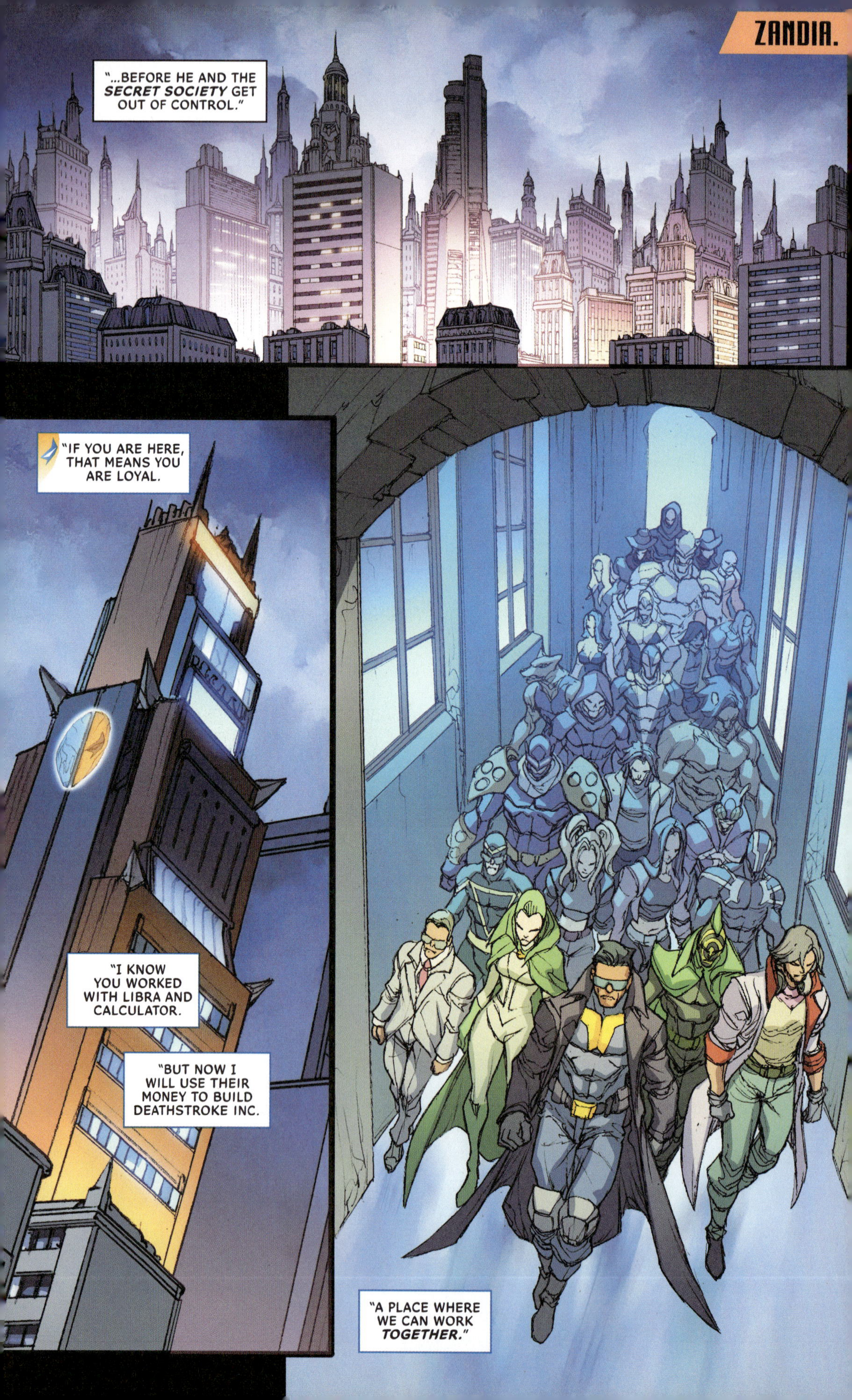
ZANDIA.
"...BEFORE HE AND THE *SECRET SOCIETY* GET OUT OF CONTROL."
"IF YOU ARE HERE, THAT MEANS YOU ARE LOYAL.
"I KNOW YOU WORKED WITH LIBRA AND CALCULATOR.
"BUT NOW I WILL USE THEIR MONEY TO BUILD DEATHSTROKE INC.
"A PLACE WHERE WE CAN WORK *TOGETHER*."

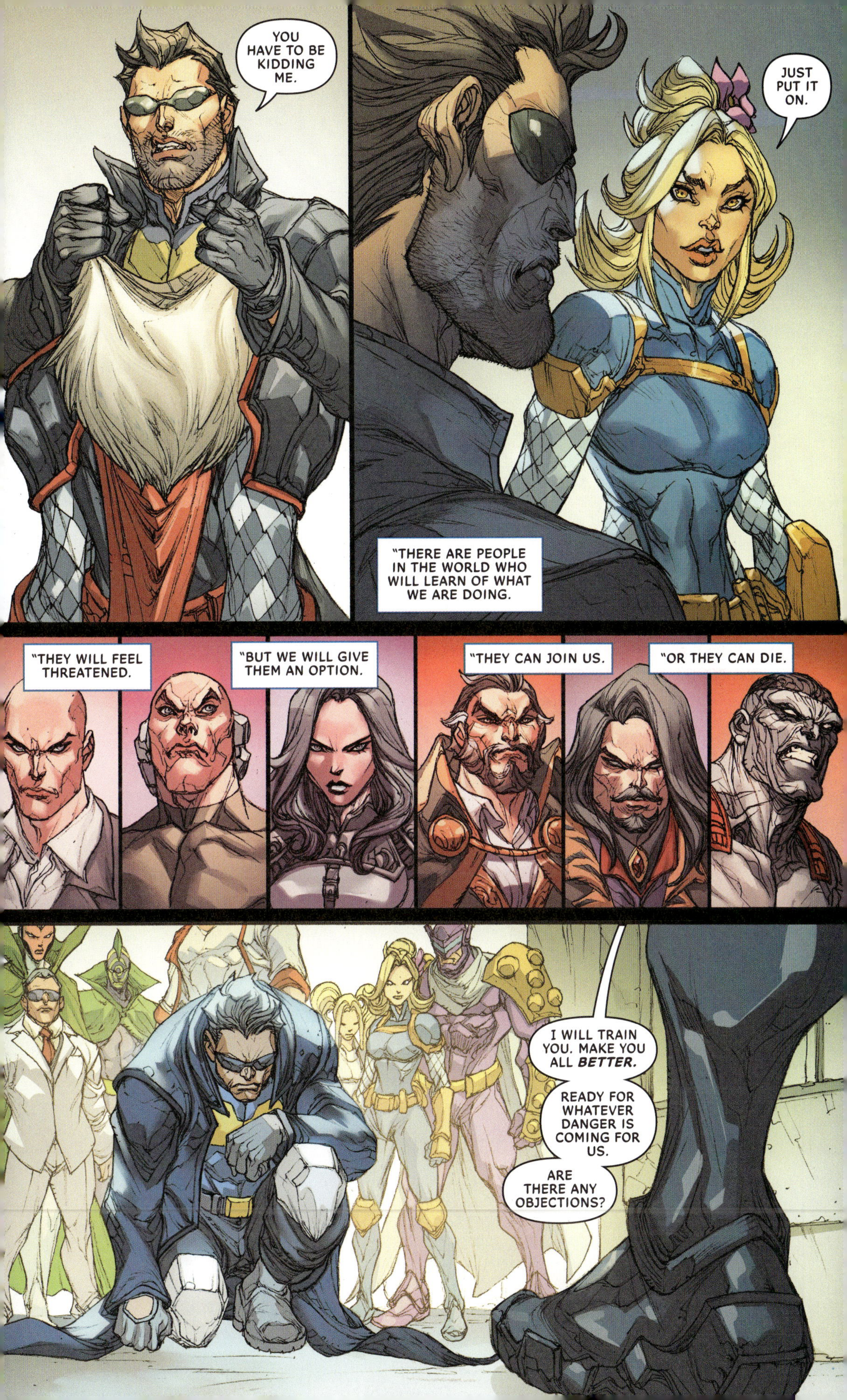
YOU HAVE TO BE KIDDING ME.
JUST PUT IT ON.
"THERE ARE PEOPLE IN THE WORLD WHO WILL LEARN OF WHAT WE ARE DOING.
"THEY WILL FEEL THREATENED.
"BUT WE WILL GIVE THEM AN OPTION.
"THEY CAN JOIN US.
"OR THEY CAN DIE.
I WILL TRAIN YOU. MAKE YOU ALL *BETTER.*
READY FOR WHATEVER DANGER IS COMING FOR US.
ARE THERE ANY OBJECTIONS?

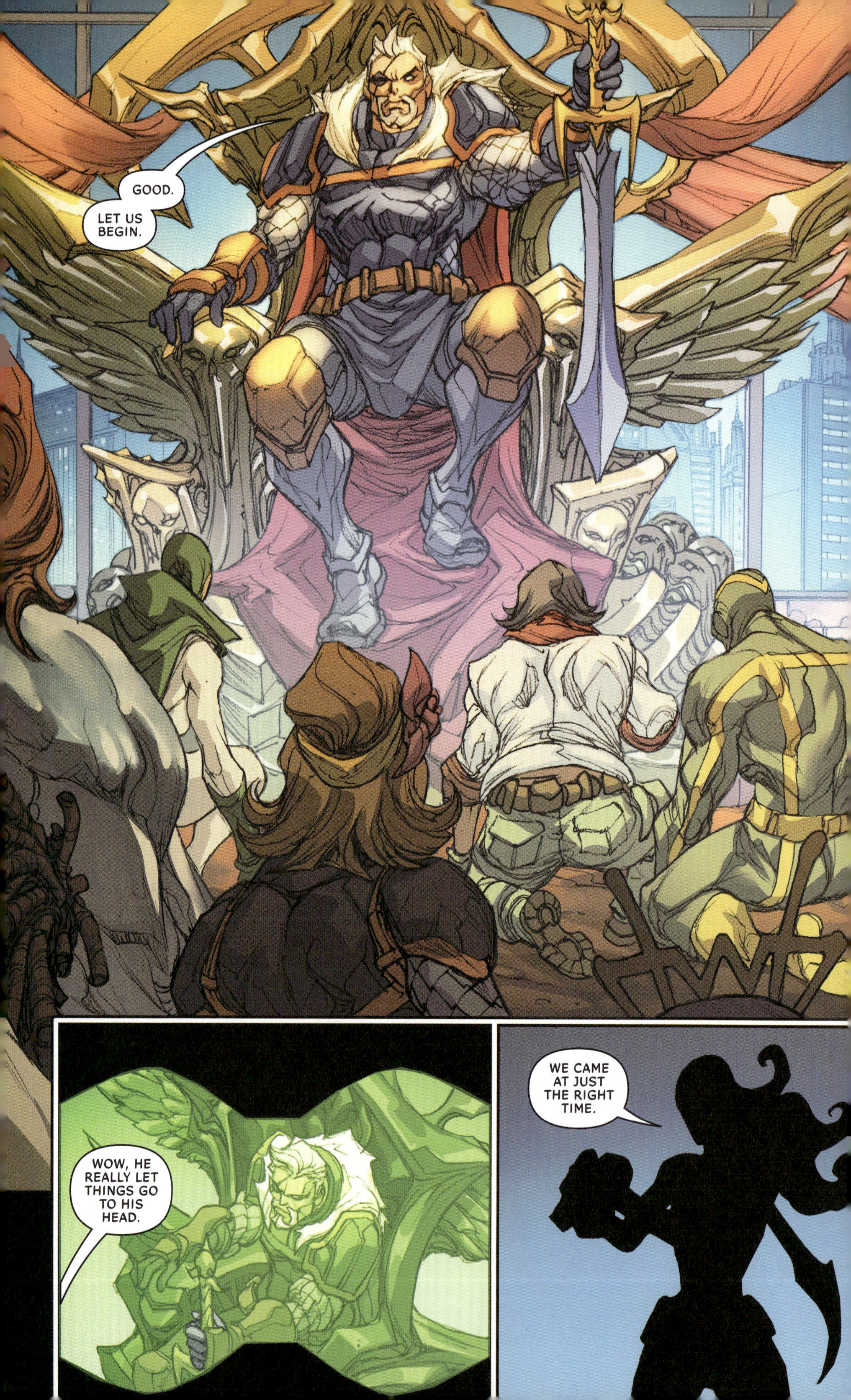
GOOD.
LET US BEGIN.
WOW, HE REALLY LET THINGS GO TO HIS HEAD.
WE CAME AT JUST THE RIGHT TIME.

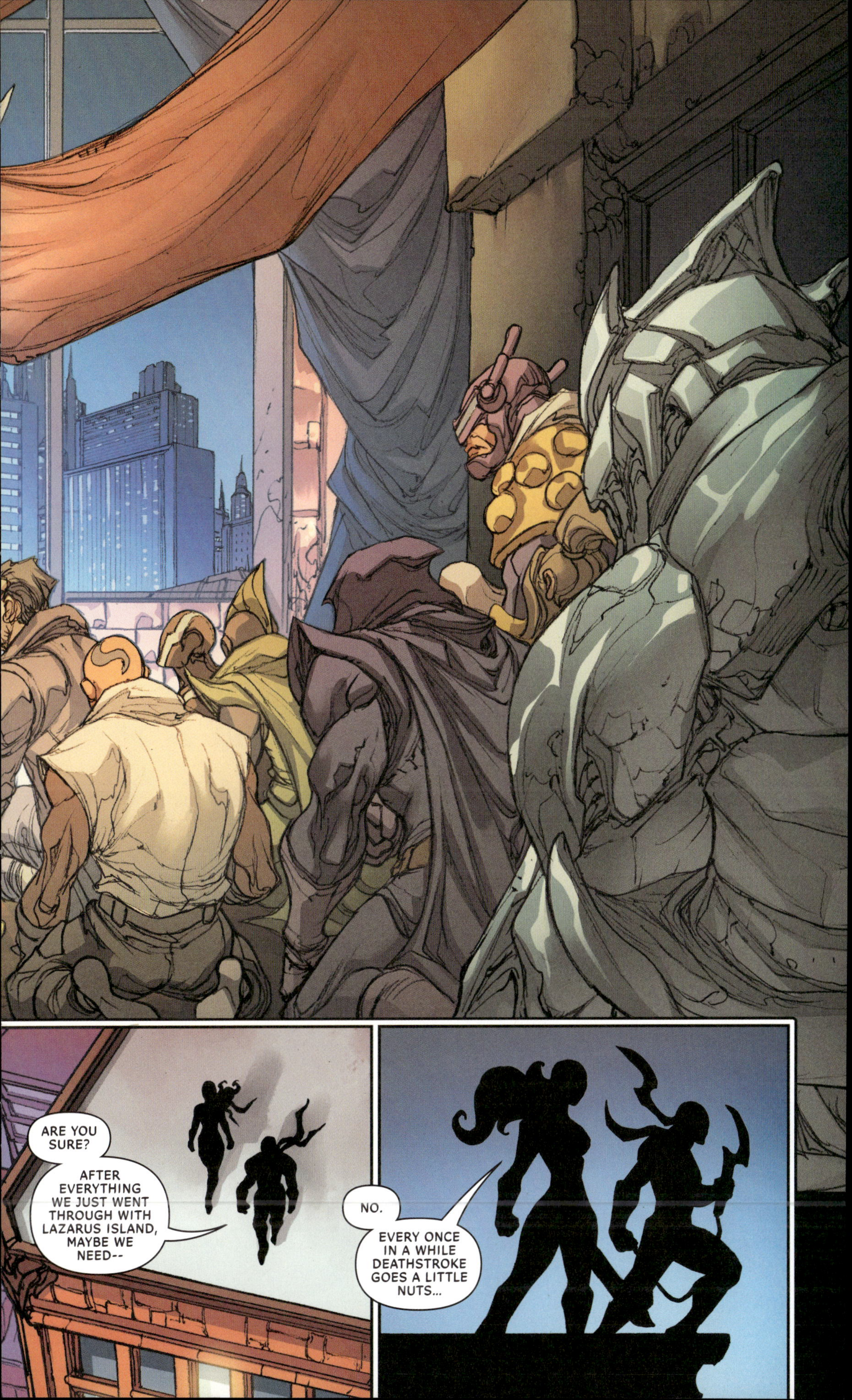
ARE YOU SURE?
AFTER EVERYTHING WE JUST WENT THROUGH WITH LAZARUS ISLAND, MAYBE WE NEED--
NO.
EVERY ONCE IN A WHILE DEATHSTROKE GOES A LITTLE NUTS...

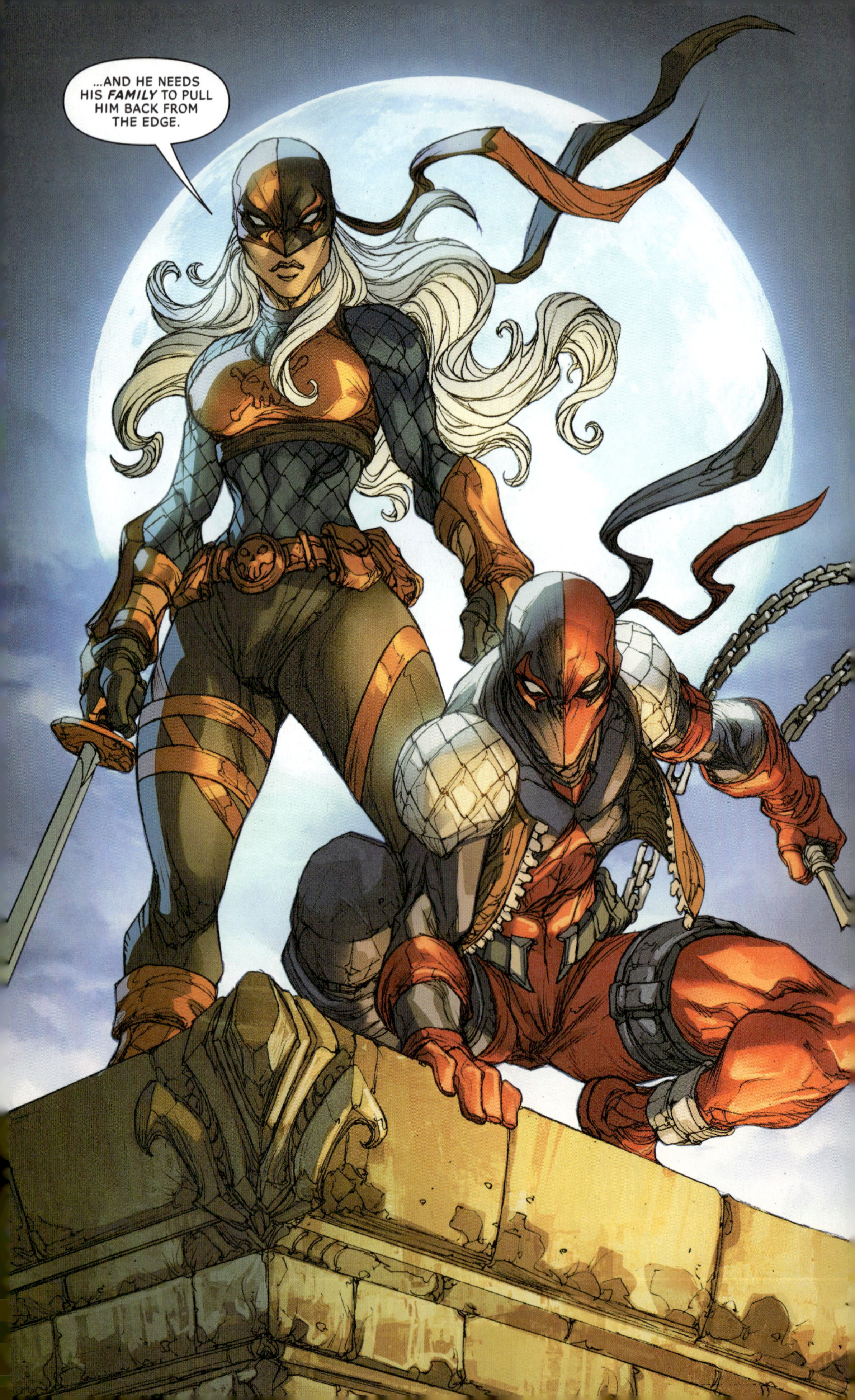
...AND HE NEEDS HIS FAMILY TO PULL HIM BACK FROM THE EDGE.

DEATHSTROKE INC. #7
cover art by HOWARD PORTER & HI-FI

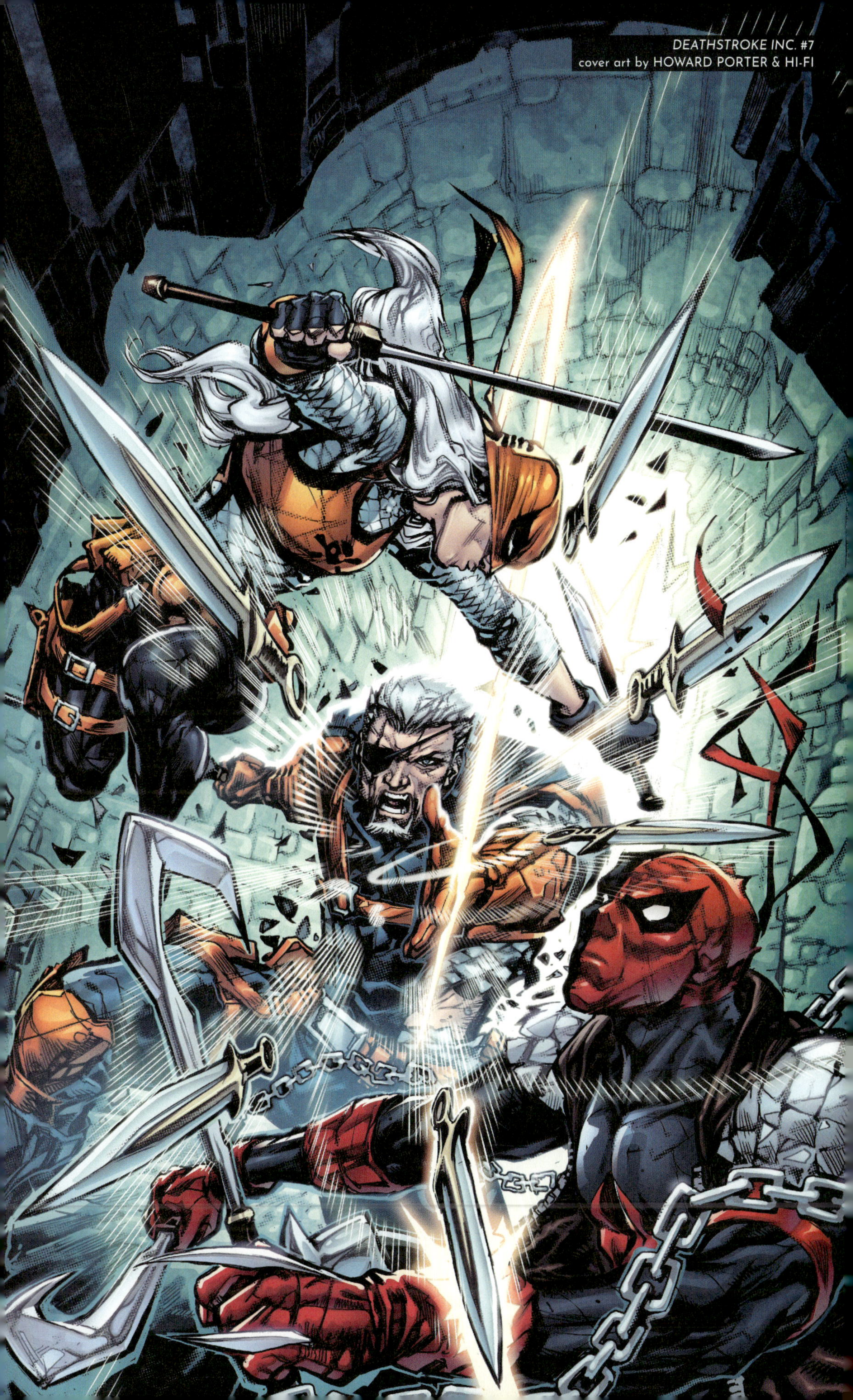

DEATHSTROKE INC. #7
variant cover art by IVAN TAO

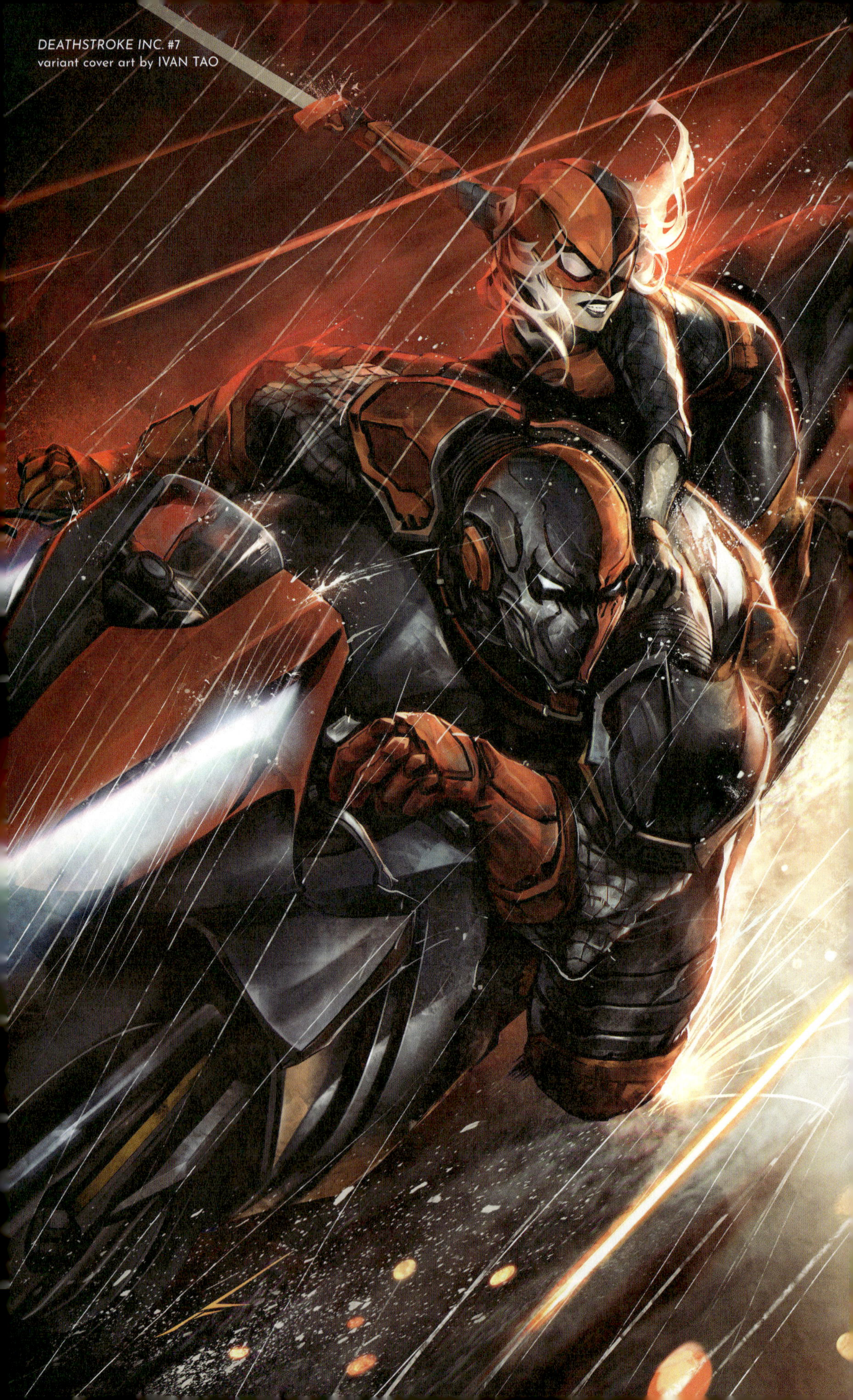

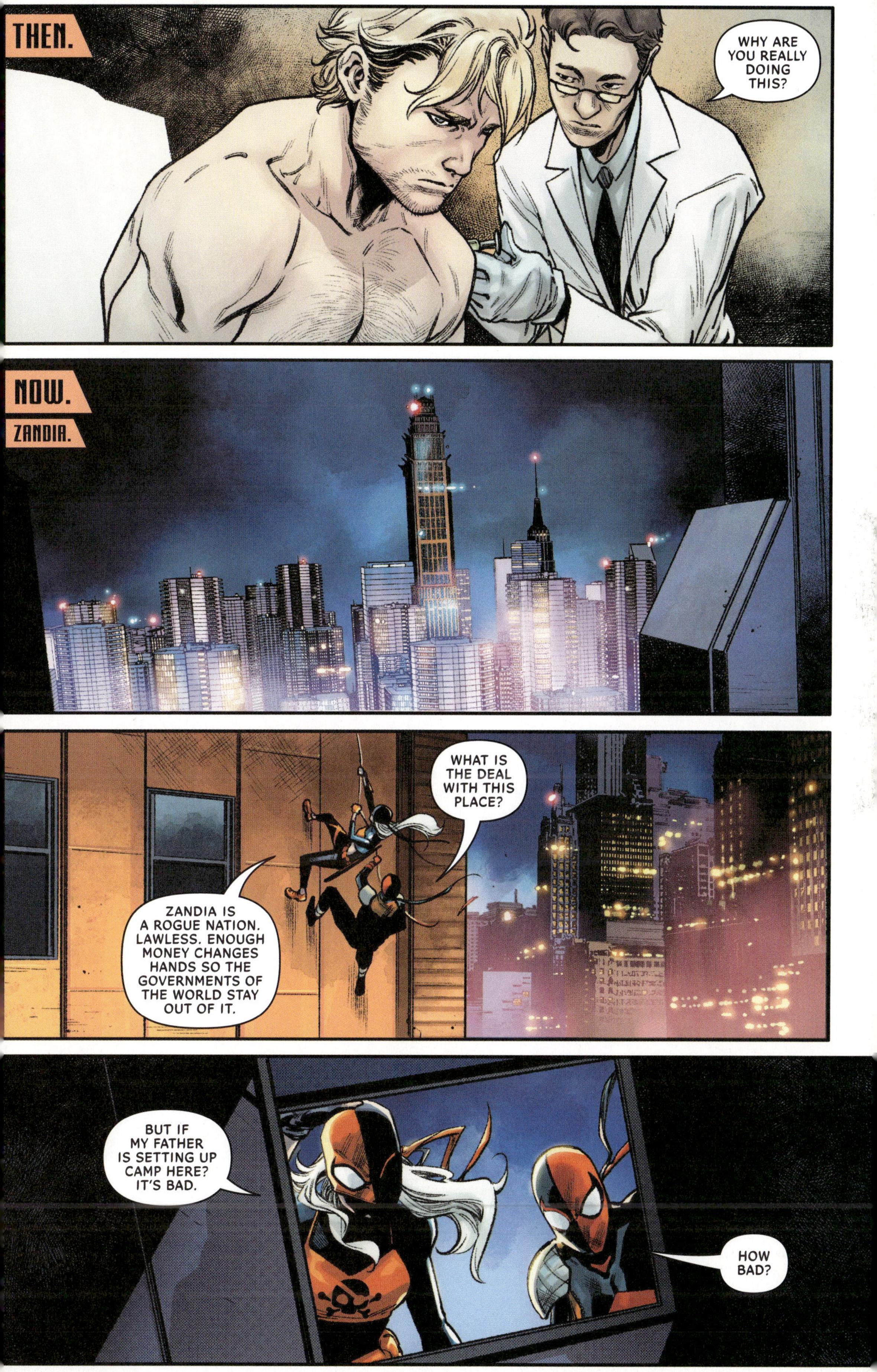
THEN.
WHY ARE YOU REALLY DOING THIS?
NOW.
ZANDIA.
WHAT IS THE DEAL WITH THIS PLACE?
ZANDIA IS A ROGUE NATION. LAWLESS. ENOUGH MONEY CHANGES HANDS SO THE GOVERNMENTS OF THE WORLD STAY OUT OF IT.
BUT IF MY FATHER IS SETTING UP CAMP HERE? IT'S BAD.
HOW BAD?

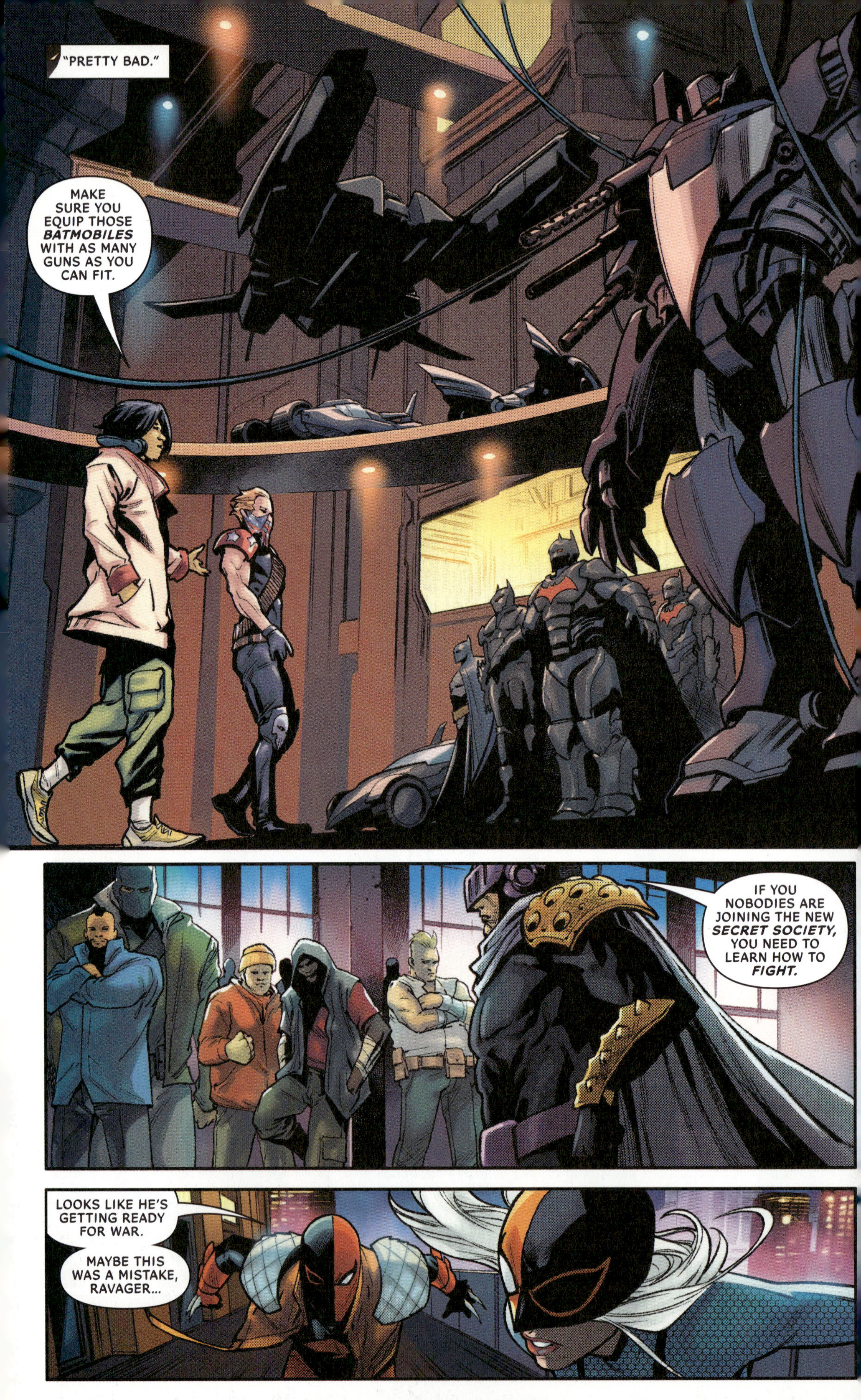
"PRETTY BAD."
MAKE SURE YOU EQUIP THOSE *BATMOBILES* WITH AS MANY GUNS AS YOU CAN FIT.
IF YOU NOBODIES ARE JOINING THE NEW *SECRET SOCIETY,* YOU NEED TO LEARN HOW TO *FIGHT.*
LOOKS LIKE HE'S GETTING READY FOR WAR.
MAYBE THIS WAS A MISTAKE, RAVAGER...

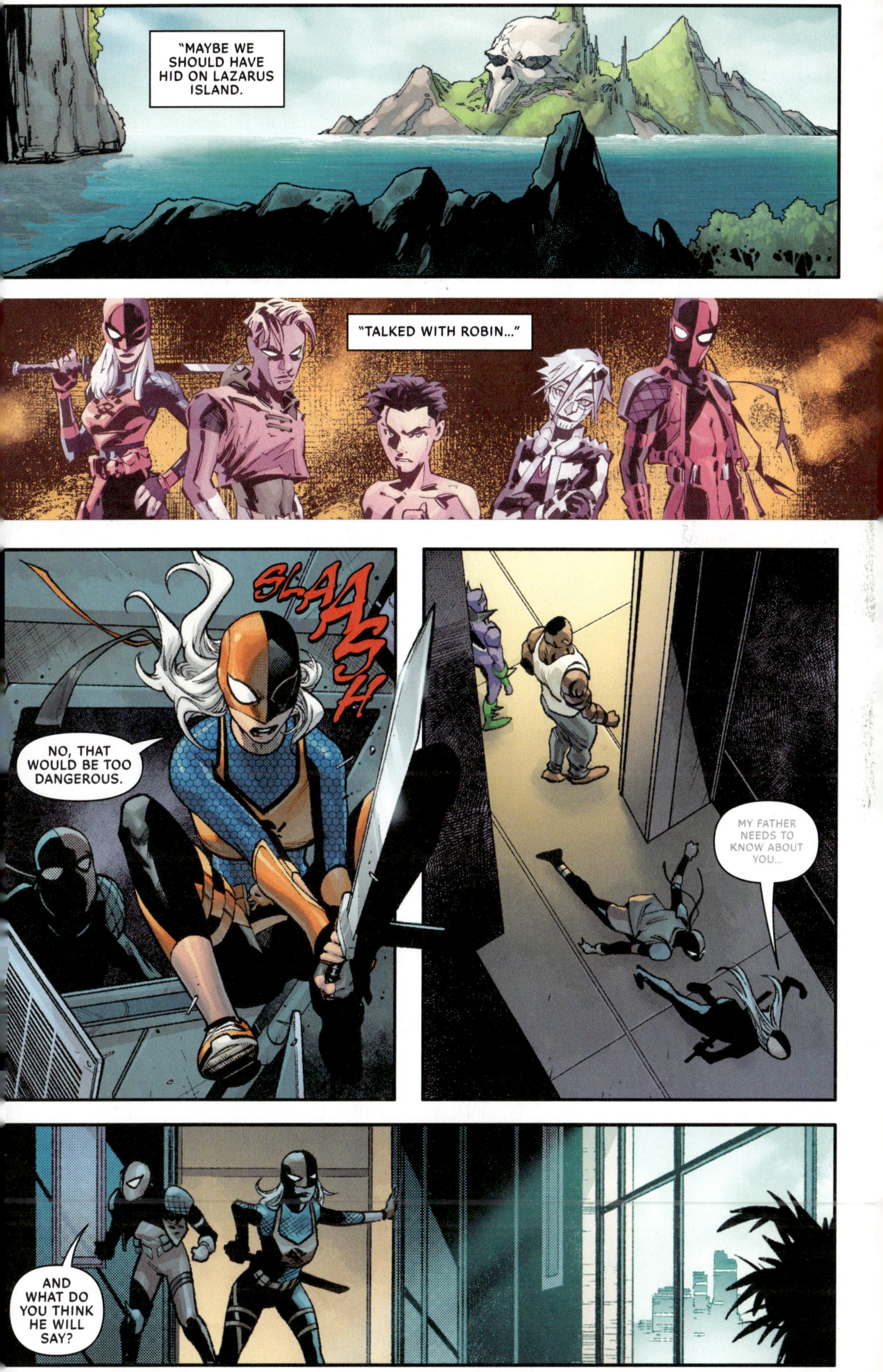
"MAYBE WE SHOULD HAVE HID ON LAZARUS ISLAND.
"TALKED WITH ROBIN..."
SLAAASH
NO, THAT WOULD BE TOO DANGEROUS.
MY FATHER NEEDS TO KNOW ABOUT YOU...
AND WHAT DO YOU THINK HE WILL SAY?

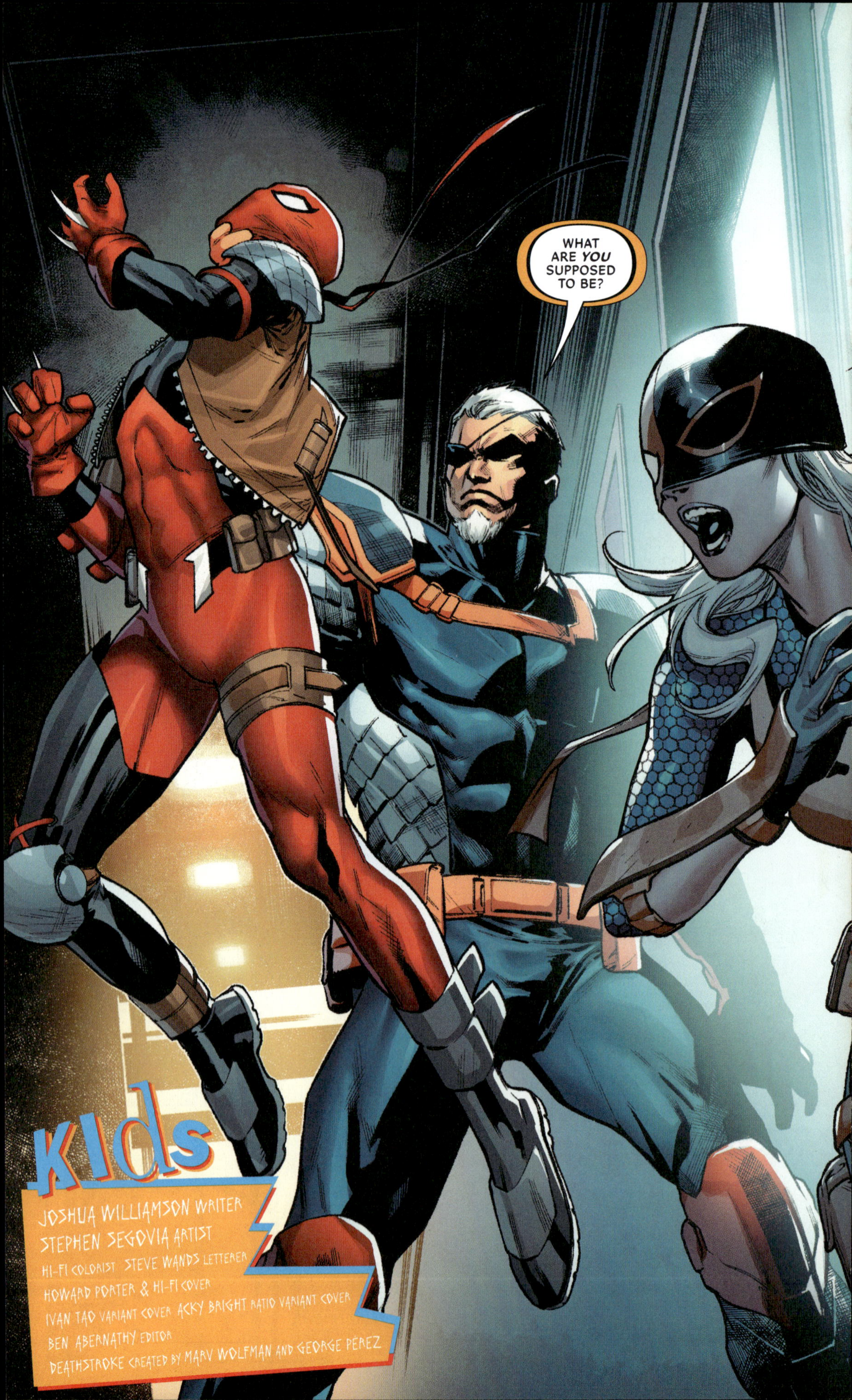
WHAT ARE YOU SUPPOSED TO BE?
KIDS
JOSHUA WILLIAMSON WRITER
STEPHEN SEGOVIA ARTIST
HI-FI COLORIST STEVE WANDS LETTERER
HOWARD PORTER & HI-FI COVER
IVAN TAO VARIANT COVER ACKY BRIGHT RATIO VARIANT COVER
BEN ABERNATHY EDITOR
DEATHSTROKE CREATED BY MARV WOLFMAN AND GEORGE PÉREZ

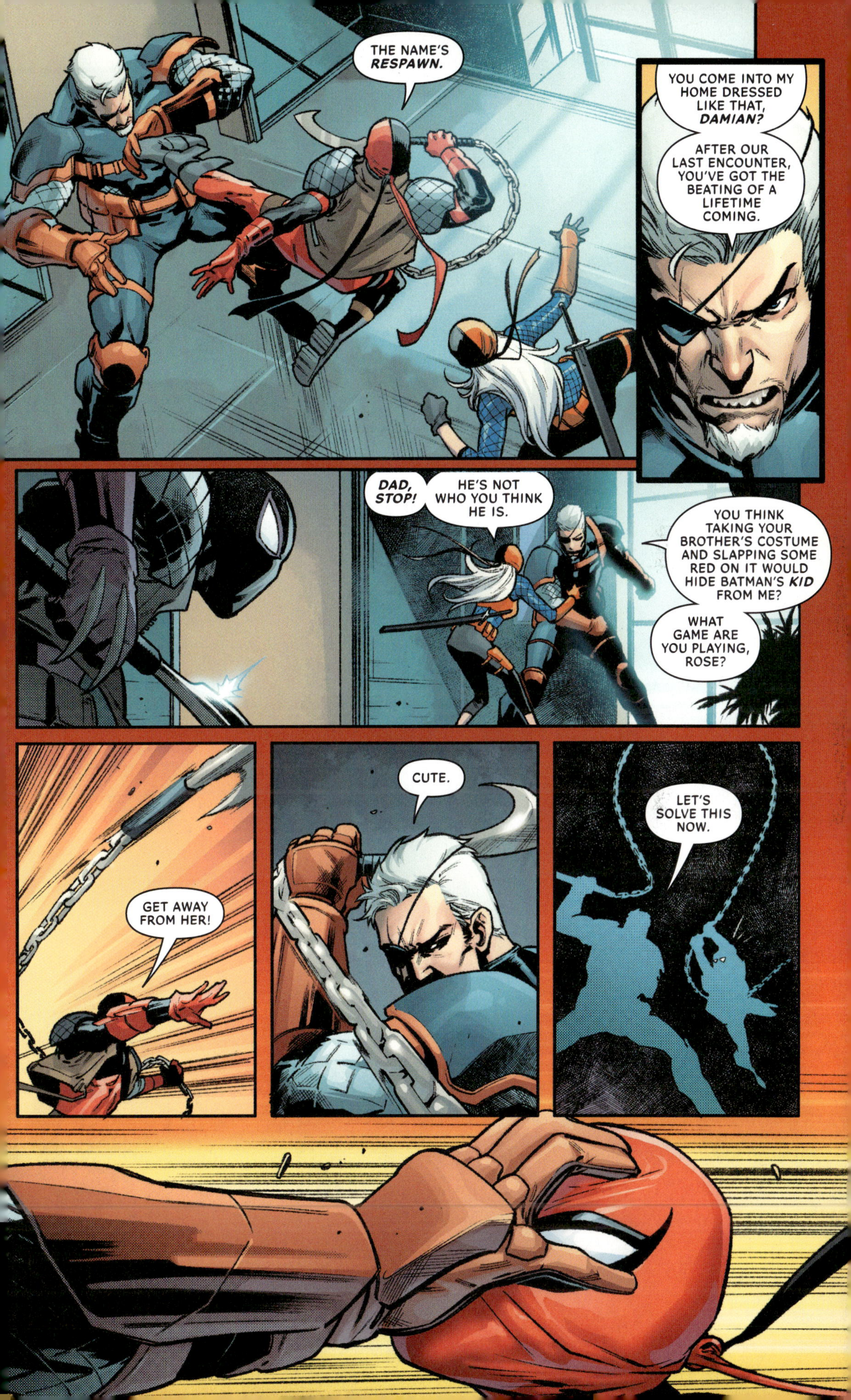
THE NAME'S *RESPAWN.*
YOU COME INTO MY HOME DRESSED LIKE THAT, *DAMIAN?*
AFTER OUR LAST ENCOUNTER, YOU'VE GOT THE BEATING OF A LIFETIME COMING.
DAD, STOP!
HE'S NOT WHO YOU THINK HE IS.
YOU THINK TAKING YOUR BROTHER'S COSTUME AND SLAPPING SOME RED ON IT WOULD HIDE BATMAN'S *KID* FROM ME?
WHAT GAME ARE YOU PLAYING, ROSE?
GET AWAY FROM HER!
CUTE.
LET'S SOLVE THIS NOW.

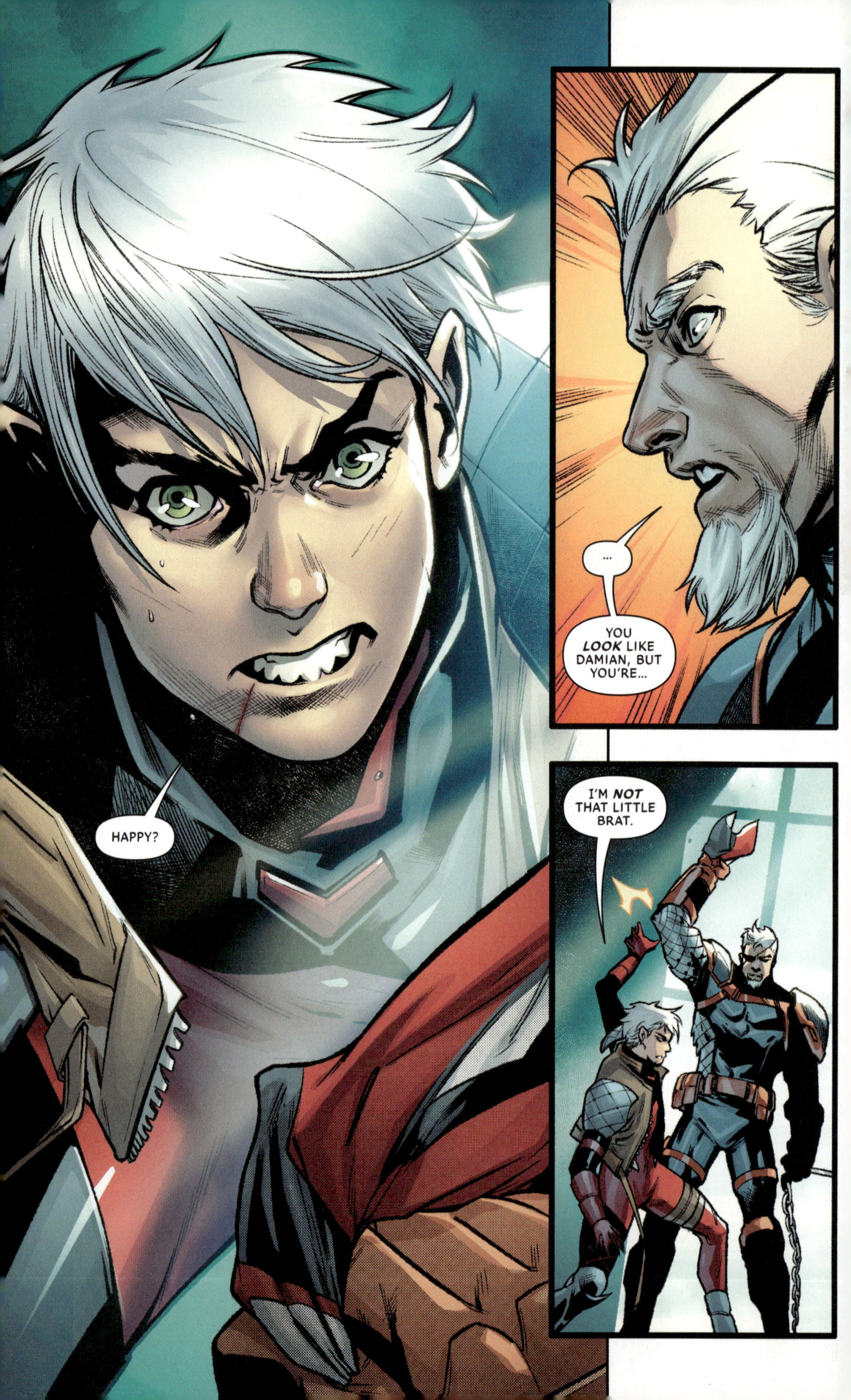
HAPPY?
...
YOU LOOK LIKE DAMIAN, BUT YOU'RE...
I'M NOT THAT LITTLE BRAT.

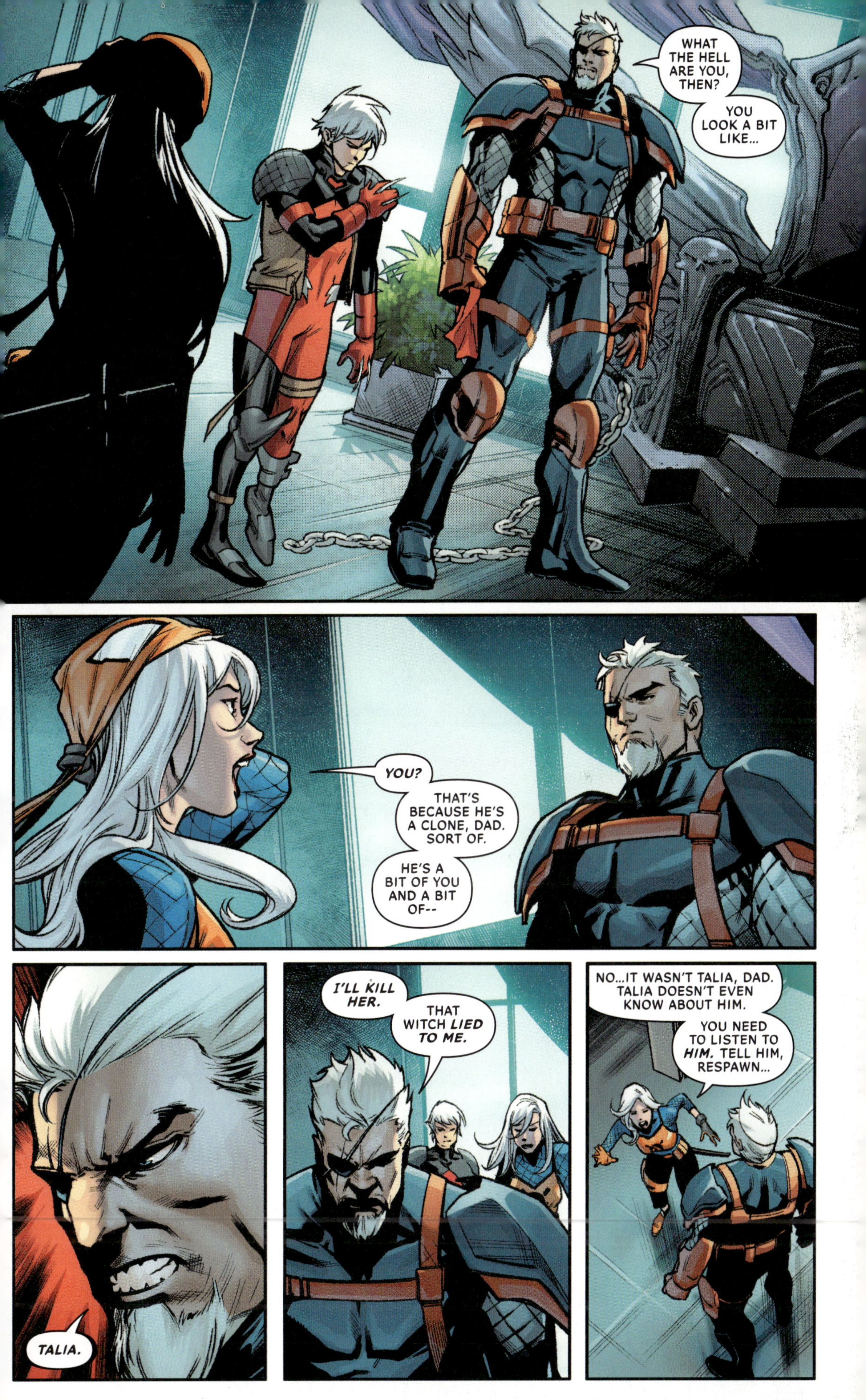
WHAT THE HELL ARE YOU, THEN?
YOU LOOK A BIT LIKE...
YOU?
THAT'S BECAUSE HE'S A CLONE, DAD. SORT OF.
HE'S A BIT OF YOU AND A BIT OF--
TALIA.
I'LL KILL HER.
THAT WITCH LIED TO ME.
NO...IT WASN'T TALIA, DAD. TALIA DOESN'T EVEN KNOW ABOUT HIM.
YOU NEED TO LISTEN TO HIM. TELL HIM, RESPAWN...

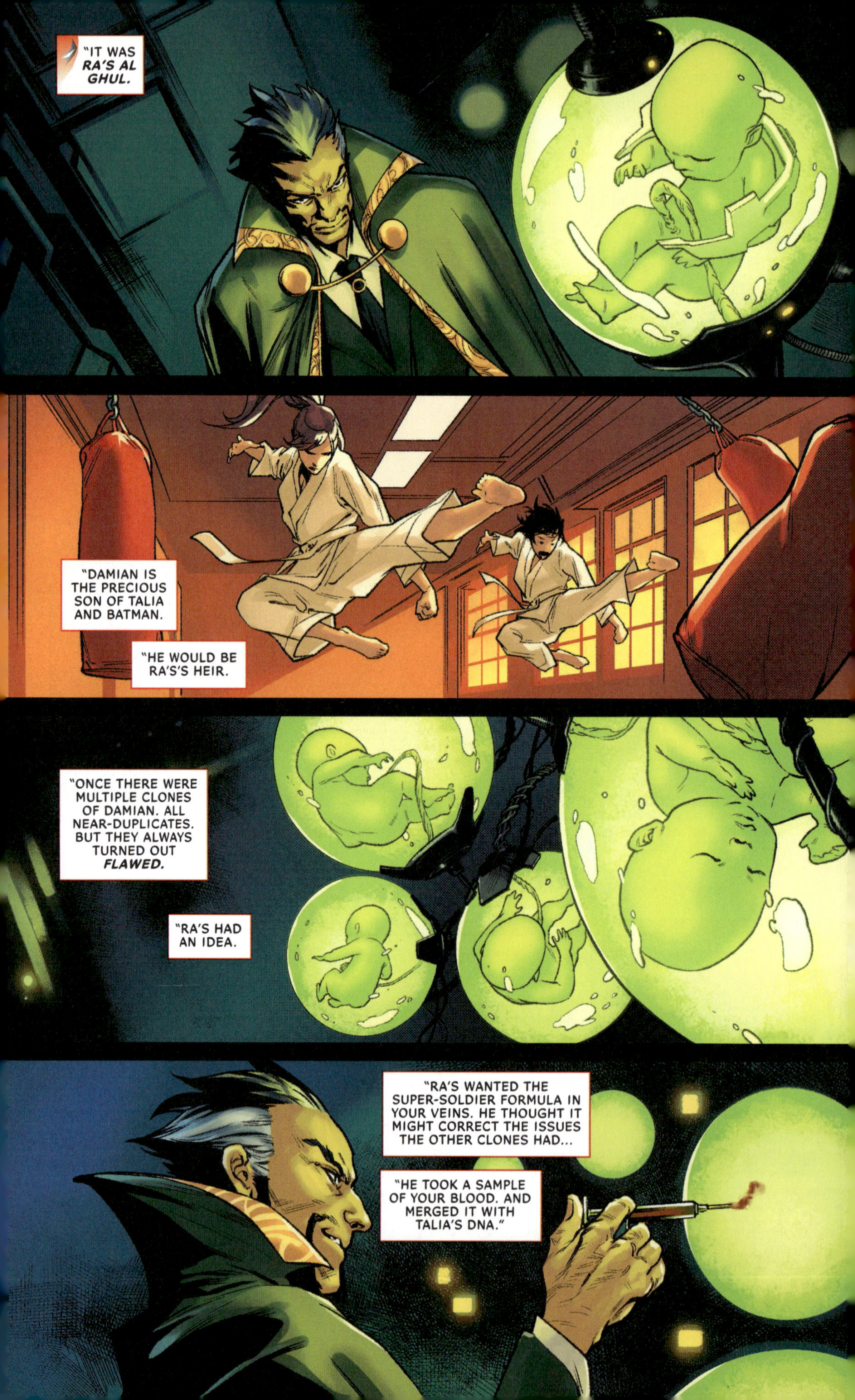
"IT WAS *RA'S AL GHUL.*
"DAMIAN IS THE PRECIOUS SON OF TALIA AND BATMAN.
"HE WOULD BE RA'S'S HEIR.
"ONCE THERE WERE MULTIPLE CLONES OF DAMIAN. ALL NEAR-DUPLICATES. BUT THEY ALWAYS TURNED OUT *FLAWED.*
"RA'S HAD AN IDEA.
"RA'S WANTED THE SUPER-SOLDIER FORMULA IN YOUR VEINS. HE THOUGHT IT MIGHT CORRECT THE ISSUES THE OTHER CLONES HAD...
"HE TOOK A SAMPLE OF YOUR BLOOD. AND MERGED IT WITH TALIA'S DNA."

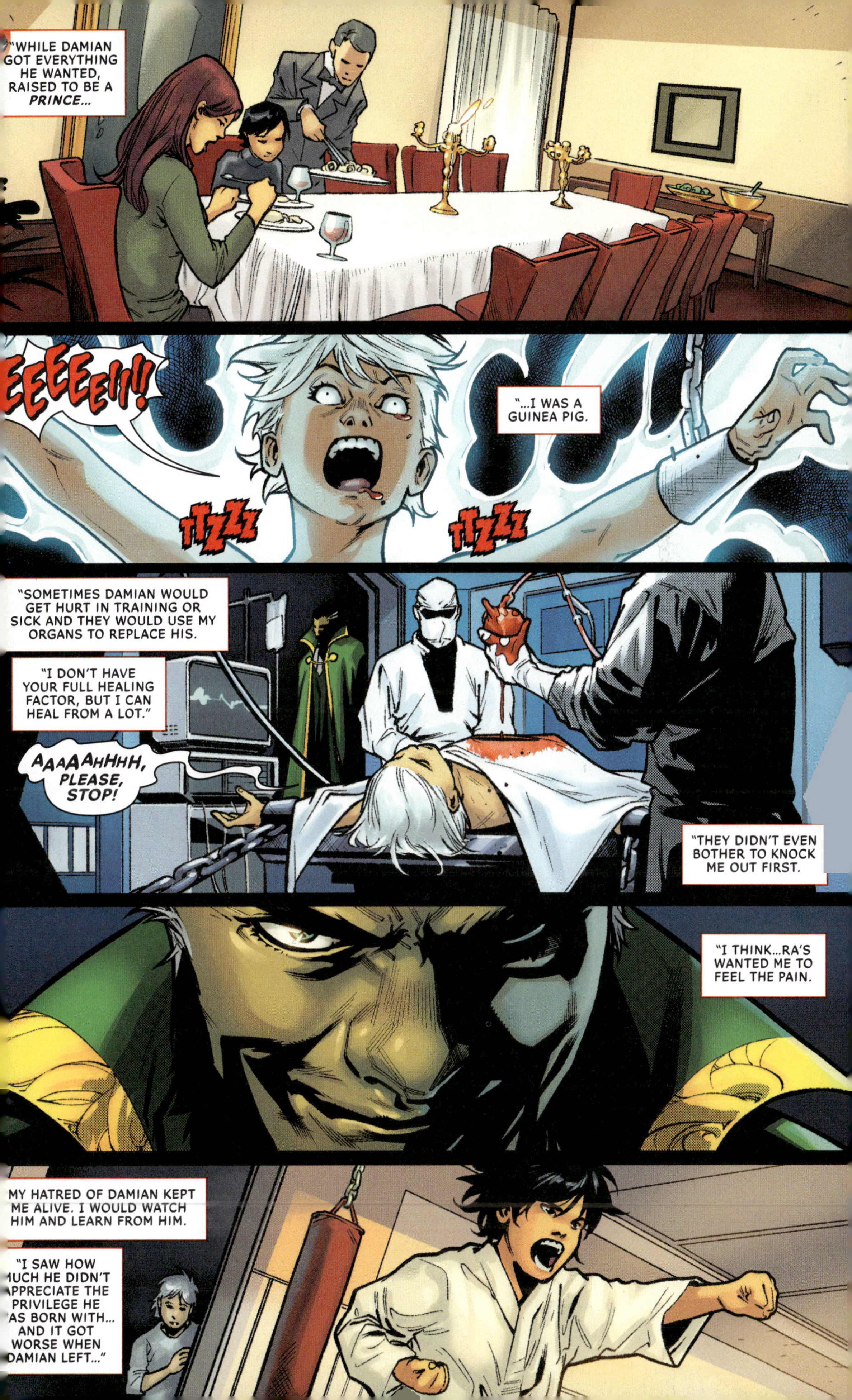
"WHILE DAMIAN GOT EVERYTHING HE WANTED, RAISED TO BE A *PRINCE*...
EEEEEII!!
"...I WAS A GUINEA PIG.
TTZZZ
TTZZZ
"SOMETIMES DAMIAN WOULD GET HURT IN TRAINING OR SICK AND THEY WOULD USE MY ORGANS TO REPLACE HIS.
"I DON'T HAVE YOUR FULL HEALING FACTOR, BUT I CAN HEAL FROM A LOT."
AAAAAHHHH, PLEASE, STOP!
"THEY DIDN'T EVEN BOTHER TO KNOCK ME OUT FIRST.
"I THINK...RA'S WANTED ME TO FEEL THE PAIN.
MY HATRED OF DAMIAN KEPT ME ALIVE. I WOULD WATCH HIM AND LEARN FROM HIM.
"I SAW HOW MUCH HE DIDN'T APPRECIATE THE PRIVILEGE HE WAS BORN WITH... AND IT GOT WORSE WHEN DAMIAN LEFT..."

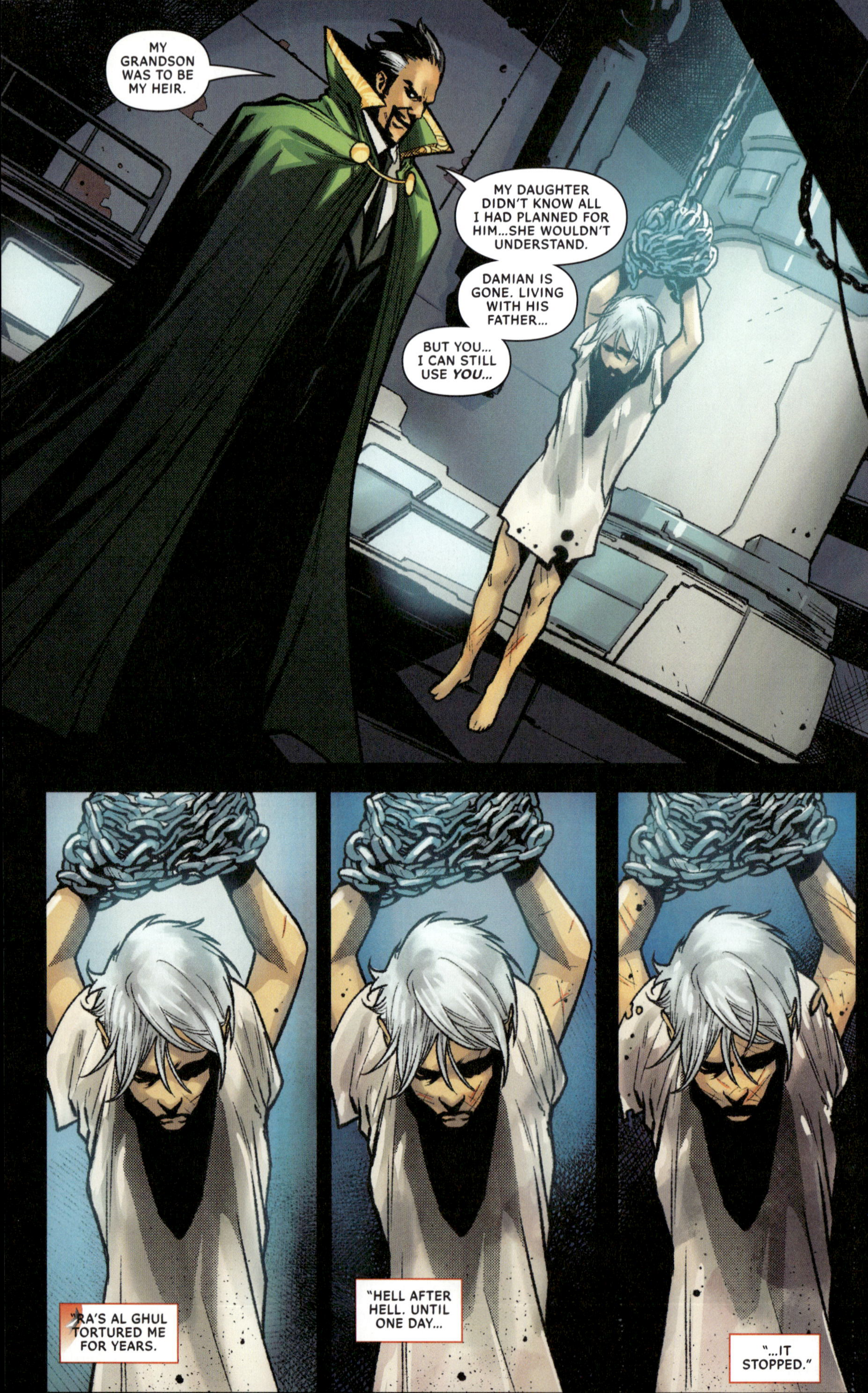
MY GRANDSON WAS TO BE MY HEIR.
MY DAUGHTER DIDN'T KNOW ALL I HAD PLANNED FOR HIM...SHE WOULDN'T UNDERSTAND.
DAMIAN IS GONE. LIVING WITH HIS FATHER...
BUT YOU... I CAN STILL USE *YOU*...
"RA'S AL GHUL TORTURED ME FOR YEARS.
"HELL AFTER HELL. UNTIL ONE DAY...
"...IT STOPPED."

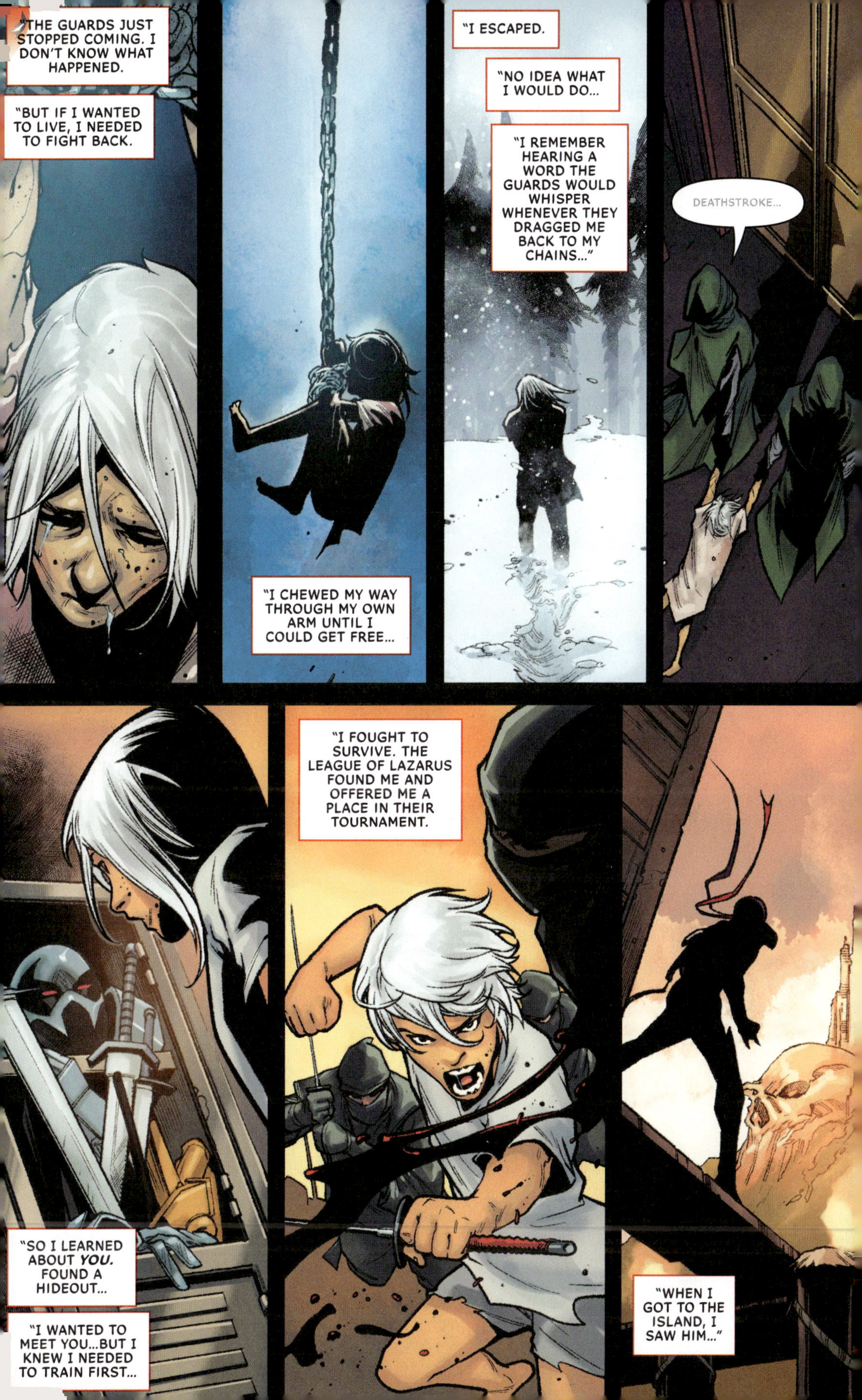

"THE GUARDS JUST STOPPED COMING. I DON'T KNOW WHAT HAPPENED.
"BUT IF I WANTED TO LIVE, I NEEDED TO FIGHT BACK.
"I CHEWED MY WAY THROUGH MY OWN ARM UNTIL I COULD GET FREE...
"I ESCAPED.
"NO IDEA WHAT I WOULD DO...
"I REMEMBER HEARING A WORD THE GUARDS WOULD WHISPER WHENEVER THEY DRAGGED ME BACK TO MY CHAINS..."
DEATHSTROKE...
"SO I LEARNED ABOUT *YOU.* FOUND A HIDEOUT...
"I WANTED TO MEET YOU...BUT I KNEW I NEEDED TO TRAIN FIRST...
"I FOUGHT TO SURVIVE. THE LEAGUE OF LAZARUS FOUND ME AND OFFERED ME A PLACE IN THEIR TOURNAMENT.
"WHEN I GOT TO THE ISLAND, I SAW HIM..."

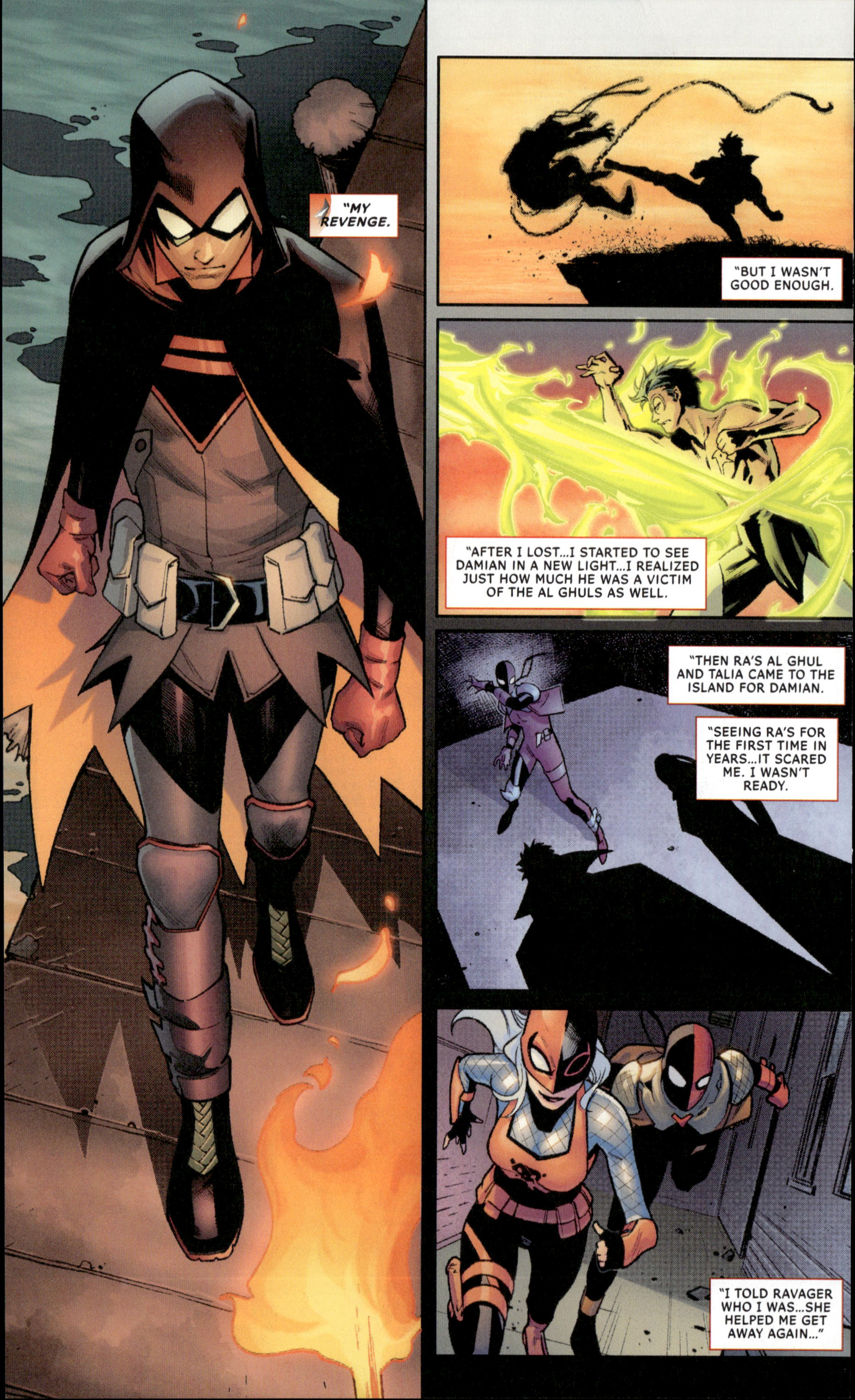
"MY REVENGE.
"BUT I WASN'T GOOD ENOUGH.
"AFTER I LOST...I STARTED TO SEE DAMIAN IN A NEW LIGHT...I REALIZED JUST HOW MUCH HE WAS A VICTIM OF THE AL GHULS AS WELL.
"THEN RA'S AL GHUL AND TALIA CAME TO THE ISLAND FOR DAMIAN.
"SEEING RA'S FOR THE FIRST TIME IN YEARS...IT SCARED ME. I WASN'T READY.
"I TOLD RAVAGER WHO I WAS...SHE HELPED ME GET AWAY AGAIN..."

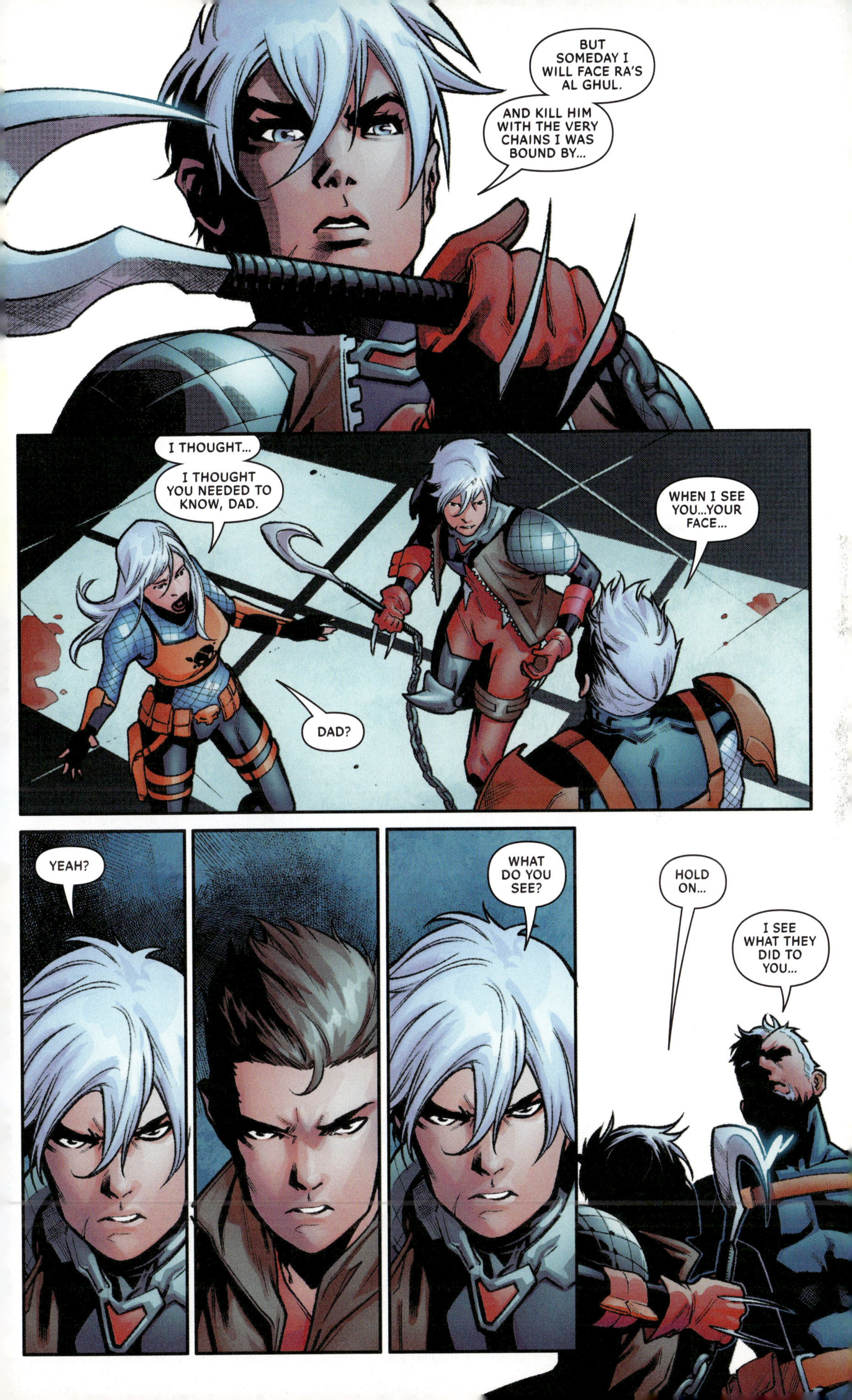
BUT SOMEDAY I WILL FACE RA'S AL GHUL.
AND KILL HIM WITH THE VERY CHAINS I WAS BOUND BY...
I THOUGHT...
I THOUGHT YOU NEEDED TO KNOW, DAD.
WHEN I SEE YOU...YOUR FACE...
DAD?
YEAH?
WHAT DO YOU SEE?
HOLD ON...
I SEE WHAT THEY DID TO YOU...

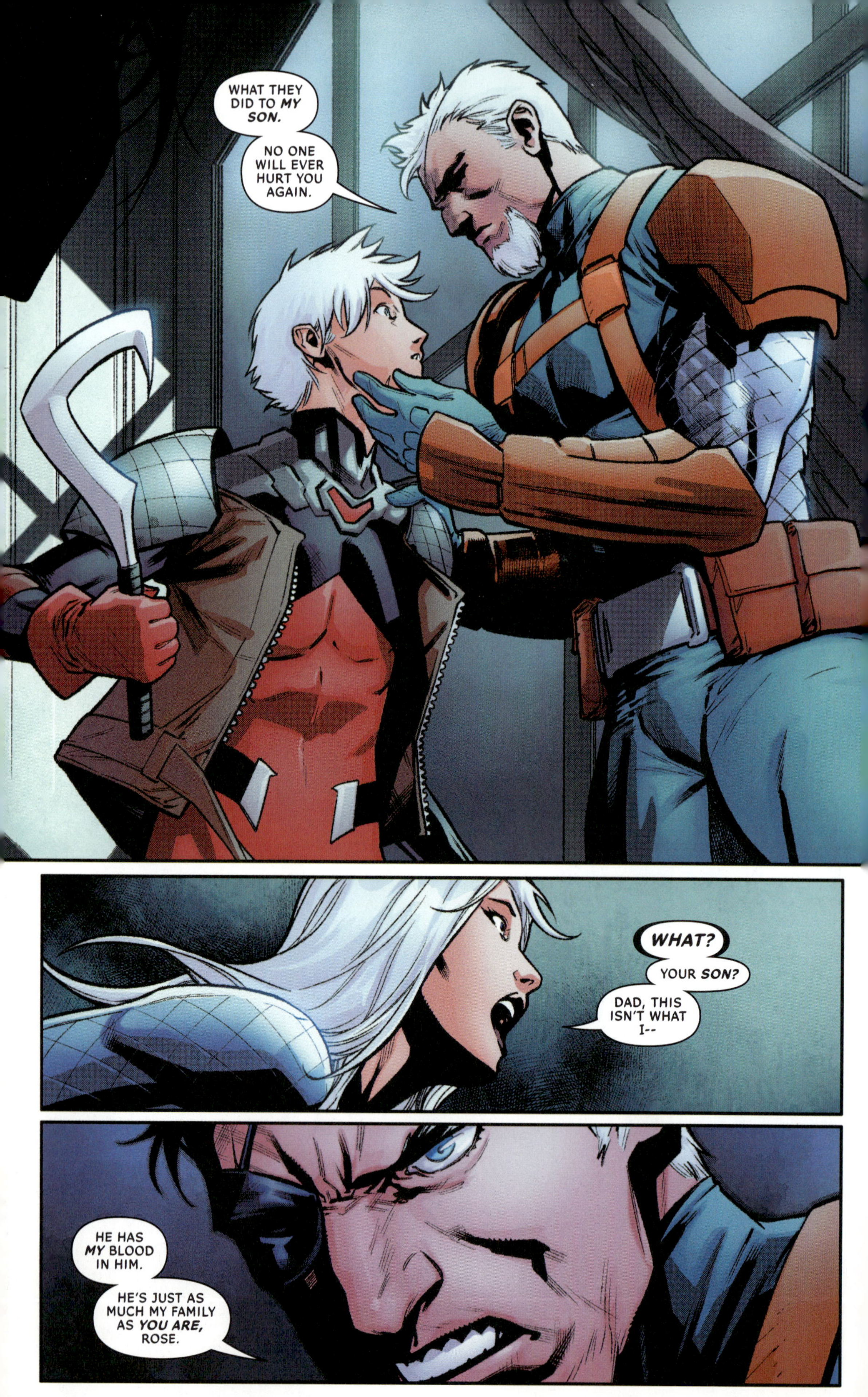
WHAT THEY DID TO *MY SON.*
NO ONE WILL EVER HURT YOU AGAIN.
WHAT?
YOUR *SON?*
DAD, THIS ISN'T WHAT I--
HE HAS *MY* BLOOD IN HIM.
HE'S JUST AS MUCH MY FAMILY AS *YOU ARE,* ROSE.

WHY ARE YOU REALLY DOING THIS? *THIS WHOLE THING?!*

BUILDING ARMIES? TAKING OVER SECRET SOCIETIES?

THAT ISN'T YOU!

I WAS ON A MISSION*...

AND I SAW SOMETHING...

* AS SEEN IN *DEATHSTROKE INC.* #2! --BEN

"DARKNESS.

AND THEN I KNEW WHAT I NEEDED TO DO.

THERE IS SOMETHING *COMING.* AND I'M GOING TO PREPARE FOR IT.

YOU KNOW IT, TOO. YOUR PRECOG POWERS...YOUR LITTLE FUTURE-VISION CHEAT...

YOU DIDN'T ENTER THAT TOURNAMENT BECAUSE OF THIS BOY.

YOU WANTED TO SEE IF YOU COULD KICK-START YOUR POWERS AGAIN, BECAUSE EVERY TIME YOU TRY TO LOOK AHEAD YOU SEE *NOTHING.*

I WAS LOOKING FOR *YOU!* WE FINALLY HAD A SHOT AT BEING A FAMILY!

AND YOU LEFT US AGAIN!

I LEFT BECAUSE OF GRANT!

MY SON DIED!

"THE TITANS COST ME MY SON.

"HOW COULD I EVER SIT AROUND A TABLE AND PRETEND TO BE A HAPPY FAMILY WITH GRANT *GONE?!* LIVE A *FAKE LIFE?*

BUT NOW...YOU'RE HERE. RESPAWN IS HERE.

WE CAN GET JOSEPH. WINTERGREEN. ADELINE.

THEY CAN ALL COME HERE AND BE WITH US.

NO.

I'M NOT LETTING YOU BRING ANYONE ELSE INTO THIS.

THERE IS SOMETHING *WRONG* WITH YOU.

DON'T DO THIS.

IT DOESN'T TAKE A VISION OF THE FUTURE TO KNOW WHAT WILL HAPPEN IF YOU CHALLENGE ME.

I KNOW YOU.

I KNOW YOU HATE WHEN *ANYONE* COMES TO KNOW YOU.

BUT I DO.

AND I NEED TO PUT A STOP TO THIS BEFORE YOU GO TOO FAR.

RESPAWN, COME WITH ME...

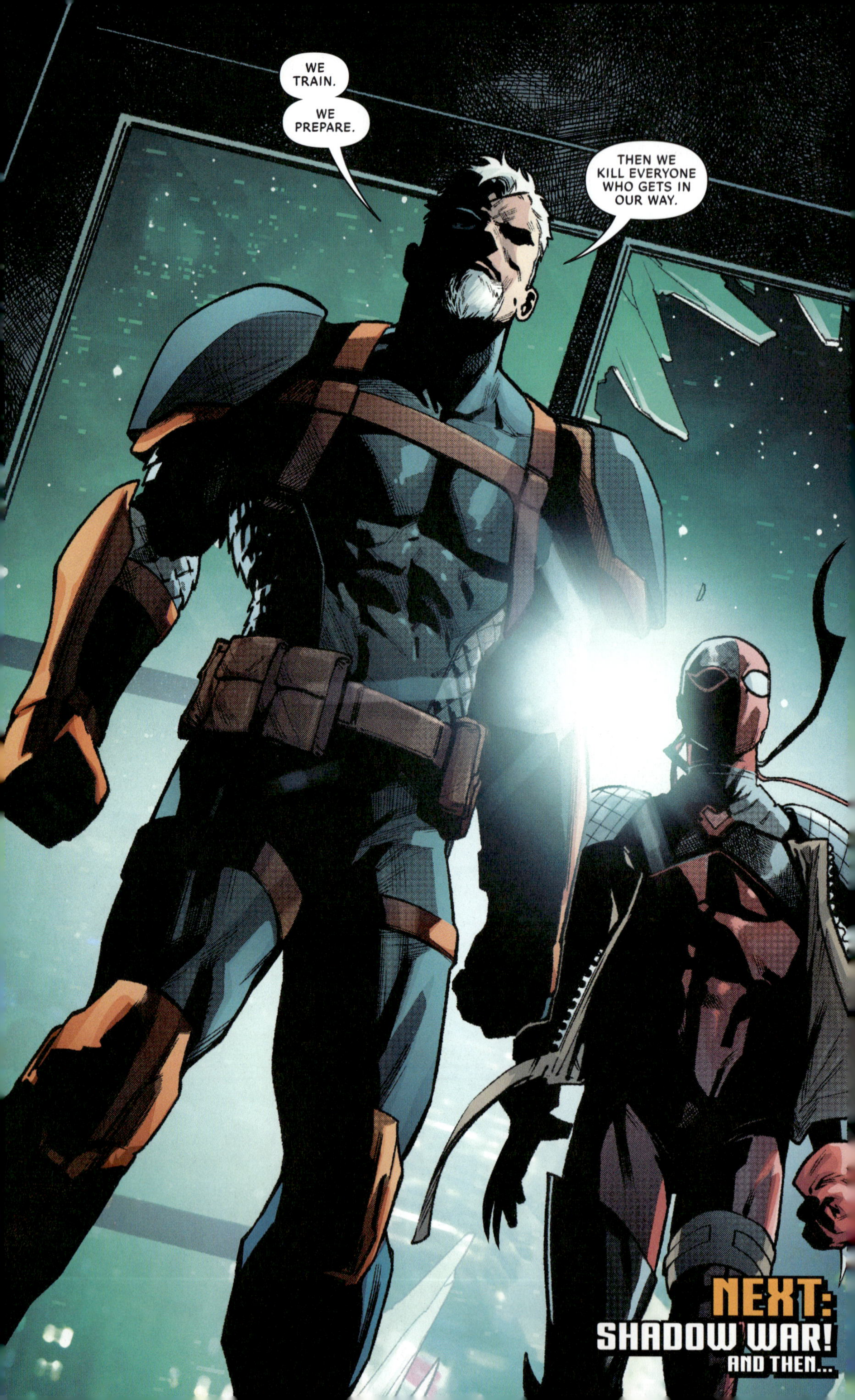
WE TRAIN.
WE PREPARE.
THEN WE KILL EVERYONE WHO GETS IN OUR WAY.
NEXT: SHADOW WAR! AND THEN...

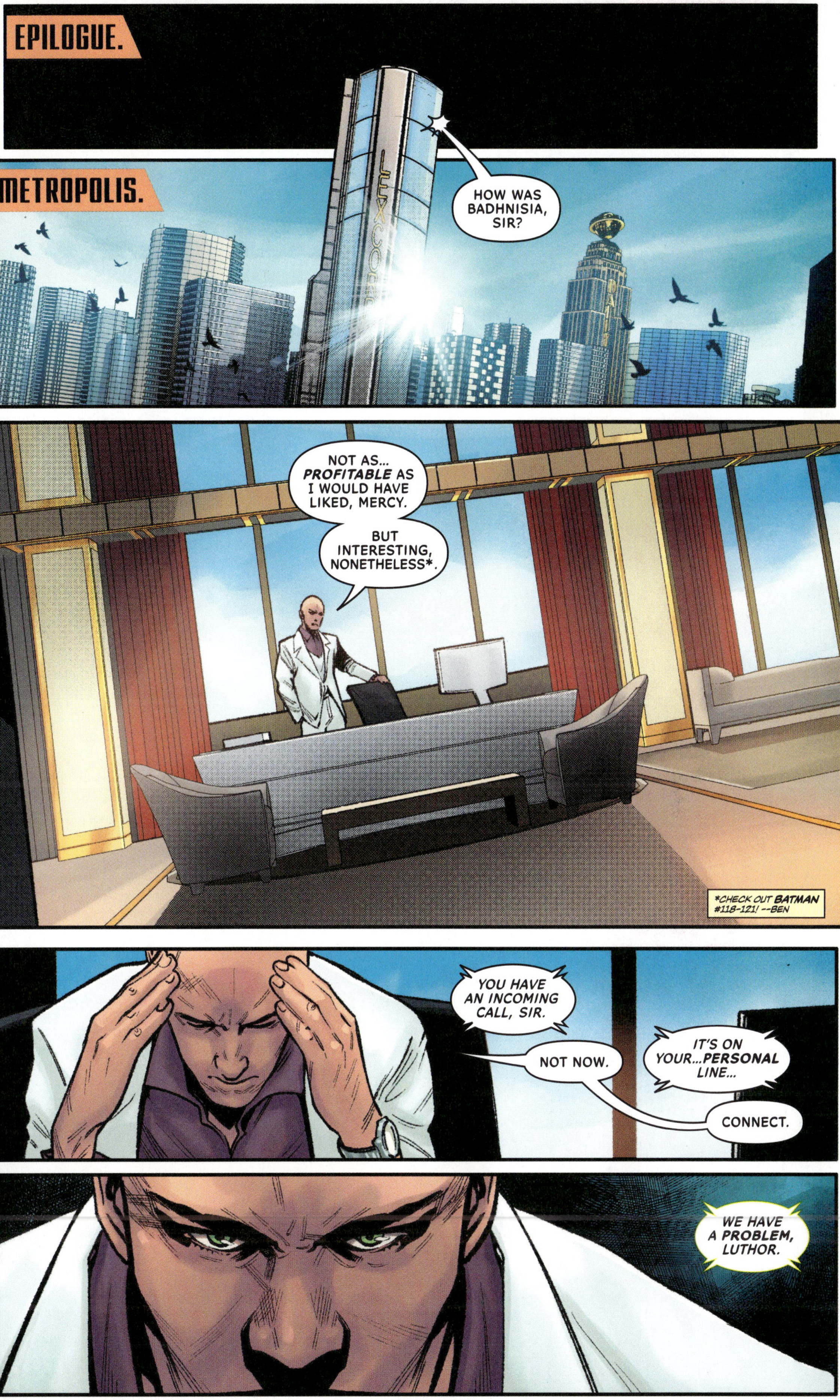
EPILOGUE.
METROPOLIS.
LEXCORP
HOW WAS BADHNISIA, SIR?
NOT AS... PROFITABLE AS I WOULD HAVE LIKED, MERCY.
BUT INTERESTING, NONETHELESS*.
*CHECK OUT BATMAN #118-121! --BEN
YOU HAVE AN INCOMING CALL, SIR.
NOT NOW.
IT'S ON YOUR...PERSONAL LINE...
CONNECT.
WE HAVE A PROBLEM, LUTHOR.

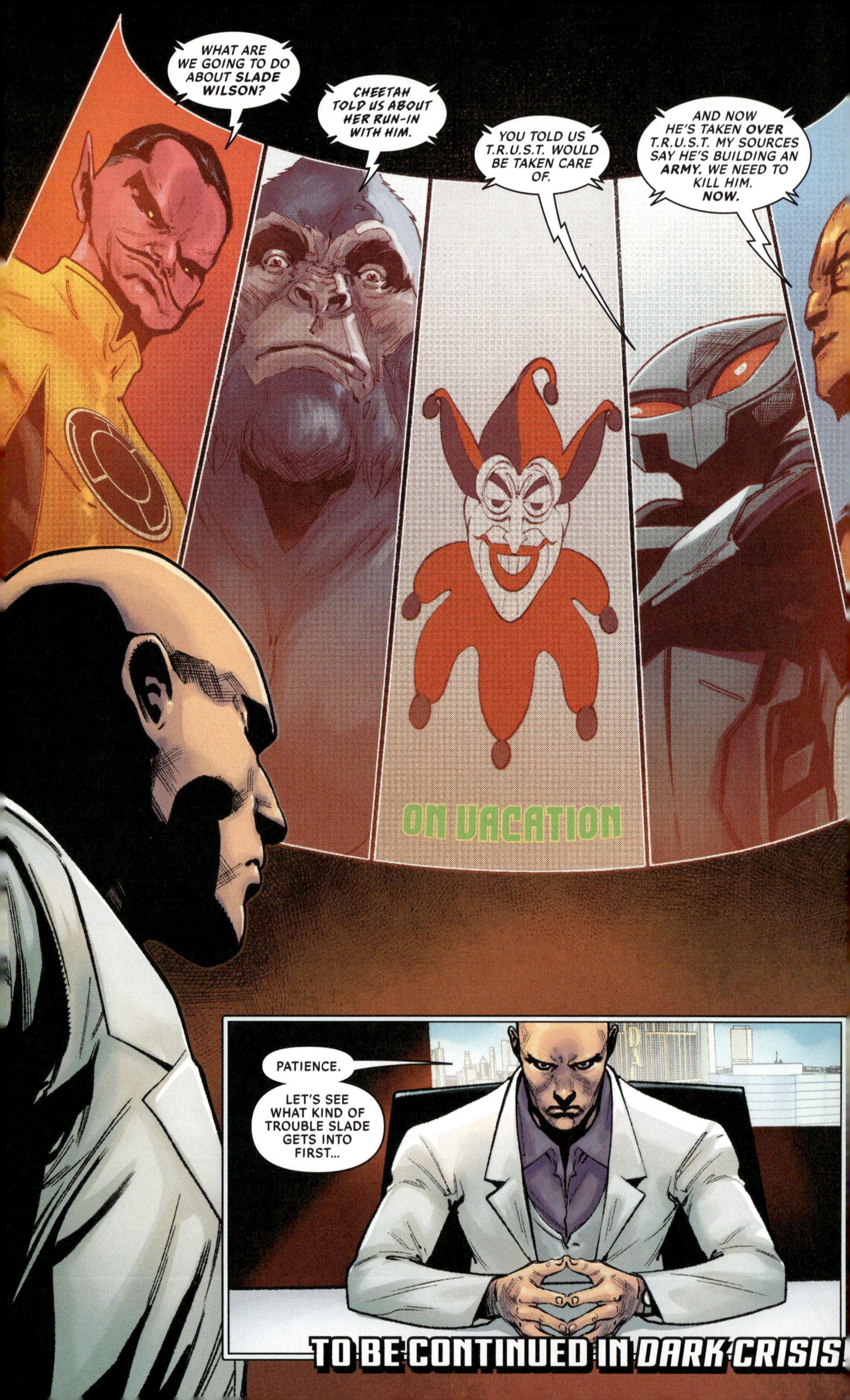
WHAT ARE WE GOING TO DO ABOUT SLADE WILSON?
CHEETAH TOLD US ABOUT HER RUN-IN WITH HIM.
YOU TOLD US T.R.U.S.T. WOULD BE TAKEN CARE OF.
AND NOW HE'S TAKEN OVER T.R.U.S.T. MY SOURCES SAY HE'S BUILDING AN ARMY. WE NEED TO KILL HIM. NOW.
ON VACATION
PATIENCE.
LET'S SEE WHAT KIND OF TROUBLE SLADE GETS INTO FIRST...
TO BE CONTINUED IN DARK CRISIS!

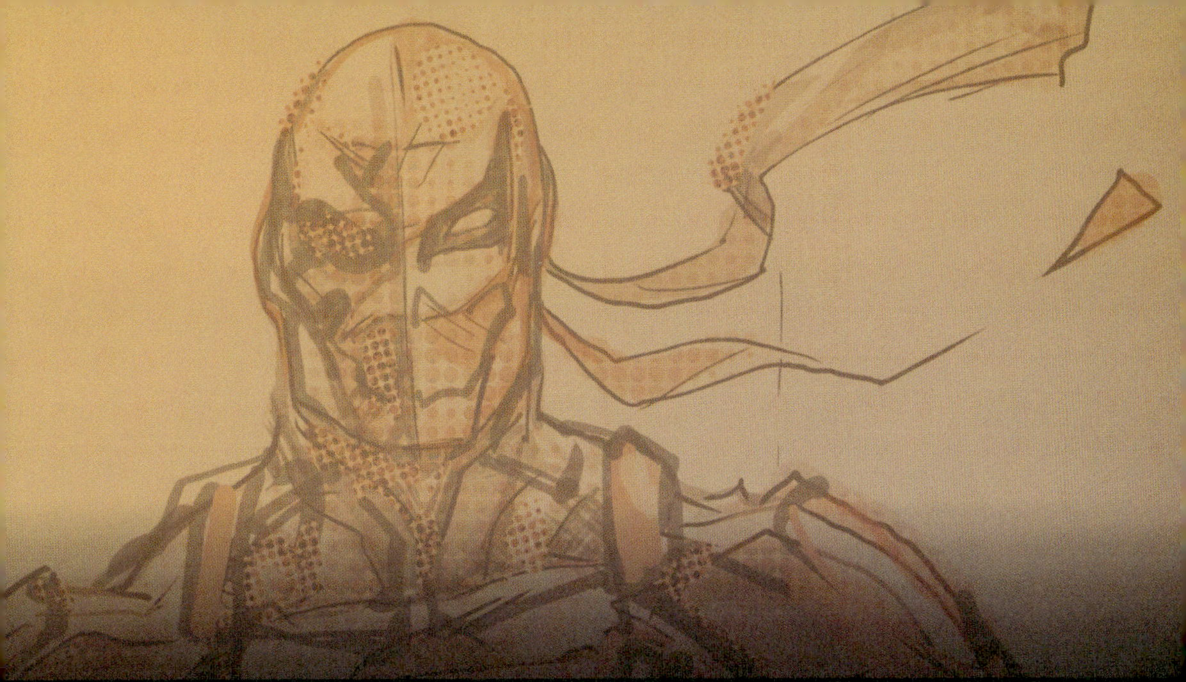

DEATHSTROKE INC.

ART & DESIGN GALLERY

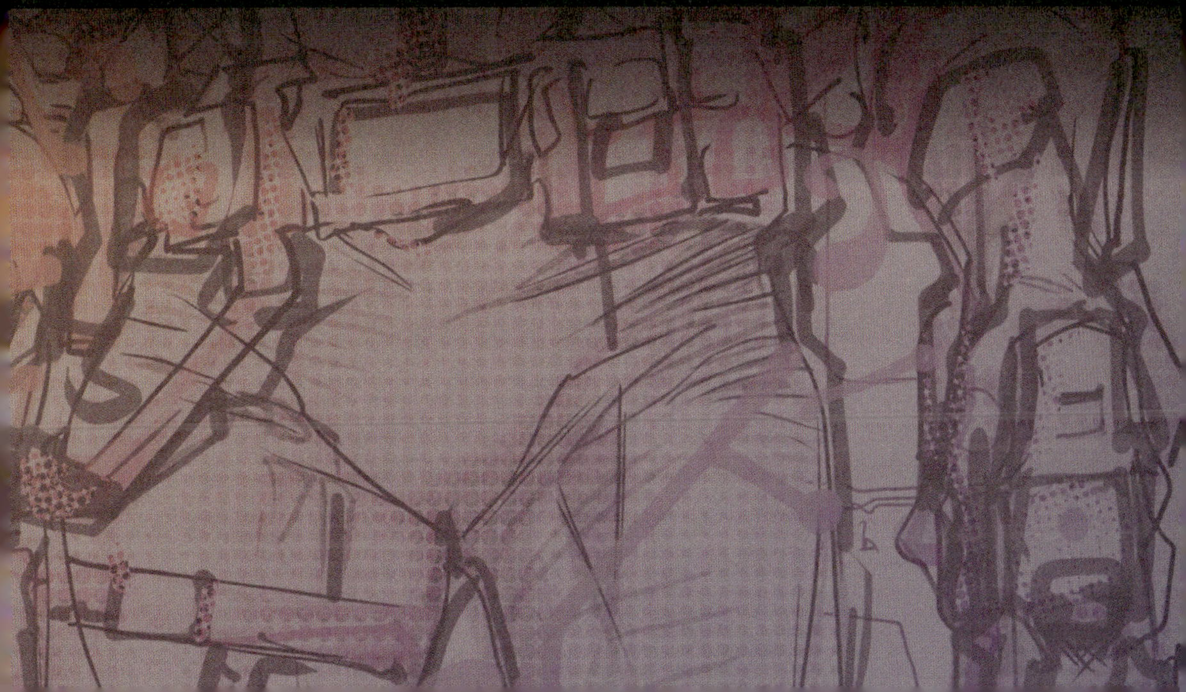

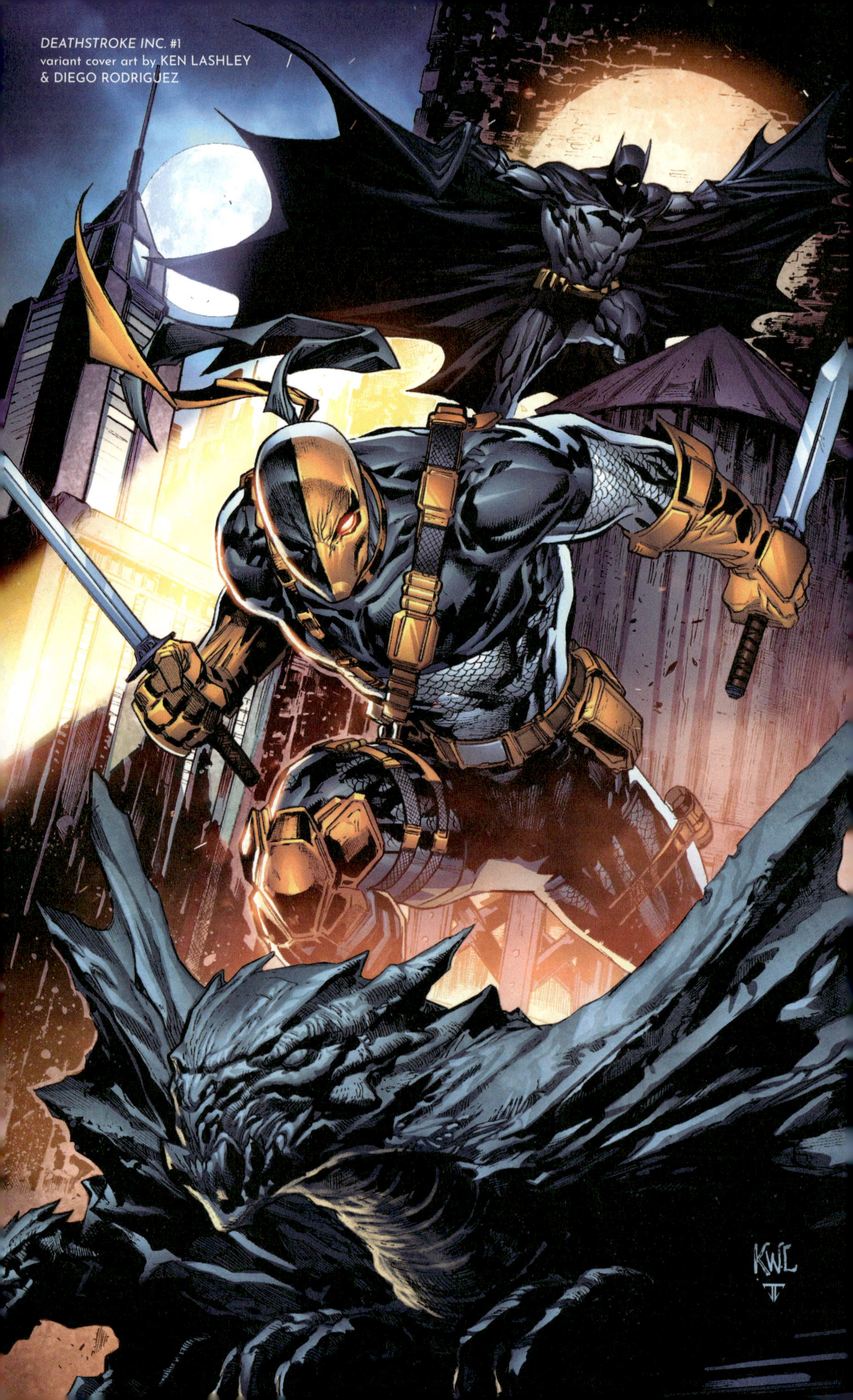

DEATHSTROKE INC. #1
variant cover art by KEN LASHLEY
& DIEGO RODRIGUEZ

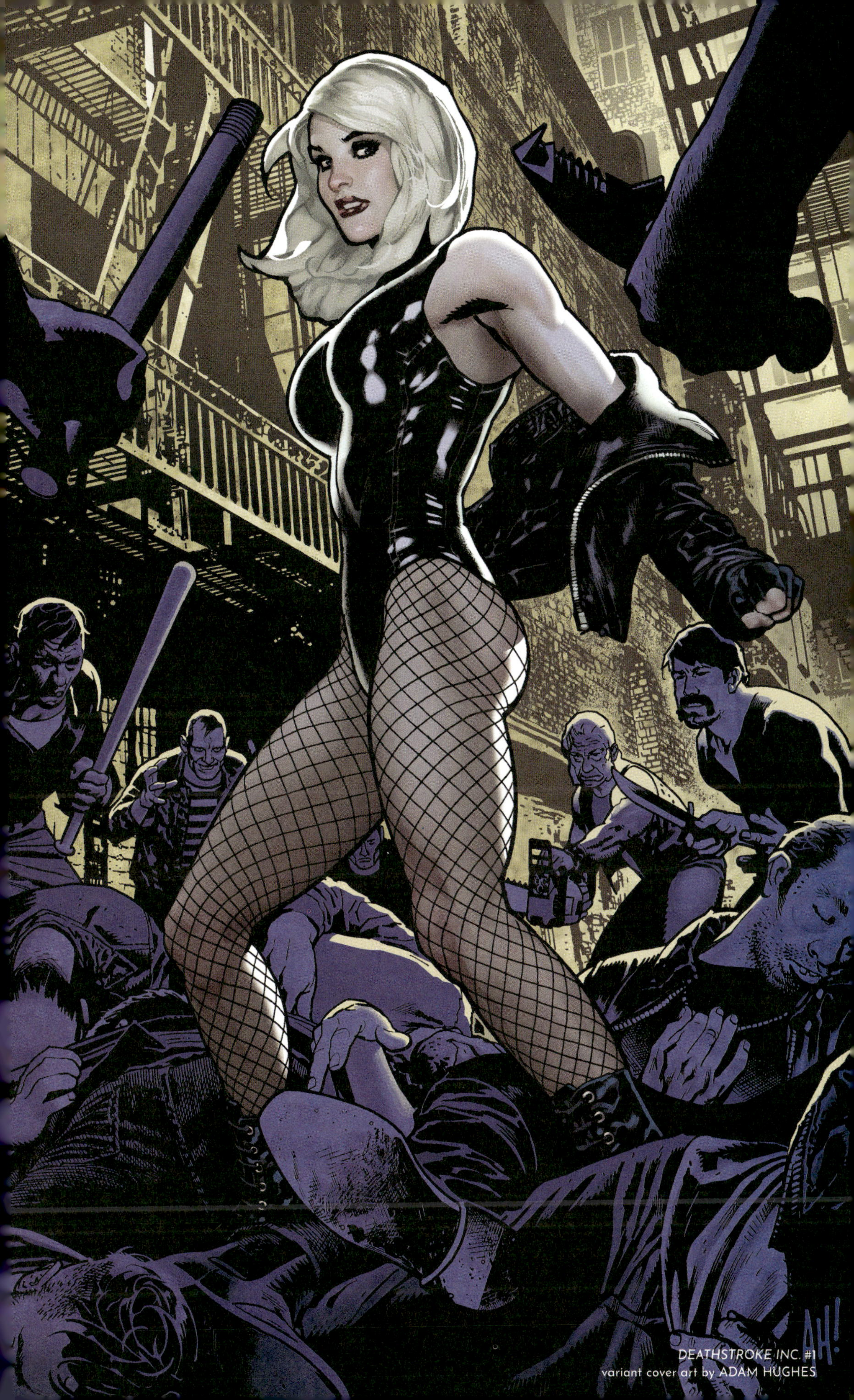
AH!

DEATHSTROKE INC. #1
variant cover art by ADAM HUGHES

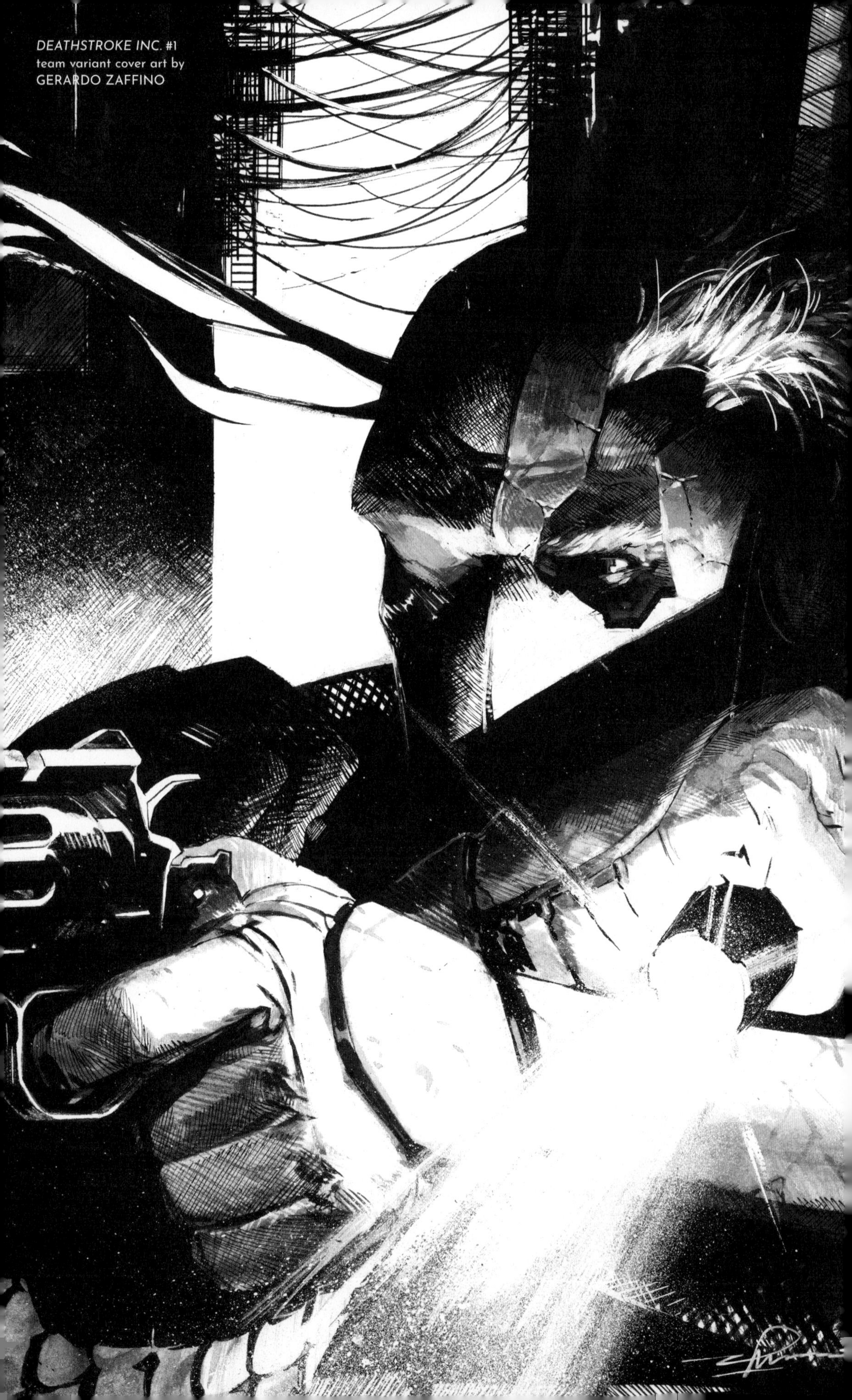

DEATHSTROKE INC. #1
team variant cover art by
GERARDO ZAFFINO

DEATHSTROKE INC. #1
variant cover art by DIMA IVANOV

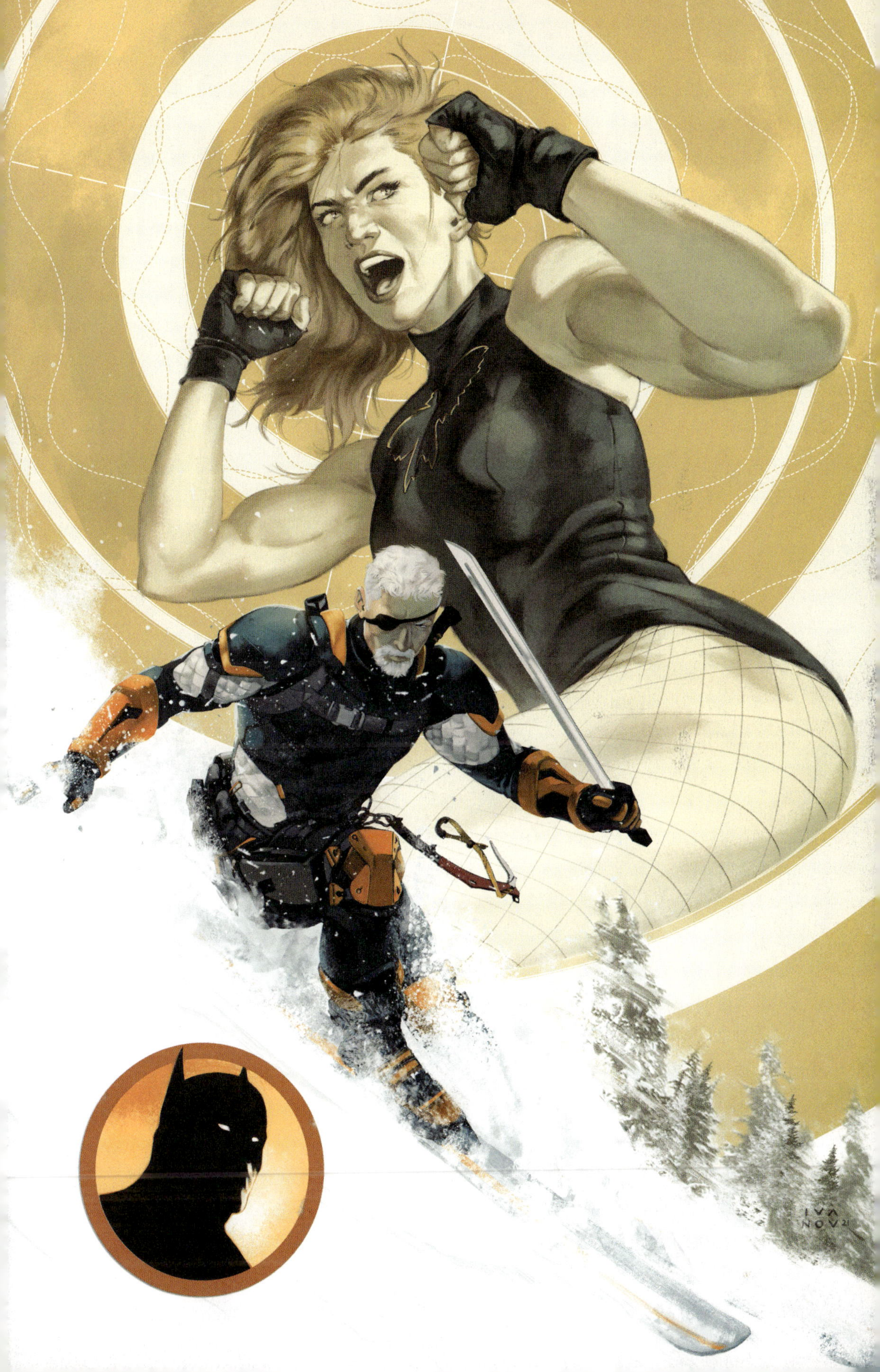

IVA
NOV'21

DEATHSTROKE INC. #1
variant cover art by FRANCESCO MATTINA

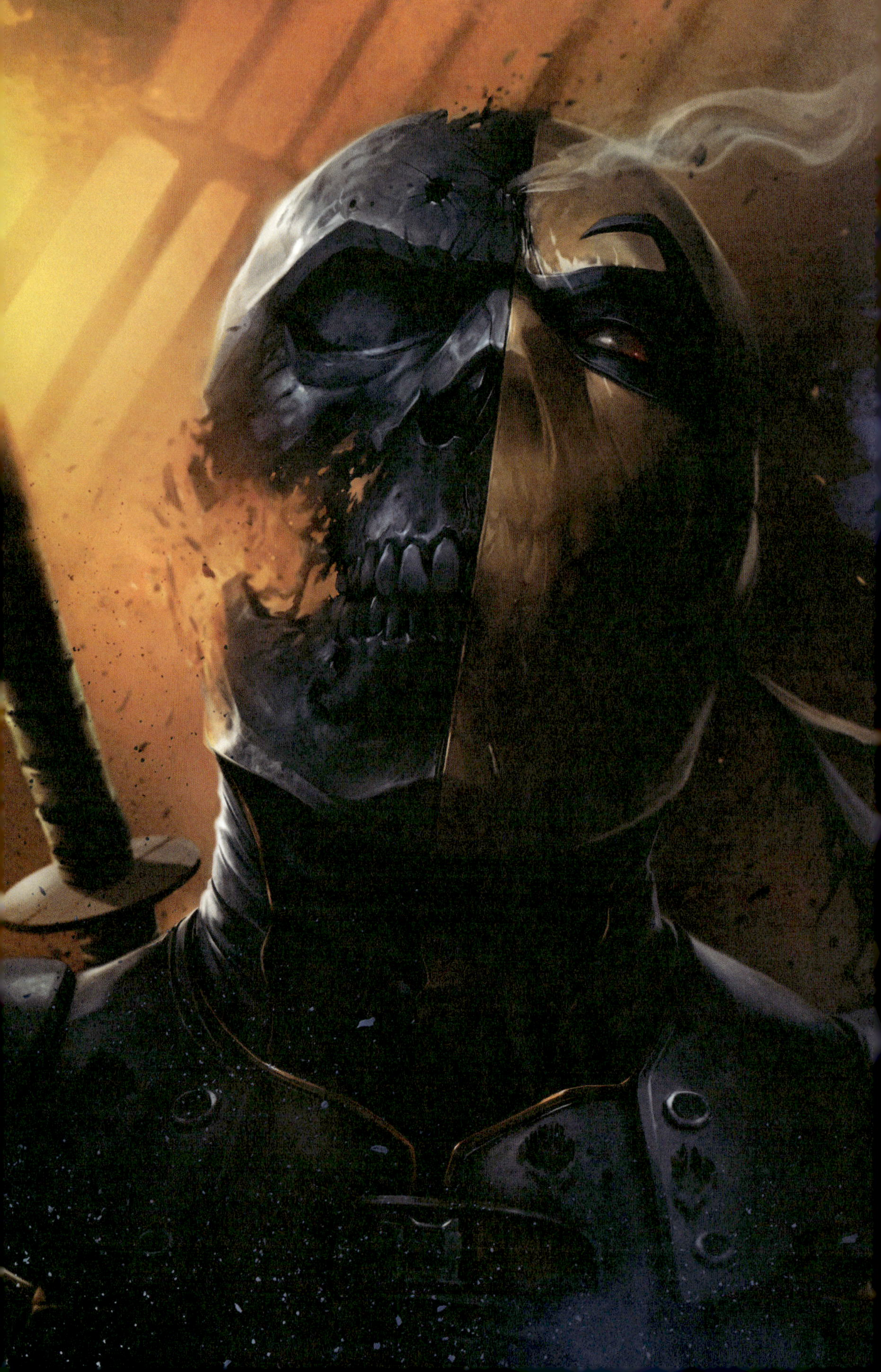

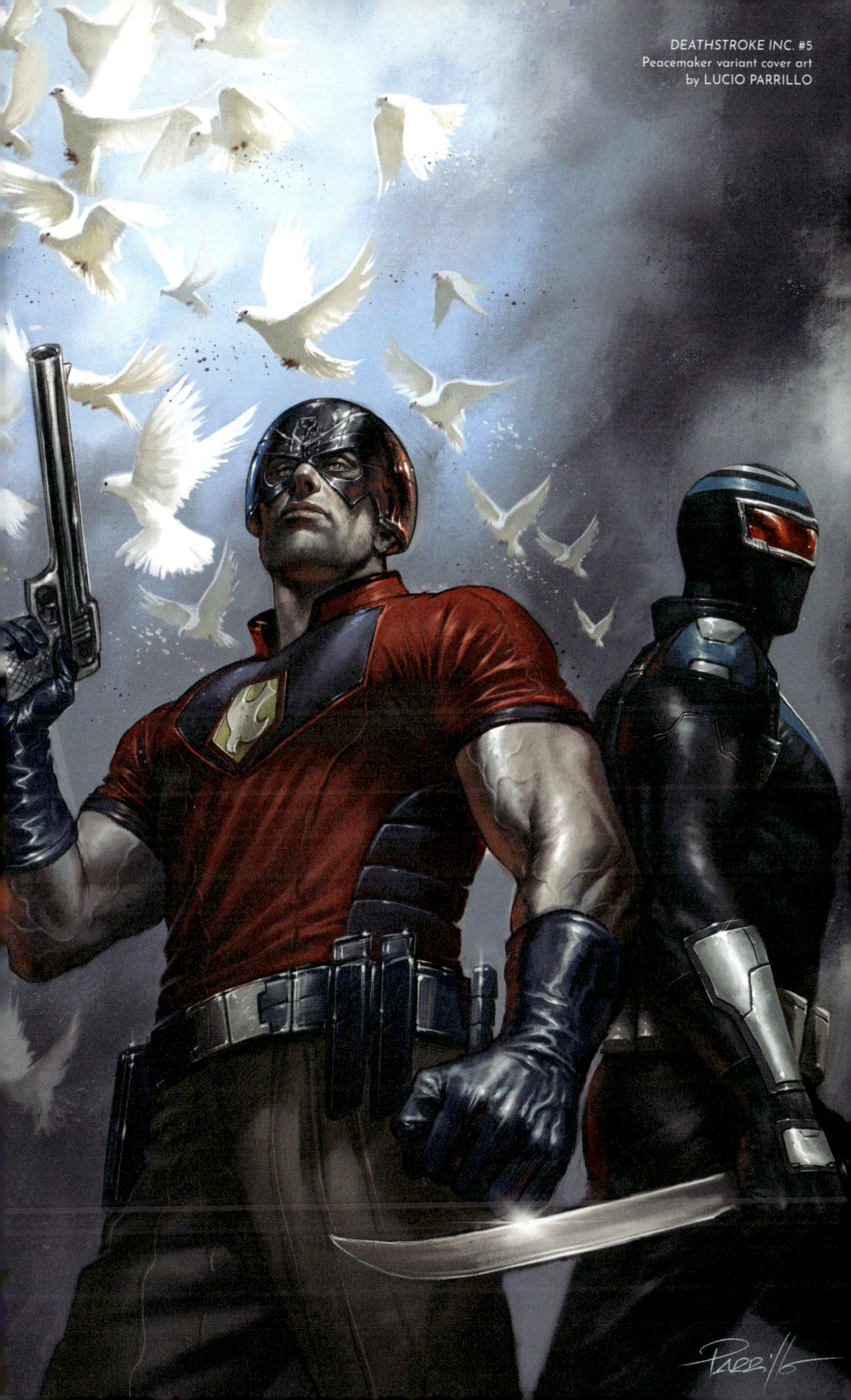

DEATHSTROKE INC. #5
Peacemaker variant cover art
by LUCIO PARRILLO

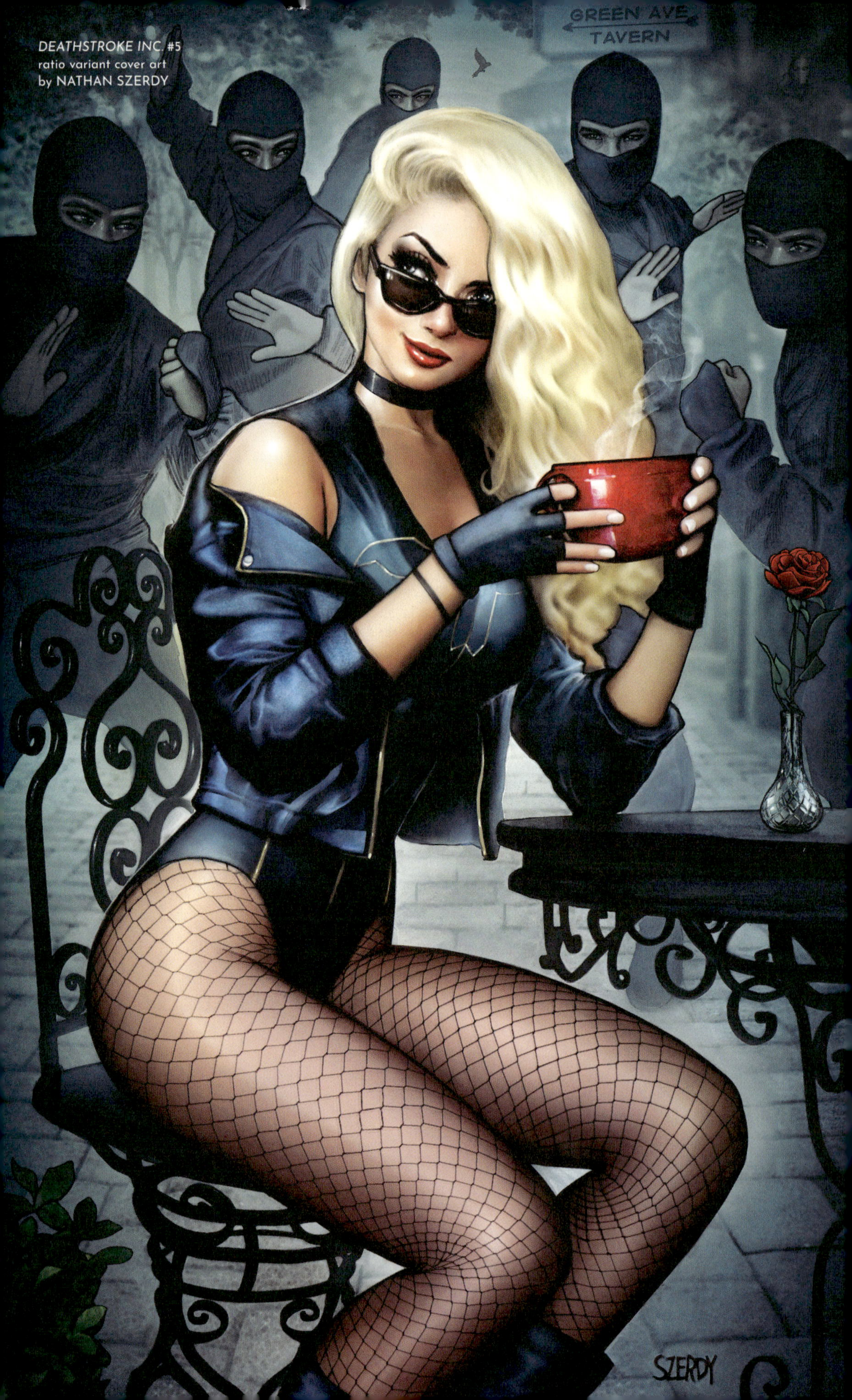
GREEN AVE
TAVERN
SZERDY

DEATHSTROKE INC. #5
ratio variant cover art
by NATHAN SZERDY

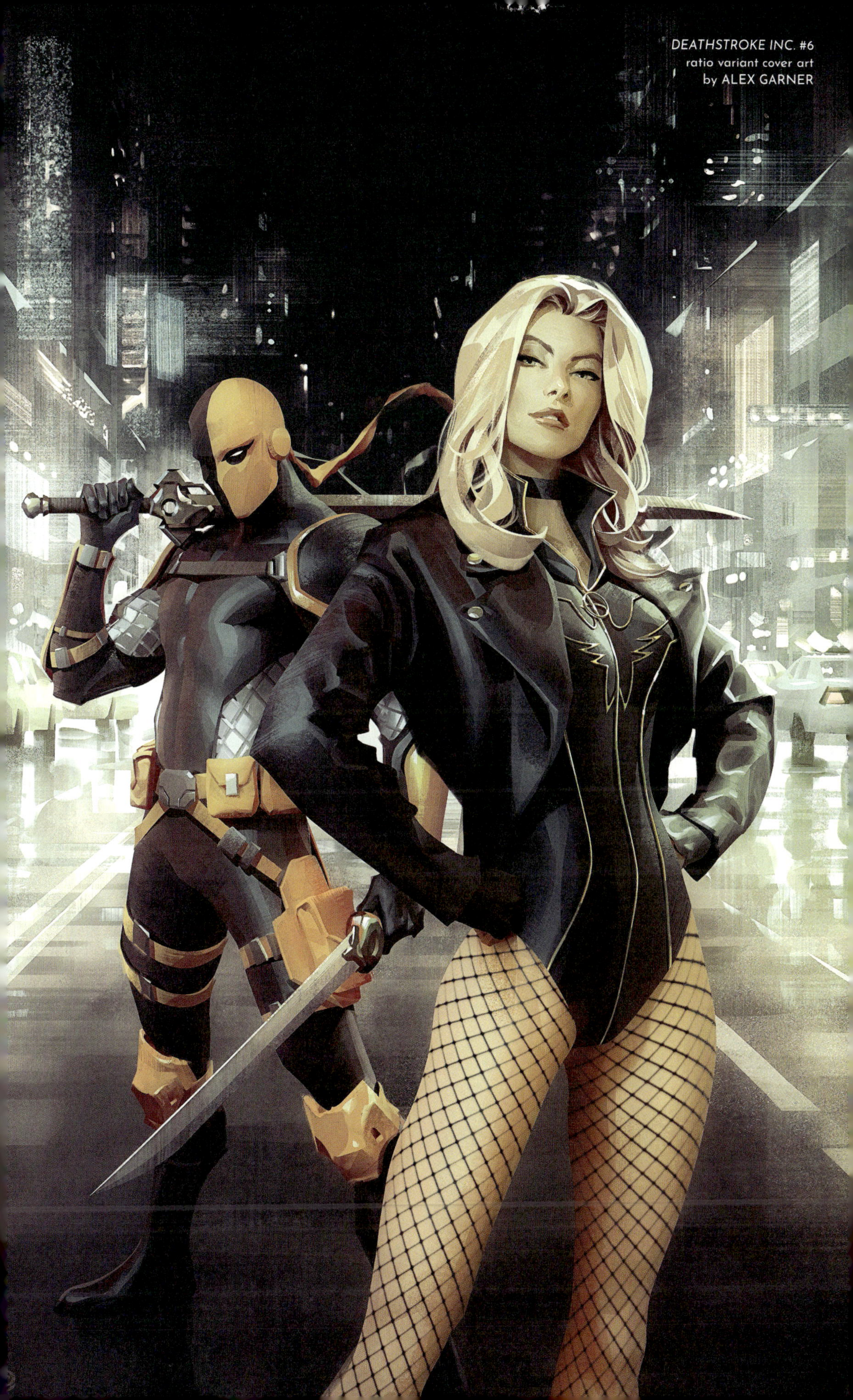

DEATHSTROKE INC. #6
ratio variant cover art
by ALEX GARNER

Character designs by Howard Porter

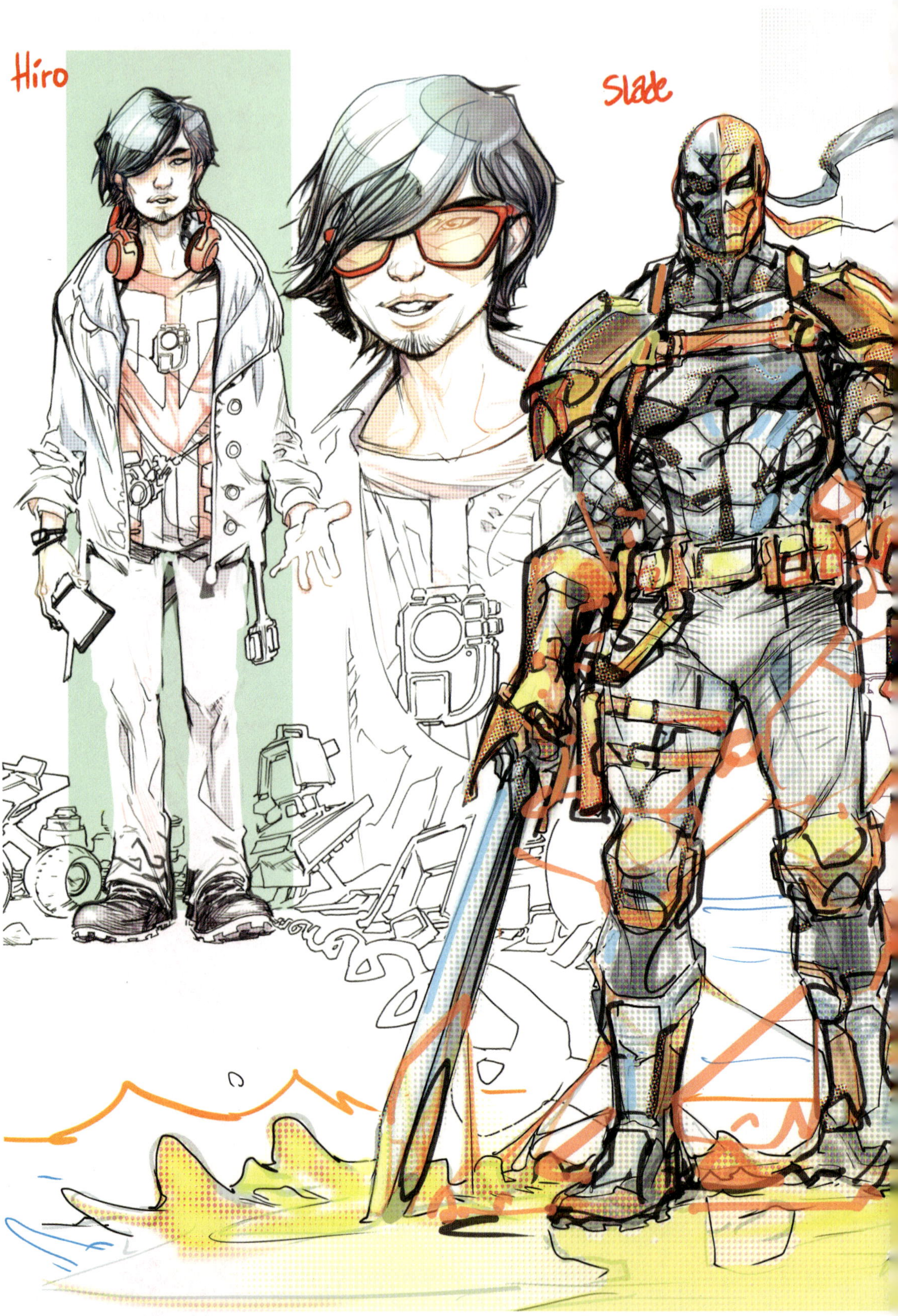
Hiro
Slade

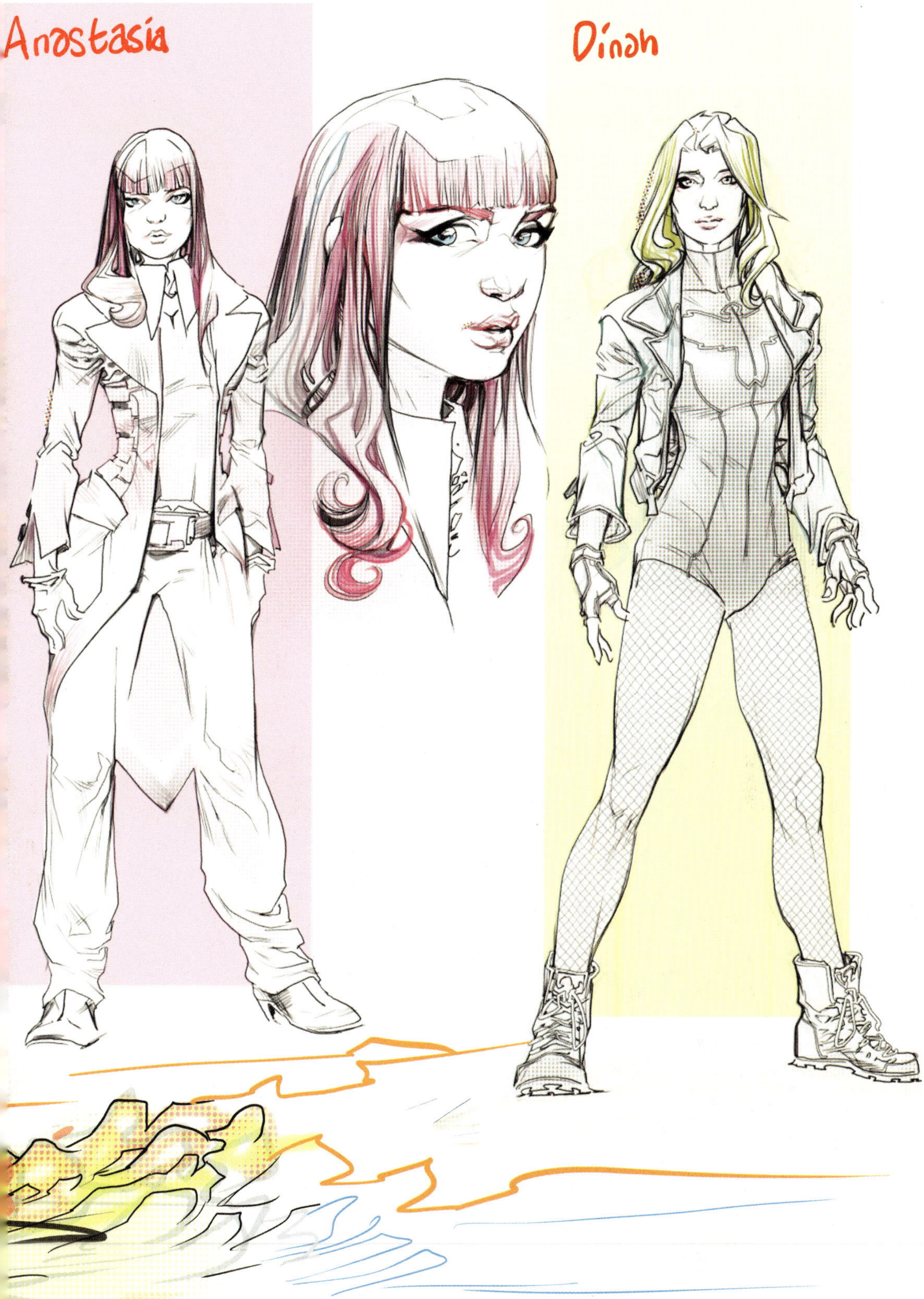
Anastasia
Dinah

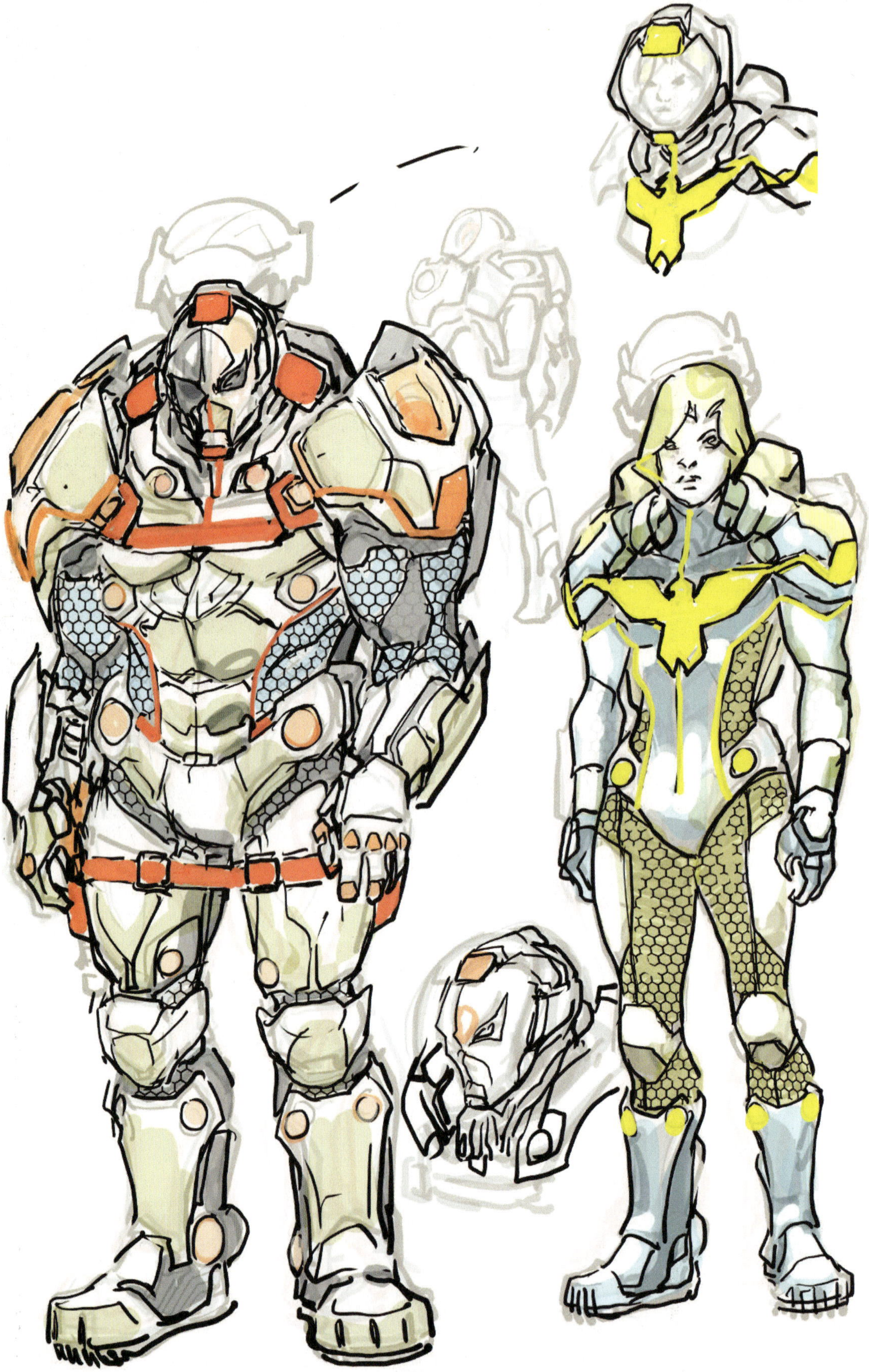

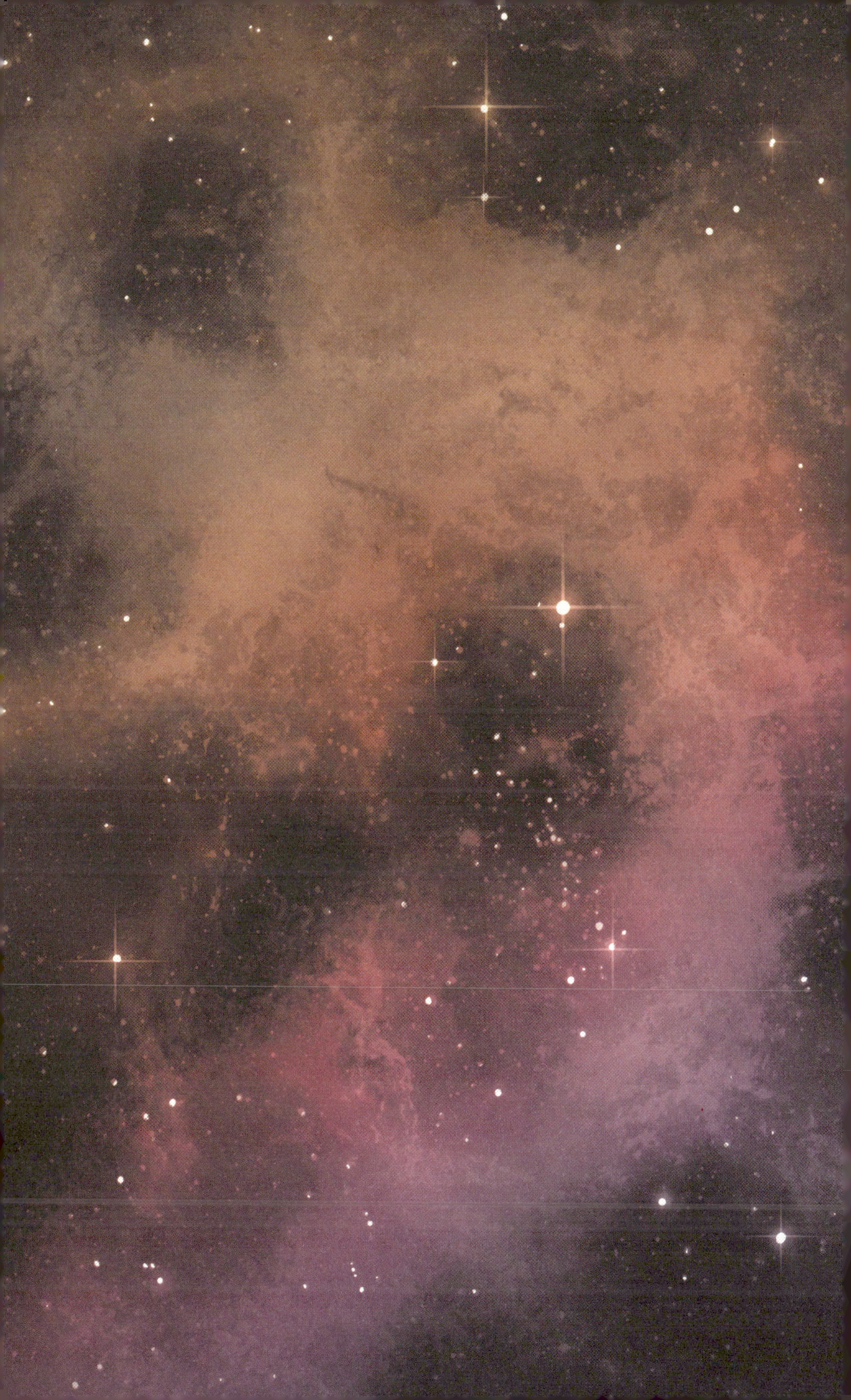